About the Author

Thyssen Carlisle was born in Great Britain but travelled and lived all over the globe.
He has lived a colourful life and lived like there was no tomorrow.
He loved and lost and met lots of exciting characters on the journey we call life.

To My Soulmate

Thyssen Carlisle

LUST IS A
FOUR LETTER WORD

AUSTIN MACAULEY
PUBLISHERS LTD.

A CIP catalogue record for this title is available from the British Library.

ISBN 978 1 78455 272 5 (Paperback)
ISBN 978 1 78455 274 9 (Hardback)

www.austinmacauley.com.

First Published (2015)
Austin Macauley Publishers Ltd
25 Canada Square
Canary Wharf
London.
E14 5LB

Printed and bound in Great Britain

With Thanks

Here is to the host of fascinating characters who have coloured my life! To the Supermodels, Photographers, Designers, Artists, Film Stars, Hollywood Producers, Pop Icons. Princes and Prostitutes and to all the people I have loved and lost on my journey through life and here is to my Soulmate. Let's hope our paths will cross again – somewhere in time.

Before you turn the pages of this novel remember.
BE CAREFUL WHO YOU LOVE.

Contents

CHAPTER 1

Chloe Cambodia 1995

A shaft of morning light darted into the room through the shutters, casting sinister shadows against the walls. Paralyzed with fear the sixteen year old lay pinned to the bed. The weight of the powerful beast on top of her fragile frame prevented her from moving, she wanted to scream but was too frightened to do so. She stared at the lace dress that had been ripped from her body, the tiny pearl buttons scattered across the polished teak floor. Frozen in time, tears welled in her eyes as with one swift sweep the man penetrated her, robbing her of her virginity. She would never forget the smell of the whisky on his breath or the odour of his sweating body as he pumped deeper and deeper into her flesh. The bed creaked and her pale cheeks were wet with his saliva as he drooled and stole his pleasure.

Suddenly the man screamed, his body shuddered and within moments it was over. His body slumped on top of her, later sighing he rolled over and within seconds fell into a deep sleep snoring like a buffalo.

Nan was trembling so much she feared that he would wake and attack her again, shaking she stepped out of the carved bed and limped towards the bathroom, a trickle of blood and sperm ran down her legs as she crawled into the shower and stood for what seemed like an eternity under the cold water hoping the cool flowing liquid would wash away the pain that had overwhelmed her.

Wrapping a towel around her wet body she crept out of the room past the sleeping guard in the corridor and through the rooms of the large house.

She was pale skinned and extremely beautiful, her parents had arranged the marriage and she had been forced to wed this fifty-three year old criminal. She had been sold for a pittance and her parents had not even turned up for the ceremony. She had been married to this stranger in an expensive lace dress only hours earlier, he was a cruel and violent man whose only female companionship had been with whores. Nan had been purchased by Chang to provide him with an heir, he was a wealthy and powerful man and her youth and extreme beauty had been the thing that had drawn him to her. Her father had been working for him as a gardener and as soon as Chang had seen Nan he had bid a meagre price, her parents had accepted and from one day to the next she had been married to this beast. After the ceremony he had literally dragged her to the bedchamber, ripped her dress off and raped her, it was her first experience with sex and she had been startled and he had slapped her and held his hand over her mouth when she tried to object, not only had he robbed her of her maidenhood he had damaged her soul. Arranged marriages were barbaric in her opinion she had been sold like a piece of meat.

She wandered aimlessly through the rooms of the great house that was to be her prison and she stumbled on the kitchen. All the staff had been given the day off, they had rejoiced at their master's wedding and everyone had seemed to have enjoyed it except her.

Nan crept back to the master bedroom, the guard had been drunk he was snoring and didn't rouse when she crept past him. Nan held her breath and with one clean sweep cut Chang's throat from ear to ear, he made no sound but his eyes opened and stared at her she dropped the mango knife and watched the pillows turn red with his blood enjoying watching the beast die.

Calmly she wandered through the house in the white lace, bloodstained wedding dress till she found the servants quarters. She plucked some jeans, a peasant's shirt and dressed as a boy, rolling up her hair she put on the baseball cap and sunglasses and walked out of the stately home by the servants' entrance. She spotted a bicycle at the back entrance and jumped on it.

Chickens were waking and morning light was breaking, as she cycled as calmly as she could past the guards, staff were arriving and the previous shift were going home, no one batted an eyelid as she passed through the large gates. She started to go faster on the bike, her heart was beating so loud that she thought it would burst. Hopefully they wouldn't disturb their master on his wedding night surely they wouldn't dare to wake him before noon and this would give her time to cross the border.

At the end of the clearing she dumped the bicycle in a verge and headed for the main road. She had no money except for the large gold chain, bracelet and diamond ring that had been a wedding present from her husband.

There were dozens of lorries passing every hour at this point all the trucks heading for Thailand passed along this road. She had been lucky within minutes of hitching a lift, to her surprise the driver thought that she was a boy. They stopped at a garage and the driver went to use the toilet, while he was gone Nan raked through his wallet and stole his ID, card he was young and slim and she would try and use his card to get over the border.

At the border she thanked him and went to join the queue of people that passed over the border every day to sell goods at the Thai market on the other side. It was busy and the guard never batted an eyelid as he looked at ID card, she went to join the entrance queue and repeated the performance at the Thai immigration side, they warned her she had to be back by six pm. The driver had no problem getting through the border despite he had lost his ID card, the guards knew him as he made he used the crossing on a weekly basis.

This is just a suggestion.

Nan felt relief sweep over her as soon as she crossed the border she had been responsible for slitting the throat of one of Cambodia's most corrupt criminals, a death warrant would be out looking for her at this very moment and there would be a fair price on her head.

Ironic that a man who had been surrounded by bodyguards twenty-four hours a day and who had spent millions on security, was wiped from this earth by his child bride. She shivered thinking of his face as he lay there naked with a red gash from ear to ear his eyes popping.

It had been so quick. Nan wished he had suffered more, she knew one thing, she was glad that she had done it, she had hated him and she would never be able to return to Cambodia again she would start a new life here in Thailand. She would sell the gold that should be enough for her to have a good start. She would get a job work in a hotel or in a restaurant. She would survive and whatever future fate dealt her it would be better than an existence being held prisoner at Chang's mercy. She had been sold as a reproductive machine for him to raise heirs for his criminal dynasty, instead she had wiped out his dynasty with one clean swift slash.

When the master of the house had not roused by three in the afternoon his right hand man had knocked on the door of the bedroom and opened it slowly, he shrieked at the sight of his master lying on the bed, his face as white as the crisp sheets. He was lying naked in a pool of blood a stray cat had come in the window and was licking at the open wound flies were hovering above his carcass. All hell was let loose at the mansion, the guard outside his room was being beaten almost to death by the other guards that were trying to glean information out of him. The whole house was searched for his bride they thought that perhaps she had been kidnapped after Chang had been murdered, all suspicions were turned to a rival drug cartel that had been threatening Chang no one even thought that his new child bride would have been responsible for his death.

Nan couldn't believe her eyes as she read a newspaper at the market, 'Cambodian Underworld Boss Brutally Murdered by Rival Cartel on Wedding Night - Child Bride Held for Ransom,' she laughed out loud as she read the article three times and could hardly absorb it, days later there was a follow-up article claiming that she had been murdered too.

It was a relieving feeling to read her own obituary, she could start afresh now, there was even a photo of her parents in a magazine who had sold their story and they claimed their daughter, the child bride, had been kidnapped and murdered after being brutally raped.

They claimed that she had called them from the kidnappers' haven, it was unbelievable the only thing that they had got right was that she had been raped, that was true, she had been raped on her wedding night by her husband and the black bruises on her body reminded her of that awful night.

She had been smart enough to slit a gangster's throat and get away with it and smart enough to escape without leaving a trace of evidence but whether or not she would be streetwise enough to survive living in Thailand was another story. She had sold the bracelet for half the price that it was worth and jumped on a bus to Pattaya. She'd heard that there was a beach there and she had never seen the sea and the first thing that she wanted to see was the sea. When she reached the bus station she hopped on a motorbike taxi, he took her to Jomtien Beach and laughed as he watched her run into the sea fully clothed with shoes on, she loved the sea instantly and decided that this would be the place that she would settle. She sat under an umbrella on the beach till seven pm at six thirty it was so beautiful when the sun dipped into the horizon and the sky turned a million shades of red, she walked along the water's edge.

The beach was filled with tourists and Thai's drinking cocktails, eating and lazing in the sunset.

Lovers walked hand in hand and children played volleyball, this was the place to be, away from the rural country, no mosquitoes, no snakes just sunshine and fun.

Selling the gold was easy, finding a room was not so easy, she had wanted to find a room on the beach but the prices were crazy and mainly rich foreigners lived there. She opted for a room in the city near the market, it was basic but had cold running water and electricity which was more than her parents' shack had, she would buy a mattress and some towels and that would be enough. On every corner of the street were vendors selling food and everything was cheap, there were lots of young people here. Where there were tourists there was money and it looked like the streets of Pattaya were paved with gold.

Pattaya was a sleepy fishing village twenty years ago now it was a bustling tourist destination with hundreds of hotels, restaurants and clubs catering to every taste, in the last two years development had gone crazy and condominiums and hotels were springing up everywhere.

Here you could play twenty-four hours a day, nightclubs seemed never to close and for most, life was one big party.

After settling into her room she went to the market to buy clothes, she couldn't help but notice that women here dressed differently than in the villages she was used to, they wore make-up and wore sexy clothes that she had only ever seen in magazines before.

The streets were full of pretty young women walking hand in hand with foreign men and she couldn't help but notice the abundance of beer bars with dozens of girls hanging around shouting at the foreign men as they passed by. Nan was too innocent to know what a whore was but not so innocent to know that most of the women here were looking for rich foreigners.

Most of the men were old and fat like Chang had been, but often she would see young women walk hand in hand with handsome men that looked like gods or movie stars.

She decided that one day she too would have a rich foreign man, a blond Adonis like the ones in the western movies. She realized that to attract such a man she would have to look like the other girls in the city she would have to wear make-up and high heeled shoes but she didn't know where to begin. She had noticed a very glamorous neighbor who usually came home around nine in the morning when Nan was going to the market, she decided that next time she saw her neighbor that she would ask her to help her with a top to toe make over.

The next morning like clockwork she heard the click of her neighbor's high heeled shoes on the stairs. Nan popped her head out and introduced herself, she was in awe of the beauty of her neighbor who was tall and elegant and looked stunning.

It came as a total shock when Candy, her neighbor explained that he was actually a ladyboy. Nan was so green that Candy had to fill in every detail and Nan looked gobsmacked as she listened to her neighbor explaining about all the surgery that he had gone through. At the end of the sermon Nan didn't care, all she knew was she wanted to look as sexy and elegant as Candy, they set a time to go shopping for later in the afternoon as Candy slept by day and worked by night. Nan was excited, Candy was going to organize everything, a haircut, make-up and a shopping spree. Nan couldn't wait, it would be a long day.

Candy worked as a showgirl at a nightclub near the beach where she did three shows a night and received handsome tips. She promised to take Nan to the club after her make over. Candy had just finished the series of operations that had transformed her into a woman, some of the best surgeons specializing in transsexuals worked in Thailand and patients came from all over the world entering the country as a man and leaving as a woman.

Nan admired how hard it must have been for Candy. Born a simple boy in the north of Thailand he had left home at fifteen and worked as a male prostitute to save money for the operation. Nan thought it sounded painful and it must have been painful both physically and mentally. Like Nan, Candy had no contact with her parents or family, she was an outcast and had made a new life for herself in the crazy seaside resort of Pattaya.

Nan knocked on her door and was shocked to see that Candy actually looked quite plain without make-up, seeing her like this she could imagine what she must have looked like as a man. They went on a shopping spree to little boutiques in side streets and back alleys that Nan would never have discovered by herself. Candy forced her to try on the skimpy, risqué items of clothing and at first she was reluctant to try them but it was amazing how good she looked in the sexy little dresses that her mentor had selected. She was tall and looked much older than her sixteen years and Candy screamed in disbelief when she told her new friend that she was only sixteen, as to get into clubs you had to be twenty. Candy promised that she would arrange a new fake ID card for her within a week. After the shopping spree they went to a little beauty salon in North Pattaya where Candy gave her over to three cackling ladyboys who were given the task of revamping the country Cambodian girl into a temptress. The process seemed to take forever, a facial, manicure, waxing, one cut her hair and set it in rollers while another applied a mask of make-up after two hours of prodding she was relieved to be told that she was finished. The girls helped her into the skimpy skintight dress and ridiculous high heels, all three laughing as she tried to balance on the killer spike heels, they added large earrings and dragged her into the next room so she could look at herself in a mirror.

Until now she had no idea what she was going to look like and as she gazed at her reflection she was amazed, she looked stunning, just like one of the girls that you see in the glossy foreign magazines even wearing trashy clothes she looked classy, she possessed an inner grace. The ladyboys stood staring at her, half proud of what they had achieved and half jealous because they knew that they would never ever look as good as this kid.

Candy roared with laughter as she watched Nan trying to walk across the room and they decided that she was way too glamorous to use the name Nan and christened her Chloe.

Suddenly the room was a hive of activity, Candy and her friends were getting ready to go to the show, two of them were performing and Chloe was invited for the ride.

Chloe couldn't believe her eyes, all the girls in the show were transsexuals and they all looked better than real women. Candy was stupendous and did an amazing play back of a heart rendering ballad. After her performance she received lots of tips when they went racing. After this they went racing to three other venues the last of which was a huge club with live acts, dancers and a comedy show. Nan had never been in a club and had never had alcohol. Tonight she tasted her first cocktail and loved the atmosphere in the club. She was oblivious to the fact that men both foreign and Thai had been hovering around her table all night and she didn't realize as she walked to the toilet that almost every male pair of eyes were on her. Candy's friends accepted her into their circle immediately having her on board guaranteed free drinks all night and lots of attention from the males. They decided to adopt her and groom her for the future.

Chloe being young and naive had no idea that they were going to use her looks to open doors for themselves. Deep down they resented the beauty she possessed, something that they had tried to emulate. Chloe was pleased with her membership to the girls' club. It meant Chloe was free to borrow all their clothes and hang out with them in the bars every night.

Chloe's money was running out and she had done little to find a job, working in a hotel paid only three thousand baht a month and that wouldn't even cover her rent and food bills.

Candy seemed worried when Chloe asked to borrow 2000 baht for the rent. She didn't know that her friend was in such dire straits and she suggested that she go to work in a go-go bar. Chloe didn't even know what a go-go bar was, never mind what the work entailed.

She had been living for six months in Pattaya and the money she had had from the gold was finished. Candy said that she would introduce her to a German who owned one of the best bars in town. On Candy's night off they got dressed up and made their way to the walking street, although Chloe had been there six months she had never been in the pedestrian part of the town, she was surprised to see rows and rows of pretty girls all lining the bars on either side of the street.

The moment they walked into the club all the men stopped looking at the lap dancers and stared at them. Diederick the owner stopped in mid-sentence and raced to the door to greet Candy he was not into ladyboys but had slept with Candy twice before, he was studying her friend eagerly praying that this kid was a real chick.

As an owner of one of the biggest bars in town he had seen many good looking girls before, however this one made the hairs on the back of his neck stand up, she was different, she had class and a kid like this would guarantee lots of dollars, he couldn't wait to try her. Diederick ordered champagne for the girls, this impressed Chloe as she had never tasted it before but she knew it was expensive and even though she didn't like the bubbly bitter taste she sipped the glass that the man offered her. He was a tall blond man with a dark tan and she had never seen anyone wearing so much gold before, round his neck there were five thick gold chains and he sported a ring on almost all of his fingers.

As she sipped the cold bitter liquid she felt slightly uneasy, he was staring blatantly at her in a way that made her feel very uncomfortable. Chloe excused herself and went to the bathroom and while she was fixing her make-up Candy verbally wrestled with Diederick, she had supplied him with fresh meat before but this one was special she wanted a 5000 baht fee.

Chloe felt embarrassed and tried not to look as the D. J. announced that it was show time and suddenly the stage was filled with six totally naked girls performing a lesbian ballet for the thirty or forty customers, she couldn't believe that Candy had brought her here and lowered her eyes feeling ashamed for the girls on the stage.

After a five minute show the stage emptied and 40 beautiful girls took their place, as soon as they positioned themselves at their poles they removed their bras and danced topless wearing only transparent G-strings and high heels, each girl sported a badge with a number and when a client wanted they could invite a girl to have a drink with them.

The music was great but Chloe wanted to run away she had a strange sense of foreboding that something bad was going to happen. Diederick disappeared reappearing moments later with two cocktails which he handed to both of his guests. Chloe didn't want to be impolite so she reluctantly accepted the drink and sipped the fruity liquid in the tall elegant glass. There was an orchid and cherry decorating the glass and this was the last thing she could remember she stared at the flower thinking how bright the purple seemed then everything seemed hazy. She remembered a narrow stairwell and a dark room with a circular bed, Candy had been with her and she remembered Diederick's naked body creeping into bed. It was like a nightmare, Candy had been licking her and Diederick had done the same to her as her husband had. She screamed and woke up feeling dreadful she was still clothed and in her own bed her make-up was smudged and her hair matted she was at home, she felt sick her head hurt and it was two in the afternoon it seemed like she had blacked out and she couldn't clearly remember what exactly had happened or how she had got home, she had flashbacks of being sick in a taxi, flashbacks of someone stuffing money in her bag trembling she opened the bag there was two thousand baht notes crumpled inside. She lay in the bed till darkness fell trying not to remember what had happened.

At seven pm she confronted Candy her friend seemed quite cool about the whole situation, she sat applying make-up expertly while Chloe screamed at her. Candy put down the mascara and swirled round in the chair looking her straight in the eye and she told her what had happened. Diederick had drugged her to loosen her up she explained that she needed money and that was the quickest way to earn it, adding that Diederick had a job for her, 90000 baht a month guaranteed and some people didn't earn that in a year, old women sweated on building sights doing heavy labour for 120 baht a day, she could guarantee her 3000 a night. Most people worked a month for that. All she had to do was look pretty, act sexy, dance a little go to dinner and nightclubs then give a little pleasure to a nameless man and that was that. Candy returned her concentration to the make-up mirror and told her to take it or leave it, Chloe walked out of the room.

She was glad when she heard the clicking of Candy's heels as she ran down the stairs.

She lay in bed feeling sick and thought about the jobs she had been offered working in a store for twelve hours a day for 200 baht, waiting tables for 150 baht a day, perhaps she should try it for a few weeks just to get herself started. Perhaps Candy was right she was trying to help she drifted into a sleep filled with dreams of demons, and for the first time in months she saw the ghost of her ex-husband, his throat slashed from ear to ear.

The next day she felt better it was Tuesday and she wanted to go to the market, she had seen a nice dress and was planning buying it from the 2000 baht that she had found in her bag.

Unknown to Chloe, Diedrick had paid Candy 5000 baht to persuade her to start work at the club. He had been phoning Candy all day and was driving her crazy, he already had six clients who had seen her at the club and had requested her.

Candy sent a text to Diederick between shows to warn him to be patient, that Chloe was no cheap trick and that he would have to be patient. This at least would give her more time to work on Chloe.

On her way to the market Chloe watched dozens of other girls, they were sitting at traffic lights in their Mercedes and walking out of beauty parlors with gold dripping at their necks. Most of these girls where nowhere near as pretty as Chloe but they had caught rich men. Most of them had been go-go ladies and retired after catching a rich foreigner. Perhaps Diederick's bar would be her passport to a better life, perhaps her beauty could trap a young handsome foreigner that would respect her and give her the security she craved.

Deciding to take the bull by the horns she decided that tonight she would go to speak with Diederick and make a deal with him, one thing was for sure she wouldn't accept a drink from him ever again. That night she dressed carefully wearing the new bright red dress she had bought earlier, it was cheap but the fabric clung to her body like a second skin and she couldn't wear underwear as it was almost transparent, the effect was provocative, one could easily see that apart from the slither of fabric she was naked. She carefully applied her make-up using all the tricks the boys had taught her, how to make her eyes larger, lips fuller.

The finished result was stunning she had never looked so sexy, she was all legs, breasts and lips. The hairdresser at the corner had put her hair up leaving one wild lock falling over one eye, tonight she emulated a sex goddess she had mastered the act of walking in even the highest heels, the boys had taught her how to enter a room, to walk like a tigress and that is exactly what she did as she entered the bar.

Like a tigress she made her way to the bar where Diederick was sitting. Every man in the room stopped staring at the forty women on stage and looked at her, all the pretty girls in the room seemed to look dull in comparison, she shone like a great Hollywood star and even Diederick was impressed. The German checked out the vision next to him, legs that didn't end, nipples that popped through the fabric, eyelashes so long and lips so moist she was a knockout. In all his career he had never seen anyone like this and his clients would die for her, she was going to break a lot of hearts this kid.

Chloe demanded first an apology from him then she requested an apartment on the beach, a guaranteed income of at least 100000 a month and a driver to drive her and pick her up from clients, she added that ugly ones would have to pay double and that she would have the right to refuse if she wanted.

Normally Diederick treated his staff like dirt, they were after all whores and came ten a penny. He couldn't believe that he was actually agreeing to her outrageous demands, sitting next to her he felt like she had him under a spell and within minutes he had agreed and without even knowing if she was able to dance had agreed to all her outrageous terms.

For a moment he thought that he would keep her for himself but then decided not too, he would make lots of money out of this one, she would be his star attraction.

Although he had the hots for Chloe he purposely kept her at arm's length reckoning that it would be better for business if he did so. There was plenty of pussy to be had so why should he jeopardize business by having a bit of fun with her, most of the girls were happy enough to service the boss for free.

Candy was wild with jealousy when she heard that her neighbor was moving to a nice apartment on the beach, she was even madder when she discovered that Chloe had approached Diederick for work, this meant that he would not get the usual commission for delivering her to him. She had had 5000 baht but was not happy with that, she should have kept a tighter rein on Chloe, she was a fast learner and manipulator. Candy claimed that she had discovered Chloe and made her what she was, Chloe moved out leaving Candy on the stairwell screaming dog's abuse. She was glad to see the back of that crummy apartment and the bitchy ladyboys.

The first night at the club was nerve-wracking the thought of dancing topless in front of all these foreigners was unnerving and she had postponed it as long as possible. Diederiek was demanding that she take centre stage, a girl wearing a sequined bikini and cowboy hat appeared at her side and gave her a shot of tequila Chloe knocked it back in one gulp it was foul but gave her a buzz and shoulders back, breasts forward, she climbed the stairs.

The DJ was playing one of her favorite songs and bathed in light oblivious to the onlookers she started to gyrate her body to the sound of the beat, suddenly she was aware that almost every male in the room was looking at her, she singled out one of the better looking ones and stared at him provocatively, she was amazed at the power she had over these men with one look she could drive them wild. She had only danced for minutes and had been called down the youngish man that she had stared at, he offered to buy her a drink so she put on her bra and slipped into the silky short robe and made her way to his table, the mama-san informed her that there had been six other clients interested and told her to drink the drink quickly and move on if he wasn't going to off her.

Jamie was a twenty-seven year old English stockbroker he spoke with a very polite accent which she could barely understand, her English was limited so she just smiled politely at him and studied his face. He had freckles and red hair which fascinated her as she had never seen a redhead before, he had interesting pale green eyes and seemed to laugh a lot. He was actually more shy than her, it was his first time on holiday alone, first time in Thailand and first time at a Go-Go Girl bar and it had taken him all his courage to request her to come to his table and his cheeks were blushing a deep pink each time she looked at him.

Chloe was glad that he was a novice at least he wouldn't expect too much from her, she had heard horror stories from some of the other girls. She felt quite relaxed sitting next to the young man he was as green as could be. The mama-san interrupted their conversation and warned Chloe that if this guy wasn't going to off her, one of Diederick's fat German friends would. If a client liked a girl he would off the girl by paying a 500 baht fine which allowed him to take the girl out of the bar or back to a hotel. Chloe dismissed the mama-san and with what little English she knew asked Jamie if he wanted to take her outside. Jamie sat speechless and Chloe added that if he didn't the gross big German would. The blushing young man paid the bar fee and a relieved Chloe went to get dressed, Jamie was her first customer, he was in Thailand for two weeks vacation it was his first night he had jet lag but had dragged himself to the club. It hadn't been his intention to off a girl, he was shocked at first when he entered to see all these young women with numbers on their G-strings they seemed like meat at a cattle market, he had been intending quickly finishing his drink and going back to his hotel, until he had seen Chloe take the stage. She was tall and classy looking with long legs and full breasts, she had high cheekbones and full lips. He couldn't take his eyes off those lips, all he thought about was kissing them, in the bar he had touched her leg accidentally her skin felt like silk.

Out on the street, Chloe decided to play it straight with him, she told him that he was her first client and that she had been dead nervous, he laughed and retorted that she was his first –go-go girl so they were equally green.

They went to eat and Chloe asked two motorbike taxis to take them up to the hill, it was quiet up there and they had a panoramic view of the city. The lights sparkled in the distance and Jamie was having fun, the idea of taking a vacation alone had been scary, he had never really been abroad before and he had booked a last minute holiday and had landed up in Thailand it all seemed so strange, yesterday he was in dreary London and tonight he was standing on a hill, stars above him, holding hands with one of the most incredible girls he had ever seen. They sat on a rock and after ten minutes asked their drivers to take them back to his hotel. Jamie watched her as she sat on the motorbike in front of him her long silky hair blowing in the cool night air.

He was staying at a five star hotel and at reception they caused an embarrassing scene saying that he would be billed automatically for taking Chloe to his room. The receptionist looked disapprovingly at her and Jamie's heart went out to her, it was her first night with a client and she was being treated like this. He informed the receptionist that he would be checking out in the morning, he didn't want to stay at this place any longer.

Chloe had not expected to be treated like this, in most hotels they were used to gorgeous girls sharing with the guests here however they had an attitude.

Jamie had been up for forty-eight hours, he was exhausted, In the room he opened a bottle of champagne from the mini bar, she went to shower and to her surprise when she returned he was lying fast asleep in bed she sat on the balcony admiring the sea view wondering what they charged a night at a place like this and how a young guy could afford it. After an hour she crept into bed hoping not to wake him. In the morning she was woken by him and while she was half asleep he made love to her, he was so excited the whole performance lasted only five minutes then they went to shower together. While she applied some make-up he sheepishly slipped three thousand baht in her bag.

Chloe had her own ghosts to deal with, the three thousand baht in her purse was a reminder that her career as a prostitute had begun she sat huddled on the small balcony of her apartment feeling dirty, the fact that Jamie had been nice to her didn't help, she had enjoyed his company he was a nice man but when he put the money in her bag she felt like a whore.

She sat on the cramped balcony all day without eating or drinking, at seven the sun set and the sky was ablaze with red it looked so pretty she sighed and went to shower and prepare for the night.

When she arrived at the club she was surprised to see Jamie sitting outside, for a moment she thought perhaps that he was here to complain about her then she saw the smile on his face. He had been waiting for her and had paid the bar fee for her for two weeks and wanted her to spend the next fortnight with him, she smiled and was secretly happy, anything was better than dancing topless in that club. He was a nice guy and he wanted her to show him all the tourist attractions.

The next two weeks became a holiday for her he treated her like a princess, splashing out, taking her on wild shopping sprees, he bought her clothes, shoes and on the last day a gold ring and pair of earrings. One week into the trip they had gone to see a Chinese Temple twenty kilometers outside Pattaya. A freak rainstorm had erupted and they stood under an awning taking refuge from the torrential rain.

Chloe looked at him and was amazed at the look in his eyes he was looking at her, the rain droplets running down her face she felt frightened it was obvious that he had fallen madly head over heels in love with her she couldn't look him in the eyes. She liked him but she was not in this game to fall in love she was in this business to meet a very rich man and Jamie was comfortable but not rich enough. She wanted to nail a really rich man, then divorce him and retain a small fortune, this was her dream and her ambition and Jamie was cute but not what she was looking for.

The last night of his vacation he took her for a very expensive meal at an extremely expensive French restaurant she toyed with the food on her plate finding it bland, she didn't like European food and didn't see the point in paying a month's salary for a meal.

Jamie didn't want to leave her and he demanded that she stop at the bar and wait three months for him, he offered to pay her rent and send her money every month, he couldn't stand the thought of her dancing in her underwear and being pawed by different men each night.

He had deposited some money in a bank account and vowed to send her 30 000 baht a month. She learned that night how to lie, she promised him to give up dancing and said she would wait for him, That evening they made love for the last time on the sofa in the room that he had rented, after showering together she accompanied him on the two hour journey to the airport he had held her hand all the way and when he kissed her good-bye there had been tears in his eyes. The taxi took her from the airport back to Pattaya, she asked the driver to drop her off at the bar, and before Jamie had even taken off she was up on the stage flaunting her body and searching for the next victim who she hoped wouldn't fall in love with her it was too heavy. She informed the mama-san that she wasn't interested in long time offs, she only wanted to go with the men for a short time from now on it was less complicated.

Within minutes a Swiss business man had taken her off and they had gone to a short time room upstairs. Jamie's flight was late, it was just taking off while he sat in the darkness remembering every single moment that they shared. Chloe was being fucked by a man whose name she didn't even know.

The man was pleased, he gave her 2500 baht for the half hour and after a quick shower she was downstairs back on stage. Before she had even removed her bra an elderly man had requested her company, it was easy if she kept this up she would be loaded, she decided she would do three a night.

Sometimes if the man was young and persistent she accepted offers to stay the night, sometimes she stayed a week with them and like Jamie, they fell in love with her opened bank accounts and sent her money every month.

Staying with one man bored her, after a few days she found it impossible to stay with these strangers twenty-four hours, she preferred short time encounters with no strings attached, she spent most days in the internet cafe sending regular emails to the ones that had been stupid enough to have fallen in love with her she emailed them claiming that her mother was ill that she needed an operation and the men believed her sending more money to the bank accounts they had opened for her.

Three months had sped by and she was expecting Jamie to arrive on the Saturday he emailed her regularly and had sent her faithfully the 30000 baht a month as promised he thought that she had stopped dancing and was working in a hotel.

She would never forget the look on his face, he had arrived a day early and gone to her apartment to surprise her. A neighbor had heard him thumping on the door and said that she had gone to the club, she had been upstairs with a client, she was kissing the old man on the cheek before returning to the stage, as usual she would focus on one man to make him feel special. What a shock she got as she stared out into the dimly lit audience and spotted Jamie's ginger head, his face was chalk white and he had a look in his eyes that she would never forget, she dipped her head in shame wondering what to do as he sat watching her drinking glass after glass of whisky, she didn't dare go to his table. The mama-san approached her and informed her that the French man from last week was waiting at the door she walked down the stairs towards the dressing room ignoring Jamie, that was when the fight began.

Girls screamed and the police were summoned as Jamie rolled about the floor almost choking the Frenchman, it took the doormen ten minutes to calm Jamie down and he was taken away by the police and charged. Diederick had warned her not to play with the clients' hearts. He hated having trouble in the club, every time the police came it cost him money, in the end the Frenchman had to go for stitches. Chloe never batted an eyelid she undressed and went back on stage smiling like it was some kind of privilege to have men fight over her.

She was glad that within ten minutes another man had taken her, she was pleased to get out of the club as she was afraid of further confrontation with Jamie. She agreed to sleep with the man who had taken her, she wanted to avoid going to her apartment in case Jamie turned up.

After spending a night in police custody Jamie was set free he appeared at the club drunk and was refused entry, he was devastated that she refused to see him, he had waited outside her apartment block for hours but she couldn't face him.

The next night at the club the police arrived. Diederick wondered why they were taking her away he hoped that she hadn't been doing drugs as she was whisked off still wearing the skimpy robe that she wore at the club.

This was the last time she would see Jamie they had taken her to identify the body.

Jamie had written her a letter addressed to the club it was still in his hand as his body hit the ground when he jumped of the twelfth floor of his hotel suite. Chloe was shocked as she looked at his crushed body, his ginger hair matted with blood, she had led this man on disappointed him and he had committed suicide.

For nights every time she tried to sleep she saw his lifeless body lying there in a pool of blood her dreams were filled with nightmares and she was sure his ghost would haunt her. She filled her rooms with Buddhas and went to the temple to speak to the monks.

The other girls in the bar nicknamed her the murderer and Diederick gave her a week off to try and sort herself out. Even worse his parents arrived as he had told them all about her and they arrived one afternoon on her doorstep, desperate to investigate why their son had killed himself. Their hearts were broken Jamie had been an only child. She learned from them that Jamie had been heir to his grandmother's family fortune.

Thinking that she was too heartbroken they had brought a photo album to show her Jamie as a child, he had been brought up in a sort of castle and she thought that he had been poor, Jamie would have been the goose that laid the golden egg for her, he had never mentioned that he had come from such a wealthy background and to make matters worse the parents left the album with her and offered to have her flown in for the funeral, she declined pretending that she was too upset and that she didn't have a passport. For a year after Jamie died his family still transferred the 30000 baht to her account but she didn't touch the money she felt too guilty to accept it.

Jamie's dead face haunted her still and she had taken to using sleeping pills, and uppers and downers to keep her going. Living by night took its toll on her body, she was still beautiful but that special fresh glow had been replaced with a desperate look. She had been dancing for a year and slept with hundreds of men, many of which she didn't remember their names she drank a lot and went out almost every night. Diederick hated seeing her slip, he never thought that she would go the same way as most of them did.

The innocence that had made her special had been replaced with a hardened savvy.

She was still a great beauty but looked tired and burned out. Diederik genuinely liked Chloe she had made a lot of money for him he decided that she needed a break. In two weeks his lesbian sister was arriving from Dusseldorf and he would send them for a week to Phuket. It would get both of them off his chest, he called the travel agent and reserved two tickets, one for Chloe and one for Carla.

His sister was thirty and she had made quite a lot of money modelling for catalogues and had opened an upmarket bar for lipstick lesbians. Her five year relationship with a tennis champion had come to an abrupt end when the tennis star became pregnant to a trainer.

She was visiting her brother to get away from it all and Diederick hadn't seen her in ten years and was dreading her visit. Sending her and Chloe on a holiday was a great idea.

CHAPTER 2

Rogillio Rio de Janeiro

Rogillio stood under the steaming shower, the jets of water made him feel awake and invigorated, he shaved carefully and stood back admiring himself in the mirror, he was tall and tanned and had an excellent physique, like all Latinos he was vain and spent almost ten minutes studying himself before going into his dressing room to get dressed.

He was twenty-four years old, tall dark, handsome and rich, he had already made his first million at twenty when a major European team bought him from the South American football team that had discovered the child striker. His good looks had been an asset and he had made millions from the modelling and advertising contracts that he had managed to get. He was the perfect sportsman rugged but possessing a smooth clean-cut look, he appealed to the male market, females adored him, he had sex appeal in a masculine way and was popular with the teenyboppers and grandmothers alike.

Young men wanted to look like him and he was signed up for major advertising contracts for a global footwear company, a sport's clothing brand, an aftershave campaign and a car company were planning on using his face to launch their newly designed car which was to be launched within a few months. Although he was handsome it was not in a way that threatened people, he was like a very photogenic version of the boy next door in a clean-cut kind of way that appealed to the mass market, his face was appealing in all countries the Americans, Europeans and Asians adored him and when he put his name on a product the sales shot through the roof.

His celebrity was at a peak and whenever he arrived at public functions or airports thousands of fans lined the streets, in the beginning he had adored the adulation but recently his popularity was disturbing, mostly he travelled with a small army of security guards which crippled his freedom, he no longer could simply go on a date, go see a movie or enjoy a shopping binge, every move he made had to be planned. Living in the eye of the public had put tremendous pressure on him and he enjoyed stealing time alone whenever he could. Being photogenic the paparazzi adored him, his face sold many magazines and newspapers and they seemed to follow his every move.

He was disciplined he didn't drink or smoke and spent hours in the gym his looks were his livelihood and he was in tip-top condition, unlike some of the other young football stars he didn't party or have wild nights out with the lads, he slept early and always turned up on time and ready for action whether it was on the football field or in the photo studio, a lot of his teammates were jealous of him he had the profile and the big bucks. Some of the players were better than him but it was his name that hit the headlines, he was skilled at football but not the best, however having him on the team was a lucrative business venture because the money that the team made from his marketing contracts was incredible, he was single and lived in a huge house that any movie star would have been proud of.

He had been poor, living in a slum area of Rio he had been abandoned by his parents and lived on the streets survival was a struggle for most of the kids, many turned to drugs and crime, little Rogillio was too religious for crime he turned to sport, a youth project for street kids had started a football sponsorship and he had been quick to audition.

Talent scouts had been quick to snap him up and with coaching he became an excellent player, one thing led to another and suddenly he was a football star a shining example to the impoverished kids that there was a way out of the ghetto. He gave large chunks of his income to children's charities and never forgot his roots, off the football field his passion was for fast cars and flashy clothes, being poor and spending the first years of his life barefoot he bought fine shoes by the dozen and owned around 300 pairs of footwear, his other passion was for beautiful women preferably blue eyed and blonde like the ones he used to see in the Hollywood movies as a kid. He would sneak in to the rundown movie theaters without paying and sit for hours looking at the beautiful women who lived in the beautiful homes and drove beautiful cars, sitting in the dark of the theatre at six he had promised himself that by hook or by crook by the time he was thirty he would have all the things that they had in these movies. He had arrived early at the destination of his dreams, earlier than anticipated, he was only twenty-four and had it all.

Dressing in a cream silk shirt and cream cotton pants he admired his reflection in the huge antique mirror in the hallway, the fabric looked great next to his bronze skin. He checked his appearance in the mirror and made sure that he had condoms in his wallet. He snapped on a chunky gold bracelet; for a bit of the bling bling effect and grabbed the keys of his Porsche, he had a lunch date with a blonde model from Sweden. The press thought that he was in Europe so there were no paparazzi camped outside his home, he felt like a schoolboy playing truant as he sprung into the gleaming yellow car and as he turned the keys in the ignition he thought about his lunch date. They had been introduced at a film premier and she was one of the hottest creatures on the catwalk, her hair was almost white and her skin was like cream, her legs went right on up for miles and he looked forward to their meeting. Lunch was at her apartment which would be cool, knowing that soon he would be between the sheets with Tiffany, she like all women would melt like butter in his arms and like all the rest would probably fall deeply in love with him.

Rogillio liked variety and rarely dated a girl twice, he was not the type for second helpings and preferred to play the field, the amazing thing was that usually the really beautiful women that he was magnetically drawn to were a disappointment in bed. He remembered one actress he had met at a party, he had seen three of her movies and she really turned him, on the night that he met her he was captivated and he couldn't believe that she was available. He had wined her, dined her and landed up in her bed four hours later. It was the greatest disillusion of his life, she was cold and icy, without an ounce of passion in her body, self-centred and egoistic was an understatement he had never been so disappointed in his life. The Hollywood Star who looked so sexy on screen was as dull between the sheets as cold as could be. In reality she wasn't even all that pretty she was as cold as ice in bed and frigid, he had felt like he was making love to a rag doll and he was glad to have left after the act and was still amazed sometimes when he watched her movies, on screen she had this animal sexuality and charisma, it was sad he thought that she could always get into character on screen but not between the sheets.

The Swedish blonde would probably be the same, all the great beauties were a complete disappointment, however she was incredible looking and he sped off to the address she had scribbled down on her set card. At the traffic lights he checked the address and licked his lips, the photo of her on the card was great she was wearing a swimsuit and looked sensational. The music throbbed in his car, the windows were tinted an illegally dark shade so that people couldn't see him. At the traffic lights he checked his appearance in the driving mirror carefully dragging a wet lock of hair letting it fall carelessly over one eye he smiled thinking that he was looking extra handsome today.

She was living in an expensive apartment block so obviously she had made a good living out of modelling, the doorman directed him to her floor and warned Tiffany that he was coming up.

She answered the door wearing old jeans and a shapeless t shirt, without make-up and her hair in rollers she looked nothing like the sex symbol on the magazine cover that lay on her coffee table. While the tall skinny girl removed her rollers he looked at the editorial of her in the magazine and wondered how many hours the computer genius had taken to retouch her photos, in the flesh Tiffany bore no resemblance to the gorgeous creature featured in many magazines, up close she had an odd profile, her nose pointed up and her teeth seemed too large for her mouth, her chest was as flat as a boy's and she seemed scraggy without an ounce of flesh on her bones.

She had just done three weeks of catwalks in Paris, Milan and New York and had just secured a global perfume campaign that would pay her more than one million dollars. The lens loved her and the designers were waiting in line for her. She was represented by six of the world's leading agencies. In the flesh she was rather plain, she was photogenic and most people were disappointed when they met her in person. The one thing she did possess was attitude. She was indeed a diva with high demand on shoots. It was not uncommon for her to turn up two hours late or storm off a set. She was after all the world's most sought after supermodel. She had been scouted at eighteen in a bus station by a model scout and whisked off to Paris where she became an overnight sensation.

As famous for her editorials in leading glossy magazines she was regularly featured in the tabloids as the bad girl from the catwalks. She smoked too much, drank too much and had a substance problem however she still was the Queen of the catwalks despite her indiscretions.

During lunch she must have answered 50 calls from her bookers, Rogillio felt about as attracted to her as a donkey. In the naked light of day without the professional make-up she looked horsey, after the low calorie lunch he found himself leaving making the excuse that he was off to train, glad to have escaped the six foot bag of bones he sat in his Porsche and wondered where he could go. He was horny and needed company but he couldn't just walk into a singles bar and pick up a girl he was too well known and any scandal could ruin his career. For a moment he thought of calling an escort agency but didn't want to, that could be too dangerous and he winced imagining that if he did the hooker could sell her story and ruin him too. Damn it, he hadn't brought his phone he did have some numbers of girls that would probably come round. Wasn't life a bitch, he was so horned up and had been so looking forward to lunch at Tiffany's and now here he was driving on the freeway with a boner.

Suddenly he decided to go to the gym, he would do a workout, cool himself off then go home and hang out by the pool or go shopping. Shopping was always cool especially when there was no press around.

He didn't really have friends on the team because they were a little jealous, he wasn't quite one of the lads he didn't drink and always got the hottest chicks. In the beginning he had tried to strike up a friendship with some of the lads on his team. He had invited them for dinner to his home and it had turned out a disaster, the drunken bunch had been openly insulting and been quite hostile towards him. The flow of drink had loosened their tongues and he had been shocked at how jealous they were of him, his team mates hated the fact that he was the only one noticed on the field, they hated the fact that he had made so much on marketing and since that disastrous night he had kept them at a distance.

Sometimes he missed having a family, he wondered sometimes who exactly his parents were, where they were and if he had had brothers or sister. He was rich now but being rich had its drawbacks it got kind of lonely and sometimes when he was on the field and heard all the crowd cheering he wondered if his father was standing in the throngs of people or if his family were watching him on t. v.

Perhaps if he had had a normal family life he wouldn't have become what he was now, perhaps if he had been loved he would know how to love but having survived on the streets it made him reluctant to trust anyone and even though he was rich and famous he trusted no one. He owed his good looks to his parents and sometimes he wondered if he hadn't been blessed with these looks if he would have ever escaped from the ghetto at all. Yes he was handsome, yes he was rich and famous, yes he liked fast cars and large pieces of jewelry, he glanced at the large diamond rings on his fingers and thought that these were the same hands that had as a child raked through the rubbish mounds outside the city searching for food. He never felt guilty about buying shoes by the dozen, as a child he had been barefoot for years, his feet blistered and scarred. He had found an old football in the trash and this discovery had been the one that developed is passion for football as he played to keep warm, played to pass the time and lost himself in the sport. The anger and despondency he felt deep down inside he had taken out on the ball and as he had kicked that ball against the graffiti sprayed walls of the back streets he had never guessed that this ball abandoned in the rubbish would be the discovery that would change his life and be his passport to a new world.

It's hard to sleep with an empty stomach, it's hard to sleep on the streets and a child grows up fast when abandoned, it was a jungle out there the streets of San Paulo were a dangerous place even now he didn't sleep well even in the opulence of his luxurious bedroom he would wake in the night, sometimes he would wake in a sweat and lie between the silk sheets thinking this was all a dream. Sometimes in his sleep he would return to the streets of San Paulo, there had been a time he had slept in a cardboard box, a gang of other youths older than him had beat him and stole his box he had walked the streets and cried till daylight broke. There were those were now jealous of him, they didn't know where he came from, one day when his sport's career was over he would write a book, he would surprise them all. Perhaps they would make a movie about him, there were so many things they didn't know about him, so many ghosts that haunted him.

He had been a thief stolen to survive, he had sniffed thinner to escape from the horror of his daily existence, his first sexual experience was selling his body to perverts and dirty old men to survive, discovering that ball in the rubbish heap had changed his life. That magic ball had a place of honor in a glass case in his study, sometimes he would look at it and wonder what would have happened if he hadn't discovered it, probably he would have died on the streets, have taken a drug overdose or turned to crime and spent his life in jail or been shot like some of his childhood friends. Sometimes he had to count to ten and thank his lucky stars that fate had brought him to this point in life but deep down inside he believed that there would be a price to pay for the luck he had had.

He wanted to fall in love, have a family that he could love but was afraid to love how, could he love? How could he trust being brought up the way he was? In a way everything had changed in his world but sometimes inside he was still the fragile child sleeping in a box on the streets waiting to be beaten waiting for the rain to come and destroy his home. Sometimes when he dreamt he was back in San Paulo standing barefoot on a mound of rubbish searching for food, the heat, the smell the desperation the helplessness would come flooding back to him and he would wake in a cold sweat. Each time these dreams came to haunt him he would promise himself to help. Perhaps God had plucked him out of the ghetto and blessed him with success so that he could help others, he wanted to help but was always too busy, all the traveling all the pressure the training, the football the marketing modelling. He was superstitious and thought that if he didn't do something major to help all these kids that were still sleeping in boxes that God would take it all away from him with one great sweep.

On the way to the gym he stopped off at a store he liked, within an hour he had bought six pairs of shoes, two suits and a dozen shirts. He couldn't resist the shoes, when he was a kid he used to beg for money and he would sit on the street and watch the people walking by. He judged them by how expensive their shoes, were for him they were a status symbol and he had been a shoeshine boy for a year. He had adored polishing the fine leather shoes, he had been after all barefoot as a child, now times had changed and sometimes he would bulk buy three pairs of the same style because he liked shoes when they felt new and rarely wore the same pair twice. He had a contract with a sport's shoe company, they gave him hundreds of pairs of trainers a year, he wore them once then stored them boxed, one day he was going to auction them and send the money to build schools for the street kids.

He would never forget one kid, she had been abandoned and was only about three she slept in a box near his with three other kids, he had given her some food because she had looked so weak and thin.

She had curly hair and the eyes of an angel, one morning he woke to the sound of dogs howling. A pack of wild dogs were hovering around her box, the other children were gone looking for food, no doubt the child with the eyes of an angel had died in her sleep. The wild dogs were eating her, at first he had sat frozen to the spot watching as the animals ripped the flesh from her loins, then screaming, Rogillio had thrown stones at the pack and foolishly charged at them waiving a stick, fortunately the beasts had had their fill and took off.

Tears spilled down his cheeks he grabbed his plastic bag of belongings and ran and ran for miles to another spot nearer the city he ran till he was out of breath and sat against a wall. Heartbroken, his cries echoed throughout the streets, no one stopped to help him, they all walked by as he sobbed his heart out. He watched the feet of the people as they went about their daily schedules not even noticing the small crumpled figure that was in trauma, to the world he was just another street kid. He wanted to be near people and was afraid that the dogs would come to him. The police arrived and beat him, threatening to take him to jail so he had to scamper away again and find an alley to rest in. He was nothing, less than a human being on the streets, there were thousands of children like him, thousands of nameless faceless creatures that nobody cared for or loved, they were regarded as less than human, like rats that infested the cities. No one respected them, how could anyone expect them to.

survive, no home, no family, no love how could they blame them for turning to crime, prostitution and drugs it was the only escape, God it seemed had turned his head from the plight of the street children. For many years Rogillio didn't believe in God. He didn't believe in anything but survival.

God had given Rogillio nothing but pain, then one day God gave him a ball, that ball changed his life. Here he was a celebrity, rich and famous, young and handsome. However once streetwise always streetwise, Rogillio knew that everything came with a price tag and for his luck he knew that one day there would be a price to pay.

Life was strange he thought, when he was living in a box he was searching for something, now he was living in a palace his environment had changed but he was still searching for something, perhaps it was love.

CHAPTER 3

Marisa Los Angeles

Marisa had arrived in Hollywood on a Greyhound bus, she was wearing torn jeans, a sweatshirt, she looked almost too fragile to carry her rucksack which contained all her worldly possessions. She was another runaway teenager that had arrived in Tinseltown with hopes of becoming something. She had escaped from her drunken father and was glad to have left the trailer where she had lived almost all of her sixteen years, she had high hopes of becoming someone and didn't want to look back. Whatever happened could not have been worse than the life she had had till now, her mother had been a showgirl and had left her with her unemployed father when she was two months old. They had lived in a broken down trailer outside Detroit, and she had looked after herself for as long as she could remember.

Her father was mostly unemployed he had been a gambler and they survived on his winnings. When he wasn't gambling he was busy conning people, selling fake insurances and mail order products that never arrived. The invention of the computer had killed his trade as everyone shopped on line and the day of the door to door conman was obsolete.

His drinking and binges had got worst and he had taken to beating Mary, often at school she would wear dark glasses to hide the black eyes.

She hated her father and had hated her childhood, when her classmates had gone to movies and played, she had done odd jobs to scrape up money for food. She had worked for as long as she could remember delivering milk and newspapers when she was ten years old. She would never forget having to get up at 4 am to start the milk rounds. In the winter she had been so cold that her nose had been blue. After delivering the milk she would go home and grab her school bag, after school she would sew doing alterations for people and sewing curtains on the second-hand sewing machine that her father had bought her from his winnings at a gambling binge in a casino in Las Vegas. Sometimes she would sew till midnight, often at school she was tired and listless and had bad results from her tests.

She had never had new clothes and wore the cast-offs that the neighbors gave her on the trailer park. At school they called her Second-hand Rose and she was quite ordinary looking till she turned fifteen. As womanhood approached her body changed. She lost the puppy fat that had made her look short and fat and the ugly duckling had transformed into the best looker in the school. At sixteen she discovered to her delight that she had one gift it was something that would change her life forever and shape her destiny.

Mary from the trailer park had been blessed with one gift, she had sex appeal. She had indeed inherited the magical quality that her mother had possessed, sex appeal. Her mother had been a Vegas showgirl and her father had been crazy about her. Mary had been conceived in the back of a rented truck the night her father had won 2000 dollars in Vegas, he had splashed the whole amount on her mother and three nights of wild sex sessions had resulted in her mother's pregnancy. After Mary had been born her mother took to drink then started to work as an exotic dancer. She had run off with one of her customers leaving Mary with her father in the run down trailer.

Suddenly at sixteen Mary realized that she was beautiful and she started making her own clothes from remnants that had been left over from the curtain fabric and she looked stunning in whatever she wore, she worked part-time in a diner and men went there just to eat dinner to see her, she had blonde hair, blue eyes and pouty lips, she had developed large breasts and looked older than her years, at the diner she made lots of tips and soon learned how to flirt with almost all of the male customers. All the best looking boys at school had the hots for her and suddenly she was popular. When she had been young she had no friends at school now she was the most popular girl in the there. When boys dated her she would always ask them to take her to the movies while the lads squeezed her breasts and became flushed with passion she would study the glamorous women on the screen and eat up their mannerisms. When she left the diner the sales went down by one third. The owner Fat Sam had been coming on to her, usually she could handle it by teasing him. One night however when she was cleaning up he had grabbed her and ripped her blouse open, she had hit him hard on the head with the cook pan she had been scrubbing and left without her pay never to return.

At sixteen she lost her virginity to the school baseball hero, the whole experience had been disappointing and had lasted five minutes from start to finish she had imagined it to be romantic like in the movies instead it was a quick, wet and sticky affair, she had sex with a few other of the students but was always disappointed since she had been ten she had dreamed of going to Hollywood and becoming an actress she had visions of herself one day getting an Oscar and imagined herself floating down the red carpet wearing a magnificent dress.

Her father had been so furious that she had quit the diner he had beaten her then gone out to a bar, he returned drunk and fell asleep in a chair while he slept she had taken the money from the cookie jar and packed her rucksack and headed for the bus depot. On the bus she had sat next to an old lady they had spoken during the long journey she had proudly shown her a photo of her newly born granddaughter she was called Marisa, Mary liked the name and decided that from the moment she stepped off the bus she would no longer be plain Mary she would be Marisa, Marisa Duval.

The gangly teenager arrived in the bus station at six am in the morning, so this was LA she thought disappointed, she had imagined that the whole of L. A. was like Beverly Hills however Los Angeles seemed like one big concrete jungle she wondered if she had done the right thing she had a rucksack with one dress three t shirts and a pair of sandals and ninety-eight dollars in cash.

No friends, nowhere to stay, she was the perfect victim for Sergio. He came often looking for new girls arriving at the bus station his radar eye caught her immediately and he licked his lips, this one was a stunner she would look great in a tight dress he thought admiring the curves of her body. Without wasting a moment he approached her offering the usual introduction by offering her breakfast, a room and before he could even discuss her working for him on the streets she had told him to fuck off. Sergio was shocked she had the face of an angel and the tongue of a fishwife she looked so fragile but was as streetwise as hell. She marched away and Sergio raced after her begging her to have a cup of coffee with him. She looked him straight in the eye and told him to be careful, that she was no two bit cheap trick and that she would boot him in the balls if he followed her. With every ounce of charm that he had he started wooing her with polite conversation and in the end after five minutes she decided to let him buy her breakfast. Over a huge plate of fried sausage, eggs, bacon and grits Sergio sat speechless as Marisa explained she was looking for an agent she wanted to be in movies so bad and wasn't interested in his offer as working as a hooker. Sergio had to admit that this kid was different, she had charisma and the sex appeal was dripping off her, he had an erection just watching her eat her brunch.

He was captivated by this kid he couldn't take her eyes off her after the plate was clean.

She looked him in the eye and asked him if he wanted a piece of the action then he should help her become a star, as a pimp he must have connections with people in the industry, she offered him a piece of the action if he could get her in movies. It was true Sergio supplied young fresh flesh for some people who worked in the movie business but he didn't know anyone at the top. She added she wouldn't do skin flicks or porn and wanted a serious contract, they talked for an hour and Sergio offered her to stay at his flat, she agreed warning him that if he tried anything she would cut his cock off. Sergio believed that she would too she was as hard as hell.

Marisa moved into Sergio's apartment and demanded that he get her connected quickly.

Sergio could have set her up with a client for sex but for a screen test he didn't know where to begin, one of his girls had been banging an assistant director called Jake so he decided to go for that angle, perhaps he could get her a screen test. To his surprise when he called the assistant director he was up for it, they were auditioning for a girl for an up and coming movie and there were seventy-five girls coming so what difference would one more make? Jake was gay so he wouldn't expect anything from Marisa.

Sergio took her shopping in a second-hand store they found a simple skimpy floral dress for her, the flimsy fabric clung to the curves of her body like a second skin, she bought a pair of strappy high heeled shoes and was satisfied with the result.

Marisa showered and changed, she took ages doing her hair and make-up and when she emerged from the bedroom Sergio looked at her in disbelief she was knockout drop dead gorgeous. A second-hand dress had never looked so good, under the flimsy fabric she was completely naked, not that that would have any effect on Jake he was gay. Sergio dropped her off at the casting and she was the last to arrive and unlike the other seventy-five she had no book, no experience and probably no chance.

Jake was getting bored it had taken him four hours to see all the seventy-five girls and no one had been right for the role, he had seen almost all of them before, and even though it was going to be a small part he wanted someone fresh. This movie had the biggest budget they had worked with and he wanted everything perfect, it was late and he was hungry he would get rid of the last girl quickly he had had enough. Marisa made an entrance Jake would never forget, she glided in through the door and struggled to balance on her ridiculously high heels. Jake didn't speak he remained silent as she sat provocatively in the chair across from him, he was speechless it was like a light had filled the room the moment she entered.

He was gay but couldn't fail to see the rampant sexuality she possessed, girls like this were not ten a penny. Before even asking her name he decided that she was perfect for the role, even if she had no experience, even if she couldn't act she was the one. They would coach her, teach her, just sticking her face on the video would sell millions of copies every red-blooded American male would go wild about her she was a new Monroe.

After five minutes of chatting he knew she was the one and he arranged a screen test for the following day and told her to turn up bright and early, no make-up and fresh from the shower. She was as green as could be and had only been in Hollywood for a weekend.

Marisa didn't sleep she lay awake all night finding it impossible to rest. She had a screen test and she had no experience, she had bags under her eyes when the car arrived to pick her up she was so nervous she could have died and Sergio had been furious that she wouldn't let him come with her.

Someone directed her to the studio and she was given a mug of coffee and whisked off to hair and make-up. It took them almost two hours to transform her into the character she had to be. While she was being preened and prodded by three people Jake turned up with a script and ran over what she had to do. He repeated himself till she was growing tired perhaps being a movie star was not all that hot after all, they discussed her skin and figure like she wasn't in the room and every flaw was remarked on, when the team had finished she was taken to wardrobe, the dress they gave her was like a slither of fabric conceived of bandages the designer was European something or other when the stylist helped her in to it she held her breath. This dress did more for her than she imagined, her body looked sensational and she could hardly believe the reflection that she saw in the mirror, everything seemed to have been exaggerated, her eyes seemed larger, her lips fuller. What they had done to her hair she didn't know but it looked great she studied herself in the mirror and thanked the team she had never imagined that she could look like this.

She was playing the role of a would-be starlet trying to get a role at an audition, the other actor introduced himself, my God he was so handsome, she didn't know guys could look like that. She hoped that she would remember her lines staring into those big green eyes he was to die for, pity he was gay.

Jake waited till the director and producer had arrived, he had called them to check this kid out. When everyone arrived they took their spots and Marisa did what she had been told to do, someone in the darkness shouted cut and everyone stopped. Marisa felt uncomfortable she felt that she hadn't done her best, had felt awkward with the dialogue and felt quite honestly that she had screwed it up. Breaking the silence she shouted towards Jake and asked him if she could do it one more time. The clapperboard snapped and she entered the room this time using her own dialogue, own technique and when Jake said cut there was a strange silence for a minute then everyone in the room started clapping.

The director was shocked, this new kid possessed something special, so special that he had never seen someone do this at a screen-test. Her presence lit up the screen like light, when the cameras rolled she was superb she possessed an animal sexuality that sold tickets. They were silent, having her in a small role would blow the star right off the screen. Everyone would pale next to her, Simon the director surprised Jake by asking them to prepare her for another screen-test he wanted to see her do some dramatic scenes, he had a hunch that this girl could get the leading role. She was new, she would be cheaper and he had a hunch that she was going to be big soon. A moment like this happened rarely on film.

Without knowing if she had done well or not she was whisked into make-up, this time someone else came to explain her role for the second test. In contrast to the last scene she didn't look beautiful. She looked sick and tired, the make-up department transformed her from a vamp to a woman that had been beaten, kidnapped and multiple raped by a gang of guerilla captors.

The torn remnants of clothing were covered in blood she had to stab one of her captors, a huge brute of a man wearing a scary knitted mask.

Talk about throwing someone in at the deep end, if she could pull this off she deserved a role Jake thought as they screamed action. At first Marisa didn't know what to do she was trembling naturally from nerves, the huge man approached her attempting to rape her again.

Suddenly she slipped effortlessly into character, tears welled in her eyes as she remembered her father, touching her, beating her, the man wrestled with her and for a moment it all seemed real the camera zoomed into her face, her eyes darted about the room bulging in fear for a moment she felt that this was all real, screaming she took the stiletto from her captor and lunged it deep into his chest the man rolled off her and slumped on the ground Marisa sobbed and collapsed wracked in tears her wails filled the studio when they did shout cut everyone was silenced by the depth of her portrayal.

All the lights went on and they instructed Marisa that Simon wanted to see her in his office the following afternoon.

Marisa wasn't sure if she would get the bit part, perhaps she had overdramatized the scene. She didn't care as it had been a harrowing experience and quite emotionally draining, different from what she had expected. She wondered what it would be like doing that every day probably screw your head up.

The next afternoon a large limo arrived to collect her, everyone in Sergio's block had their heads out of the window, they had never seen a limo in that neighborhood. In the back there were bottles of drinks and a television it was like a living room she thought.

Simon greeted her with a wide smile and together with a crew of people they went to a screening room to watch her two screen tests. Once everyone was seated the lights dimmed and she was shocked as her face lit up the screen it was weird to look at yourself on such a large screen.

She held her breath as she watched the finished results, first they ran the dramatic scene, it was scary and even she could hardly believe that that woman up there on the screen was her, the two minute of film was compelling she looked like she had been raped and beaten and the emotion she expressed was truly amazing in contrast to the first scene. They showed the second scene and she looked sensational, she laughed to herself at the rampant sexuality that she emanated on screen she never thought for a moment that she looked like that, the lighting was great she looked sensational from every angle.

After the screening in the privacy of Simon's office he offered her the major role in his new movie it was a risk he knew, this kid had no experience and no history, however he had a hunch, a gut feeling that this kid was gonna make the studio millions.

Marisa was so elated she grabbed the pen and signed the three year contract without even reading it. Hey Presto the little girl from the trailer park was a Hollywood film star overnight just like Cinderella it was a dream come true.

Chapter 4

Tyrese

Tyrese lived in Harlem his mother Laticia was a lap dancer at a sleazy bar in New York. As a child he had pretty well brought himself up, sleeping on the sofa in his mother's run down flat. He hated the nameless men that frequented their house, his father had been a drug dealer gunned down in a hit and run while delivering a fix. He couldn't remember his father as he had only been eight months old when he had been shot. His mother did a lot of grass and all her income went on hash and uppers, her career had taken a dip and by the time she was thirty she was doing tricks on the street, she had been beaten several times by pimps and customers. Tyrese hated drugs he refused even to try a joint, for as long as he could remember the stench of weed had filled their apartment it stuck to his clothes and hair, he was tall and skinny as a rake and all the kids on the block bullied him and called him snake. For most of his life he was a loner, the outsider he didn't possess a knife didn't do drugs and spent most of his time cleaning the apartment and looking after his mother who was mostly always stoned he had learned to cook at eight and since then Laticia had never once served him food.

Sometimes he was so goody-goody it scared Laticia, how could he survive Harlem with that attitude she didn't know. For as long as he remembered there had been no money, he got used to seeing eviction notices pasted on the door when he returned from school. However bad it got they always managed, he loved his mother in his own way, sometimes he would have to put her to bed as she would collapse with a combination of too much pot and wine. She had been stoned for as long as he remembered.

The kids made fun of him as he had holes in his sneakers, all the clothes he had were hand-me-downs from the neighbors who felt sorry for him. Often he would eat at Big Mama Blacks on the floor above him, she had six daughters and often would invite him in to eat Mama Black didn't seem to care about feeding another mouth all her girls were huge just like her, they were a fat family and Big Mama could hardly walk she was so big she almost filled a whole armchair by herself. Tyrese was devastated when he learned that she had died of a heart attack, he missed her and when her daughters moved out to live at an aunt's he felt like he was losing his family.

Laticia's career was slipping, who wanted to pay to watch a middle-aged junkie dance round a pole? Her career on the streets was slipping too, the deep dark circles round her eyes frightened the clients so she had taken to wearing shades all the time.

When he was thirteen Tyrese got a part-time job in a gym, he collected the towels and cleaned up he was tall and skinny as a rake and dreamt of looking like some of the dudes that were members. After work he would work out every day for two hours, the boss was cool about it, he wanted to help the boy develop his physique and he was a good worker he worked harder than the two previous cleaners. By the time Tyrese was sixteen he had the physique of a sportsman with wide shoulders and a six pack, no one called him snake anymore he was the coolest guy in the school and the booty had the hots for him, tables had turned and the kids paid him for his company, it was cool to be seen with Tyrese. He was one hot dude because he was so physically developed he looked older than his years at seventeen using a fake ID he got a job as a stripper with a dance troupe that entertained women, they paid him well and he loved the adulation the real bonus was he got to sleep with lots of white pussy and they actually paid him handsomely for his black ass. They travelled on the road in a bus, there were nine white guys, one Latino, an Oriental and he was the only black, lots of the women were fascinated by him and the pride he took in his body. It was his temple and meal ticket. Somewhere along the line the gangly boy from Harlem had turned into an Adonis and sex machine, each month faithfully he sent a cheque to his mother, he had been shocked the last time he had seen her, she was on crack and every dollar he sent went on drugs. He was glad he was on the road as he didn't want to be confronted with that. Being on the road meant he didn't have to a have an apartment he was saving money to start his own troupe he was clever enough at eighteen to realize that a career like this wouldn't last forever.

When he wasn't working he was exercising, he had a passion for football and was good at it he didn't drink or smoke and was disciplined, never missing a work out.

One night at a show in Detroit he received a card in his dressing room it was from a middle-aged blonde who owned a record company she had asked him to dinner which meant that she wanted to be screwed by him. As far as he knew she was filthy rich, he had seen her in the front row she looked like a business woman in a pink designer suit and she looked younger than her forty years and had obviously had surgery. When Tyrese left the theatre her limo was waiting at the stage door, the driver was waiting on the kerb and opened the door for him. Pippa was nestled in the back seat she was drinking champagne and preparing a line of coke on a little mirrored table Tyrese shot her a million dollar smile and they headed towards her penthouse. She lived in a sprawling penthouse apartment with an indoor pool and a panoramic view of the city, it was obvious she had the hots for him and he decided that he would make her beg, she might be rich but he was a star in his own right she had a passion for black cock and he wanted to play it cool with her. She kicked off her high heels and dragged him into the living room. The stereo system looked like a spaceship and the sound system was to die for. There was champagne in a bucket on the table waiting, he guessed she must have called the staff to arrange this, there was no one in sight he wondered if they were hiding in a cupboard somewhere in the massive penthouse.

Pippa asked him to strip, he looked startled and joked that a private show could be expensive he had no intention doing one for free and wanted to make it clear that it was gonna cost her.

Pippa did another line and looked him dead in the eye and asked him to name his price.

Tyrese retorted 1000 dollars, Pippa didn't bat an eyelid she simply nodded her head in agreement and ordered him to continue.

Tyrese removed his clothes slowly, dancing around the sofa teasing her then quite unexpectantly he grabbed her stuck his tongue down her throat, stripped her and stuck his cock in her mouth, he fucked her on the sofa, on the glass table, in the bedroom and by the pool. The sun was coming up and he hadn't stopped, they fell asleep at six am in her massive circular bed between ivory silk sheets.

When Pippa woke he was still asleep she studied the perfection of his body, the contrast of the ebony skin against the creamy sheets he was divine, something special she decided there and then that she wanted him not as an escort but as a lover. Pippa wondered if he had a girlfriend probably some nineteen year old black piece of ass with hot booty, she was forty-four he was probably in his twenties. She did have money and power, she wondered how much he made displaying his wares and wondered how much it would cost to buy his fidelity. She knew that everything had a price, she herself had married Scot, he was the head of the studio, filthy rich and ugly as sin and she had been delighted when he had passed away and she had inherited his estate and the recording company that he had worked for years to have.

She was now the one pulling the strings and had major names signed to the label, since she had taken over profits had doubled, the money was rolling in she had enough money to live for the next century even with her extravagant taste she could never spend the wealth that she had amassed she had been married to Scot for twenty years.

Right from the start she had told herself that one day she would take over his business, she herself had gone with Scot to try and get a recording deal, marrying him was even better than getting a recording contract she had the money and the power without even having to sing a note. The truth was that she had an average voice anyway, Scot had fallen in love with her showgirl figure, mile long legs and silicone breasts.

She drifted into the huge marble bathroom and applied her make-up she didn't want this god to see her without make-up, she wanted to look her best. Fortunately it was Bruno her butler's day off. Bruno would never have approved of Tyrese. Bruno was thirty-five he had been her PA, butler, bodyguard for years, he was Latin with dark good looks and he had had an affair with her for a year after her husband died. She had kept him on and he had been good to her and she trusted him even though the passion was gone he helped her run her life and was a shoulder to cry on when things got too much to bear. Bruno was secretly still in love with Pippa, he hated it when she had a regular boyfriend and tried to be as blunt to them as possible he imagined that one day she would come back to him.

Pippa sat on the balcony of the apartment, beneath her the city slept, she heard a noise and watched as Tyrese walked as naked as the day he was born across the room towards her sitting unashamed and proud of his body he sat across from her. Pippa's eyes ran over the perfect body her loins filled with desire, as if reading her mind Tyrese scooped her up in his strong arms and led her to the Jacuzzi, she marveled at his body wet with oil and water as he made love to her in the bathroom with technique and skill he brought her to heights no one had before.

As he penetrated her body he reached parts of her soul that no one had touched. Just as he came he opened his eyes and stared into hers with an haunting intense look that she would never forget, his skin was so black it seemed almost blue, his teeth were the whitest she had ever seen and his eyes were light and clear, sometimes they seemed to change colour from green to blue it was these light eyes that made him different he could speak with his eyes.

Up against the cool marble tiles in the bathroom he brought her to orgasm, throwing her into positions she had never tried he watched her come. For a moment she sensed a look of contempt in his eyes, she cleaned herself up while he was dressing, they had breakfast on the balcony he seemed awkward as she pulled out a wad of notes from her designer bag, discretely she slipped the 2000 dollars in his jacket pocket along with a card bearing her private number. Tyrese left without even saying goodbye, he entered the lift without looking back. The moment he left, the apartment seemed empty perhaps she had been alone too long perhaps it was time she settled down, she dressed for the office and was glad that she had a busy schedule.

She had a problem with an artist, she had been playing prima donna and Pippa wanted to can her, it would cost them a fortune to withdraw her contract but Pippa didn't care, the bitch was more problem than she was worth and her last album had been a flop.

All through the meeting with the lawyers Pippa couldn't focus, her mind drifted and she kept thinking about Tyrese, his lips, his eyes, his body seemed to flash into her mind and to her horror she had lost track of the complete conversation. The moment the meeting finished she tried his number, the line was dead, he had given her the wrong number she was infuriated who the hell did he think he was, he was a stripper an escort, she was sure that he would call her, and was flabbergasted that he didn't. The show was moving out of town in three days she had to see him again that night she had her driver park at the stage door Tyrese came out looking startled, he didn't notice her car but jumped in a red Ferrari that had been parked outside the stage door. Pippa was filled with jealousy watching as he drove off with a middle-aged woman with bleached blonde hair.

The next night she had her driver park right up on the kerb she had waited a half hour for him to emerge and when he did he was surprised to see her, pinned up against the bonnet of the limo she asked him to come for a drive. He was reluctant and explained he had an appointment but Pippa begged for ten minutes of his time and reluctantly he jumped in. He hated when women thought they owned him sometimes he felt like a piece of meat, a big black cock to amuse bored middle-aged women. He wondered how his mother must have felt all those men invading her body, penetrating her soul, no wonder she was on crack.

The car circled the block he was tired, he didn't have an appointment he was exhausted, the bitch last night had had more than her 1000 dollars worth and he hadn't slept a wink and his dick was sore. Tomorrow was the last show, they were splitting up for a two week holiday and he had planned going back to New York to check out what condition his mother was in. Some of the guys in the troupe were heading for a villa on South Beach, he had never been in Miami and wanted to visit them in the second week, sun, sea and sand and lots of blondes in skimpy bikinis.

Pippa was talking, he wasn't listening he wasn't going to bang her tonight he was tired out.

They had been on the road for three months he needed a break. He asked Pippa to drop him at the hotel she looked at him and laughed, he didn't have a date, he was tired she looked at his face and for the first time saw the person under the mask he looked so young and vulnerable and she laughed seeing him for the first time. She asked how old he was and was shocked to learn that he was only eighteen he had a fake ID she had thought he was twenty-four suddenly he dropped his head in her lap, she played with his hair and he actually fell asleep. He had put a lot of muscle, sex appeal and pure charisma into the last show and was exhausted.

Pippa instructed the driver to take them home, the boy was half asleep as she helped him up in the lift, Bruno looked disapprovingly as she buzzed him to help her.

He was surprised to see that Pippa wanted him in the spare bedroom, they managed to get his shoes off and loosen his shirt, within seconds of lying down Tyrese was snoring loudly quite a contrast from playing the role of superstud he looked like a schoolboy that had been kidnapped by a middle-aged woman.

Tyrese woke at three in the afternoon the following day and was grateful that Pippa had not disturbed him he emerged from the bedroom with frizzy hair and looked more like a sleepy student than stripper. He was wearing geeky glasses that she had never seen, this was the real Tyrese and she kind of like it.

Pippa joined him for brunch and he seemed to relax for the first time in her company. His troupe would have checked out of the hotel already over breakfast he opened up to her telling her of his mother how he was dreading going back to New York. Pippa listened, before she had only seen him as a sex machine, she hadn't even taken the time to see the real kid. He had clawed his way out Harlem working his guts out while his school mates had turned to crime, she realized for the first time that he was very young, his size and physique led you to believe that he was Mr Superman however, deep down inside he was still a teenager. He told her about school, Big Mama Black and his junkie mother he admitted that he had been the wimp of the class an outcast till he had been fifteen. She could relate to this, at school they had hated her too she had been too good-looking to fit in.

Pippa invited him to stay the weekend, offering to have his baggage picked up at the hotel, just a weekend no strings attached, Pippa laughed when she saw his belongings he had two suitcases one contained what he termed working clothes, thongs, sexy underwear, skin tight t shirts and pants the other contained shapeless washed out sweatshirts, baggy jeans and hats these were his real clothes nothing too much, nothing sexy just shapeless outfits that hid the great lines of his body.

When he was working he liked to show off his physique when he was free he liked to hide it, strangely enough Pippa kind of liked his geeky image when he dressed in his sexy clothes women looked at him with his worn rapper clothes no one gave him a second glance.

Pippa invited him for lunch they passed by her office on the way to the restaurant, she had to sign a contract, when they arrived at her office Tyrese felt intimidated he had had no idea that she was so important she had two assistants and an army of staff, the walls were lined with famous faces that were signed to her. She was the one behind many of the careers of stars that he listened to on his MP3 player. Tyrese was impressed, the following week she was having the annual record company bash. All the stars would be there Tyrese hoped she would let him hang about, he was desperate to meet some of the artists that were signed up on her label.

Pippa noticed the wide-eyed look on his face when her assistant ran through the guest list.

Without batting an eyelid she added Tyrese's name he smiled a toothy smile so big she laughed out loud. Her assistant thinking that Tyrese was the new hip hop act, asked if Tyrese would be performing on the night Pippa replied he would be performing but not on stage.

Tyrese laughed and the assistant blushed feeling like an idiot. He couldn't believe that Pippa was banging this geek he was a just a kid. Tyrese did all the things that he had done to her the first night and a lot more, she called in sick the next morning and they slept all day. She liked Tyrese one moment he was a kid, the next a super stud, he had two facets and she was falling in love with both.

She guessed that his animal hunger for sex was second nature he was after all only eighteen she never imagined that she had become a cougar and would have a toy. Boy her sister would be in a state of shock she couldn't wait to present him at the party.

Tyrese was enjoying his stay at Pippa's, he slept all day and fucked all night and when she took off to the office around eleven am he would sleep, work out in her gym and basically laze around listening to music, she had the most amazing sound system, it worked in every room in the house including the pool area and in the bathrooms.

Tyrese was soaking in a huge tub the bath was filled with foamy oils, the acoustics in the bathroom were great. Pippa spent a lot of time in the tub listening to the dozens of new demos she got every week, many life changing discussions had been made in that tub. It was there six months ago that she had first heard Vito Toscanis demo he was number one now and had a platinum album, Tyrese wondered if she had slept with him too and he was surprised that he had felt a tinge of jealousy when he imagined Vito and Pippa in a carnal embrace. Pippa had an insatiable appetite for sex.

At the office Pippa was checking the arrangements for the yearly bash it was a red carpet happening, there would be lots of stars there and the paparazzi would be covering it. She had also taken the time to have an appointment with Carlos, he had been waiting nervously in her reception for an hour. Carlos ran a football club his team were on a losing spiral and the club were in debt up to the eyes, she had invested a large chunk of money in the club and till now there had been no sign of improvement or pay back. She wasn't one to sit around waiting for something to happen and had tried to sell her shares no one had been stupid enough to sink any cash in the team and she was getting nervous, however she needed a favour and wanted Carlos to arrange something for her and for the first time in the six months she was actually glad that that she had pumped some money in his club.

Carlos hated Pippa she was a hard and callous bitch and would castrate you emotionally, physically and financially without batting an eyelid. The palms of his hands were sweating, he was sure she was gonna pull out, the team had been doing their best things and were improving. Pippa noticed that his palms were sweating when he shook her hand, she ordered coffee and made three more calls to prolong his agony she was enjoying watching the six foot hooligan sweat. Pippa didn't get to where she was by being sweet, in business she was ruthless.

Pippa raised her eyebrow and inquired how things were going explaining that she wanted to see progress, then to his surprise she handed him an invite to her party. A smile of relief passed over his face and he accepted gratefully, he was dying to attend her party, there would be enough pussy there for sure. Pippa concluded that she needed a favour, she had had an idea and that Carlos would have to help her. Over the last few days she had become obsessed with Tyrese she didn't want him leaving after the party she couldn't stand the thought of him flaunting his body and sleeping with all the middle-aged women who lusted after him. Stupid as it may seem she wanted him for herself she had decided he was going to be hers, lock stock and barrel. That morning as he had brought her what must have been the most intense orgasm she had ever experienced she had decided that he was going to stay. She knew that he was independent and that he had too much pride, simply being her toy boy would have been out of the question he would have bolted like a wild tiger if she had tried to buy him. In an odd way he had principles and she admired that.

That morning soaking in the tub she had devised a plan and Carlos was going to execute it otherwise she mused she was going to execute him. She explained her wishes to Carlos, at the party she would casually introduce him to Tyrese.

Tyrese was football crazy, Carlos would engage him in conversation and offer him an audition, whether the boy was good or bad was indifferent he would take him on, pay him a large salary and train him even if he was hopeless, he would train him no matter the cost he would mould him into team material she added sarcastically that he couldn't be any worse than most of his team. Carlos hated to be put under pressure like this, he liked to think of himself as professional, he knew immediately that this guy must be banging the boss, he promised to oblige and asked what kind of salary and contract he should offer, Pippa thought a year's contract would be sufficient she may tire of him after all like all the men that passed through her sheets. Smiling she showed the sweaty man out her office and smiled and rubbed her hands together she was a genius.

Tyrese was excited he couldn't wait for the party he could hardly believe that all these stars were going to be there at arm's length. Pippa was the boss they would all be licking her ass, that's what she told him. Bruno ignored him making it clear that he disapproved of the young Black Panther, he was less than half her age and obviously taking her for a ride. Pippa made sure that Bruno had lots of things to do outside the apartment and she had also given him some holiday as she sensed that one day he was going to lash out at her new flame.

Pippa surprised Tyrese by not going to the office the day before the party. Her car picked them up and he presumed that they were going shopping and he was stunned to see they were going to the hairdresser. Usually a hairdresser came to her, she explained that she would be there all day and begged him to stay she hated it so, the hairdresser was in a rundown area outside the city, he didn't expect her to go to a joint like this he thought she would have been the type to go to one of the flashy salons that they had downtown. The place was a clip joint and when they entered a cloud of marihuana hit them both, everyone inside was high as a kite. This Pippa explained was where all the stars came. These guys were the best. Pippa never failed to amaze him, the first time he had seen her she was wearing a Couture suit but all week she had been slopping around in a baseball cap and men's jeans he mused what the next step would be. She was like a chameleon she explained that as queen of the recording industry she would have to look even better than the stars she signed up. Tyrese flicked through some magazines and drank endless amounts of coffee- while two girls and a guy whizzed around her head, for eight hours they pulled, kneaded and added dreadlocks. The finished result was astounding. She had a mane of rainbow coloured dreadlocks to her waist. It was like instant cool and her head ached. The whole process cost 1500 dollars they finished the main of dreadlocks by adding little silver charms and bells and piercing rings to her hair, it was really the fattest hairdo he had seen, she tinkled when she moved. Tyrese joked that he wouldn't be able to sleep for the bells, Pippa retorted with a hearty laugh.

While she had been getting her hair extensions he had gone downstairs to have a haircut himself, she didn't know he had been away for an hour and a half and he had pretended that he had fallen asleep, he had hidden his haircut under his hat and wanted to surprise her when they got home. He had decided that he was gonna be cool too, his haircut had been 300 dollars they had put it on Pippa's bill and she hadn't even noticed. Tyrese couldn't stop looking at her in the back of the car she looked so cool, he was embarrassing her every time he tried to have a sneaky look she would laugh. She told him to enjoy it while he could for right after the party she would have them cut off. She couldn't stand it she told him last time she had it done she couldn't sleep and had cut them out herself she had made such a mess she had to wear a bandanna for a month. She told Tyrese that she was not the type to suffer for beauty's sake, the hair extensions were the nearest thing to torture she could imagine, she looked like Medusa he mused, her hair was red, orange, yellow, pink, black and lime green every time she moved she tinkled he was highly amused. When they got home Pippa went to her study, there had been literally hundreds of messages as she had had her mobile switched off. While she answered the important ones Tyrese checked out his hair, it was too cool they had shaved his head with tribal motifs and it was no longer a haircut he thought, his head was a work of art he looked proudly in the bathroom mirrors at the back and sides, he was so cool he studied himself for fifteen minutes,.

Pippa was tired of talking on the phone she smelled pizza, the smell was floating into her study at first she thought that she was dreaming because she was hungry, she hadn't eaten all day. She followed the smell and burst out laughing when she entered the kitchen, Tyrese was standing totally naked trying to scrape black burned edges off an overdone pizza, buns like coconuts she thought. She startled him and smiled approvingly at his new haircut, it was different it was red hot Tyrese grabbed her within seconds she was naked too he was making love to her like there was no tomorrow, after a half hour session of sexual acrobatics they ate cold burned pizza and washed it down with some chilled Chablis. Pippa would never forget the smell of Pizza again for years to come every time she passed a Pizza store she would think of that night, it's funny how things stick in your mind. If time had stood still right there in the kitchen she would have been happy, funny cold burned pizza had never tasted so good.

Tyrese sat cross-legged on the floor proudly feeding her his home made pizza, she savoured every mouthful, she had been suppressing her feelings for days and for the first time in years she was honest with herself, like it or lump it she had fallen deeply in love with this eighteen year old Adonis whether it was good for her or bad for her all she knew is that he opened doors that had been closed for years.

After dinner he scooped her up in his powerful arms carried her to the bedroom and made love again this time with a new intensity that she had never noticed before, just as he ejaculated he looked deep in her eyes and she was sure at that moment that something for him had changed, a look of love filled his eyes. Was it possible he loved her too after he came he fell asleep in her arms like a baby she nestled his head, his naked skin glowing in the candlelight, what an odd couple they made, him with the tribal symbols shaved in his head, her with a main of rainbow dreadlocks, after an hour Tyrese stirred woke up looked at her smiled, complained about the tinkling of her bells cuddled her and fell fast asleep again.

Pippa didn't sleep, she had too much on her mind, all the pressure of the party and she fretted what would happen if he didn't accept the football deal. She couldn't imagine life without this young man, odd she thought a week ago she didn't know he existed it's funny she mused how fate catches you by surprise.

She had gone to court that day and lost the case against a star, she was so depressed she had gone for drinks with Melanie her friend and she had dragged her to the strip show promising that it would cheer her up. The moment he had walked on stage she had felt something, it was like a bolt of electricity had shot through her loins from the first moment she had seen him she had butterflies in her stomach. Perhaps he was just staying for the party perhaps he was just using her, did it matter if he was as long as she was getting something from it.

The morning of the party had arrived and Pippa hadn't slept her eyes were red and bloodshot.

Her car was downstairs and she hadn't even showered she needed to get in to check everything even though her staff were terrific she always insisted in checking everything herself, the flowers, the venue, the menu, the guest list. Before she left she scribbled a note to tell Tyrese that she would be back at seven to be showered, she would arrange their clothes kiss kiss, she checked out the large man lying in her bed spreadeagled and fast asleep and thought that it must be great to be a toy boy today she sported a tracksuit and sun glasses there was no time for fashion today.

She arrived at ten past seven back at her penthouse the stylist and make-up artist had been waiting for an hour in the hallway.

Pippa had a quick shower and took an upper she would never have gotten through the night without it she introduced Tyrese to the stylist and sent them off to her dressing room so he could select an outfit while a rather effeminate man made up her face, Tyrese marveled at the selection of clothes he wanted to try them all on but opted for an outfit the stylist put together, black baggy Versace pants, Burberry socks, Prada shoes a Gucci belt and a custom made sleeveless skin tight shirt from some American designer, his outfit was too cool he was like a fashion cocktail all the labels merged into one statement of pure Bling. The low cut hipsters were daring almost to the point of indecency the shirt was so tight you could count his six pack, with the haircut and all he looked quite something and Pippa smiled in approval when he bounced into her bedroom to show off his outfit, she joked not to spill anything on them as they were all borrowed Tyresse sulked and pouted like a kid he had thought he could keep them. Pippa added they were all samples from the press office and they had to be returned for fashion shoots they were next season's styles.

Tyrese had never seen her professionally made up, the skinny guy with the nail varnish was a genius she looked like a screen goddess, her lips were exactly the same shade of pink as her dreadlocks and her eyes had silver glitter on them the stylist had dressed her in a skimpy chain mail metallic halter she was wearing designer jeans encrusted in silver rings and to top it off she had an ankle length lime green fake fur coat this was serious bling bling standing together they made a big fashion statement they looked like they just had stepped off a catwalk.

They were arriving in a shocking pink limo, the clash of the colour of the car and her coat was amazing. They arrived at the venue where the event was taking place, it was an old warehouse outside the city. There was a mile of security and Tyrese was amused, Pippa had fallen into the role of Pop power queen she looked different, walked different. He liked it when the car door opened, he was blinded by the flash of cameras, people screamed as they walked up the red carpet a TV camera was stuck in their faces and Pippa gave a small speech, paparazzi pushed and photographers snapped away,.

Pippa grabbed his arm he was trembling, this was all new for him. Pippa waved to the crowd and cuddled him as they posed for the cameras they made a dashing couple and the press had a field day no one recognized this man which made him even more interesting if he was with Pippa he had to be important.

Tyrese tried to smile as they walked up the red carpet, it seemed like a mile long and he was nervous. Limos were arriving every minute and cheers from the crowd made him glance back, Vito had arrived with an army of bodyguards and hangers on, stoned out of his mind. The new star received a warm welcome from the fans that must have waited hours to see them.

Vito raced up the carpet and kissed Pippa, without her he would still be working as a dishwasher in the Italian restaurant, she had made him a star. Pippa introduced Tyrese to him. Tyrese was like speechless he couldn't believe that Vito was talking to him he was like his hero he played his album every day, they stopped and posed for the press Tyrese in the middle. Pippa pouting and proudly clinging on to him on one side, Vito with his arm round him like they were best friends, it was this photo that would be published on the front pages the following morning everyone knew who Pippa was and the whole world knew Vito but no one knew who the guy in the middle was. Some papers said that he was Pippa's new hip hop star others claimed he was a top model from Europe.

Tyrese couldn't believe that it was him the next day, where they had posed the lighting had been set up, Pippa didn't leave anything to chance, Vito looked good, Pippa was gorgeous. And Tyrese looked so handsome he couldn't believe it was him.

When they arrived the party was in full swing and he had had no idea that Pippa was so powerful everyone was licking her ass big time she was the centre of attention all night.

While he waited in the wings, she had introduced him to so many superstars and film stars he had lost count, most of them were disappointing in the flesh except for a girl he noticed she was a new Hollywood starlet called Marisa she apparently was working on a movie, he had never seen her before but she looked stunning and was encircled by admirers all night.

While Pippa did what she had to do, Tyrese had a chat with a guy named Carlos it was a pleasant relief to have met him, he was director of a second division football team.

Tyrese had dreamt all his life of playing professional football he had asked the guy how you get into and it the guy had said they were searching all the time for new talent, he had invited him for an audition the following Tuesday. Tyrese was so excited he couldn't wait to tell Pippa.

Pippa was surrounded by people and he didn't want to interrupt her so he went to the bar and hung out. He was waiting for a drink when he turned round, it was the great looking girl he had seen at the staircase, he looked down and was surprised up close she was tiny and she had a deep voice which didn't match her size. She nudged him in the ribs and demanded he get her a drink. Tyrese introduced himself, like every other man in the room he couldn't help looking at her, she had the most perfect breasts he had ever seen. The bar was crowded and she pressed herself so close to him accidentally rubbing her hand against his crotch, surprised she drew her tongue across her lips suggestively and winked at him fully aware that she had just given him an erection, she thanked him as he handed her the champagne and introduced herself as Marisa she warned him to watch out for her new movie and disappeared into the crowd leaving him hard and horny as hell.

Whilst Tyrese had been chatting with Marisa, Pippa had retired to the men's room with Vito, after doing two lines of Columbian coke she unzipped him and gave him a blow job. Vito exploded in her mouth listening to the sound of the jingling dreadlocks. Pippa straightened her top and applied her lipstick Vita would perform better after a blow job, he always did. At his last gig in Vegas she had had sex with him and his guitarist in the back of their bus.

Tyrese was so excited about the trial, they were the last to leave the party and Pippa had tried to look wide-eyed and surprised when in the back of the limo he had told her that he got a football offer, the party had been a wild success there had been lots of press and media cover and Tyrese had looked impressed he had certainly turned a few heads at the party. Pippa had noticed Marisa hovering around him, she felt a pang of jealousy and made a mental note to blacklist her at any future events, she was stunning looking, perhaps too stunning strutting her stuff like a superstar her film hadn't even been released and she was signing autographs.

The next day the tabloids and newspapers were full of pictures from the party the shot of Pippa, Vito and Tyrese was published everywhere, Vito was after all her hottest property at the moment the press were extremely interested in Tyrese he was extremely handsome and photogenic in one tabloid they had described him as Pippa's new secret weapon, that was true in a sense but not the way that the press had meant.

Tyrese was driving her crazy, he was like a child he was so excited about the damn trial he couldn't sleep, he got up at six to jog then spent hours in the gym then he would go play football all day then retire early, the quicker this trial was over the better, he was becoming boring, sex was out of the question he was saving his stamina for the big day. This annoyed Pippa beyond belief, sex for him was a major work out, since she had arranged this bloody trial her coke consumption had doubled, she fretted perhaps she had made a wrong move.

She couldn't bear if he was going to be as boring as this when he got a football contract, after looking at the press she should have suggested he tried making a single, he was good looking and would look great on video, his voice was ok she had heard him sing in the shower, the voice could have been mastered they could manipulate it in the studio, she would rake through some of the demos of new material perhaps there was a song for him. Vito had rejected one, perhaps it could be a winner for Tyrese.

Pippa was in the shower with her vibrator when Bruno walked in with towels. He undressed and had sex with her then within moments got dressed and left her. She felt guilty having oral sex with him when Tyrese was around. Bruno saw it as a victory, he had been her lover once.

The night before the trial Tyrese had gone to bed early, he had tossed and turned and found it impossible to sleep, the girl from the party kept jumping into his mind. Marisa, every time he thought of that chick he got a raging hard on she was the hottest creature he had ever seen and she had slipped him her card. He wondered if the old man that she was with was her lover or producer, she was a looker every straight guy on the planet would have fancied her. He wondered when her movie was going to be released he couldn't wait to see it. He had grinned from ear to ear when Pippa had shown him the tabloids, him hobnogging with the jet set. He wondered if his mother had seen it or any of his friends, he doubted that they would have recognized him with the haircut and the flash clothes.

He hadn't missed the guys from the troupe and he wondered how they were doing in Miami.

In around ten days he was supposed to be joining the troupe, they had bookings in Canada of all places and there was even talk of going to Europe. He wanted this football career since he was a kid if he got a contract he would leave the troupe, it was two am he was still awake but pretended to be asleep and lay on his stomach to hide his hard on when Pippa came to bed.

The next morning he was so nervous he begged Pippa to drive him to the trial, she was honored to do so and it was fun to see him behave like a kid. God she thought if he ever knew that she was behind it all he would freak out, she had warned Carlos to be discreet and he was not stupid he knew if he crossed her he would be out on his ear. Pippa was ruthless she had connections with people who had connections with some rather nasty underworld figures if any one crossed her it would be a matter of one phone call and she could have them wiped off the face of the earth, she was a powerful woman in the music industry she always got what she wanted, she could make you or break you she was a great person to have on your side but not someone that you wanted to make enemies with.

Pippa dropped him off at the entrance blew him a kiss wished him luck and promised to pick him up. She watched him enter the stadium he looked so cool in his white sweat suit.

Oh! She thought revving up the engine sex tonight.

Carlos hadn't expected him to be good in fact he expected him to be pathetic, obviously this was Pippa's new toy boy. She owned seventy percent of the shares so he had no option other than following her orders, after a talk he introduced Tyrese to the guys that had already started training, Tyrese changed and they gave him his chance.

Carlos watched him and was surprised the kid was good, better than good! He didn't have professional training but was fast and sharp and gave even his best boys a run for their money, they were second division, they needed new talent but Pippa wouldn't increase their budget. Perhaps Tyrese would add a bit of zest to the team, perhaps if he had a serious course of training he could do it. At his trial he scored two goals and dribbled his best with skill.

He introduced Tyrese to the captain, trainer and masseur and after he had showered they went into his office to talk turkey.

In the locker room the rest of the team sulked they had slipped to second division and fans were turning against them, last season they had lost three of their best players to European teams their egos were deflated. They were needing professionals with a name not novice inexperienced pretty boys. They had seen him on the tabloids and thought that he was a pop star, they didn't like him at first glance he would never be one of the lads to them.

Tyrese called Pippa from a pay phone, in the excitement he had left his mobile at the penthouse he was so excited she could hardly understand him. He was shouting that he had a one year contract. He was to begin immediately with an intense three month training program before he went on field, the salary was good and he was giving up dancing.

Pippa replaced the receiver and grinned from ear to ear she asked her driver to take her to the stadium and cancelled all her appointments for the day.

Pippa came in a limo to collect him. The driver opened the door for him, she had an open bottle of champagne waiting and he stared in amazement, apart from a pair of black high-heeled boots she was completely naked. The window between them and the driver was sealed, they celebrated with chilled bubbly champagne and within five minutes she had stripped him and they were making love in the back seat of the limo. Tyrese came quickly he was so excited and hadn't had sex for three days. After sex they drank the remainder of the champagne, both naked, Tyrese was so happy he looked out of the windows and sipped the drink while Pippa lowered her head and gave him the best blow job he had ever had. He couldn't believe his luck, here he was in a stretch limo drinking vintage champagne, getting head and he had just signed a football contract.... it was the coolest day he thought as he orgasmed again and spurted deep into Pippa's throat.

It was easier to undress than dress in the back of a limo and both he and Pippa bumped into each other as they scrambled into their clothes they were going to lunch at Tony's.

Pippa had arranged that one of her tabloid press contacts would turn up accidentally and snap their picture. The headlines read Pippa celebrates with football star, the press delighted Tyrese, but infuriated Carlos the kid hadn't even played a game and he was a fucking star. The boys would be up in arms about this.

Pippa invited Tyrese to stay with her on a move in permanent basis, he accepted of course.

Actually he would have agreed to anything, he was so high at getting the contract. Seven times he tried to call his mother, eventually he learned that the telephone had been cut off. He wanted to tell her he had a football contract, he called a neighbor and asked if they could bring her to the phone, after ten minutes the neighbor came back and explained that his mom was too wasted to move, he hung up feeling lost and disappointed. Pippa tried to cheer him up, she had seen the disappointment in his eyes. To lighten the atmosphere she lit lots of candles, poured some drinks and showed him the video of the party, Marisa was in some of the footage she looked so sexy he laughed at himself dressed like a pop star he was the coolest dude there, they watched the film twice and he couldn't help being proud of Pippa she was an important lady, if he hadn't met that guy at her party he would still be dancing. Pippa jokingly asked if he would still be her private dancer, he agreed smiled then turned away he hated to be treated like a gigolo. He was a football player.

Tyrese took his training very seriously and in a way was gaining respect from the rest of the team. He had been in reserve but never played a game, Carlos wanted him to be ready when he went on pitch and the young man didn't disappoint him when the day arrived for him to play his first game he was more than ready.

Carlos had a feeling that this kid was gonna make it big. The impression was he was hungry for it, he wanted it and that hunger for success compensated for the experience he lacked. Pippa hated football, however she made an exception and turned up for his first game and to her surprise he was exceptional. They beat the opposing team to the ground and won three nil. Tyrese had scored all three goals making him an instant sensation with the fans and team mates alike, Pippa had gone into the locker room after the game, it was quite cool, all these naked sweaty hunks. Since Tyrese had been training their sex life had diminished, she never had imagined that her sex god would have cooled down so much, she too had been busy and there had a mountain of paper work, legal battles and record releases, she had fired Bruno. It had been impossible when he returned from his vacation he had been so moody to learn that Tyrese was staying permanently at the apartment he had been hostile to her lover and one evening when she arrived home she found them beating the shit out of each other. Bruno was still in love with Pippa he was so extremely jealous of Tyrese it was an impossible situation so with a heavy heart she had fired him and written him a cheque for six months salary, she missed him he had taken a lot of the pressure off her.

After the game Tyrese was ecstatic he looked like a schoolboy all grins and teeth an overnight football hero the press called him the Black Panther; he was sleek and fast and was dragging the team out of the darkness. Every week the fan base increased, the empty seats in the stadiums filled up and the crowds roared his name. He had made wacky haircuts a trend and had sported a Mohican hairstyle the first time he played, he was easy to spot with his dyed blue neon blue Mohican and whatever style he had the fans copied.

He trained three days a week played on a Saturday and exercised as much as he could.

One morning at breakfast Pippa threw him the idea to release a single, he thought that she was joking and was stunned to see she was serious. He was merchandisable, good-looking and visual, she knew if he made a good video the single would sell his voice was not important they could work miracles in the studio. She had a track, it was one that Vito wanted badly and she was sure that it had all the ingredients to be a hit also she wanted to piss Vito off. He had been impossible recently and was forgetting that she pulled the strings, he had delivered three number one singles but that was beside the point, an artist was nothing without good management and she was considering dropping him. His ego had outgrown him, he was not doing the radio shows, showing up late for gigs and in general being a bastard. His drug abuse had become a major problem, his last tour had been almost cancelled, there had been a mountain of bad press, squabbles and fights the last blood bath at the airport had resulted in him being jailed. All this negative press was bad for sales and she was tired of his demands, giving Tyrese the song that he wanted would freak him out and she hoped that it would be a hit, that would hit him even harder.

Pippa produced a CD from her bag and slipped it in the stereo, Tyrese loved the song it was an upbeat dance number the kind that when you heard it once you couldn't get it out of your head.

She kissed him on the forehead told him to keep the disc listen to it in the car and master it. She had booked him into the studio the following week for a recording session.

Tyrese had often gone with her to check on artists' progress when they were in the studio.

He knew the set-up and was aware that they could do great things with technology he fancied making a single and was glad to have the chance. Secretly Pippa hoped that he would have success with music perhaps if he did he would give up football she had preferred him when he was staying up late and having fun, this football lark was boring he was always exercising , training or sleeping.

By the time the recording day arrived Tyrese had mastered the song, his voice wasn't exactly the best in the world but they had had worse in the studio and the recording was going well.

Pippa treated Tyrese like any other artist on her books, the fact that he was her lover made no difference, in that respect she was professional. He had wanted her to come to the recording but she had point blank refused, she had dozens of other artists on her books and a major record company to run so as a rule she never stayed at recording sessions or video shoots, having her around would make everyone nervous and result in overtime and over budget productions. She told him that she would, as always, appear at the end of the day to listen to the tapes and check how it had gone, Tyrese sulked, she was a stubborn bitch sometimes.

It was so difficult for him to keep stopping and starting, he couldn't just take up where he had left off he liked to start from the beginning and build the track up. He must have sung the chorus two hundred times and hated it every time he heard them saying let's take it one more time.

Eventually around eleven in the evening Pippa showed up and together they sat and listened to what had been done, she sat expressionless and asked to hear some parts a second time, she criticized the parts she wasn't keen on and said nothing about the parts that she approved of. The track would have to be mastered and remixed. They had chosen two producers that would come up with two different versions so on the single there would be the original mastered cut, a disco version and mega mix club cut with some rap thrown in. Pippa had sprung the rap bit on them and she left them with Tyrese to record it, she wanted Tyrese to do the rap himself, she never told Tyrese but she was impressed. The song would be a hit she was sure, he sounded good not great but the finished product would be mastered and perfected, Vito would be sick with jealousy.

From her car she called her assistant and asked her to arrange a video shooting with one of the hottest directors in town, she gave her the budget and asked her to have a copy of the song hand delivered so they could hear the track and come up with a concept.

Who knows maybe she would make some money out of her lover boy.

Two weeks later Pippa called Tyrese and told him the mastered tracks had just been delivered, he raced over to her office his heart beating. He had been training and hadn't even bothered to shower or change he was sweaty, smelly and wearing his football shirt when he arrived.

His management team were called and they sat waiting as Pippa slipped the disk in the stereo. Tyrese was pleased, it sounded hot, the mega mix with the rap was particularly strong, his voice sounded so powerful it had been mastered so well. They played the three versions twice all sitting motionless like dummies, Tyrese wondered what they were thinking perhaps it was crap, perhaps they were going to shelve it. At the end Pippa asked her team what they thought, it was a unanimous decision they loved it, it was an out and out hit.

Pippa called Justin herself she asked him if he could rush over to hear the track and bring his video concepts.

Justin was red hot, his last two clips had won best video in two categories at the music awards.

He was a bit weird and stoned a lot but he was a genius, he was a pain in the ass to work with. No one understood what he did, most of the genius came out in the editing and he could take a simple scene and make it block busting, he had become so much in demand and ridiculously expensive it was crazy, however Pippa had known him from the start she had in fact gave him his first clip so he felt in a way indebted to her, when he had started and everyone had thought he was just another crazy young guy she had seen the potential and given him the chance. She knew if she asked him to do Tyrese's clip he would put his heart into it. They would shoot that week, the concept was basically they would shoot on field, him playing football but flying in the air like they did in Chinese movies, he and his ball would be suspended in the clouds. They would also do a dance scene in the locker room, not the actual locker room they would build a set on the studio, Tyrese would be oiled up and naked surrounded by all these scantily clad chicks, there would be sex in the video lots of skin some black and white scenes and a bit of CGI computer manipulation.

That night they went for dinner to Tony's to celebrate, Tyrese was so excited, he had forgotten all about football. Pippa couldn't wait till the damn football season was over recently he had been hotter on pitch than between the sheets she knew she shouldn't complain, his star was rising and at least his career was keeping him here.

Tyrese was just spooning a bit of heavenly crème brulee off his plate into Pippa's mouth when Marisa approached their table, she smiled at Tyrese and complimented him on his football success. Pippa looked her up and down from top to toe remembering her instantly, she was the young starlet that had been at the party she had to admit that she was stunning.

Pippa looked at her with distain, the blonde oozed sex appeal, she wondered if the breasts were real, she disliked her immediately she had never seen anyone so beautiful and to her absolute horror Tyresse invited her and her manager to join them.

Pippa had read in the tabloids that her movie had been released. It was one whopping great success and the blonde bimbo had shocked the world by actually being able to act. The press were saying she was tipped for an oscar nomination.

Marisa returned hanging on to the arm of her middle-aged manager who loved the fact that every eye in the room was on Marisa. She was in Detroit to film a sequence of her second movie, she absolutely hated the city and couldn't wait to get back to Beverley Hills. Pippa wanted to throw up. Tyrese never took his eyes off her and Pippa laughed when he actually missed his mouth with the champagne glass because he was so focussed on her breasts. Actually Marisa was quite sweet, she was witty in a dumb blonde sort of way. Tyrese made the mistake of telling her he was shooting a video that week, Pippa was horrified when Marisa offered to be in it, Pippa chimed in that they were already over budget and couldn't afford a movie star, Marisa offered to do it for free, there was a film crew with her doing a documentary drama, 'A Week in The Life of a New Starlet', she would do it for free if she could bring the film crew around, she threw in that it would be good PR for Tyrese's new single, she was after all hot property at the box office.

Pippa had to agree it would be good hype, Tyrese got a potential oscar nominated actress in his clip for free, her docudrama would be aired all over America and the press would love it.

Pippa's manager agreed that she could take two hours and Pippa called Justin and asked him to write a bit in the script for Marisa, she warned him that she would only be available for two hours so they would have to be set up to do her scenes the moment she arrived. Justin was stoned, she hope that he remembered in the morning.

Tyrese wanted to tell Marisa that he had loved her movie but he couldn't, he had sneaked off to the cinema after training and he hadn't told Marisa in case she had been suspicious. He had worn a hat to hide his currently red dyed hair and sported sunglasses when he went, he didn't want any of the football fans to recognize him.

He had been mesmerized by Marisa, on screen she was drop dead knockout gorgeous and looked even sexier in the flesh than on screen. Her heart-rending debut had almost brought tears to his eyes at the end of the film when she committed suicide. Half the audience were in tears and the other half had a lump in their throat, she was just magical on screen and he could hardly believe that she was sitting in such close proximity and he was stunned that she was literally begging him to be in his clip, her manager didn't look too enamored that she was doing it for free. She was doing it actually partly because she was bored, she thought the new movie she was forced to make was crap and partly because she really had the hots for Tyrese.

Pippa not being dumb sensed this and decided that for once she would bend the rules and turn up on set when miss hot tits was there. Usually Pippa would turn up at the end of a day's shooting, not this time.

On the day of the shooting Tyrese was collected at 5 am Justin wanted to shoot all the stadium outdoor shots at 6 am he said the light was right. Tyrese was rushed into make-up and they filmed him in his football strip from six till nine, he had to jump in the air hundreds of times. They had erected a trampoline and he had to jump and kick the ball in the net, he also had to walk down the entrance to the field, they would mix this with some previously shot material of a real game with the stadium filled with fans. They did some shots of him on a wire on a green screen and concluded filming him in the shower, which was kind of embarrassing taking a shower in your birthday suit with cameras up your bum. Tyrese had to laugh at himself, he used to be a stripper and he was getting cold feet to remove his pants for a film crew.

After Justin was satisfied with the outdoor shots they moved to a sprawling great studio outside the city where they had set up a locker room set and the dance scene would be filmed here. The place was a hive of activity, already there were twenty good-looking girls in make-up and stylists and lighting men were racing around. His hair had been dyed bright red for the shoot and he had again that crazy Mohican style haircut with tribal symbols shaved on the sides. Tyrese burst out laughing when they introduced him to the dancers, all the girls had exactly the same haircuts as his, they were like clones with their dyed red Mohicans. It would look great, all these girls in skimpy punk style outfits like gang girls in leather bras and miniskirts with ripped fishnet stockings and high heels, they were made up like whores with dark eyes and bright red lips. The make-up artists were skillfully tattooing his name on their breasts, arms and other body parts, the girls were hot.

Tyrese finished in make-up his video outfit was simple, he got a pair of super low cut hipsters which were so low he couldn't wear underpants. The jeans began at the top of his penis and his butt, his butt was popping out the back. Well sex sells in videos so they say. The make-up lady clipped away at his pubic hair, trimming it down so the low cut hipsters would look cool.

He went over his routine with the choreographer and did the lip-sync rehearsal. He was sweating a little, he had to lip-sync his song and he had never done it before, all this fuss just for him was unnerving, there were about thirty-five people on the set.

Justin started Tyrese with scenes while the stylists dressed the girls. The first scene was shot against a wall sprayed authentically with graffiti. He did his rap section, that was easy and he did it on three takes, the next scene was a killer he had to lip-sync sections of the song in close-up, the camera was real close and the make-up artist kept powdering and preening him between every take. This seemed to take forever, he was cold and hungry and his feet ached, they filmed parts of his body, his six pack, his muscles then he grabbed a cup of coffee which was the best coffee he had ever tasted and suddenly it was four in the afternoon and everyone was in a panic they were behind schedule and hadn't even done the dance scene. The girls didn't mind hanging about they were used to it, the making of a two minute pop video was a gruelling job, they had started at six am and would no doubt go on till two or three in the morning. Pippa had warned him that this was quite normal. She had turned up and seemed pleased with the progress.

The girls looked fantastic when they arrived on set the dance sequence was what Tyrese had been looking forward to. It would be easy for him he had after all been a star dancer in the strip troupe, he was in a locker room surrounded by sexy gang girls, they were dancing round about him making suggestive erotic movements then they went into a major sequence where they all had to do the same routine which had been created by a top choreographer.

Tyrese was oiled up and his black skin gleamed like bronze, they shot the dance scene four times it was a weird feeling to be there in the centre of all these girls listening to the sound of your own voice. They had played his song a thousand times during the shooting it was getting irritating, in the middle of the last take of the dance scene there was a flurry of activity at the entrance to the studio, it was Marisa with entourage she had just entered the building with her manager, media representative, film crew, make-up artist, hairdresser, personal secretary and stylist. She had just come from filming an action scene from her last movie and had arrived perfectly made-up wearing a Japanese dressing gown with her hair in rollers.

Justin was mesmerized by her, he stopped filming and approached her, her eyes were wondrous, she was magnificent and he studied her from every angle she was a knockout and he couldn't wait to film her. He had written in a small part for her, she was to roll around a bed, dance with Tyrese with rain pouring on them then he would roll about the ground with her and kiss her. They would both be covered in oil and the rain would make them shine and that would be the end of the video.

She was interviewed and filmed while the hairdresser did her hair, she was dressed in a flimsy slither of fabric and high heels, the designer dress barely covered her nipples and Justin liked the look. The set was still and Tyrese and a tight lipped Pippa stood at the side and watched as Marisa rolled about the bed and followed Justin's instructions, he shot her in one take and was so enthusiastic he got behind the camera himself. They were using three angles and on the day she looked great on all cameras. After the take she walked over to the screen to check what it looked like, bending towards Justin she pouted and said, 'Justin darling can I try out my way honey, just once more take please?' Everyone on the set stood still, no one questioned Justin or suggested things to him or they would be thrown off set. Pippa had seen him go into rages before and it could be quite ugly, after a silent minute to everyone's surprise Justin agreed, dived behind the camera and executed what Marisa suggested, 'Justin honey I'm gonna do it two ways baby, just tell me what you think.'

The clapperboard clicked and someone said action, Marisa walked across the room stopped turned, pouted, rolled on the bed and it was magical, she ran her tongue over her lips and let her fingers run down her body, he zoomed in close up and her blatant sexuality was captured on film he shouted cut and she did her second take this time shy, almost virginal. Tyrese stood in the wings he had an erection just watching her. Justin had only planned a small part for her but when he edited the video he would land up using lots of her footage she was sensational.

The last scene of both of them only wearing their low cut jeans was fantastic, rain lashed his muscles enveloped her naked torso he threw her on the ground and kissed her the shot was all muscle, breast and sex they would love it. Tyrese danced with her and the synthetic rain felt good on his skin for a moment he forgot the cameras he pinned her down and kissed her when Tyrese felt her soft pink tongue dart down his throat he was erect she felt his manhood pressing against her and when Justin shouted cut she retorted can we do another take my way. Pippa thought the she was joking but to her horror she wasn't and Justin agreed, they caressed and cuddled and this time she took control she twisted Tyrese arms behind his back and pinned him down on the ground she kissed him passionately and then dragged her tongue down over his chest towards the waistband of his jeans, Tyrese lips parted in ecstasy it was too hot to use, Pippa was furious and screamed it is America it's for the music channels not the porno net.

It was three am when they finished, Marisa let her film crews film her while they were taking off her make-up and to Pippa's disappointment she noticed that she looked just as great without make-up as she did with it. Pippa was tired, the shoot had been great, the video would be superb, Justin was really high about it. Pippa had a migraine and she just wanted to go home, Tyrese was on a high, it was his first clip he wanted to take the whole crew to Beluga's to the VIP room. Pippa couldn't bear the thought of going clubbing so she declined and Tyrese looked genuinely disappointed he wanted to come home with her but she refused she wanted peace and quiet, she called the club to warn them that they were coming and told them to bill her all the charges.

The shooting had been tiring but Tyrese was too excited to sleep he was glad that Pippa had gone home with a headache, unknown to Pippa, Marisa was also ditching her manager and coming to the club she arrived ten minutes after him with her two bodyguards, she kept her distance from him but gave him a signal when she went to the powder room,.

Tyrese followed her to the restroom, she was naked except for her heels and waiting for him when he walked through the door. She unzipped his pants and went down on him within seconds he was so filled with lust he fucked her crazy while her two bodyguards stood outside the door.

Their passion had been rampant and they had ten minutes together. Marisa was incredible to look at, every man who had her fell madly in love with her, Tyrese was no exception she was like a drug. While they scrambled into their clothes she explained that she was leaving the following day at three in the afternoon, she asked if he would come by her hotel, gave him the room number and kissed him on the cheek. Tyrese was supposed to be training he had never missed a moment's training but tomorrow he was going to call in sick. After she made her exit he washed his face and cleaned himself up, he hoped that Pippa would be sleeping, he needed to shower before going to bed, he still smelled of Marisa's perfume.

Everything was special about her, she smelled like flowers, her pussy tasted like strawberries she was something else man. A cleaning lady entered the bathroom and informed him that he was in the wrong station, he smiled and excused himself, she looked again at him and said, 'Oh you're the sports star,' and asked for an autograph for her son.

It was daybreak when he returned to the penthouse smelling of vodka and sex. Pippa pretended to be asleep as he crawled beneath the Egyptian cotton sheets.

The next day Tyrese had faked being sick and asked Pippa to call his team to say he was ill. She thought that the video had knocked the stuffing out him and never expected for a moment that he had a date with Marisa. While Pippa was working her butt off in the office Tyrese was in bed with Marisa pumping her raw. He had turned up at noon at her hotel suite and she had still been in bed, he had joined her and they had enjoyed a sex marathon. He had fucked her three times and had enjoyed every minute of it. It was now two thirty and they were both naked eating a room service breakfast. He was going to miss her like mad, they exchanged telephone numbers and he helped her to pack. The limo was waiting and she had to catch a plane, he confessed he had been crazy about her film, she said she was crazy about him, they parted in the car park and he felt a pang of loss as her car sped off in the direction of the airport. After she left he put on his hat and went to see her movie again, all the guys in the audience were drooling over her, it felt kind of strange just have having stepped out of her bed.

He watched her grace the silver screen and he still could smell her perfume on his body she was dangerous like a drug he mused, like a drug.

Tyrese had been miserable since Marisa left, Pippa thought that he was just nervous thinking about the clip. He had done exceptionally well and even though she hated that big-boobed bimbo it was good to have had her in the clip, according to the dailies her film was a box office hit.

It took a week to edit the video, Justin had been living in the editing room this was where his magic touch would kick in. He called Pippa at ten o'clock one evening to let her know it was ready. Pippa woke Tyrese who had fallen asleep on the sofa, they were in the car in five minutes flat and speeding towards Justin's studio flat.

For a guy that earned so much he lived like a junkie, the place was a mess with half-filled coffee cups everywhere he must have been a millionaire but still lived in the same studio he had when he was a student, weird Tyrese thought how could he bring a chick back here? Pippa and Tyrese sat in the darkness of his studio holding their breath, Justin pressed the remote and the video began. It started with surrealistic shots of Tyrese suspended in mid flight, muscles tense and legs kicking in slow motion, he scores a goal, there is a cheer of the crowd and the music begins. The video was better than good it was shit hot there were great shots of Tyrese's wet naked body dancing with the girls, it was just so cool then Marisa entered the scene, he had cloned her and there were hundreds of her, she looked sensational and the finishing scene in the rain was too hot. He had edited two versions, the steamier one for Europe and the more decent one for the States. Marisa just oozed sex appeal she was amazing and blew all the twenty other girls off the screen. He had captured a magical chemistry between Tyrese and Marisa. Pippa could see that at the finishing scene when Tyrese had kissed Marisa he wore a look on his face that Pippa recognized all too well he looked like that when he reached orgasm she thought. The chemistry between them unnerved her, she hadn't realized at the time but she would watch out for this bitch.

They watched the video ten times, it was fantastic the young girls would get the hots for Tyrese and the guys would buy the single because he was a football star. It was gonna be a hit. Justin spread a generous pile of coke on the table and skillfully divided it into nine lines they celebrated the clip and even Tyrese broke the rule and snorted one line. He was nervous he was a pop star he never thought that he could look or sound so cool and he owed it all to Pippa. He had seen the look on her face when she watched the clip she was suspicious of Marisa he would have to be careful or his singing career would be axed.

He hated making love to Pippa now, she felt so old and colourless next to Marisa. He missed her, the taste of her lips, the smell of her hair she had driven him wild, he thought of her all the time and it drove him crazy. He wanted to call her but she was promoting her movie in Europe she hadn't called him and he was disappointed. He had to focus on his training, on the promotion of his single it was due out this week and he was nervous as hell.

It was really weird, he was driving to the stadium one morning and he had switched on the radio and just as he did the DJ had announced his single, it was weird man to listen to your own voice on the radio what a buzz. When he arrived at the stadium there had been thirty or forty fans all waiting, they were screaming as his car passed and each day the number increased.

Pippa called, she sounded strange and she asked if he could come after his training to her office.

He asked her why and she said to attend a press conference because his single Your Body had gone right in at number three in the charts. She warned him to look good, she hadn't warned him that she had arranged for thirty photographers to be there all ready to snap snap snap photos. He was right in at number three without any major promo it was amazing Vito was sick with jealousy it was his song.

Tyrese was greeted by an army of photographers who blinded him with perpetual flashes, they were outside the building and inside the building after an hour of press conferences and interviews Pippa introduced him to some of the pluggers that she was paying to get him more airplay.

She wasn't sure if it was because he was a footballer that they had bought the single or if it was because of single that his fan base on the pitch had soared, whatever it was, he was a hit with the team. He also would be heading for the first division, the team were financially out of the red and he had put their name back on the board. The football season was finishing and she wanted him to record an album of eleven songs and shoot four videos it would all have to be done quickly because he was a hot item now. She had never for a moment thought that his single would have been quite so big, having the blonde bitch on board in the video had been a plus point, the European music stations were playing his video because of her and his single was about to be released in the UK, Germany, France and Japan they were considering trying it in Thailand too as the Thai's loved football and he was a household name there.

Pippa had reckoned on everything except the fact that Tyrese might not be ready for all this, he was tired and the pressure of the football season had really exhausted him. He had hoped to take a vacation with her and now he had all this on his plate, interviews, tours, live shows, recording and filming and on top of that a soft drinks company wanted to use his song and put him in a commercial. They were offering a fortune and Pippa got twenty percent he had to do it tired or not she thought.

She wished she had never introduced him to Carlos, he was still determined that kicking a ball was his future and he had the whole music industry caressing him.

The night he was number one and Pippa arranged a surprise party at the club, he was so shocked that he was number one he couldn't believe it till he read the listings himself. Here he was number one in the charts, he was releasing an album and was a superstar on the football field it was all too much to take. Pippa was dancing with Justin and the party was in full swing, Tyrese had gone to the toilet when his mobile rang he recognized the voice immediately and his heart raced when he heard the it, it was Marisa she was filming in Croatia, it was cold and miserable and she missed him. She congratulated him, telling him he was very popular in Europe she thanked him for the copy of the clip and said every time she heard his single on the radio she remembered their ten minutes in the powder room. This was a great day he was happy just to have heard her voice, when he hung up he returned to the party. He was in the middle of the floor dancing by himself grinning like a Cheshire cat, Pippa laughed, she was sure that someone must have spiked his drink because he looked like he was actually having fun. Justin and her did a few more lines of coke for the sheer hell of it, she was glad her baby was happy, she was happy too he was gonna make her a fortune.

She shouldn't have invited Vito he was aggressive and security had to drag him away, he was wasted and shouting that it was his song, his hit, she hoped that the press were outside with their cameras when the security dragged him outside, his popularity was failing.

She danced over to Tyrese and danced with him, he was hers she loved him to bits and he was going to make lots of lovely dollars for her empire, wasn't it wonderful, she had never seen him so happy.

Tyrese wasn't happy for very long he didn't have time to be happy he was exhausted.

The football season was over but he still had to train to keep in condition. His holiday was spent in the recording studio trying to accomplish in a month what most artists took over a year to do. He had to try and record eleven songs and after that there would be at least three videos to shoot plus all the press interviews and photo shoots. He started at seven and was never in bed before two, everyone was pressing him, no wonder everyone in this industry were doing drugs.

Pippa also had him pencilled in for some appearances on TV shows, performing live was scary for him on top of that his new celebrity status had come with a price wherever he went, they were always there, cameras and paparazzi were outside his apartment in the morning and there when he went home. They were bastards they wouldn't leave him alone for a moment, he no longer could go shopping or sneak off to see a movie. Next month Marisa's second film was being released – how on earth would he be able to go.

Some of the songs were difficult and out of his range Pippa had employed a voice coach and he had daily singing lessons. Seven of the tracks were already being mastered and he had five days left to complete the album and a cover of an eighties pop hit then it was on to the videos.

Most artists hated making clips he actually liked that side of the business.

Pippa had offered him some speed to keep going, he was infuriated and refused to start taking anything like that. His mother was a junkie and besides as a footballer he could have spot checks at any time and he would be suspended if they traced any illegal substances in his blood. He had no intention no matter how tired on starting to take drugs.

His single had been successful in Europe, they wanted him to fly out there, the team had seen a big increase in the sale of merchandising products since he topped the charts.

Pippa was driving him crazy she was never satisfied, he was up at seven in the studio till after midnight then she expected him to come home and screw her rotten every night.

It was too much and sometimes he wished that he had gone to Miami and stayed with the.
Strippers at least there he had fun. Apart from Pippa and the people who were producing the album he didn't have any contact with anyone, he was lonely he missed the camaraderie of the troupe. Funny he thought that being a star would be fun, it wasn't all that it was cracked up to be, he missed the freedom of going to a shopping mall, checking out a movie and hanging out with friends. On the other hand

if it worked, Pippa had said that he would make millions of dollars, he just didn't know how he was gonna fit it all in when the football season began. He did do a commercial for a power booster fizzy drink, they also used his track and he got a whopping great cheque for that. They filmed the commercial in a half day, Pippa also got a huge amount of commission, just how much he didn't know but she had been pleased, his stunt selling fizzy drinks would pay the costs of the album and video shoots.

Pippa was careful not to moan when Tyrese was too tired for sex, she was a business woman and she realized that if this project scored she would make millions. She was handling him with kid gloves now as he was as sensitive as could be and it seemed that he was near boiling point, the hours he spent training were a pleasure, he took his aggression out on the ball.

On the other side of the globe Marisa was standing in her underwear her head full of rollers, she was having a mad turn in front of the whole crew, her manager had her under extreme pressure, she was on her fourth film that year without a break and she had snapped. She was sick of being preened and prodded and treated like an object, sick of being a sex symbol, she yearned for serious roles where she could keep her clothes on. Her manager ducked as she threw a heavy pair of curling irons at him screaming like a banshee she walked off the set swearing that unless he did things her way she was finished, she was a sex symbol - but didn't have time for sex, she was always traveling and working and she too was at the end of her tether, in tears she dialed Tyrese's number and was so relieved when she heard his voice she broke down and cried. They spoke for an hour he explained he was in the same boat as her, she was despondent she had still two months to shoot this film and the script sucked. Both successful both lonely they now had more in common than they thought.

To be honest Tyrese didn't even want to hear the mastered finished album he was sick of listening to the tracks and was glad to see the back of his voice coach.

Pippa sprung another surprise on him before she even played the disk, she wanted him to do the three video shoots in one week, one day shooting one day rest she had arranged a package deal with Justin to do all three clips. This was a mistake on her part to have chosen the same producer for all the clips, Justin was hot but it would have been cooler to have three different people shooting the videos.

One clip was made on location in a diner it was fun and they had all been happy with that.

The second was in the studio again with the usual formula a black guy, bikini clad chicks all that and a fast car it was too cliché. Lots of bling bling and racy dance scenes. The last clip was a ballad called Cry of the Panther this was interesting, Tyrese had sat for six hours in the hairdressers, the one that had done Pippa's dreadlocks, they painstakingly dyed it twice, his hair was first bleached then tinted and with paintbrushes they made his hair like a leopard skin it really suited him.

Tyrese was grateful having six hours to chill out, it was a luxury. He was exhausted by being preened and pampered. The video they made for Cry of the Panther featured only Tyrese it was shot in black and white with a hint of colour like an old photograph, there was no bling bling no cars no chicks just Tyrese all muscle, barefoot and naked except for a linen sarong, with his leopard skin hair he looked divine, this was one for the ladies and he looked quite stunning in the finished product singing his heart out. They had filmed him against a worn linen sail cloth and then on a blue screen using computer technology they had him in a jungle backdrop with him reclining in a lair of leopards and at the end he was running with a pack of black panthers.

The effect was startling and his voice haunting. The album turned out quite unique it had something for everyone there was dance music, ballads, hip hop they had integrated orchestral sections and opera and the whole effect was different from anything that they had ever expected, Against Pippa's advice they released the Cry of the Panther track first as a single, there would be a disco version of the ballad this would keep all audiences. She had been outvoted and was concerned that they would expect a ballad from him.

Within a week of being released the song raced up the charts the plan was to release the three singles then the album Pippa had been wrong, the teenage girls loved it and the grandmothers loved it the ballad was played on all the radio stations and the clubs played the dance versions in all the major cities young men were getting their hair dyed like his.

When Pippa saw the video she had been silent he looked so handsome, half man, half boy. Justin had an eye he had caught that look that she had seen in him the first time she had seen him dance with the troupe on film he looked almost too handsome, untouchable.

She wanted to release the single with a DVD version of the video, every woman in America and every gay man would be queuing up to buy it.

Who wouldn't be pleased to look like that on film Tyrese was flattered that they had made him look so good, he was well aware that he didn't look as handsome as that and that they had computer manipulated him to create a demi-god. He was driving in the new sports car that Pippa had bought him he passed a movie theatre, they had a huge billboard outside it was Marisa's second film in the poster she looked so untouchable. He parked the car and thought he would try, he found a bandanna in the glove compartment put it on his head and put up the hood on his sweatshirt he sported the sunglasses he always carried with him and went to queue up for a ticket. Two women behind him joked that the guy in front was trying to look like that guy that sang the panther song, the other laughed saying no way, no one could look like that, the guy in front don't even come near.

Tyrese sat through the movie twice, savoring every moment Marisa was on screen, it wasn't as good as her last film but she looked great and when he left he called her, it was her answering service.

He left a message saying that he had loved her film and that he hadn't forgotten her.

CHAPTER 5

Bangkok, Thailand

Carla arrived in Bangkok and was met at the airport by Diederick, he had booked her into a hotel in the city thinking that she would like to shop. She was tall and thin and her hair was white her clear bright blue eyes had sold lots of goods in catalogues and although she was still an attractive woman for her age, she walked with a masculine gait and dressed in a masculine way preferring pants to skirts she never showed the great long legs that she had paraded on the catwalk. He drove towards her hotel it was early morning and the traffic was bearable, on the way he explained that he had arranged a holiday for her on an island.

He said he had a friend that wanted to accompany her. Typical she mused, he hadn't seen her in years but he was packing her off already, he added that Chloe was waiting in their hotel, that she was good fun and needed a break too, he lied that he would try and join them later in the week, Carla knew that he was lying she didn't care, a week on an island sounded better than a week with him.

Carla was tired after her flight but was pleasantly surprised when he introduced her to Chloe.

She was absolutely striking with long legs and beautiful hair she could earn a fortune modeling lingerie Carla thought as she admired her perfect body. Usually Carla liked masculine women, she had fallen in love with a tennis player who was as stocky and butch as you can imagine she had never till this very second thought that Asian women were beautiful until she had seen Chloe.

Diederick had warned Chloe to take good care of his sister in Phuket, Chloe was excited, she knew that Carla was lesbian she could handle that, she had done threesomes before for clients and didn't really care as long as they paid she could be anything they wanted and Carla was cute she had blue eyes and white hair. They decided to let Carla sleep for a few hours and promised they would come back to take her for lunch. Diederick was planning escaping after lunch going back to Pattaya and planned dumping Carla on Chloe, they had tickets to go to Phuket the following afternoon and he had paid Chloe in advance her normal day price.

Carla was still asleep when they arrived, at midday she woke up and showered and didn't bother to unpack her case there seemed no point if she was leaving again tomorrow. She had been broken-hearted since she split with her tennis playing friend, she missed her and perhaps spending a week on a tropical island with a beautiful Thai girl was just what she needed to heal the wounds.

She arrived in reception showered and changed looking crisp and smart in a white shirt and pants, after an excellent lunch at a five star hotel Diederick raced off leaving Carla in Chloe's hands. Carla was surprised that Chloe spoke such good English she had wit and charm and was fun to be with.

They spent the day shopping and Carla went mad buying clothes and souvenirs, at seven they went to Patpong market and bargained for handbags and watches. Chloe got everything for an absolute snip, it was so cheap Carla couldn't believe it. Around nine they headed back to the hotel laden with bags, Carla was tired she hadn't slept off her jet lag and she didn't think that Chloe was a lesbian and wondered what the sleeping arrangements would be. There were twin beds in the room so it didn't matter, she was attractive she thought soaking in a bubble bath, Carla was startled when the bathroom door opened and Chloe naked as the day she was born proudly walked in and jumped in the tub with her. Wow thought Carla Thailand wasn't so bad, Chloe found a sponge and was soaping her up, her skin was like silk so smooth and golden she was one of the most amazing women that Carla had ever seen.

After the bath Chloe led her to the bed and lay her on her stomach then for one hour she massaged her with cream, taking all the aches and pains out of her body. Carla fell asleep and Chloe was glad she preferred dick to pussy and couldn't wait till the week was over she was expecting a bonus for this, she wanted to kill Diederick. She hated staying with clients, it was only because it was his sister she had agreed, however she did want to see Phuket if there was money to be made she might not come back she was sick of Pattaya and even sicker of Diederick.

To Chloe's relief Carla was more interested in her companionship than sex when they arrived at the Spa Resort that Diederick had reserved for them, Carla requested a room with separate twin beds. The island was beautiful and Chloe was impressed with the charm it had, unlike Pattaya it wasn't overcrowded and everywhere was lush and green, everything seemed to be expensive on the island, it was a favorite with upmarket tourists, there were no cheap Charlie's or backpackers here.

They stayed at a luxurious spa resort in the north of the island, each day they had steam baths and massages it was the first time that Chloe had experienced being pampered and she adored the experience. They went on excursions round the island and they enjoyed the wonderful sunsets and divine cocktails, they went only once to Patong beach, that was the busy part of the island Carla had not been impressed, she found it too busy. Chloe wondered if she had even been in Pattaya she imagined she would detest it there Patong Beach was quiet compared to the bustle of Pattaya.

Chloe enjoyed Carla's company and Carla was grateful that Chloe had accompanied her.

Since she had split with Natasha her professional tennis player lover of five years she had been so lonely, she owned a lesbian bar but didn't mingle with the clientele and apart from Natasha she had had no real friends, when they split up Carla had buried herself in the renovation of her villa which was just outside Dusseldorf. She had made a small fortune modeling and had invested the money in her bar she earned a comfortable living and was grateful that she had earned so much so easily. They say that it never rains but it pours, as far as Carla was concerned it had been the worst year that she could remember. Natasha had left her and run off with another tennis player, the same week her mother had taken a stroke and died, Diederick had left all the funeral arrangements to her and in the end hadn't even turned up for the funeral, it had taken her a month single handedly to empty her mother's villa.

She had no relatives except for her brother she imagined that he had booked this holiday to make-up for the fact that he had done nothing when their mother died she presumed that he was trying to make amends, it was a shock to learn that actually Diederick had booked it to get rid of her.

Carla thought that he ran a hotel and spa in Pattaya she was horrified to hear that he was running a brothel, she had had no idea that Chloe had been a go-go girl, her brother was nothing more than a pimp, she was repulsed to hear that Chloe had to dance topless with a number pinned to a G-string. She had a lesbian bar ok, but it was a classy establishment, a private club with membership only, her clientele were closet corporate lipstick lesbians, doctors, lawyers, professional sportswomen and politicians. There was nothing sleazy about her establishment she was furious and couldn't believe that for years he had lied to her. Perhaps this was the reason he had always made excuses in the past when she had suggested bringing mother out to rest at his spa, some spa, a bloody brothel.

Chloe had drunk a lot of wine with dinner and she wasn't used to it so it had gone straight to her head, she had perhaps told Carla too much. Diederick would be absolutely furious with her.

Carla couldn't wait to confront Diederick and one day while Chloe was having a manicure she called him, she had told him that she was bored in Phuket it was the rainy season and she asked if she could come for a week to stay at his spa. When the telephone had rung Diederick was asleep, sandwiched between two new girls from the north and he had been caught by surprise and was nervous to hear his sister's voice. She told him that they would come back to Pattaya the following week she was dying to see his resort.

Diederick ordered the two whores out of his bed and flung two thousand baht in notes at them, the girls were confused they thought that they hadn't pleased him. As quickly as they could they scrambled into their clothes and made a speedy exit.

Chloe arrived and proudly showed Carla her newly painted nails, the tall elegant German woman felt a pang of sorrow for the poor Thai girl she was ravishingly beautiful and deserved more than a career as a prostitute, at least if she had been working in Germany she would have made money, they would have paid 1000 euros a night for a girl like her in Dusseldorf.

Diederick called back his voice sounded nervous and Carla couldn't wait to hear what kind of lie he was going to invent. To her total surprise he leveled with her, he explained that he ran a Go-Go bar and that Chloe was one of his top girls, he said that she was welcome and added that if she fancied a bit most of them swung both ways. Carla was appalled she resented his remark and disliked people who thought that just because she was lesbian that she would sleep with anything that had boobs. They talked for an hour on the phone and one thing led to another she had told him how furious she was that he hadn't even bothered to go to his own mother's funeral and how tasteless it had been to fax her and ask to transfer his share of the inheritance, in the end Carla hung up on him and wracked into sobs. Chloe didn't not know what was happening they had been talking German on the telephone and she had guessed form the tone that things were not going well.

Carla told Chloe everything, about their mother dying, about Diederick being her only relative alive and how she had made this trip to try and patch things up with him. She cried openly and told her that when she had been thirteen Diederick had raped her together with a friend, she had been too afraid to tell their parents, too afraid to tell anyone, they both had spent their teens in boarding schools and had little contact with each other after the sexual assault. She was sure that is why she had become lesbian, she had had an affair at the Swiss finishing school with another French student, she had hated men since her own brother had robbed her of her maidenhood and the only real love that she had ever had was with Natasha, she had met Natasha quite by accident and they had lived together for five years.

Carla had been nursing her mother who had had a stroke and she had neglected Natasha, one day she came home and Natasha had left, she had packed her bags and gone to live with Imogen a new tennis player. The week Natasha had left her mother died.

Chloe cradled her in her arms and promised that things would get better she told her to focus on the positive things she was good-looking in her prime and had a good business.

Carla sobbed even harder and shoved her away, Chloe didn't understand what she had said to upset her. Carla locked herself in the bathroom for an hour. Finally when she had pulled herself together she came out she sat Chloe down and told her that she was going to tell her a secret and that she needed her help.

In the privacy of the bathroom with the door firmly locked Carla had sobbed her heart out. She was not religious but in a fit of pure rage she asked God why he had dealt her such a mean deal, she had pulled herself together and lay for half an hour in a bath, she thought about things and thought about her brother he had abused her he was nothing to her, soon she would die too, the cancer was malignant they had said that she would only live for a year maximum, she had intended to tell Diederick that she was dying as he was the only family left, he would inherit what she left behind and probably open another brothel where he could abuse more women. She didn't want that to happen, she didn't want to die alone.

It was then the idea sprung to mind, Chloe! She would ask Chloe to stay with her as a companion she would make her a business deal, pay her a monthly salary, she liked the girl. Her brother had made her into a whore, Chloe had told her that she was from Cambodia and had arrived in Thailand and been so desperate, that Diederick was her only way out. He was a bastard and she hated him, if he even imagined that she was dying he would be all over her like a vulture waiting for her to drop dead so he could cash in. She had an idea and Chloe would be part of that plan, she wouldn't die alone she would ask Chloe to be there like a friend, like a nurse, she didn't want to end her days in a clinic or in a hospital ward connected to tubes and hanging on. She wouldn't go to hospital and she wouldn't suffer any more chemotherapy, it wasn't helping and made her feel worse, she wanted to travel, to see the world for as long as she was mobile and capable. Apart from her obvious good looks Chloe was sweet she was good fun and she enjoyed her company.

Chloe was shocked to hear that Carla was dying she was even more shocked to hear that Carla wanted her to go to Europe with her and work for her as a companion at first Chloe refused point blank. Carla asked what she earned from Diederick she was shocked when she heard. Carla offered her triple the amount, paid monthly into her bank account in either Baht or Dollars whichever she preferred. She would give her an open return ticket and pay her in Thailand an extra three months salary into her account in advance so that if she didn't like the job then she was free to leave.

Chloe sat speechless on the bed, at first she thought Carla was joking but seeing the stern look in her eyes she realized that she was serious. Chloe always had dreamed of traveling, as a child she fantasized about going on planes to countries far away.

Carla's emotional outburst had done something to her, Carla had confided in her and told her about the rape for twenty-two years Carla had carried that secret with her, she had never dared to tell anyone, just getting it off her chest had made her feel better. Now it was Chloe's turn to shock, they were in the room and darkness had fallen, Chloe sat on the bed her head dipped in shame she told Carla that she would love to be her companion she would love to come to Europe but couldn't.

Carla watched her as she cried, silent tears ran down her cheeks like crystal beads on her golden skin, she tried to speak but the words wouldn't come out. It took her ten minutes to pull up the courage, it was dark in the room and the darkness helped, her for some strange reason she trusted this woman.

Carla sat frozen to the spot as Chloe told her story that she was from Cambodia that her family had sold her at sixteen and that she was too raped she admitted to slitting his throat.

Carla was weeping too, she said to her never tell anyone else this story she said that she did the right thing cutting his throat, if she had had a knife she would have cut her brother's throat too. Together they sat on the bed in the darkness cradling each other. Chloe wanted to run away, she hated Diederick and the nameless men that invaded her body, she told Carla that she had to sleep with three men a day. Carla was shocked she warned her about the dangers of aids, Chloe said that she didn't have a passport, she said that they would never give her a visa.

Carla held her like a baby in her arms, she had an idea she would get a visa, she would get a passport. Carla knew people with influence, she knew people that worked in embassies and that could pull strings. Fate that Carla was dying, but poor Chloe was dead already. She tried to calm her and told her that money talks. That night as Chloe slept

Carla felt more compassion for the golden skinned girl than she had ever felt. She made a silent vow to help her.

It hadn't been easy but Carla had been able to pull a few strings it had cost her an arm and a leg and had taken three weeks but it worked Chloe had her passport and visa they had left Phuket and gone to Bangkok. Carla had flown back to Germany to arrange things there, she had arranged a bank account for Chloe in both Thailand and Germany, she had called in some favors in Germany and had managed to get all the documents within days. She had flown back to Bangkok four days later.

At first when she had announced that she was flying back, Chloe didn't believe her, she had stayed in Bangkok in their hotel for four days, she had eaten room service and watched every program on TV. She could not believe it when Carla walked in the door, she was tired out but had all the paperwork they needed. It took them another ten days to get the visa and it had cost Carla a small fortune but it was worth it, she never told Chloe how much that she had paid people she would have been upset.

Diederick had no idea what they were scheming, he had not spoken to either of them since they were in Phuket. Together they took a taxi to Pattaya. Chloe wanted to get her clothes, her apartment was paid for by Diederick she didn't care about anything, there were some photos and bits and pieces that she wanted to take to Germany with her. Carla wasn't impressed by Pattaya she preferred Phuket it took them only one hour to pack all Chloe's belongings, they had did a deal with the driver to wait for them. That night they slept like logs, strange how life changes thought Chloe looking at the thin blonde woman sleeping in the bed across from her, she had never ever dreamed of possessing a passport in her life. She had a new identity now and a new future, she liked Carla a lot and wondered what she would do when she died, she had grown so close to her in the last month, mentally close to her, she was not a lesbian, she liked men she had made that quite clear and Carla had been enraged that Diederick had paid Chloe to sleep with her, the poor girl wasn't even that way inclined.

She hated her brother even more now. Diedrick was furious when he learned that his bitch sister had ran off with his best girl he couldn't believe that Chloe was so into pussy, the bitches. Well he thought his sister sure had good taste he couldn't imagine how on earth that she had been able to arrange a passport so quickly. He pondered whether to keep paying Chloe's flat, he could also use it to stick some of the new girls in there till she got back, she would hate Germany he thought too cold and boring for her. He bet the doorman that she would be back in two weeks it was low season anyway and he had enough girls, it would do the bitch good to lick pussy for a few weeks she would come crawling back he mused.

She was a cracking looking girl and he would miss her, she was the favorite even though she had gone off the rails recently. She was the best eye candy, the men at the club were missing her everyone thought that she had met a rich guy. No one believed that she had taken off with his sister. He was glad that Carla hadn't come, he had lied for years about a spa resort she would have freaked out if she seen his bar talk about the kettle calling the teapot black she had a fucking lesbian bar in Dusseldorf. Oh he mused that was different that was a classy joint she had always been odd, his sister always been a problem.

Chloe was nervous she had only flown to Phuket and was scared of being in a plane for so many hours, she had got some sleeping pills for the flight and wanted to take them the minute she went on board, the pharmacist had said that she would sleep like a baby and waken up in Europe.

Carla was amused that she was so scared of flying and she did everything to put her at ease, they had both overweight baggage and Carla was shocked that the baggage cost just as much as a seat. Chloe looked nervous as she handed the immigration officer her passport he stared at her for a long time making her nervous as hell he was however only admiring her, she was beautiful probably a model he thought. Carla warned her not to look so guilty when she went through passport control, she didn't want any unnecessary problems.

Chloe was fascinated by the pop up TV screens in business class. Carla followed Chloe's idea and also took a sleeping pill, it had been a great idea before they realized a thing, both of them were being shook by the stewardess she was telling them to put their seats in the upright position as they were landing in Dusseldorf.

The sun was shining as they landed and Chloe couldn't believe how different the city looked to Bangkok it was Sunday morning and there were hardly any people in the street. Carla lived almost in the centre of the city in a palatial abode that had recently been expensively refurbished. Chloe couldn't believe that one person lived in this home, she had five bedrooms and bathrooms and two lounges it seemed so extravagant for one person to live like this. She was impressed it looked the houses you seen in the movies.

Carla showed Chloe to a bright room with a balcony overlooking the garden, this was to be her room. Chloe tested the bed it was big enough to get lost in, she had found it chilly outside and Carla had given her a sweater it was the first time she had worn a sweater and she felt it scratchy on the skin. The following day Carla promised that as soon as they had slept off their jet lag they would go shopping for some winter clothes for Chloe. Most of the clothes she had brought she wouldn't be able to wear because they were too skimpy and too sexy.

Both of them slept for hours, it was Carla who woke first and headed to the kitchen to make some coffee, fortunately the maid had got the message that they were arriving and the fridge was full of goodies. Carla thought that Chloe would never wake up she looked like an angel with her dark silky hair cascading over the pillows, she was a beauty Chloe mused as she quietly closed the door to let her sleep. It felt good to have someone in the house, her home was too big for one person she was crazy to have bought it, crazy to have spent so much decorating it.

CHAPTER 6

ROGILLIO

Rogillio's heart raced as he approached his house, there were two police cars parked in the drive and his housekeeper was outside talking to four officers. He braked and jumped out of his car still wearing the shorts he had worn in the gym, he imagined that he had been burgled and regretted not having put the box that he kept his jewelry in the safe. As he approached the doorway two officers came to meet him, the police man explained that they needed to talk to him and that they wanted to take him down to the station. Rogillio was confused but jumped in one of the cars, he asked a hundred questions but was told that everything would be explained in the police station. Part of him was happy that he hadn't been burgled, the other half wondered what the hell they wanted with him.

Rogillio was infuriated when they fingerprinted him and asked to take some DNA

Rogillio was objecting and asking to call his lawyer when the police chief arrived.

The chief inspector apologized that no one had explained what the situation was, he had wanted to speak to him personally, Rogillio was put in an office and questioned about his day he told them clearly everything that he had done. The police looked at each other, them explained to him that shortly after he had left Tiffany's apartment she had died of a heroin overdose, the problem was that the dose had not been self-administered there had been a struggle, they believed that he had been the last person to see her alive. They asked him dozens of questions over and over again, almost as if they were trying to trick him. Rogillio couldn't believe that this was happening and an hour later he found himself in a line up for attempted murder. He had called his lawyer but as yet the jerk hadn't turned up there was chaos on the freeway and he was stuck in traffic.

The police were trying to calm the old concierge, he had worked at the apartment block for twenty years and there had never been any trouble and the man was overwrought, he trembled as he eyed the men behind the glass and recognized Rogillio immediately. His hand was shaking as he explained that Rogillio was there visiting Miss Tiffany, he left about ten minutes before the other man arrived. He said that after Rogillio had left, a tall man had arrived and he called Tiffany to tell her that he was on the way up. Miss Tiffany had said that it was ok, he had not waited till the concierge had called her, he had dived into the lift. After half an hour he left in a hurry. The police asked why he had not said that there had been two guests that visited her, he said that he was so upset that he had forgotten to mention it.

The lawyer was embarrassed that he had taken so long to get there, the freeway had been blocked, the police apologized for the way they had treated Rogillio they had disrespected his feelings too.

He was shocked to hear that Tiffany was dead he had just spent the afternoon with her.

The police explained that Tiffany was a diplomat's daughter, she had been beaten and someone had filled her up with heroin.

Rogillio hated drugs, his lawyer drove him home, it was chilling to think that she was gone that seconds after he left someone had done this, if he had stayed to make love to her he might have been murdered too.

He wondered if she was a heroin addict, a lot of models took it to stop their hunger.

He hadn't noticed any needle marks on her arms but then again he hadn't really looked.

He was silent as the car sped towards his home, a fat lot of good his lawyer had been.

Turning up after he had been humiliated he wondered if it was because he was famous that they had given him such a rough time, the interrogation had been grueling. He was glad that the press hadn't been there, it was pure luck that they hadn't been around his house when the police cars were there, luckily they had thought he was in Europe. He had postponed the trip a few days to get some peace, he was glad now that he was going to London he had had enough of this place it would be refreshing to get away. He asked his lawyer to keep him informed if there was any progress on the case and explained that he had to go to Europe. In two days he was in the clear, a neighbor had also said that she had seen Rogillio leave and had seen the other man come out of the lift and thump on her door. Rogillio asked his lawyer to find out when and where the funeral was and send flowers.

An Italian team had wanted to have Rogillio he had had talks with them before, they wanted to make him an offer and were meeting him in London for talks. Rogillio liked his home he was reluctant to move to Europe even if it did mean more money. He earned a lot and was happy with all the extra money he earned with promotion and advertising, his public relation company had also arranged appointments with a sportswear company and a soft drinks company who were offering him a handsome contract to advertise their products.

The trip had been scheduled to tie in with an appointment he already had. They were shooting a commercial for a new line of sports shoes, he had signed a two year contract with the shoe company and they had paid him handsomely.

The meetings went well, the Italian team were offering him a massive transfer fee and although it seemed like a golden opportunity he hadn't said yes, he wanted more time to play they had given him a deadline as they were desperate to buy another player and had apparently their eye on a new rising star, some black guy named Tyrese he had never met him, but he heard that he was a mean machine on the pitch. Ironically the soft drinks company had approached this guy also, suddenly out of the blue it seemed he had a rival.

He had a free day in London and went wild with his credit card in Knightsbridge and Sloane Street. There were so many cool stores in London he wished that he had longer, it was also cool to be able to shop without being pestered for autographs, back home they knew all his disguises, here with his shades and hat no one looked twice at him.

He was collected at six am on the day of the commercial. These people didn't like to sleep they always had to get you up in the middle of the night.

He had fallen straight back to sleep after the wake-up call, which was really unusual for him. The shock of what had happened back home with Tiffany had knocked him off balance.

They were shooting in a studio way outside London, it was a cool studio with huge sound stages when he arrived the whole team were already there his PR company had given him a brief of what was happening. It was simple really, a football hero, all muscle, wears the shoes, does some sprints and jumps and kicks all against a blue screen then the computer wizards would add some magic. Weird, Rogillio thought, they flew him half way across the world to film him on a blue screen, well no problem it was cool to be in London and they were paying him handsomely.

While a make-up girl named Janine applied his make-up he read the script, he didn't know that there was a girl in the script, 'Who's the chick?' joked Rogillio.

The make-up artist said she was in make-up, it was Marisa Duval she said emphatically.

Rogillio felt a little dumb he had never heard of her, Janine looked at him like he had been on another planet and explained that she was the hottest thing on the screen at the moment. Her first two movies had been blockbusters she raved how incredible she was and admitted that she had been real disappointed that she had to do his make-up instead of hers.

Rogillio had no idea who this film star was but was curious, as soon as his make-up was ready he went to see the stylist and put on his outfit, he was on his way to her room, yes, she had her own make-up room, he was just approaching the door when he was called for a lighting check. Life sucks he thought as he walked towards the studio, he knew how it worked with films this was gonna be a long tiring drawn out day. Silly how he was complaining, it sure beat the shit out of sleeping in the streets of San Palou.

The light check was taking forever, there he was bathed in light in an absolutely huge studio.

The blue screen seemed to be endless it was indeed almost as big as a football pitch. He had to run around and kick a ball then jump as high as he could. After what seemed like forever they were ready and he had to do his thing for the camera, he ran and jumped for almost fifteen minutes with cameras filming from every angle.

After the director was satisfied they put him back into make-up he was, they said perspiring, some wonder he thought under these lights they were blinding. He showered they applied the make-up and an attractive redhead did his hair, he was given another costume and a great pair of sports shoes and he went on the set. After doing endless close-ups of his feet they attached a harness on him and suspended him from the rafters. A screaming stylist stopped them in action and he was lowered and asked to change his shoes, they had forgotten to change them, it could have been fatal Rogillio thought if they had to fly him back in to reshoot. The harness was strapped round his crotch and they elevated him in the air, he joked that he felt like Peter Pan. They were arranging his lighting when he saw her, she walked into the studio, a make-up artist was adding finishing touches to her lips, another guy was adjusting her hair, a stylist was tying the laces of her sports shoes and two huge gorillas of bodyguards were standing behind her. Suspended in mid-air it was like time had stood still she stared right up at where he was suspended and shot him a big smile, Rogillio's heart seemed to beat faster, he didn't know if it was the height or her presence she looked so stunning Rogillio was lost for words.

He couldn't wait to finish the scene he wanted to get on the ground and meet this Marisa movie star chick, just by luck the lighting was wrong they had to lower him and were going to do the suspension scene later in the day. They let him have a break as they wanted to focus on Marisa's shots, 'I'll bet thought Rogillio. The lower he got the closer he was to her, she was so breathtakingly perfect that he hardly could speak when she introduced herself. It was weird when she walked on the set it was like the room lit up. Up close she was even more beautiful than he had imagined she was small and petite with long legs and the most perfect breasts he had ever seen, she had the most incredible body imaginable but what made her different was her face, she radiated sex appeal like nothing you could imagine.

She checked her reflection in the mirror and asked the make-up artist to put more gloss on her lips, satisfied with the effect she smiled directly at Rogillio and lowering her lashes pouted and inquired do you have a tongue, Rogillio stuttered and realized that he hadn't introduced himself. She teased him that she believed that in the commercial they had to kiss and that she never kissed men without knowing their names. Rogillio stuttered his name and she laughed, she was well aware that she had sent his temperature rising. It amused her that she had that effect on men, they were always speechless when they met her - little wonder she didn't have a permanent boyfriend she thought everyone was afraid of her.

The commercial was intended to look like a computer game, both Marisa and Rogillio would be suspended as they travelled through time and space. They would fly through the universe with their cooler than cool sports shoes and hopefully after showing the expensive commercial global sales of the product would soar. The scene would end when of course the football hero got his leading lady and they would close the commercial with a kiss. Rogillio couldn't believe his luck, being paid a small fortune to wrestle and kiss this girl.

She did some scenes alone everyone stood silently watching Marisa in action it was obvious why she had become a star so quickly, she was not only incredible to look at but could really act. On the monitor when she flew through the air she had a strong look of sexuality on her face it was captivating. The filming in the harness was uncomfortable and took ages, Marisa never complained and kept on doing whatever was requested. At last they had to film the kiss, this was the scene Rogillio had been looking forward to doing, he could have done it all night if needed, having her in his arms was electrifying and she seemed to be enjoying the scene. Just after the director shouted that it was a wrap and everyone thought that they could go home, Marisa asked if they could try a little something her way.

The director was fascinated with her and agreed, they had the shots but why not, it wasn't every day he had someone like her around and he wanted to work with her again. The more footage of her the better, he had imagined she would have rushed everything and gone off, she explained that she wanted to try a mid-air kiss, she suggested that they swing both of them in slowly and they would do a mid-air love scene, that way they could shoot the shoes and arms and legs and the kiss.

As soon as the cameras rolled the director knew that was the scene they would use. Marisa glided through the sky into Rogillio's arms, she kissed him with sensuality and passion, the camera on the dolly rolled round taking in the scene, catching the shoes, the kiss, her breasts. They stopped kissing and heads together looked right in the camera it was one of the best scenes the director had ever shot. He was so pleased he knew that it would be knockout.

Rogillio was getting changed, he was standing in his underpants almost naked at the sink washing the make-up off when she came up behind him, startled he turned round and was surprised to see Marisa. She said that if he was taking her to dinner then she would keep her make-up on, he agreed eagerly and she disappeared to her dressing room to slip into something more appropriate.

Rogillio was wearing a baggy sweatshirt and jeans ten minutes later Marisa emerged in a silver lame dress Rogillio felt he was underdressed, she laughed claiming that she liked her men Au natural. Her bodyguards ushered him to her car which was a gleaming vintage Rolls Royce with ocelot interior. She looked embarrassed as they entered and she told him it was the studio's they were trying to impress her with this sugar daddy car as she called it.

They had a great dinner at San Lorenzo and the place was ablaze with gossip when they entered. After some of the best Italian food he had ever tasted they made their exit and as they left the restaurant the flashbulbs popped, an army of paparazzi had arrived.

Marisa actually enjoyed the intrusion of her privacy, she said this was the part that most stars hated, she claimed that this was the part that she enjoyed most. She had called the studio to tell them to inform the press where they were eating. She reveled in the press attention and had booked a table for two before he had even accepted her invite.

Marisa was so bubbly if you got over her beauty, there were a lot of things to discover. She was witty, she had humor, she was a million miles from being the dumb blonde that the press portrayed.

She was modest and even a little shy, under all the make-up was a very intelligent woman and Rogillio like every other man who crossed her path was besotted.

They went to Annabel's to finish the evening, she was impressed that Rogillio could dance so well and when they were on the floor all heads turned, she was a great dancer and she knew how to attract men. Rogillio couldn't take his eyes off her and the closer she got, the hotter he became, she was the sexiest woman in the world he thought as she rubbed her breasts against him. He had never seen lashes so long or lips so full without thinking he kissed her full on the mouth, at first he wanted to pull away thinking that she was angry instead she pressed her thighs against his and her tongue darted down his throat.

The following day a photo of them in a deep embrace hit the tabloids, the headlines were SCREEN GODDESS MEETS SUPER HERO. Someone obviously had snapped a photo of them with a spy cameras.

Rogillio was proud when he saw the picture, he was elated to have his name linked to her, they hadn't slept together but he was meeting her at her hotel, she had been amused that he had not seen any of the two films that had been box office hits. She had joked that she would take him the following day to see one of her films he thought that she was joking but when he arrived at her apartment he was surprised to find her wearing a black bobbed wig and gold rimmed glasses the great body hidden in a shapeless coat and jeans. Rogillio thought that she was joking she told him she went out like this all the time, when she got tired being a public figure she wore her frumpy Freda outfit and it always worked, sometimes she had walked out past the Paparazzi and they hadn't batted an eyelid. When she had invited him to see her movie he had imagined a private screening, she said, 'No way, the way to see me on the big screen is with lashings of popcorn and soft drinks too.' They left by the back entrance of the hotel and haled a cab on the corner. The two films were playing in Leicester Square and they landed up going to both, she liked watching herself up there on the big screen she liked to see the reaction of the people that paid money to see her.

Rogillio was so mesmerized by the sheer intensity of her performance he forgot that she was sitting next to him, the truth was she too was fascinated by the raw emotion she portrayed on screen no one was more surprised than herself of how she looked on film.

Of course she owed a lot to lighting and the make-up was fantastic, the camera loved her and she loved the camera she glanced at Rogillio he was so handsome, she could not wait for the second film to end so she could get him into bed. It had been months since she had been with a man, her filming schedule just hadn't allowed her to have any sexcapades whatsoever.

Marisa was on such a high that she had actually been able to sit in a movie theatre and watch her own movie, the audience had obviously loved it and she much preferred to watch it like this than at the premier or in a private screening room. Rogillio had been so impressed he was speechless when he left, Marisa told him that he should be in movies too he had Latin good looks that women adored, he was photogenic and she thought there was a market for someone like him in the industry, she concluded that she could pull a few strings. Rogillio was flattered but somehow didn't see himself up there on the big screen he was just a boy that kicked a ball he said. Marisa wanted to go to lunch at a diner but had second thoughts and in the end they went back to her hotel suite. Her manager was waiting in reception. Red-faced and furious that she had ditched her bodyguards he screamed at her in front of Rogillio telling her that as long as she was filming under contract she could and would not go out alone in public. Her contract stipulated that, what if something ugly happened or some stalker kidnapped her? Did she realize how much that that would cost the studio? She was a movie star not a checkout girl and she had to obey the rules.

Rogillio was surprised how badly she was treated but realized that the guy was right, there were plenty of crazy people out there on the street. She was a major movie star and if something did happen it would cost the studio millions of dollars. Marisa said nothing and slammed her room door. Once inside she ripped off her wig and looked him in the eye, being a star was like being a prisoner she cried, then she pulled him into her arms and kissed him.

Rogillio was sure that the bodyguards must have heard her scream as he brought her to orgasm twice, she made love with all the passion that she put into her acting and Rogillio wondered if she was acting when he made love to her. He propped himself on his elbow and studied the sleeping beauty that lay beside him, she was too good to be true he thought studying her amazing naked breasts and full lips. He smiled, thinking that even her pussy was special, she had shaved her pubic hair into a heart shape, looking at her he couldn't believe that he had just made love to her and that he was actually lying in bed with the girl that had stirred his emotions on screen.

He wondered who it was that he had made love to, the real person or the screen goddess. He fell asleep at her side and was woken two hours later. Marisa was leaning over him sucking his cock, within seconds he was erect and threw her on the bed. He plucked two silk scarves from her closet and tied her to the four-poster bed taking total control.

After a very satisfying sexual workout they ordered lobster and champagne from room service, Marisa enjoyed expensive food, for years she had lived on a diet of tinned beans that she cooked on the one ring cooker in the trailer that she had shared with her bastard father. She had been real surprised that he hadn't turned up in her life looking for money. The truth was that he had seen her several times on TV when he had been drunk but had never thought that the slick sexy girl was his daughter, he had joked that they bore a resemblance but he had never imagined that his hot-tempered little Mary Lou and the sex symbol Marisa Duval had been one and the same person.

Sergio had been a problem he was on her payroll and getting a fortune for retaining a low profile and keeping his mouth shut. The situation suited him and he was planning opening his own lap dancing bar, the project of course was to be financed by Marisa, anything to keep him away she had thought as she had signed the cheque to finance his establishment. In a moment of weakness she had let Sergio know her real name, he alone knew her identity and could ruin her future.

The studio had invented a history for her for the press, she was according to their press release the daughter of a ballerina, her father having had died in an accident when she was a child, the bed ridden ballerina was living apparently in the South of France.

Marisa didn't care about her past, she cared more about her future and was determined to be a screen goddess for as long as she could, she was desperate to be admired as a serious actress and didn't want to be a flash in the pan three hit wonder brainless bimbo.

She had argued with her management team that the next film would have to be a serious role, no sex scenes, no glamour. She had shown interest in a script where she would be a teacher who is blind, the studio thought the whole project was crazy the public wanted to see her in glamorous roles. She was a fucking sex symbol not Meryl Streep. Stubborn as an ox she rejected all the roles they were pushing at her and demanded that they let her do this low budget film which she thought would showcase her acting talent instead of her boobs.

In the end the studio had agreed she could do the serious movie if she signed up to do an action movie right after it. She had hated the script of Galaxy Warrior the moment she had seen it but signed anyway, she was so desperate to film Blind Vision that she would have done anything.

She persuaded Rogillio to postpone going back to the States for a week, he didn't need much persuasion and soon the season would begin again so he would be unable to return to Europe for a while. He was still unsure about a transfer to Italy but the idea of being near to Marisa appealed to him. He had promised himself to train vigilantly every day to keep in condition, he wanted desperately to be in top form when he returned.

Marisa left her hotel suite at five thirty every day often she would be on set till midnight.

Rogillio usually went to the studio in the evenings to eat with her and enjoy her company while she hung around waiting to be filmed. She explained that they were trying to finish the movie a month ahead of schedule so that she could do two other films before the end of the year.

She was tired but never complained and Rogillio was amazed at how professional she was. He enjoyed standing in the wings in the darkness of the sound stage and watching her in action she had a magical electric presence that made the screen light up.

The director was not too enamored that Rogillio had turned up every night but he had to grin and bear it. Marisa had demanded that he was allowed on set and that was that, at night they would eat together she had insisted in having menus from all her favorite restaurants and they delivered whatever she wanted.

It was strange to watch her, one evening doing a love scene with her handsome young co-star Rogillio felt a pang of jealousy as he watched the athletic blond man simulate sex with her in a love scene. He had joked with her at dinner asking if she had enjoyed it, Marisa had said yes adding that it was always easier when her co-stars were gay then she knew it was acting. Rogillio could hardly believe that her co-star Cameron Sandors was gay he was so macho and a real hit with the ladies, he thought that she was joking until she called him and invited both Cameron and his make-up artist boyfriend to join them for dinner.

Rogillio was surprised, Cameron, every woman's dream was gay. He arrived with a cute young guy named Jason and it was obvious that they had a thing going on. Cameron roared with laughter when Marisa told him that Rogillio had been jealous when they filmed the love scene, Jason had added he was jealous too. Cameron had actually teased Marisa that he would like to try a love scene with Rogillio, the footballer blushed awkwardly, he didn't like faggots. It reminded him of the days way back when he had to do tricks with perverts to earn money for food. In the film industry there were lots of gays, half of Marisa's entourage were gay and she wished sometimes that Mr Macho Rogillio would relax more in their company, he got so uptight. She had no idea that as a ten year old boy he had sucked old men's dicks in back alleys for a few dollars, that was a part of his life that was buried forever, no matter how successful he was, ghosts of the past still haunted him. He was homophobic he couldn't help it. Once when he was eleven a man had nearly cut his throat, he had not been satisfied with the blow job and had ripped off his pants and buggered him, he had fought as hard as he could but the man had been strong, after he had abused him he ran off without paying, leaving Rogillio bleeding on a pile of garbage. Even after all these years he still could remember the smell of his sweat, he could still clearly see his face and would have stabbed him if he had had a knife. No one had come to help him when he screamed, everyone knew what was happening but no one cared when the beast had covered his mouth to stop his screams Rogillio had bit the man's finger so hard that it almost came right off. For a week after it happened Rogillio had returned there every night to the same spot with a knife he wanted to cut off the bastard's cock. The man never returned and after that week Rogillio had never gone back to the street where the perverts came looking for street kids. Instead he worked as a shoeshine boy and stole money from drunks, instead of selling his body he robbed people to survive.

Suddenly the day arrived when they had to part, Marisa had her car take him to the airport.
They said their goodbyes in the back of the car and as he kissed her he felt a knot in his throat. He had to play football on the other side of the globe and she was off to Africa to film for two months. He waved goodbye till her car was out of sight. She had been wearing her dressing gown and her hair was full of pink rollers, funny every time he thought of her he saw in her in those ridiculous pink rollers. When he entered the airport he was mobbed by journalists, they had had a field day with Marisa and him and the tabloids had

been full of photos. He raced through the passport control leaving the press behind, as he disappeared they were still asking if he had plans to marry Marisa he was glad to have given them the shake and headed for the sanctuary of the VIP lounge where he wanted to bury his head in the papers till the flight took off.

The dailies were full of photos of him and Marisa he was angry but proud too, she looked so cool on his arm. When he read the articles he got angry they had written so many lies it was too much. According to one paper they had bought a house together, in another he was giving up football, in another they were engaged where he thought, do they get this information.

He was glad to get on the plane and as soon as they took off he put on his eye mask and fell asleep, he tossed and turned as they flew across the Atlantic dreaming that Marisa was with another man.

The stewardess woke him asking if he would like dinner she was pretty and quite blatantly flirting with him, normally Rogillio would have arranged to meet her after the flight but he was not interested, somewhere along the line in the last two weeks he had fallen in love for the first time in his life and he wasn't sure if he liked the feeling or not. He had fallen head over heels with a movie star, him and half the planet were in love with her.

He was glad to walk into the dressing room and change into his strip, he couldn't wait to get back on pitch and score some goals. He had missed the euphoria of running on field and hearing all the fans scream his name, he was in good shape and was gonna kick some ass this season.

Rogillio played football, trained and that was that, he stayed at home and watched TV and didn't go to parties. Every time the telephone rang he had hoped that it was Marisa but she hadn't called in a week. He wasn't worried as he knew she was in some remote part of Africa.

The last time she called she had been almost in tears, it was so hot and sticky and she had hated the location and still had to go to Tibet.

The PR company had sent Rogillio a copy of the commercial that they had shot together for the shoes. It was an amazing commercial, he had been really excited both himself and Marisa looked incredible and the computer effects were unbelievable. The screen kiss that they had shot suspended in mid-air was magical, they were flying through the universe heading for Mars, watching his image on film had excited him. He wondered if perhaps he should try and get into movies, he watched the commercial about fifty times and couldn't wait to tell Marisa all about it.

Every time he thought about her his heart skipped a beat, she had changed him, he had stopped going to parties and stopped sleeping with girls and to his surprise was quite content to stay home. He had no interest in other women they just seemed pallid next to Marisa and he was content to wait for her.

While Rogillio was curled up on the sofa watching their commercial Marisa was in a tent somewhere in a remote part of Africa, she was lying beneath a six foot two inch tall negro extra with the best physique that she had ever seen. He was making love to her like a savage and she was enjoying every moment. While Marisa was reaching her multiple orgasm the whole film crew were waiting, hoping that she would appear on the scene quickly. The director was embarrassed and the whole crew knew that she was having an affair with the striking extra that had been employed for a two minute scene. Marisa had insisted that they expand his role, he was an incredible looking man but the director was tired of her demands and he would have preferred to have got rid of the boy, since she had met him she seemed to spend more time in her tent than on set and they were way behind schedule.

Marisa had hated being on location in Africa the conditions were too primitive for her and the role was demanding. Blind Vision had been her dream and now it was her nightmare the temperature was unbearable and the catering was inedible. She was sure that they were giving her a hard time, she had rows with her manager but he had simply said that she was the one who wanted to make a low budget film and she was the one who had twisted everyone's arm to star in it. They still had to do some shooting in the Himalayas and she had heard that it would be just as primitive there. She had been despondent till she had met Guame. He was an extra that was playing a tracker, he would save her from being attacked by a panther, the first day he arrived in set she had spotted him immediately he was extremely handsome twenty-two years old and didn't speak a word of English. She had personally taken him under her wing and had pretended to give him acting lessons in the privacy of her tent. She had experienced the best sex that she had ever had, the boy was like a wild beast and she had fallen a little in love with him. He was not an actor he was an extra he didn't know that this blonde was one of the biggest stars in the world, she was the first foreign girl that he had ever seen and out there in the bush any woman would have pleased him he was fascinated by her light blue eyes and golden hair. Their off screen romance had created a bond between them that was electrifying on screen, the producers had agreed to add more scenes with him and the writers had been requested to write a piece where she fell in love with the tracker and he was killed by a snake. They had argued that this would be crummy and were infuriated that this was being done to please their megastar they agreed to shoot the scene but warned her if looked plastic or trashy that it would be shelved in the editing. What happened was that this extra scene written and shot on Marisa's insistence would be the scene that gripped the audience and made the movie a hit.

The on screen magic of the primitive tracker that fell in love with a blind teacher was so intense that they used those scenes in the promotion trailers. The forbidden love affair between the black and white odd couple was electrifying, the rampant sexuality between Marisa and Guame was sizzling and when at the end he died on screen in her arms the scene was so moving that audiences worldwide burst into tears.

One evening the director had argued with her about her love affair with the extra, she had argued back and threatened not to finish the film unless they filmed things her way and in her contract it stipulated that she would have a say and she wanted this kid in.

The night of the premier in New York after rave reviews she had whispered in the director's ear that if she hadn't had that affair with Guame she could never have given such a performance. Guame had attended the premiere, he still didn't speak English and had a surprised expression on his face most of the time. He didn't even recognize Marisa when she appeared by limo, he had never seen her with full make-up and dressed so glamorously. In the movie in Africa she had worn a dirty linen skirt and top and wore no make-up she had greasy hair. When she approached him on the red carpet at the entrance to the theatre to pose with him for press photos he looked nothing less than terrified, he had never seen a woman like this before, only when she spoke did he realize that this was the girl that he had made love to under the red skies of his home town.

Marisa's fascination had ended with Guame the day they stopped filming, she had left without so much as saying farewell, he had been nothing more to her than someone for her to steal inspiration from. She had not recognized him either with his clothes on, she thought that he looked ridiculous in the hired dinner suit. They had not told her that he was being flown in for the premiere and was sure that they had done it to embarrass her she had invited Rogillio and she didn't want him hearing any gossip about her screwing the extras.

Rogillio posed with Marisa for the press, they made a striking couple. Guame stood in the wings realizing his place. He wasn't alone for long the two notorious Winger twins had hijacked him.

Stella and Anna Winger were heiresses they had taken the six foot actor under their wing, Marisa was sure that after the party they would all land up in bed together the twins were rather kinky so she had heard.

The press loved the movie, except for one love scene with Guame she had kept her clothes on and her stunning performance as a teacher going blind was faultless. This was the first time the world had seen her act in such a role, they had expected the worst and got the best, as usual she was a winner. The fireworks on screen between Guame and her had alerted suspicion in Rogillio's head he wondered if she had had something with the tall dark man. She seemed to have be avoiding her co-star all evening and Rogillio thought it rather odd that he was not at their table.

That night another couple had turned up unexpectedly at the premier, it was Tyrese and Pippa.

The moment that Pippa had seen the tabloids she had arranged an invite to the Premiere. Rogillio's and Marisa's love affair had been splattered all over the tabloids and Pippa was delighted. She had been hearing rumours that Tyrese had been banging the starlet and she had wanted to confront him but didn't want to cause problems, he was under extreme pressure with the album release. She did however want to see what kind of chemistry was between them at the premier.

Tyrese had tried to get out of attending the film premiere, his heart was saddened by the photos in the tabloids of Rogillio and Marisa. He was crazy about her and had planned on leaving Pippa after the release of his album, he had wanted to be with Marisa and had imagined that when she had finished her film she would have come back to him.

Each time he made love to Pippa he imagined it was Marisa it was the only way he could rise to the occasion. Pippa had opened doors for him in the music business, he was grateful for that but didn't want to be in her debt. In many ways nothing had changed since he'd met her, he was a stripper that sold his body to her, in a way he was still selling his body to her. She gave him stardom and he fucked her. He didn't care about the album he had a football career she couldn't rob him of that, he knew that Pippa was ruthless she would be bitter when he left her and would without a doubt shelve his music career, he was glad that he had the football she could never interfere with that.

Pippa had dressed with care, she wanted to look her best at blonde bitch's screening. She couldn't wait to see the reaction between, them she was already convinced that Tyrese had been screwing her and she wanted to see how he felt sitting next to her and her new love. Mr Rogillio it was ironic that this Rogillio was also a footballer and a rival, apparently an Italian team was bidding to buy one of them and they were toying between which one to make the offer to. Also it was weird, but the shoe commercial that she had clinched the deal for and had fallen through had been shot using both Rogillio and Marisa. It was a terribly small world and if Tyrese had a rival it was the handsome man on Marisa's arm. He was rather dashing Pippa thought wondering if he could sing too. If Tyrese ever left her she would ruin him, she perhaps should offer Rogillio a record deal too just to piss Tyrese off. Recently she had felt that he was slipping away from her, at first she had thought that it was the pressure of the album but now she knew he was in love with this Marisa creature, thank God that the shoe commercial had been given to Rogillio. She had had no idea that they were using her in the commercial. Tyrese had been disappointed that the shoe ad had fallen through, he had seen the commercial, it was fantastic and if he had done it he would have been able to spend a week with Marisa. He was shocked when had read in a glossy magazine that Marisa had fallen in love with Rogillio and they had met on the shooting of the shoe commercial. It was too depressing, this guy seemed to be poaching his jobs, he didn't like him and resented the fact that he was dating Marisa. Since they shot that fucking shoe commercial she had not taken any of his calls. Pippa and Tyrese were last to be seated at the large round table, they were sitting across from Marisa and Rogillio. The actress ignored Tyresse which hurt him deeply he watched in envy as Marisa spoon fed Rogillio some champagne sorbet, it was obvious that they were in love.

'Don't they make a stunning pair?' Pippa piped up, 'she was the one in your single video wasn't she?'

Tyrese was too wounded to answer, Pippa could see in his eyes a look of pain she had never seen before, this was her way of making him suffer and she was enjoying every second of it, everyone had known, everyone except for her that Marisa and Tyrese had been fornicating. Pippa would revel in his suffering.

After dinner Marisa had passed the word round the table that they were going to escape the boredom of the premiere and go to 'Soul City' the new private club that was the hottest place in town. Pippa had been dying to go. Tyrese had been positively sick all night and she wanted to rub his face in it. He was obviously heartbroken and he refused point blank to go to the club, lying that he had an upset stomach. He ordered their driver to take them back to their hotel.

In the privacy of their suite Pippa couldn't contain herself, she verbally lashed out at him squealing and shouting like a woman possessed. She mocked him that perhaps Rogillio was better in the sack than him, this comment infuriated him beyond belief and he slapped her hard on the face, crocodile tears sprang to her eyes and he tried console her thinking that half the hotel must have heard their argument. Like always when they argued she wanted to make it up her way, which meant a heavy long and boring sex session.

Tyrese was too wounded, he couldn't bear the idea of being ordered to make love to this woman, she had helped him with his music career which was something that he was grateful for, but he didn't feel indebted to her she had creamed a nice profit off his single and she would make more than him from the album. He played along with her feeling guilty that he had indeed been unfaithful to her, she was high and demanded he tie her to the bed, it was a four poster and Pippa always carried her lilac velvet handcuffs in her bag. Tyrese wasn't in the mood for games, she could be very demanding and sometimes her taste verged on the sadistic when he made love to her she always made him feel like a gigolo and he hated her for belittling him. His head was indeed thumping he couldn't get the image of Marisa out his mind.

He hated that Latino in the cream suit, it had been painful for him to sit at dinner so near them with her in such close proximity and even more painful that she had totally ignored him all night.

The truth was that Marisa had been shocked that he was at her table, she still had some carnal feelings for him and had avoided talking to him in case Pippa had blown a fuse. She had been scowling at her all evening, Rogillio had commented on it, casually he had seen the clip and had found it odd that Marisa had not introduced him to this singing footballer who had apparently attracted the eye of the Italian team that were considering giving him a contract.

He obeyed her orders and tied her to the metal legs of the modern four-poster. Pippa lay spreadeagled on the bed, naked except for a large necklace that she had forgotten to remove, she asked him to strip for her like he did the first time they met. The sarcasm in her voice pierced his ears and feeling like a slave he mechanically started to remove his clothes, after he had removed his underpants he moved towards her she mocked his flaccid penis and sneered, 'What's wrong darling? Missing Marisa,' at this he saw red, he had had enough of her, he looked sadly at her lying there naked and stoned and as viscous as could be.

He snapped back that he couldn't get it up for a middle-aged woman with saggy tits and a flabby ass. She was outraged at this comment and threatened to ditch the release of his album, she screamed that without her he would be a two bit stripper come rent boy, he laughed and said he knew she wouldn't dump the album, there was too much lovely money her for to lose and money was her god wasn't it? She gyrated in the bed and demanded he open the cuffs, at this he just smiled and she struggled and screamed till the bed was nearly off the wall. 'You are washed up already,' she threatened as he quickly put on his clothes, 'You impotent black bastard I'll ruin you she screamed. Your album is officially shelved,' she scoffed. To which he retorted, 'That he didn't give a shit,' he told her to take his album and shove it up her saggy middle-aged ass 'cos he didn't care, he hated the music business and had a football career. At this she roared with laughter and exclaimed, 'Football career, did you really think that you would get a contract that easy? Did you really think for one moment that you had talent?' she paused and sneered and looking him straight in the eye told him that she had organized the whole thing that she owned fucking seventy per cent of the shares in his club and that she had forced them to take him on. The words she said hit Tyrese like a rock, he didn't care about his singing career that wasn't important to him, but if what she said was true he would have been devastated, he had truly believed that he had gotten his football contract because he had talent.

Pippa stopped talking, she had never seen such a broken look on anyone's face as he walked out the door. She burst into tears, the one thing that she had not taken into consideration was that she couldn't live without him. She regretted deeply what she had said, she knew how proud Tyrese was. She was a fool to have lashed out at him like that.

Tyrese waved down a cab, he had tears in his eyes which surprised him. He never thought that he would cry, as a child he didn't cry so why was he so emotional now. He was broken inside, if what she had said was indeed true what future did he have? He was good at football, he had dragged the team from second division to new heights, without talent he could never have achieved that. He wished that he had gone with the guys to Miami and stayed working at the strip revue. All the success he had achieved in the last year seemed meaningless. The taxi speeded through the city and his head was clouded with problems. Thinking back, if he hadn't met Pippa he would never had made a single, if he hadn't made a single then he wouldn't have met Marisa, if he hadn't met her he wouldn't be so broken-hearted now. He smiled, thinking that the bitch was chained to the hotel bed she would be going mad, he hoped that the maid would discover her. She would be so embarrassed, he had taken the keys. He asked the driver to take him to Soul City, at the door they recognized him immediately, he inquired if Miss Duval's party had arrived and was pleased when the doorman told him that she had.

He wanted to see her so desperately, to talk to her and ask her why she had cut him out her life.

The moment he entered the club he spotted her right away, she was in the middle of the dance floor her arms round Rogillio's neck. They were both so lost in the music that they never even noticed he was there, he joined a group from the premiere at another table and tried his best to be sociable, perhaps he could be an actor too he mused he was smiling at people and having nice little conversations but inside he felt like he was dying.

The DJ played his single, it was a really weird feeling to be in one of New York's hippest clubs and stand there listening to your own voice, never for one moment would he ever have dreamed of having a number one single he also had never dreamed that a woman could have made him feel so miserable. Someone nudged him in the ribs, he turned and was surprised to see Marisa's face smiling at him. 'It's your single darling and I want to dance with you,' she pouted, dragging him by the hand she forced him on to the dance floor. She danced circles round about him aware that he had never taken his eyes off her, she felt guilty about Tyrese, she whispered in his ear that she had not forgotten him and that she had ignored him because his girlfriend had been beastly to her in the powder room. She had tried to ignore him to avoid confrontation with Pippa. It had been her premiere and any hint of an argument would have delighted the press.

Within seconds Tyrese was under her spell, it was true he was living with Pippa he was happy and sad all at once she asked where the old bag was when he told her that she was at the hotel she grinned and dragged him off the dance floor insisting that he sit at their table. When they reached the table Marisa casually introduced Rogillio and mentioned that since they were both in the same business they should have a chat, she also added that she was so pleased that the old battleaxe had gone back to the hotel. Tyrese shook hands with the man that he considered his enemy but he refused to engage in conversation with him instead he sat and watched Marisa. She was so near he could smell the perfume of her hair, he had never forgotten that smell, it was like jasmine, she always rinsed her hair with jasmine.

Rogillio was Hispanic he was good-looking in a Latin kind of way, he had a special charm and it was painful to watch Marisa swooning over him. Tyrese sat watching them dance. There was an incident on the dance floor some man had grabbed Marisa's ass, but before her bodyguards had reached the floor Tyrese had sprung onto the dance floor and punched the drunk guy so hard he nearly broke his jaw. Somewhere in the distance a camera flashed Marisa's security guards whizzed her out of the door while six of the clubs other guards jumped Tyrese, he had just hit the owner of the club's son.

Tyrese put up a good struggle and socked two of the bodyguards, the police arrived on the scene. The owner dropped all charges and Tyrese was free to go back to the hotel by cab. Pippa was humiliated beyond belief, she had already checked out, the maid had opened the door to turn down the sheets and leave a chocolate mint on the pillow, she had been shocked to see Pippa spread-eagled naked and handcuffed to the bed. She had covered her then called the manager he had discreetly called a locksmith to open the handcuffs. Pippa wanted to die when she had checked, out they had charged her 200 dollars for the locksmith and 300 dollars for the damage to the bed as the handcuffs had scratched the headboard of the designer bed.

Tyrese packed his clothes and left the hotel, he was in New York he didn't know where to go. It was three thirty in the morning, he jumped in a yellow cab and asked the driver to take him to Harlem he wanted to go see his mother. He knocked on the door for half an hour no one answered, an angry neighbor appeared and asked him what the fuck he wanted, Tyrese knew the neighbor but he didn't seem to recognize him. He introduced himself to the drunken sleepy old man as Tyrese. The man looked shocked he asked. 'What you doin' here? Your mother passed away three months ago.' The world stopped and Tyrese stood trembling almost unable to reply, he hadn't noticed that the monthly cheques were not being cashed he had been so busy working on the album.

His momma was gone she had had a paupers funeral no friends there, the neighbor shook his head and slammed the door in his face. There he was, stuck in Harlem at three thirty am wearing expensive clothes, he would probably get mugged. He started walking, a car crawled along the kerb, it was full of gangsters he was gonna lose his credit cards and get a beating, at the worst they would just shoot him he thought. They shouted at him, 'Hey buster!' Four of them jumped out of the car and approached him, in the streetlight one of them shouted, 'Hey man that's Tyrese, he is cool man,' instead of getting a beating he paid them to drive him to the city. He signed autographs and when they dropped him off the driver said, 'Hey man I'm real sorry 'bout Lutecia man, she was a good woman.'

Tyrese booked into the first hotel they had come to, what a fucking night he thought.

Singing career fucked, football career fucked, his mother dead and buried and Marisa being fucked by his rival.

He couldn't sleep, he called one of Pippa's pushers and asked him to deliver some Qaludes he never did drugs but needed something, his head was busting.

He slept the sleep of the dead and woke the next day at noon, the first thing that he did was call Carlo he wanted the truth straight on the phone. He wanted to know if Pippa had ordered him to get signed up, Carlos had sounded reluctant on the phone but in the end had admitted that Pippa owned seventy per cent of the shares and he confessed that she had been behind his contract.

Tyrese hung up he was broken, he had been at the club for ten months there were only two months left of his year contract. He decided there and then that he would accept the Italian offer and transfer to Italy. He wanted away from all the shit that had suddenly taken over his life.

He would fly home face the problems, and get a lawyer to see what rights he had, he tried Pippa's number but she was not taking his calls. Her secretary had said that she had been asked to tell him that his video shooting had been cancelled and that Pippa had said that his belongings had been dropped off at the club, she added that she would not be accepting any calls from him and gave him the number of a lawyer who would be dealing with his contracts.

When Tyrese had arrived in Detroit he had tried to contact Pippa at her office, they told him that she had gone to Europe with Vito on his world tour. Tyrese made an appointment with her lawyer, he laid out a deal he would be free to transfer to whichever team he wished if he completed the promotion tour for his album and shot another two videos he would be paid royalties accordingly on a percent basis for the album he would then be free to move to another label if he wanted.

Pippa was not in Europe she was at very expensive clinic in Hawaii recovering from the breakdown that she had had. She was finding it extremely difficult to remain balanced without Tyrese she had slashed her wrist the first day that she had returned from New York, she loved Tyrese he was the first thing that she couldn't buy and he had turned against her.

The deal that Pippa was offering him was an insult, the only one to make any money from the album was going to be her record company. If he didn't comply and sign the deal and complete the album he would be liable for all the costs to date, in other words if he didn't do what she said then he would have to pay three hundred thousand dollars costs for producing the album and then he would be sued for loss of profits. Tyrese had no option really and as he signed the piece of paper he felt his blood boil she was a bitch.

Tyrese realized that he didn't have any friends at all, everyone he knew was connected in some way to Pippa. She controlled their lives and careers and no one took his side, Marisa had refused to take his calls and he had read in the papers that she had gotten engaged to the Latin guy.

Reluctantly he agreed to shoot the two videos, to his surprise she hadn't skimped on budget, he had the best producers the best directors and he was looking forward to being free of her and her control.

He was not looking forward to the day of shooting but somehow professionalism kicked in and he sailed through the day like a carefully programmed robot doing the dance sequences as the choreographer desired.

Pippa was angry that he had accepted her plan she would rather have dumped the project.

Three singles had been released and all of them had been in the top ten in a week, the album was being released with a big bash at a warehouse in Detroit and as head of the record company she would have to show up. It would be her first public appearance since rehab, she would meet Tyrese at the party and the thought chilled her, she couldn't bear to see him again.

The promotion of the album was a drag, he hated chat shows and felt uncomfortable when being interviewed. Once on national TV live a chat show host had asked him how he had felt about losing Marisa to another football hero. The unexpected question had taken him so by surprise that he had refrained from answering and walked off the set, from that day on he made it clear to his press office that there were to be no questions about his personal life.

The night of the release arrived and he was dreading meeting Pippa, she arrived on the arm of a handsome young hip hop artist and Tyrese hoped that she had found a new love there was no way he would have anything to do with her at the party. Pippa took centre stage and thanked everyone who had worked on the album for their hard work, she also made a small speech about how successful their label was and told everyone that they were expanding. She introduced some new faces and they were going to perform, the young hip hop artist took the stage first, the second new act was a young girl who was so stoned her eyes were like saucers, she did however have a totally new sound and a haunting melancholic voice. The last artist took Tyrese by completely by surprise, standing on stage singing his first debut single was Rogillio, he looked great and on the monitors they showed the video of his single. So this was her way of sticking the knife in deeper, on all three screens they played Rogillio's clip. Marisa was in the video, she was naked and rolling around with Rogillio on a beach, the surf lapping against her naked breasts. Tyrese walked out of the room, humiliated that Pippa could stoop so low. Tyrese wondered if Marisa was in the changing room, he wondered if she had been on stage standing in the wings while Rogillio had performed.

Pippa smiled as she watched Tyrese grab his jacket and leave the room, now the party could begin she thought.

She would get her revenge on that black bastard she thought she did three lines of coke one after the other in the ladies room, she needed something to get her through this release.

She had shivered when she saw him he still made her weak at the knees and even weaker between the legs.

Tyrese walked out the party that celebrated the release of his album, he was infuriated that that the bitch had humiliated him and he had been glad that Marisa had not been there. He had read in a tabloid that she was filming in Eastern Europe. He went to bar on the outskirts of town and wearing his hat and killer shades and hoped that no one would recognize him. It was ironic that he was sitting in a rundown bar whilst right at this moment his album was being celebrated at a lavish party hosted by his ex-lover. She must have moved as fast as the wind to have produced Rogillio's single and video so quickly, the song was ok and the dude did look cool on film but he had almost flipped when he saw Marisa on the monitors. He wondered how low Pippa could actually stoop. He was depressed, he downed two beers and had three shots of bourbon, normally he didn't drink he never had liked the taste.

Tonight however he needed false courage, he had never felt so alone and even though he was a star he had no friends, even the boys on the team had been cool towards him recently. They had never exactly been warm to him but lately they had been extra frosty, in one month his contract was over and there had been no decision about the transfer and he was getting nervous. After another couple of double whiskies he stepped into his car and headed for the city, it was raining and he felt so down the whiskey had given him false courage so he slowed down at the area where the hookers picked up tricks. It had been weeks since he had had sex and he suddenly felt horny, the women on the sidewalks eyed up the flashy sports car thinking that he was probably a pusher. They were a miserable looking bunch and he mused that people would actually pay to fuck them, most of them looked sick. He crawled along the sidewalk, under a lamp post there was a blonde girl she looked young about twenty or so, unlike the rest of the girls she was not heavily made-up, in the lamp light she actually looked quite pretty. He opened the window and she reluctantly stepped forward she was real cute with red hair and to his surprise had an Irish accent. He had kept his hat on and dark glasses and she hadn't recognized him, she looked nervous and asked if she could step in the car, the moment she sat in the seat he locked the door, her blouse was wet and her nipples were shining through the cheap fabric of it. He asked her how much, her cheeks seemed to blush and she stammered that this was her first night on the game, that she was new to this and if she didn't do some business her pimp would beat her. He offered her 50 dollars for a blow job, he needed to blow some steam and his balls were full, he said that he would stop at the next rest stop and she smiled unbuttoning the buttons of her wet shirt. The sheer idea of paying for it gave him an odd kind of buzz, the whiskey had given him the courage to lose his inhibitions and as they drove along the freeway he glanced at her firm young breasts and felt himself grow hard. The moment he had parked the car she asked for the money up front, he slipped her three twenty dollar bills and she skillfully unzipped his jeans and went down on him her red hair fascinated him and he reached orgasm, within minutes he shot his load all over her face and the bitch licked at his sperm like it was ice cream.

The police had approached the car so silently he didn't even know that they were there, she still had his cock down her throat when they banged on the window. There were four officers at the car, they had parked in front of him and he hadn't even noticed. Tyrese's dick went limp and the girl wiped the jizz off her face and tried to fasten her blouse.

The officer asked for his licence and requested that he step out of the car. Suddenly Tyrese sobered up, at first he had thought that he was dreaming, this was the worst thing that could happen. The officer who checked his ID was surprised and exclaimed, 'Hey that's Tyrese the striker,' one of the other men added he was a singer too. They were delighted with their celebrity catch, both he and the girl, an underage illegal alien were taken to the police depot, he was also over the alcohol limit. They wanted to hold him overnight he called his lawyer who was still at the release party. At first his lawyer had thought that it was a prank till the police chief took the line. Thinking that he was still involved with Pippa, his lawyer had explained the whole situation to her and she had been delighted and personally had called the television news and newspapers. By the time he was bailed, the place was swarming with paparazzi, he left the police station with a jacket over his face to avoid the sea of flashbulbs.

Pippa sat in her office with the biggest smile on her face the papers were full of it, it was front page news just like that politician who had been caught on the hop. Tyrese had really been a fool, the timing was superb, on the same day his album was released he was on every front cover on the planet, the record company telephones had been red hot all day, fans had been calling, the press had been calling and angry mothers had called in hurtling abuse down the line.

Tyrese had taken refuge at a rented apartment which was costing him an arm and a leg.

Outside the apartment block it was swarming with press, photographers and film crews it seemed as if there was nothing else happening.

He called Carlos he also sounded funny on the telephone he had had an email from Milan.

The Italian team were withdrawing their offer they had suggested that he was a superb player but had hinted that his character was not suitable. Tyrese could understand that in a Catholic country he didn't think that they would think that he was setting a shining example. Pippa had been so ecstatic with the news that she had invited ten people to dinner at a Greek restaurant, the bitch was celebrating his shame.

Just when Tyrese thought that things couldn't get worse it did, a tabloid ran a five page story about him, they had done their homework and they had the whole shebang. He was born in Harlem, his mother had recently died of an overdose she was described as being a prostitute and crack addict they had also dug up a photo of him stripping they had put a censored box over his dick and the story claimed that he was using the stripping cover to work as an escort. There was no stone left unturned and Tyrese couldn't even sue because it was the truth. After reading the article he had punched the wall so hard that his knuckles bled.

What Tyrese didn't know was that it was Pippa who was behind the article she had under a false name sold the story to a major tabloid and made a lot of dollars.

Pippa felt good she treated herself to a wildly expensive new outfit for the dinner at Kolonakis. The press had been calling her they knew that she had had an affair with him and wanted some dirt from her she had made no comment she wanted to pretend she was unavailable for comment. She was clever, it was far safer to let other people do the talking. Secretly she had contacted the room maid that had discovered her chained to the bed and she had paid the maid a huge amount to sell that bit of information to the press.

The room maid had been reluctant at first but eventually succumbed and accepted Pippa's generous bribe. The same tabloid run the maid's story, an outrageous three pages of dirt as the sixty year old described how shocked she had been to find Pippa handcuffed to the bedposts, how the poor woman had been stripped and abandoned and how she had to be rescued by a locksmith. Pippa thought that it was cool that they could actually run a three page article about what the maid saw, as for her own embarrassment she didn't care, most of the people that were close to her knew that she was kinky anyway. The article portrayed him as a sex mad sadistic beast with no morals. Pippa had paid the woman handsomely and the magazine had paid her for the story too, the old lady had been on the cover of the tabloid a cover girl at sixty she had retired early and given up being a maid.

Pippa applied her make-up carefully, she felt triumphant. Tyrese would never suspect that she had destroyed him, she had read the fax from Italy, they didn't want him either. It would be back to stripping or porno films for that bastard she mused as she applied her sparkly lip gloss.

Tyrese really did think of suicide, the maid's story was the tip of the iceberg, he felt like a rat in a trap. The circus outside his apartment was getting larger, foreign paparazzi had also arrived. He had no one, no family or friends or place to hide. The fizzy drinks company had decided to withhold the release of the commercial, they wanted the money back that they had paid him, his empire was crumbling at such a rate he didn't know what to do.

He had drunk almost a whole bottle of vodka and he was wondering if he should take an overdose and was just about to call Pippa's dealer when the phone rang. At first he didn't want to answer he was scared that it would be the soft drinks company's legal team. The radio stations were not playing his records and Pippa had put the album on hold as she had threatened.

He reluctantly answered the phone and was surprised beyond belief to hear Marisa's voice, he was ashamed and wondered if she had read about his dilemmas over in Europe. She tried to calm him and said that she had only one word to say to him, he asked what it was and she retorted Holiday, at first he didn't understand, she told him she felt sorry for him, that she was still with Rogillio but he too felt sorry and she advised him to clear out and get away from it all till the heat went off. She invited him to join them in Tuscany, they were going for two weeks and added that if he could make it to London within two days that he could travel with them on a private jet that had been set at her disposal by an Italian count who was fascinated by her. They would be staying at a superb hideaway in the Tuscan hills. She had said that she wanted to chill-out wear no make-up and be a slob and said that while she was being a slob that he and Rogillio could talk football. At first he was reluctant, he couldn't imagine that this Latino would want him to come on vacation with him, she put Rogillio on the line and to his surprise he was up for it he told Tyrese to get his butt over there as fast as he could.

Tyrese called his lawyer to check if he could travel, apparently there was no problem and there had been an interesting discovery, the girl that he had been caught with was not underage, she had a list of offences and had lied. She wasn't illegal she was married to a pimp all he would get was negative publicity and a large fine but he would be free to travel as long as they knew where he was.

Tyrese took a cold shower to sober up and packed a small bag, his biggest problem was to get out of the apartment. He had an idea and he called his laundry service he asked if they could send the van into the car park. Tyrese bribed the driver of the laundry van by giving him three hundred dollars to drive him to the airport. The van had arrived at the building and went inside the parking lot, Tyrese had left the building in the back of the van, at the airport wearing his disguise he purchased a return first class ticket to London the flight was due to leave in one hour, he texted Marisa's mobile to inform her of his flight number and arrival time. He hoped that she would send a car to the airport, just before he boarded he received a text from Rogillio, there would be a driver at the airport waiting for him. Tyrese felt a huge weight lift off his shoulders he couldn't wait to get out of this place.

The flight to London was uneventful, the first class section was almost empty, he watched two movies and slept a little. At Heathrow he went through passport control the official smiled at him as he walked through, Tyrese didn't quite know how to take it. Rogillio was waiting for him just outside the terminal he had a nice new shiny Ferrari. At first Tyrese didn't know what to say to this guy who he had regarded as a rival. Rogillio was furious with Pippa, she had approached him with a track and asked him to record it, he had done and so she had specifically asked for Marisa to be in the clip it was only after he had arrived in Detroit that he had realized that she had tricked him. Rogillio had flown in thinking that he was arriving for his own release party he didn't know that he was doing support against Tyrese, he had left after his performance. He had thought that Pippa had done it to humiliate Tyrese he was not in to that.

Tyrese found himself warming to Rogillio, he was an ok guy, he had even thanked him for smashing the guy's face who had touched up Marisa in the club in New York.

They went to an apartment in Mayfair that the studio had rented for them, she was not working on a film so the heavies had been sent home. There were no bodyguards on the door. The apartment was opulent and Marisa answered the door wearing of all things an apron and pyjamas, her hair was a mess and she was not wearing make-up she joked that she had thrown away her dreadful pink rollers and hugged Tyrese when he walked through the door. Glancing at his rucksack she smiled and asked him if he had made a quick getaway.

Tyrese was glad he had come, he was looking forward to going to Tuscany he had never been but had heard that it was beautiful. Marisa announced that while Rogillio had been at the airport she had been cooking, Rogillio laughed out loud, Marisa's idea of cooking was calling up Harrods and grilling a pre-prepared meal. The first time she had attempted it she had put the plastic cartons under the grill, there was smoke everywhere, 'What do you expect?' she pouted sheepishly. 'I am a screen goddess not a housewife.'

It was amazing how relaxed Tyrese felt in their company, it felt good being able to talk to someone. They both were sympathetic to him and Marisa thought that Pippa was behind the whole plot, she had regretted doing the video with Rogillio, she had done it for her boyfriend not for Pippa. She had promised that the single would be released in Europe but till now there was no sign of it being released at all.

They had a simple dinner which Marisa had proudly prepared, with lashings of wine. In the morning they were all flying to Pisa on a private jet, from Pisa they would be driven to a villa between Florence and Sienna an absolute heaven they had been told, where they could rest and recharge their batteries. The villa belonged to a Count, apparently he was a friend of the head of the studio and he had been quite taken with Marisa when he had been introduced to her and had kindly offered them his villa for two weeks to get away from it all. The Count would be staying at the villa of a friend ten kilometres away and said that the only thing they would have to do is attend one of Pavel Jovavits' dinner parties before they returned to London. Pavel was a famous violinist from Prague. Marisa warned the boys that except for the evening that she had to attend the dinner she was leaving her star status behind. Strictly no glamour, no make-up, no heels, no dressing up, the boys looked disappointed and agreed they would only come if she signed a contract that she was never going to attempt to cook again. Marisa pretended to sulk, she knew that there was an army of staff at the Count's villa all she intended doing was lazing around and reading some scripts that had been sent for her approval.

The next morning Rogillio prepared breakfast and they packed at eleven, the Rolls Royce arrived to take them to the airfield where the Count's Lear jet was waiting. The Count was in his seventies and he adored being around beautiful women he was reputed as being extremely jolly and extremely generous. Their trip to Pisa was straightforward there was not a reporter in sight. Tyrese liked the casual uncomplicated attitude that Marisa had adopted and he was glad that she had left her glamorous image in the studio, he liked her simple it suited her.

It took them almost two hours to drive to the villa and on the way they marveled at the Tuscan landscape.

It was idyllic. Rogillio had suggested that the second week they went to Florence and Sienna. Tyrese and Marisa were enthusiastic about the idea they could check out the museums and shop, shop, shop.

Quite unexpectedly they turned off the main road and entered through two large bronze gates, they continued for two miles up a tree lined road and approached the villa, it was incredible, more like a palace than a villa. The gardens were meticulously designed with cascading waterfalls and fountains, to say that the villa was grand was an understatement, Marisa was very impressed. As the car approached, a line of servants waited to greet them it was like a scene from a film she thought as she looked the neatly dressed staff. A foray of butlers took their luggage and they entered the hallway, Rogillio thought that it seemed more like a museum than a home, the walls were lined with priceless paintings of the Count's ancestors and there were so many sculptures in the hallway it resembled a museum, the main staircase was a masterpiece in itself.

A young butler approached them, he spoke perfect English, he showed them to their rooms, the villa was huge and it took almost ten minutes to reach their rooms which were in a refurbished wing of the building. Marisa stared at the frescos on the ceilings, it was an honor to have the privilege to stay here, she wished that she had brought more formal clothes, it was obvious that they would be expected to dress for dinner. After Marco showed them their rooms he gave them an hour long guided tour of the villa and gardens. Tyrese hoped that he was going to get lost, the property was huge.

Marisa mused that she could easily get used to living like this, in opulent decadence.

Life at the villa was superb, by day they would laze around in the grounds, catching the sun by the pool or playing tennis in the early morning mist. In contrast to the rather grand main building, the west wing had been recently renovated and it was almost like staying at a luxurious hotel, the west wing had a pool area, tennis courts, a football field, a games room, a screening room where they could watch movies and a small gymnasium. The grounds belonging to the main building were sprawling and picturesque, they had fountains, carefully tended rose gardens and a maze, the place was a haven of peace and tranquility which was exactly what all three needed. The staff were kind and discreet they each had a maid and valet, their food was cooked by a chef that had worked in a top French restaurant in Paris, his meals were divine and all three enjoyed being spoiled, there was also a driver at their disposal should they have wished to escape to do some sightseeing,.

Tuscany was picturesque and on the Friday the trio had decided to go to Florence, the staff had prepared a picnic hamper for them so that they could stop off on the way and enjoy.

Damien's home-made bread with fresh jams made from the fruit grown at the villa.

He had packed a selection of wild fruits and berries with two bottles of sparkling rosés, it was an idyllic day and just outside Florence the driver stopped on a hill and spread a crisp white linen table cloth on the ground, their picnic was served on porcelain plates and the wine was served in antique crystal glasses, the bread was the best bread that Marisa had ever tasted. They stood on the hill and enjoyed the view of the city in the distance, the red roofs of Florence were a sight to behold and Tyrese couldn't wait to reach the city.

Firenze as the Italian called it, was a bustling charming city steeped in culture and history.

It seemed like one great open air museum with its amazing architecture and breathtaking pieces of art, motorbikes made their way through the crowded streets and the smell of pizza and pasta seemed to spill onto the streets from the dozens of restaurants and cafes.

They visited the Ufitzi Museum which was a treat in itself there was so much to take in.

They had wanted to come back after stopping to rest their aching feet at a busy street cafe on the Piazza Della Signorina, they went on a shopping spree spending a small fortune at the designer shops Marisa went absolutely mad buying shoes and bags and the men snapped up some great designer clothes.

They had wondered what they could give the Count to repay him for the hospitality, he was a wealthy man and seemed to have everything, it was a difficult objective and they decided that they would return the following week and search for a little object of art.

They were also looking forward to visiting Sienna, apparently on the way to Sienna there was a magnificent medieval mountain village called San Ginarmo the landscape there was supposed to captivating and they planned to go on the Sunday.

They got home at ten in the evening and the chef was off duty but had prepared a small banquet for them in the formal dining room. This is how movie stars should live, sinking into a deep sofa in the drawing room it was absolute heaven there.

In the morning they received a handwritten invitation to go to Pavel's estate for dinner it was about ten kilometres from the Count's Villa, the Count himself would be there as well as around thirty or so other guests.

Tyrese had grown to like Rogillio they had played football and tennis together and over fine brandies at night they had become close friends. Tyrese still felt a pang of pain each night when they both retired, he couldn't stand the fact that Rogillio was sleeping with the woman of his dreams. He was glad that their rooms were on different levels and that he was not wakened by the sound of their passion. Sometimes he would catch Marisa looking at him and sometimes he thought she had a look of lust in her eye, sometimes she would brush against him accidentally and an electric shock would surge through his body, he was after all still in love with her, he had never have imagined that he would have grown fond of Rogillio. It was inevitable the man had been the next best thing as a best friend to him. When he really thought about it they were the only ones in the world that he trusted.

It was after six p. m. the sun was setting and the Tuscan skies were ablaze, fluffy white clouds hovered in the bright red sky, they were sipping cocktails in the rose garden Marisa sighed and grunted, 'Well boys it's show time,' she retired to her room to search for her pink rollers and make-up bag, after a week of being a total slob she had to get the glamour out and be a movie star again. The Count had said that there would be a string of influential guests at dinner so Marisa wanted to look her best. Tyrese wore a new Dolce and Gabanna shirt and pants that he had bought in Florence. Rogillio wore a cream well cut Armani suit with a handmade silk shirt with his hair slicked back with gel he looked every inch the aristocrat himself he thought admiring his reflection in the mirror. They sat in the drawing room of the villa waiting on Marisa, she had been in her room for almost two hours and they were running late she had been soaking in a bath filled with rose petals and jasmine oil, she had for the first time in a week painted on a mask of make-up and did her hair as best she could she had worn a semi transparent silver sheath that clung to every curve of her body leaving nothing to the imagination. She had piled on a mass of costume jewellery and completed the effect by adding and ankle-length silk coat, looking every inch the Diva the boys whistled as she glided down the staircase in her new extremely uncomfortable but dazzling shoes. Tyrese held his breath as he watched her descend he had almost forgotten how beautiful she was.

Taking a man in each arm they summoned the driver, 'Well boys here we go,' she winked, 'it's show time.' Walking with the grace of a gazelle Marisa transformed into her screen goddess persona.

Pavel's estate was a huge mansion tucked away in the Tuscan hills set amid its own vineyards, he had his own wine, the house was less formal than the Count's but was still grand.

A butler dressed informally showed them to a room, all the guests had arrived and Pavel was sitting at a grand piano playing a beautiful classical piece of music, when Marisa entered the room all eyes turned to her, the Count greeted her kissing her hand. Marisa had fallen into star mode and was pouting and giggling like the sex symbol they saw on screen. Pavel was intrigued by her beauty and even more impressed that she was accompanied by two handsome men, their host was openly gay and made no point of hiding it.

They were introduced to a ballerina, a famous opera singer, a duchess and the others who were Pavel's closest hangers on, his manager, lawyer and entourage.

At first Tyrese had felt out of place, he was placed next to a stunning looking Asian girl who was with a rather thin woman in a wheelchair.

The dinner gong alerted them that it was time to eat. Everyone fawned over Marisa and she adored the attention. The whole evening had a surreal edge. The setting seemed more reminiscent to a film set than to reality.

Rogillio and Tyrese drank goblet after goblet of chilled Crystal. Conversation was relaxed and informal and everyone seemed to get on famously.

Chapter 7

Chloe

The first few weeks that Chloe had been in Germany were depressing, she missed the hustle and bustle of Thailand and didn't understand a thing, most of the Germans understood English but didn't want to. She thought that everyone looked so miserable, she missed the smiling faces of her home and hated the cold chilly weather. Carla had been an angel trying to help her adjust but at one point she considered returning home she knew that she would never earn as much as this working in Thailand and she was glad to be out of the prostitution business. Carla told her to try another month so she did, Carla's health was ok for the first three months it was in the fourth month that it spiralled downwards, the cancer had spread through her body and she had become weak and thin. Carla had sold her business and had arranged for Chloe to take German lessons, she also had opened doors for her in the modeling world, the agency had been glad to take on Chloe she was stunning they made her a portfolio and she worked quite a bit. Carla was pleased because it gave her some independence, got her out of the house and made her feel beautiful. Between her part-time modeling, for which she was paid handsomely, her German lessons and looking after Carla the time flew and she grew more acclimatized to Germany, its people and their attitude. She was amazed that they paid her 3000 Euros a day to pose in underwear for catalogues and she enjoyed the thrill of doing fashion shows for the wholesalers and retailers at the fashion fairs.

Carla had wanted to travel but was feeling too weak she refused to have more chemotherapy as it had made her feel sick, she knew her time was limited and she wanted to enjoy what time she had left. During the last six months she had become very close to Chloe, it was a feast for the eyes to watch her, she was so breathtakingly beautiful and she was glad that she had met her, over the months a deep bond had developed between them and Carla had grown to regard her as a sister.

In the beginning she had had occasional sex with her, she was intrigued by her skin it was like silk, she had known that Chloe was not lesbian and had been impressed that she had given her body so freely. Recently the women had enjoyed a platonic relationship as Carla had lost her sex drive and the company was a godsend.

The last time that she had been at the hospital her doctor had warned her that she would only last three months, she hadn't told Chloe this as she didn't want to upset her, in Dusseldorf she had no real friends, her housekeeper had been with her for years, Fräulein Muller had been a faithful employee for years and kept her house as spic and span as one could imagine. Her only real friend lived in Italy she had met him quite by accident at a party when she had been a model.

She had accompanied a male called Kurt to party in Cologne he was gay and had been having an affair with a famous classical musician she had met Pavel through Kurt, they were both shocked when they heard that Kurt had been killed in a car crash and his death had brought Pavel and her closer together she had stayed with Pavel for a week till the funeral was over.

Pavel had been overwrought and had been indebted to her. She had remained friendly with Pavel and their friendship had blossomed. After his lover's death his career rocketed, Carla always said that Kurt was his guardian angel every time he played at concert halls he claimed that he felt Kurt waiting in the wings.

Carla hadn't told Pavel how sick she was, one day when Chloe was at German lessons she called her old friend, they chatted for a while and then she told him that she would be going to visit Kurt soon. When she told Pavel she had cancer he cried openly on the phone after that he had called her every day, he hadn't seen her for a year and she had never seen his home in Tuscany so he insisted that she come with her friend for a week or so to enjoy the clean Tuscan air. Pavel was insistent and refused to take no for an answer he sent them two first class tickets and he promised to meet them at the airport. After dozens of calls Carla agreed it would be nice to visit him, it would be perhaps the last time that she would see him. She had missed him since he had become famous. Chloe was excited about the trip but she was worried about Carla and hoped that the journey would not be too much for her.

Pavel met them Linate airport in Milan he was shocked as the wheelchair came towards him. Carla looked so different her facial features seemed drawn and birdlike, her body was as thin as a rake, he had not thought that she had been so ill and tried to hide the tears in his eyes.

Carla introduced him to Chloe, she was obviously a model friend who was rather stunning. On the long car journey to his villa Pavel told Chloe ridiculous stories from the past, they had met when she had begun her modeling career and he his musical career they had been poor and had had lots of laughs. Chloe liked Pavel instantly he was different from she had expected.

Openly gay he made camp jokes whenever he could, it was nice to see a smile on Carla's face Chloe was pleased that she had come.

Pavel had taken them to Florence, Carla had at first refused to go saying that she was too tired to travel. Pavel had refused to take no for an answer he had propped her in her wheelchair and slapped a floppy straw hat on her head and wheeled her round the city himself, they had had a great day marveling at the wonders of Florence. The day however enjoyable had knocked the stuffing out of Carla she had slept for a day after the tour.

Pavel's villa was impressive he had his own vineyards, he had bought the house from an aristocrat it had a sort of faded glory that was comfortable but unassuming. 'It sure beats the bedsit you had in Cologne,' Carla joked as he showed her around the rooms.

It was easy to see that their friendship was special and Chloe enjoyed watching them together she herself had never really had a friend, only Carla. She wondered what she would do when Carla did pass away, the thought terrified her.

Pavel secretly had cried himself to sleep at night, although he hadn't shown his emotions he was shocked when he had seen Carla, yes she would be visiting Kurt soon he thought choking on his own tears. Carla had been beside him when Kurt had died she had held his hand through the most difficult part of his life, all his success was no replacement for Kurt he would have given it all up to have kept him alive. Pavel was glad she had come, something inside him told him that this would be the last time he would see his dear friend and he had wanted her to stay longer than the planned week but she had refrained saying that she had to go to the hospital every week. One night Chloe had excused herself pretending to be exhausted, she wanted to leave Pavel and Carla alone that night. Carla had told him that she was making him executer to her will and at first Pavel had changed the subject he didn't want to be confronted with death it chilled him, she insisted he listen and handed him a sealed letter out of her bag, 'All the instructions are here,' she said with a smile.

Pavel had put his head in her lap and cried, all the emotions of Kurt's death flooded back.

Unknown to Chloe, Carla had made a will making Chloe the sole beneficiary, she had considered leaving Pavel her money but he had enough money for two lifetimes, she didn't want Diederick to get a penny and Chloe in a way had meant so much to her she wanted to give this girl a chance.

She knew that Pavel would understand, money had never been important to him and in a way she had grown to love Chloe, she marveled in her youth and relished her beauty, she had been a life support to her. When Carla died Chloe would become very wealthy, she had sold the bar for two million Euros, her home was worth almost a million and she had capital and stocks and shares. She hoped that Chloe would be happy and do something good with her money, Pavel sat with his head in her lap for an hour they never spoke, she was the bravest of the two she hoped that Pavel too would find someone again he had been too long alone. As he nestled in her lap she sniffed his hair, he smelled like a garden, she mused promising to remember this aroma forever.

The weekend that they had to leave Pavel had threatened to hold a grand party for them.

He had promised to invite aristocrats, musicians, artists, movie stars and celebrities, Carla had thought that he was joking, he was not. A string of guests arrived in their honor and Carla's eyes twinkled as she inspected the colourful guests as they arrived, just like the old days she joked, referring to the parties they flung in their youth. Pavel played songs that she liked and Marina Grimaldi sang arias, her voice was like a nightingale. The room went still when a sensational young woman entered with two handsome suitors, it was Hollywood starlet Marisa Duval.

Carla was impressed she had seen all her films, she was a wonderful actress.

Pavel had pulled out all the stops and Carla was delighted that they had come together, they enjoyed a dinner fit for a king and Carla sat at the table. Here she was in

Tuscany surrounded by talented beautiful people, she herself wasn't blessed with life she was going to meet her maker this was her going away party she thought sadly just after dessert she excused herself. Pavel understood the excitement had been too much for her she retired to her room Pavel escorted her to her chamber and waited by the bed till she drifted to sleep.

He studied the thin skeletal woman in the bed and remembered her as she was when he had first met her, she was a beauty on the catwalk always the tallest always the most elegant.

God was cruel he thought as he tucked her in and returned to his guests. He was intrigued by the movie star she was drop dead gorgeous and the two guys she was with were total dreamboats. Marisa had been seated next to the Count she had teased him and flirted relentlessly with him all night and he was enjoying every minute. Rogillio had been locked in conversation with a Spanish artist and Tyrese had started to talk to the beautiful Thai girl that had been seated next to the lady in the wheel chair that had retired.

The Thai girl was rather striking with a clear golden complexion and shoulder length black hair that gleamed in the candlelight she was at the totally other end of the spectrum to Marisa.

The more he studied Chloe, the more beautiful she was unlike Marisa she wore no make-up, she had dark almond shaped eyes with long lashes, her lips were full and their natural shade was a blushing pink, her teeth were as white as pearls and her beauty was a natural one rather than manufactured. He noticed when she stood up that she had a beautiful body with ripe breasts and long legs.

The more he watched her, the more he had become fascinated by her, she had an inner light like Marisa's. During their conversation he noticed a strange sadness in her eyes, he wondered where she had come from and where she was going. After a few drinks she seemed to loosen up, she told him that she had come from Thailand to look after her friend who was dying and that she modeled in Germany he told her that he was a football player. The Thai's loved football and he was surprised that she as a woman knew so much about the game. She seemed more impressed that he had made a single when he hummed the words of it she stared at him open-mouthed and exclaimed, 'You're the one,' she explained that she did her yoga classes to his single every day.

Pavel had refurbished the basement into a bar with a grand piano and dance floor, he had rented a DJ and after dinner the guests danced the night away, the Count was old but managed to outdance Marisa. Rogillio danced with the rather portly opera star and Tyrese danced with Chloe, at one point, after too many drinks, Tyrese sang his hit ballad 'Cry Of The Panther' Pavel played piano and the female opera singer provided backing vocals, he sang with a passion that he had never known and the sound of his voice spilled out of the open windows waking Carla, she snuggled up in bed and fell back to sleep with the velvety sound of Tyrese's voice. Sitting in a corner Chloe felt that he had been singing just for her, whilst at the other end of the room while Marisa waltzed with the Count she thought that Tyrese had been singing just for her.

The party was a success and they left for home at three am, everyone had eaten and drank too much, Chloe had enjoyed the evening she had liked the tall black man with the voice like velvet. Marisa had joked that Tyrese could bring a woman to orgasm with his vocal chords.

Tyrese had given Chloe his number and she had given him hers they had promised to keep in touch and he had kissed her on the cheek before he had left.

Marisa was in turbo party mode she didn't want the night to end when they reached the villa she threw off her dangerously high heels and insisted that the party continued, they took two bottles of champagne rosé and three glasses to the pool and decided to have a pool party. The live-in staff were in the other wing they wouldn't hear them, all three had drank too much, there had been cocktails, champagne, fine wines and cognac served at dinner and now they were drinking vintage pink champagne. Suddenly without warning Marisa stripped of the expensive silver sheath and jumped in the pool Rogillio stripped and joined her and he waved Tyrese to follow their example, unlike Rogillio Tyrese kept his underpants on. He dived in and the cool water invigorated him, Marisa was the one who started it and they both took Tyrese by surprise, she kissed them both simultaneously pressing her body close to them she grabbed Tyrese's erect cock and Rogillio's together both men took turns of making love to her she sucked Rogillio's cock in her mouth while Tyrese fucked her doggy style. Rogillio and Tyrese brought Marisa to an explosive orgasm after their bodies were spent they retired to her room and slept in the enormous four poster bed.

Tyrese woke first, he had a headache and was embarrassed that they had all slept together, he was just going to creep out of bed when Marisa stirred, she smiled at him and rolled over on top of him. Rogillio was angry he pretended to sleep while Tyrese made love to her. The sound of their lovemaking had excited him he opened his eyes and joined in, sticking his cock in her mouth, after a few minutes they changed positions Marisa screamed in ecstasy when both men came on her breasts.

Tyrese went to his room to shower he felt strange and wondered if Rogillio was feeling like he did. While Rogillio showered Marisa nestled in the frothy foam bath she felt completely satisfied, for days she had fantasized to have them both, she had planned it for the night of the party it had been her first threesome and she felt comfortable that it had been with two men she liked. Closing her eyes she ran her finger over her heart shaped pubic hair and imaged having sex with three men, Rogillio, Tyrese and Guame! He had been divine, so primitive and well hung he had been like a wild beast in bed. She wished that he had been there last night the last she had heard about Guame was that he had moved in with the twins, she couldn't blame them and fully understood their fascination for him, no brain just a body and a cock.

Marisa orgasmed again thinking of Guame then tossed her vibrator out of the tub for the maid to clean.

On the other side of the Atlantic, Pippa was sitting in her office she had sniffed three lines of coke and was hyper. She didn't have any left and her dealer was not answering his phone. The qualudes she had taken the previous evening had made her drowsy and she swallowed two speed tablets with some vodka.

Vito had just called her, he had signed with another label, she had lost three of her most important artists this year and financially it would be crippling. Most of the new artists had been flops and except for Tyrese none of them had scored hits. She was having a rough time and couldn't get him out of her mind, her apartment and her bed seemed empty without his presence and she regretted having treated him so badly, hell hath no fury like a woman scorned was an understatement when it came to Pippa, she always acted first then thought about the consequences. Carlos had told her that he had raced off to Europe to avoid the press, his football career was washed up and so it seemed there was no turning back the clock, the board of directors were pushing her to bury the hatchet so to speak and release his album. The negative publicity had not affected his record sales and his last single had actually sold more copies since all the publicity had started. Her scheme had backfired and it seemed that the record buying public did not give a shit that he was caught with his pants down or had been a stripper, the fact that his mother was a junkie just made him hipper.

Pippa knew she would have to launch the album, she didn't know how to approach him or where he was on the planet he had changed his damn number or was rejecting her calls.

Perhaps if the album was a whopping great success he would come back to her she thought high on coke, it was the only way she could survive since he left.

She had tried other men she had been disappointed no one did to her what Tyrese did, she resented the fact that he had this magical power over her and hated him with a vengeance.

In sheer desperation she emailed his lawyer and asked him to have Tyrese contract her at the record company as she was willing to launch his album. Tyrese couldn't believe his ears, she had destroyed his life and now she expected him to play ball, no way he sent her a text telling her to go fuck herself. Two days later she called Rogillio, she had no idea that they were all together Rogillio was the last person on the planet that she would have expected him to be with.

Pippa had been charming on the line she had apologized for the delay in launching his single, she promised that it would be released in the UK, France, Belgium and Spain within a week. She apologized for the fact that he had had to perform at Tyrese's launch and promised that he would have a proper launch in London, it would be a lavish affair with lots of press coverage. Rogillio was dry and told her that in future she should contact his media company or lawyer that he did not want to deal with her personally again he reminded her that he had not as yet signed the contract and that she could not release the single without his permission he politely told her that he didn't give a shit about the single and that Marisa would sue if she dared release the video, that she wanted a huge retainer and that her lawyers were already contacting Pippa's lawyers.

Pippa was having a bad day, her empire was crumbling she was sure that Tyrese had put a voodoo curse on her, footballers she cursed as she picked up the phone to check if her talent scouts had discovered any new talent.

The holiday was coming to an end and Tyrese wondered what the future would bring, he had enjoyed being with Marisa even though he had shared her with Rogillio, she was an extremely complex woman and he felt that she had cast a spell on them both, deep down they both knew that no one could win Marisa's heart, one man was not enough for her one night drunk she had confessed that she had been having an affair with Guame.

Tyrese looked at Rogillio the pain in his eyes was devastating he was hooked on her she was like a drug. Her great beauty would destroy men, that was for sure Rogillio thought, as he wondered why this woman had been the one that would destroy him. Tyrese was beginning to see her in another light, she was beautiful on the outside but melancholic on the inside. She was unashamedly selfish and took her pleasure as she pleased with no regard for the person whose heart she had captured.

CHAPTER 8

Dusseldorf

Chloe sat in the darkened room, she was tired and strained as she sat vigilantly at Carla's beside. They had returned from Italy only three weeks ago and since then her health had deteriorated in leaps and bounds. The doctor was visiting every day and Chloe had placed a makeshift bed in the room so that she could sleep there. The heavy painkillers were making her drowsy and she looked so weak. Fräulein Muller had been a godsend she had been there till all hours giving Chloe moral support.

They both had enjoyed the trip to Tuscany it was a pleasure to see Carla so happy.

Suddenly without warning Carla woke up, she looked bright and cheerful and Chloe propped up the pillows so that she could sit up it was lunchtime and Fräulein Muller had made a creamy soup, Chloe spoon fed Carla like a baby and after a few spoonfuls she rejected the soup claiming that she was not hungry. Carla asked Chloe to go upstairs and bring her the crocodile bag that was on her dressing table, Chloe left the room leaving Fräulein Muller to try and persuade her to eat the soup.

When Chloe returned with the bag Carla propped herself up and although her voice was weak she spoke clearly to

Chloe so that she would understand everything. She had asked Fräulein Muller to stay and act as a witness. Carla opened the bag and handed her maid a letter and box, 'Not to be opened Fräulein Muller till I'm gone.' With a serious note she took Chloe's hand and with tears in her eyes she thanked her saying, 'God knows what I would have done without you dear.' Chloe had tears in her eyes, Carla explained that when she died she wanted to leave her house to Chloe, she added that there were substantial funds in the bank and that Chloe would be the heir to whatever she had.

She gave her friend the address and telephone number of the lawyer that had her will and stated that she had left firm instructions that her rogue brother was to receive nothing. She said that the moment she passed away that she had to call the lawyer and Pavel, he was executer and she said that she was not to worry as they would take care of everything.

Chloe sobbed openly as the woman she had grown to love clasped her hand tightly, she finished by saying that she had left everything to Chloe and that in return she expected Chloe to do one last thing for her, Chloe choked on her tears and asked what it was that she wanted. Carla asked her not to be sad when she left and made her promise that she would fall in love and settle down. She made her promise that she would go on holiday and look up that dreadfully handsome man that they had met at the villa.

Chloe wondered which man she meant Carla said, 'The one with the voice like velvet,' Chloe was surprised she had thought that Carla had retired when he had sung, her friend added that his voice had floated all the way up to her bedroom and that she had noticed the way he had looked at her, 'He has an eye for you,' she laughed before falling into a deep sleep.

Chloe sat in the lamplight, she had lost all track of time she herself had dozed off for an hour and she stared at her friend thinking that she looked so peaceful, it was only then she noticed that she was not breathing. Gently she kissed the pale woman's cheek. Carla had left this earth forever she closed her eyes and prayed to Buddha for strength, then called the doctor, Pavel and Fräulein Muller.

The maid arrived within twenty minutes and took control of the situation.

The funeral was a quiet affair, Fräulein Muller, her husband and Pavel were the only guests.

Pavel sobbed openly at the graveside Chloe held on to him, feeling weak herself.

Pavel was beside himself with grief, her funeral had brought back all the bitter memories of Kurt's death, he had died at twenty-three when a drunk driver hit his car. The vehicle had toppled down a ravine and had set on fire. Pavel cried as he told her how he had to identify the body, Kurt was a model she had seen his photos he had been a striking Pavel had broken down when he saw his lovers mangled burned and charred body on the marble slab of the mortuary, the sight had haunted him for years.

Since Kurt had died he had not had a regular lover he lived alone, his career had flourished and he said that he was sure that it was Kurt up there that had blessed him with the luck. Pavel invited Chloe to visit him the following week in Tuscany, he didn't want to be alone in that great big empty house. Chloe had things to tie up for Carla she was shocked to discover that Carla had left her almost three million marks in properties, bonds and assets she was sure that Diederick would appear out of the woodwork and cause problems he had not even been decent enough to turn up for the funeral.

Chloe was rich, she had no idea that Carla had been so wealthy she had never had security before and it felt strange to have so much money at her disposal. The house seemed empty without Carla and she missed her more than she had imagined. She had been like a sister to her and she hated staying in Carla's house every time she went to the bathroom she expected Carla turn up.

Fräulein Muller suggested that she should sell the house with all its memories and told her to go visit Pavel and that when she was gone she would keep the keys so that the estate agents could let people view the property. Chloe called Pavel, he was in Paris playing at a concert hall.

He was finishing his tour in ten days he asked her to meet him in Paris the following week.

She could come to his concert on the closing night of his tour.

It was so quiet in that great big house without Carla she wondered why her friend had bought such a large home. It was scary to sleep every night there. One night she dialed the number that Tyrese had given her, since the villa she had not spoken to him and thought perhaps that he might have forgotten who she was.

Tyrese was dripping wet, he had just stepped out of the shower and was expecting a call from his lawyer. His football career had gone down the drain, but much to his surprise when he returned he discovered that his single was number one in the hit parade. Since the scandal the radio DJs had been giving his single lots of airplay, instead of having a negative effect the bad publicity had actually boosted his record sales. Pippa had contacted him, she was literally crawling but he refused to talk to her personally, but through her lawyer agreed to a deal that suited him, he gave her the permission to launch that album and remaining video clips in return he would get a large chunk of the royalties plus a lump sum. He would have to do promotion tours in Europe for three months, he had his lawyer build a clause in stating that he would have no direct dealings with Pippa. This hurt her as she had wanted to meet him, however money was money and she had agreed to his terms.

Tyrese was pleased to hear Chloe's voice he had thought about her a lot recently and had been meaning to call her, she broke down on the telephone as she told him that Carla had died. He expressed his condolences and they chatted for an hour. She told him that she was going to Paris to meet Pavel, he was delighted, he was going to London to promote his album so he could meet her in Paris he could fly there before moving onto London.

When Tyrese hung up he smiled from ear to ear he had liked that girl she was beautiful, till he had met her he had never really looked at Asian women before.

He hadn't seen Marisa since their wild weekend in the Tuscan hills, she was apparently filming in Tokyo, in her new movie she was a martial arts super hero. Rogillio had called him regularly he got the impression that things between him and the screen goddess were not all that they were cracked up to be, he had been taking coke a lot, one day they had done a drugs test he had been picked and was suspended for using illegal substances.

It was his turn to get sour press and Tyrese felt sorry for him, he had started on coke he confessed, because he suspected that Marisa was having an affair with her Japanese co-star. Tyrese had seen the tabloids himself the photos of Marisa and the Asian kick boxing champion had been in all the gossip magazines, he was a handsome man and just Marisa's type. Tyrese knew that Marisa couldn't live without sex for five minutes. She was forever falling in love with her co-stars, she claimed that it helped her screen performance, he advised Rogillio to stop taking drugs and told him that there two things that he could do, one option was leave her and find a monogamous girl or accept it. Rogillio thanked him and hung up, the next day at the airport he noticed that Rogillio's photo was in the paper he had taken an overdose of sleeping pills and was in hospital.

Tyrese dialled Marisa's number, she sounded like she was in bed he had forgotten that there was a time difference, in the background he could hear that someone was lying next to her. No wonder Rogillio had overdosed, he told her about the papers and gave her the number of the hospital and told her to call. She did eventually, after hanging up she made love to Yoji they had breakfast together then went to the studio after shooting all her scenes she called the hospital. Fortunately Rogillio was sleeping she left a message that she was on location and hung up.

Tyrese had never been to Paris it was large and he found it difficult to get his bearings, he had called Chloe she was arriving that evening and agreed to book into his hotel she wanted to meet him for dinner in the evening, the following night she was going to Pavel's concert she had invited Tyrese too.

Chloe was even more beautiful than he had remembered, today she was wearing make-up and had her hair up, she was wearing a sexy black dress that enhanced the curves of her body and a small pair of diamond earrings that Carla had left her.

They went to the Buddha bar for dinner, Chloe was impressed, the meal was delicious and the atmosphere electric. Early in the evening the music had been soft and relaxing, by the time they had ordered dessert the beat had livened up and people were dancing.

It had been a wonderful evening and as they walked just round the corner to their hotel
Chloe spotted a dress in a window that she planned buying the following day, suddenly she felt that her clothes were too simple for Paris.

Tyrese invited her into his suite, she had wanted to hear his album and he had brought her a copy, he popped the disk in the CD player and his voice filled the room, she remembered the Cry of The Panther track from the villa and that was her favorite. She was delighted that he had given her a copy and asked him to sign it, he looked so handsome on the cover of the album he assured her that they had airbrushed the photo to the limit, they had used a naked shot of him with the leopard skin hair she thought that the hair was super cool and thought that he should get it done like that again.

They sat drinking champagne till two am then Chloe went back to her room, she wondered if Tyrese was attracted to her perhaps he was married or had a girlfriend she had forgotten to ask him that.

She had told him that she had noticed him watching Marisa, he claimed that Marisa and he went back a long time. He told her that she had been in his first clip and lied that that's what had made her famous. She was amazed that he had never really performed or had concerts, it seemed odd that you could be number one without all the tours, he told her that it was because the music channels had aired his clips that he had been so lucky.

The next night they went to Pavel's concert, she had bought the dress in the window and looked stunning, it had cost an absolute fortune and she would have to wear it for the rest of her life. She wondered how much the movie star girl spent on clothes, it must have been a fortune.

They enjoyed the concert and rushed backstage to complement Pavel. The whole troupe were going for a farewell dinner, they had booked a table at Cabaret, Tyrese and Chloe joined them, when she looked at all the other girls in the club she was glad that she had invested in the dress, they all looked stunning.

They reached the hotel at three am and Tyrese kissed her lightly on the cheek to wish her goodnight, she was disappointed, obviously he didn't find her attractive. After she showered she decided to take the bull by the horns, grabbing a bottle of champagne from the fridge and wearing her dressing gown and slippers she knocked on his door. Tyrese crawled out of bed, she said that it was room service, he sounded confused but when he opened the door she jumped on him letting her dressing gown fall to the floor. Half asleep Tyrese felt her soft silky skin against his body and roused, they spent the next day in bed together ordering from room service between making love, the following day was their last, they had intended going sightseeing but didn't, instead they stayed in his suite and had lots of sex. Chloe had told him that she hadn't been to bed with a man for almost a year, looking at her with disbelief he scooped her up in his arms and said, 'Well let's make up for that,' Tyrese hadn't had sex since he had stayed at the Count's since the incident with the hooker he was reluctant with whom he slept. Chloe was something else, her skin was like pure silk and she was certainly no virgin, she had taught him

171

a position or two, he wondered where she had come from then, didn't care. He was more concerned about her future than her past.

Tyrese headed for London to promote his new album he had some television interviews and autograph signings at record stores, he was there for a week then he had a weekend free. He had been asked to go to Germany, at first he had been reluctant but now he wanted to go, he could meet up with Chloe there. She had gone with Pavel for a week to Tuscany the timing was perfect. He did two television interviews the first day, he was glad to have finished the interview, one of the TV hosts had been quite crazy, he was nervous at first that they would ask him embarrassing questions but in the end everyone had been polite they loved him.

In England he called Chloe every night, usually he was on the phone for at least an hour which drove Pavel crazy, Tyrese did lots of shopping in London he loved the shops there, Harrods was his favorite it was an amazing store that had absolutely everything.

His media company took him to Rouge, a new night-club the rest of the time he lazed about his hotel believe it or not writing lyrics for a new album. He had never written before but had ideas, the music seemed to fill his head and Chloe had inspired him, suddenly words were springing into his head he had written three songs already.

Unknown to Pippa he had a meeting with a major record company, he had plans to switch labels after his contract was finished. His first two singles had been well received in the UK and they were impressed with the album, he had told them that he was working on a concept for a new album.

The Panther Strikes Again, things were looking promising and he was sure that they would come back to him with a deal. He couldn't wait to leave Pippa's company he would meet her then to personally tell her to fuck off.

In Chloe he had found inspiration, he found it odd that he missed her and his heart skipped a beat when she called him, he was kind of scared. Could it be he was falling in love with this chick, he hoped not, look what love had done to Rogillio.

After Rogillio had checked out of hospital he had gone on the booze, Marisa had ignored his calls and was having a full blown affair with Yoji. They had finished shooting in Japan and she had taken off with him to the Caribbean to Mustique or somewhere dreadfully exotic.

He couldn't face the fact that their relationship had finished, there had been no argument and no confrontation. He had been suspended and without football and without Marisa he had nothing in his life, he considered flying to Mustique for a confrontation with her but Tyrese had advised against it. In desperation he had stared living it up going to clubs every night doing coke and drinking, he wasn't training or exercising and had put on weight.

There were no shortage of bed mates, he was handsome and well known and each night he picked up girls and brought them back to his flat, no matter how high or drunk he was, he was always ready for sex but no woman seemed to satisfy him. He wanted Marisa, compared to her the others seemed bland, every time he saw a photo of her in a tabloid with her 'Muscle Mary' he cringed he was obsessed by jealousy. He had recently read that she was taking a year off, the tabloids had suggested that she was pregnant to Yoji he wept with anger.

When he read this he cried and in a fit of rage went to the closet and cut up all the designer dresses that she had left in his closet, after he had slashed and shredded them to bits he sat on the torn garments and lifting one in his hand he smelled it he could still smell that fragrance of jasmine from her clothes. Tyrese had warned him drugs were dangerous, nothing he thought could be as dangerous as Marisa, she was cruel and heartless. He went to the kitchen snorted some coke and swallowed an upper washing it down with neat vodka. He wandered aimlessly through the two dressing rooms tripping on the racks of brightly coloured shirts. He had hundreds of pairs of shoes and endless rails of Saville row suits, after an hour of deciding he changed into some clean clothes and headed for the bright lights of the city, in search of more drugs, more liquor and more sex.

Two months later he learned that her latest film was to be premiered in San Francisco, using his contacts he managed to get his name on the guest list he packed a nice suit and headed for the airport he knew that she would be at the premiere. Yoji would be there too. He arrived in San Francisco the day before the premiere, he had booked into the same hotel as her, hoping that he would catch a glimpse of her. He wanted her to look him in the face and tell him what had happened, the day of the premieres she gave a press conference to announce that she was indeed taking a year off she looked sensational on TV. He had never seen her so happy she plugged her film and did her usual pouty thing then showed the cameras her vulgar oversized engagement ring, she concluded the interview by announcing their wedding, she was marrying Yoji and that she was two months pregnant. Rogillio threw up on the carpet, he watched as she hugged the oriental kick boxer turned actor and switched off the TV. That night he shaved carefully and wore the same suit that he had worn at the villa, before leaving for the theatre he took two pills and a line of coke.

He would see her tonight. As he walked up the red carpet his legs trembled, he waited, talking to some of the press, her car arrived and he watched her she looked stunning in a gold lame dress, the vulgar diamond ring sparkled in the light as she waved to the fans. She was clinging lovingly onto Yoji, he was smaller than Rogillio had imagined, but all muscle and very handsome. As she sashayed up the red carpet hundreds of flashbulbs flashed, she was too high, drinking in the adoration of her fans to have noticed Rogillio waiting in the wings.

He had walked up the red carpet with her dozens of times he knew her routine she would reach the entrance then turn and pose for the cameras for two minutes, she was so near him he could smell her perfume. Blinded by the lights she didn't even notice him, her lover, her man. His nostrils flared and he looked like a man possessed as he lunged forward and in full view of the cameras live on TV he stabbed Yoji with a ten inch blade, his face filled with contempt, he stabbed him seven times, the blood spurted over the crowd and Marisa screamed as Yoji slumped on top of her, his blood spouting all over her gold dress. Seven security guards advanced trying to control Rogillio he waved the blade at everyone who approached him and pulled a gun from his pocket. The onlookers screamed, the camera men let their cameras role even though they couldn't believe what they were seeing. Yoji's lifeless body fell to the ground and Rogillio stared deep into Marisa's eyes, with one hand he ran the blade across her belly screaming, 'It should have been mine I love you more than he did.' he then he pulled the trigger and shot Yoji in the head at point blank range the bullet hit and Yoji's head exploded. Marisa was covered in blood her screams could be heard for miles, the whole incident had happened in what was a matter of seconds but it had seemed to Marisa like it had been in slow motion.

Marisa felt to the ground she was in shock she didn't know if he had slashed her belly or not, she was numb with fear and dripping in blood. The young starlet cradled her lover's headless torso, the sounds of her screams echoing through the air. The scene was like that of the worst horror movie.

Collapsing on the street she heard the faint sound of sirens in the distance she looked down and saw blood running down her leg, realizing that she had had a miscarriage she lost consciousness.

All this had happened live on TV. The horror footage was shown all over the world.

The police arrived and Marisa blacked out.

Twitter, Facebook and all social media platforms went crazy. Tyrese watched the image on his television set, at first he thought that it was a trailer of one of her films, realizing that it was real he sat down and cried feeling almost guilty that he hadn't helped Rogillio more. Falling in love with her was like playing with fire. That night he couldn't sleep, they had repeated the shocking images in breaking news all night. He sat down and wrote a song for Rogillio it was called 'That's What Love Can Do'.

When Chloe called he wracked into sobs, she hadn't seen the news she couldn't understand him.

He was choking as he tried to explain that Rogillio, his best friend had just killed Marisa's lover live on TV.

Marisa was rushed to hospital she had lost her lover, lost her baby and almost lost her mind. This was God paying her back she thought as they sent her into a drugged filled sleep. She would never forget the look of hate in Rogillio's eyes, never forget Yoji's eyes rolling as he took his last breath.

She would never make a film again and never return to the spotlight, she would retire, she would live like a recluse for the rest of her life she promised herself as the drugs took effect.

The world would be stupefied when, three months after the incident, she would return to the screen and be photographed again dangling on the arm of a business Tycoon. Marisa would never change she was just born bad.

Pippa sat like most of the rest of the world open-mouthed as she watched the live footage on the news channel, she couldn't believe what she was seeing. 'Shit!' she exclaimed, she could never release his single now, where would she pay him the royalties? The State Penatentiary? She hadn't particularly been fond of Marisa but felt sorry for her.

She did have the unedited video clip featuring Rogillio and Marisa, it was uncanny she thought the title of the song had been 'Love You To Death'. Smiling she picked up the phone and called Simon Clairmont at the tabloid magazine she dealt with. The next morning he ran a story on the front page the headlines were LOVE YOU TO DEATH and showed six pages of photos some of the bloody attack and some stills from the video with Rogillio and Marisa in a passionate embrace.

Pippa's business partners couldn't believe that she was serious when she called a meeting with her lawyers to see if she could launch Rogillio's single, it was beyond bad taste but Rogillio's face was on the front page of every newspaper worldwide and she had a hunch that she could make a lot of money out of a murderer's last single.

Rogillo had fallen to his knees, half crazed with drugs, half crazed with passion. An army of security guards descended on him and within seconds he was cuffed and in the back of an armored car. Just before he stepped in the van he turned and looked at Marisa she was kneeling in her blood drenched designer creation cradling Yoji's lifeless body.

Marisa had to be taken in an ambulance, Paramedics tried in vain to peel her away from Yoji she held on to his bloody carcass and refused to let go. She was in a state of shock, the cameras kept rolling and for a second before she collapsed she thought that she was in a movie, the funny thing was that she couldn't remember what her part was she couldn't remember her lines.

In the back of the ambulance two men held the hysterical woman down while a tall nurse stuck a syringe in her arm they had to sedate her she was totally out of control.

Marisa woke up two days later in a darkened room at a private clinic.

She bore no resemblance to the glamorous screen diva that had walked up the red carpet in her golden sandals she was pale with black circles under her eyes.

The clinic was surrounded with Paparazzi, the incident had caused shock waves across the world. Yoji's torn and shattered body had been flown back to Japan, the funeral was in two days. Marisa was in shock the only way that she could attend was to be totally drugged up.

The doctors thought that she was too ill to make the journey to Osaka but she insisted.

She had to say goodbye to Yoji, they made the travel arrangements, she was to fly with a small army of bodyguards to keep the press at bay and two nurses. She was so drugged up that everything seemed fuzzy and unreal she couldn't believe that the studio were flying out a hairdresser and make-up artist with her, they wanted to make sure that she looked good. The whole world was going to be watching.

Marisa went to the airport straight from the clinic she was wearing a dressing gown, pyjamas and dark glasses. When she left the hospital there were more than 150 journalists and photographers waiting for her. Being a star was a nightmare, the security guards thought as they tried to shuffle Marisa into her limo. The airport was also crawling with press and they had permission to drive their car to the tarmac where a private jet was waiting.

Yoji's family were angry that she was coming to the funeral they knew her presence would stir up a media frenzy and they were afraid that their son's funeral would turn into a media circus. They didn't want this woman there, they blamed her for their son's death. They hadn't even formally invited her and had learned from the news that she was already on her way.

In the penthouse suite of a luxury hotel in Osaka, Marisa sat motionless in a chair, sedated to the limit she stared into oblivion while a make-up artist and hairdresser she barely recognized preened and groomed her, the result was scary. Without her persona, Marisa looked like a geisha the glamorous face that the make-up artist had painted on her looked like a mask. Two people dressed her in a black suit, she didn't like it she looked funny, she wondered where they were taking her dressed like this as the fleet of cars set off for the burial grounds.

The cars forced their way through a sea of photographers all hopeful to get a snap of the heavily sedated screen goddess. Marisa was so drugged up that the nurses had to put her in a wheelchair. The service was finished, Yoji's body had been so badly mutilated that his coffin was sealed, as they lowered the coffin into the ground Marisa sat staring into space she knew a secret no one knew.

She smiled and ran her hand over her belly, it had been published in the papers that she had had a miscarriage but the doctors had confirmed the baby was ok. She had not lost Yoji's child, she never wanted to subject this child to the invasion of the press, she had an idea to disappear for a year have the baby, let no one know.

After the funeral she asked her bodyguards if she could speak to Yoji's parents, they had made it quite clear that they had not wanted to speak with her but Marisa had been persistent, being Japanese they had perfect manners and reluctantly they agreed to speak with her for five minutes only.

Their first impression of Marisa was that she looked like a courtesan with the heavy make-up and dyed blonde hair they knew she was under sedation and were curious what she had to say. Marisa ordered her bodyguards and nurses to wait outside as she wanted to talk to Yoji's mother and father in private. The five minutes that the parents were to have was extended to half an hour. Marisa tried to control her emotions and explain everything, she knew that his parents hated her, knew that they bitterly disapproved of her, she understood that and knew that they held her responsible for his death to them she was nothing more than a harlot that had used and abused many men. For what it was worth she wanted them to know that she had loved Yoji, she needed to tell them that they had planned to marry and she wanted them and only them to know that she was carrying a part of Yoji in her womb. She confided in them how important that it was that this was kept a secret from the press she wanted Yoji's child to lead a normal sheltered life without being surrounded by media.

Yoji's mother softened to her when she heard that she was carrying Yoji's child, with tears in her eyes she hugged the broken Japanese bereaved couple and whispered in their ears that as soon as their grandchild was born she would come to Tokyo to let them hold it in their arms at least there was a piece of Yoji left she cried.

Yoji's father remained silent, he wrote an address and telephone number on a piece of paper and slipped it into Marisa's hand. They bowed towards her and left. For ten minutes Marisa sat alone in the room trying to gather her thoughts and emotions, she wished that they would stop sedating her she wanted to be alert and aware of what she was doing.

She flew back to New York the following day, they had obeyed and cut her medication and she was feeling a little better. On the way back she asked her personal assistant to remember to thank the Studio for the plane, to her surprise the plane did not belong to the film studio, she was curious and asked who the plane did belong too. To her amazement it was the Italian Count that she had met at the villa, he had laid on the plane and had been sending her flowers almost every day.

Marisa could not believe how generous he had been, she had only met him occasionally and had danced a few dances with him at Pavel's. He was an absolute angel she thought looking out at the fluffy white clouds as they headed towards the Big Apple.

Marisa checked out of the Clinic and went to a friend's house in the Hampton's. She badly wanted to rest and avoid the press, they had gone to great lengths to get her out of the clinic undercover and as far as she knew no one knew where she was.

She called the Count to thank him for his generosity, they spoke for an hour on the telephone and she had cried. He was a dear man and he felt heart sorry for the bubbly little girl and offered that if she needed peace and to escape from the world that she was welcome to spend some time alone at the villa in Tuscany. He was in Madrid now, if she wanted to go he could arrange for his Lear jet to pick her up, all she had to do was call.

Odd, she mused when she hung up, in times of disaster your friends disappeared and strangers from out of the blue turned up out of nowhere, they were the ones to save your soul.

What did she have here? Nothing, she was sure that the press would discover her whereabouts eventually and decided that she was going to take up the Count's offer and go to Italy, it was beautiful there and peaceful. She called his number the next morning and he said that his plane could pick her up the following evening, he added that she was free to stay for as long as she liked, no one was there except for the staff, he also let her have Pavel's number he was going to be there in a week or so as he was on tour.

Marisa packed the bare necessities and called the studio to see if they could arrange a way to sneak her into the airport, her manager suggested she go in one of studio prop vans, limos and bodyguards would only attract attention. He would try and arrange that the van could be permitted onto the tarmac. She couldn't bear the idea of facing a paparazzi onslaught.

Marisa climbed into the worn out van and giggled, the paparazzi would never dream of spotting her arriving like this but just in case of trouble they had sent three bodyguards.

They were wearing overalls instead of smart suits. Marisa pulled on her hat and dark glasses and they headed for the airport. The officials had been all too happy to comply with her wishes they realized that if the press knew she was in the airport that there would be a frenzy. On the flight she patted her belly and said to herself that her and baby Yoji were off on vacation.

CHAPTER 9

Chloe

Chloe had spent a week with Pavel in Tuscany, he had shown her endless photo albums of him and Carla. She was just beginning to understand how insecure Pavel was. She was sure that he would never get over Carla, she had been like a mother to him.

Tyrese called her every night and Pavel moaned and groaned, as he always seemed to call at dinner time. Chloe had become quite accustomed to eating cold pasta. It was autumn and the Tuscan landscape was a multitude of golds, reds and amber, she was captivated by the beauty of the landscape. Pavel had driven her around the countryside, it was awesome.

Diederick had sent her lawyer a letter, he had been trying to contest the will, her lawyer had assured her he could do nothing. Diederick was like a madman when he heard that his sister had died, he imagined that he would have inherited everything. He had heard from a friend that she was worth a couple of million and he had been infuriated when he learned that Carla had left everything to that slut Chloe. Probably she hadn't died of cancer he thought, probably that bitch had bumped her off to get the money. He hated Chloe with a vengeance and was considering flying to Germany to try and sort things out.

Diederick did fly to Dusseldorf but when he learned that there was nothing that he could do and that Chloe had indeed been the sole heir he went wild.

He demanded a meeting with Chloe and she turned up with her lawyer, Diederick had been positively hostile towards her and she was glad that the lawyer had been there. He called her a whore and a lesbian bitch, he threatened to have her visa revoked and even suggested that she had murdered his sister. Chloe had retained her cool, he was after all embarrassing himself, after half an hour of balling at her, he spat at her and raced out of the room shouting that he would get his own back on her.

Her lawyer had been shocked he had never seen such a shocking display.

While Chloe had been in Tuscany three people had looked at the house, two had actually put in an offer and she had got much more than the asking price. She didn't regard Germany as her home and now that Carla was gone she didn't see why she would have to stay there.

She wondered what Tyrese was doing, perhaps she could move to wherever he was going to be based, his album was going well and she knew that he was perhaps going to get a deal with a European country. She hoped that wherever it was t she could tag along, she was crazy about him. Tyrese surprised Chloe by turning up on her doorstep at midnight with a bunch of flowers. She had been angry, it had been the first evening that he had not called her and she thought that perhaps he had found another lover in London.

He had a week in Germany to do promotions he had three TV programs where he had to perform, lip sync, he hated it. The new label had warned him that if he got a contract for a second album then he would have to do it the old fashioned way, he would have to tour and do concerts, he would have done anything to escape the evil eye of Pippa.

Tyrese made love to Chloe in the dining room, then he made love to her in the hallway and later in the bedroom, she couldn't get enough of him. In the dining room he had fucked her on the table while they listened to his new album it was weird Tyrese thought, as he reached orgasm, weird to listen to your own voice singing whilst screwing.

Tyrese hadn't asked Chloe much about her past, she in turn hadn't asked him about his, as far as he knew she didn't know about the scandal, the hooker or how he had been suspended. He hoped that she would never find out, she was so sweet and refined, she was probably from some wealthy Asian family with a rich family heritage. She had mentioned that her family were dead, he didn't want her to know where he had come from, he was afraid that she would leave him if she knew his background. She was the first girl he had really ever loved, Marisa had been a physical thing. Chloe was something else, he had never imagined he would have fallen in love, he thought that love was a sissy kind of thing, he realised now that love was what he had been missing in his life.

Chloe opened her eyes and stared at him, he was snuggled up to her watching her while she slept, he liked to do that when they had made love and she drifted to sleep. He would just lie there and watch her, the almond shaped eyes the sensuous lips every time he looked at her lips he wanted to kiss them he thought she was fantastic and he was so proud that she was his woman.

The following day she had told him that she had a show and asked if he wanted to come and watch.

She modeled five outfits at the show and he was filled with pride as he watched her slink down the catwalk, she looked so beautiful. His expression turned sour when she appeared back on the catwalk wearing a semi transparent item of lingerie, a pang of jealousy pierced him as he looked left and right and saw two guys ogling at her. He wanted her out of this business, he thought he didn't like her flaunting herself like that.

Chloe had been surprised that he was so jealous, at first she thought that he had been joking, she didn't know this side of him. She asked what about his videos, all these naked women dancing about letting it all hang out, that was different he snapped and he remained moody all day. She was relieved when his spirit lightened and he announced that he wanted to go shopping alone. She was a bit miffed thinking perhaps that he was bored of her. Tyrese had noticed a fantastic jewellers on the Konings Alee, he wanted to go and buy her an engagement ring, he had taken one out of her jewel box so that the size would be right and intended surprising her with it that evening. The diamond was wildly expensive but he couldn't resist it, this was the girl he wanted to spend the rest of his life with. She was the one so why not splash out. The jeweller promised that he could have it re-sized within an hour. Tyrese went shopping while he waited, he went a trifle crazy buying of clothes in the designer boutiques that lined the street for a mile. That night he showered and dressed in a very smart suit, he wanted to look as smooth as possible, this would be one of the most important days of his life and he did so want to get it right.

Chloe put her hair up and wore a bronze metallic strappy dress that Tyresse had surprised her with, they went to an Italian restaurant and Chloe thought it odd that it was empty,' 'Are you sure it will be ok here?' she asked Tyrese, they were the only guests and she had never seen an empty restaurant in Dusseldorf before. Carla always said don't eat in a restaurant if it's not busy Tyrese explained that it was a wonderful restaurant and explained that it was empty because he had booked the whole place just for them.

They sat in the middle at a table overloaded with candles Tyrese had even hired a pianist, Chloe thought that he was the most romantic man on the planet. The meal was heavenly, six waiters served them a four course meal with fine wines the piece de resistance was the dessert, it was served with fireworks and it was only after the waiter had placed it in front of her she saw the box, 'Oh,' she screamed, left between the crème brûlée and the chocolate fondant was a velvet box.

Her fingers trembled as she opened it, the huge diamond sparkled in the candlelight and Tyrese thought that it had been worth all that money just to see the look on her face. Tyrese's voice trembled as he announced that this was an engagement ring and that she could only accept it if he would accept his proposal of marriage.

Chloe's eyes glazed with tears of joy as he spoke, 'Yes, yes, YES,' she replied thinking that it was like a scene out of a movie. He asked her to dance, she hugged him close and a soft voice in her he told her this is the moment, the one you always dreamed of. She had always wanted security, she had wanted a rich man and here he was, rich had been her objective she had never reckoned that he would, however, be so young and handsome.

The waiters smiled, watching the young couple, they knew he was a pop star and hoped that he would remember to give them a generous tip they looked at the rock sparkling on the beautiful models finger and wondered how much that something like that would cost.

That night Tyrese made love to Chloe with passion and intensity, she was naked except for her spikey silver sandals and dazzling engagement ring. That night she kept glancing at the ring to remind herself that she was not dreaming, fate had been kind to her, too kind perhaps, she hoped that her luck was not going to change. Everything had happened so quickly, here she was, a poor girl with only a few years education lying in the arms of a pop star.

Over breakfast they spoke about Rogillio. Tyrese was so upset about it he had nightmares about what had happened, only in his dreams it wasn't Yoji that was mutilated it was himself.

He remembered making love to Marisa sharing her with Rogillio at the villa in Tuscany, God what if Rogillio had snapped then. He wondered how Marisa had survived the experience, they had said in the press that she had lost a child, he wondered if it had been Yoji's child, Rogillio's or his own.

That night at the villa they had been so drunk that they had not used condoms. What if it had been his child? He guessed that Marisa was hiding somewhere.

He had wanted to send flowers but didn't know where to send them. When Marisa's name was mentioned Chloe piped up that she had seen her.

Tyrese was amazed and inquired where, 'She was staying at the Count's villa,' Chloe exclaimed while chopping the vegetables, she had called Pavel as she was bored and they had gone over to the villa. Chloe raved about the Count's villa, it had been the first time she had seen it.

He casually inquired how she had been Chloe said that she had this haunted look on her face and she was reading scripts and avoiding the press, she also added bitchily that without her make-up she looked rather plain. Tyrese laughed knowing that there was no way that Marisa Duval could ever look plain. He told her that he thought that it would be a good idea to send flowers to her from both of them, she agreed but added that she hadn't mentioned to her that they were having an affair.

Chloe like everyone had been shocked at the live footage of the bloodbath, she knew that Marisa was a survivor, under the helpless glamour girl image she was as hard as hell. Friends had said that Marisa had had an affair with Tyrese, that was why she avoided telling her that she was seeing him. Pavel didn't like her, he had felt sorry for the Count, he couldn't understand why he was so taken in by her. On the way back to his estate he had joked with Chloe, 'God help the servants and gardeners she will eat them alive.'

Chloe arranged a huge bunch of flowers to be sent to Marisa, she would freak out when she saw both of their names on the card. For privacy they addressed the flowers to Miss D. care of the Count.

Rogillio had been in the maximum security wing of the state penitentiary. He had suffered endless beatings from the inmates and was now enjoying solitary confinement. Rogillio sat on a cardboard seat, his head bandaged like a mummy as time dragged on. Some said he would get life, others thought that it would be the death sentence. His life here was already a death sentence as he sat in the small room and stared at the brick walls. Every time he closed his eyes he saw Marisa lying in a pool of blood, they said she had had a miscarriage, maybe he had killed his own child.

Rogillio hoped that he would get the death sentence, he was after all dead already, he had been dead from the moment she walked out of the door. They thought he was mad, he should have killed her instead of the Jap.

He thought he should have slashed her face, stuck the gun down her throat. He imagined the scene she liked sucking cock he should have made her suck the gun then pulled the trigger. In his mind her head exploded and her brains splashed over the paparazzi, he laughed and laughed imagining the scene, pulling the trigger, pulling the trigger. It was a crime of passion. Perhaps if he claimed he was mad he would walk free if he did he would get her next time, trigger in her mouth, trigger in her mouth.

Tyrese wondered what future Rogillio would have with a life behind bars. He remembered so many young boys in Harlem that had thrown their life away.

He must have gone mad Chloe thought to have done something like that.

For Marisa it had been the biggest publicity stunt in the book, her mediocre film was the biggest grossing movie at the box office, it seemed that everyone wanted to see the woman that drove men crazy.

Tyrese enjoyed sex with Chloe she was hot between the sheets and sometimes he wondered just how many boyfriends she had had, perhaps she had just one he mused just one very experienced one that had taught her all these sexual tricks. He never mentioned ex-lovers he was afraid that she would delve into his past, he had enough skeletons in the cupboard and he was wondering what the outcome would be about the charges with the redhead. He would have to tell her one day about that before she read it in the press. Tyrese was becoming prolific in his TV interviews, all the play back lip sync performances had gone well and Chloe liked watching him on television it made her feel proud.

She had escaped the poverty of Cambodia and landed up with her very own Prince Charming, she dreaded to think what her life would have been like if she had remained with that old criminal man that she had been sold to.

Soon Tyrese was going back to the States and she had wanted to join him there but apparently it was going to be difficult to get a visa. Tyrese had actually mentioned that he wanted to marry her, he said that he would check with the Embassy in New York, he couldn't stand the fact that he was leaving her there. He had suggested over dinner that perhaps they could go on honeymoon to Thailand. He wanted to meet her family and friends, he thought they could go for a month to visit Vietnam and Cambodia. His suggestion had taken her so by surprise her stomach turned as he spoke, eventually when she retained her composure she suggested that she would adore to go to America, see Las Vegas, San Francisco and Florida, her eyes lit up like a child when she admitted that secretly she was aching to go to Disney World and be a big kid.

Tyrese thought perhaps she was right it would be fun and it would be a new horizon for her, he felt that he had been selfish and promised to take her to Florida.

They made love all night on his last evening, Tyrese went to the airport by cab he said that he wanted to remember her lying in bed looking tired and lovely.

When Tyrese left she fell into a deep sleep her dreams were peppered with demons.

Her ex-husband had appeared. Diederick and even Carla she woke in a cold sweat.

Being superstitious she feared the worst, she knew that something was going to happen.

Before she went to sleep she made a vow that she would go to see a monk who lived in the city, she needed some inner peace and missed the Temples.

Tyrese smiled remembering the face of his lovely fiancé she was so special, perhaps too classy for him. She was right, it was better to go to America it would be fun they could be big kids again.

Tyrese called Chloe at three am in the morning, she woke up with a start thinking that something was wrong, to her relief there was nothing at all wrong. He was so excited that he couldn't wait till morning to call her, his debut album was racing up the charts and his single was number one in Japan. The time had come now for real promotion they had arranged a small tour of eight venues he had enough material to do a show, now the best news was that his record company wanted him to record his own song. The one he had written for Rogillio, they had liked the demo of 'That's What Love Can Do' and they wanted to release it as his new single worldwide. He was busy now in the studio recording the voice track and had an idea, they needed a female backing vocalist and he had heard Chloe sing in the shower. He wanted her to come, they had loved her photo she could also feature in the video Pippa had been delighted with the idea, it would be cheaper to use a new girl than use another artist to do the female vocals and she was a real looker so she could do the video, also the main idea was trying to keep Tyrese happy. She was making a fortune out of him and although he still point blank refused to have any direct confrontation with her she didn't want him to leave, his contract was ending in 6 weeks and she wanted to keep him happy hoping that he would stay with her label that was why she wanted to rush this project.

She wanted it in the can before his contract ended, God forbid if he did try to leave at least she would have the profit from this one, it was a great track the heart rendering balled version was haunting and she was intending having it remixed and mastered into an upbeat dance track. She hadn't told Tyrese but there was a film studio looking for a theme track for a new blockbuster she had a feeling that this was the track, if they did select this one it would be a hit in almost every country on the planet.

Tyrese saved the best for last, he excitedly told Chloe the record company were going to give her a contract for the project. They would arrange her visa within days, he told her he loved her, to fax a copy of her passport immediately and to go pack her bags, they needed her there early next week to record the background vocals and the video would be shot the following weekend after the track had been mastered.

Chloe was so excited she couldn't get back to sleep she was terrified at the thought of singing she couldn't believe that he had done this. The great thing was that she could get her visa and work permit the record company was one of the best on the planet it handled many major names, for them it was easy to break and bend rules.

Chloe raided the designer stores on the Konings Allee, she wanted to look her best when she arrived in the States it was sale time and she managed to find lots of bargains.

As Tyrese had promised within days they requested her at the embassy, her visa was at the visa office and she was given star treatment by the clerk who thought that she was a famous singer.

It had been a hectic few days she had moved all her personal belonging into storage, her home had been sold and the furniture that she had had been given to an auctioneer. Everything had been such a rush, she had spent hours with the lawyer and estate agent signing the papers for the transfer she was looking forward to relaxing on the long flight to the States.

On the plane she wished that she had done more karaoke in Thailand, the Thai's loved karaoke fortunately she slept almost all of the way, one hour before landing she went into the toilet to put her face on and change into a slinky skin tight jumpsuit.

Tyrese's heart skipped a beat when he saw her disembark, she was stunning perhaps her beauty was more intense than Marisa's. It was gonna be a hot video he thought, as she approached the vulgar stretch limo she had never seen a car so long it looked like a joke.

Pippa had tipped off the paparazzi that a new singer was arriving from Europe, a supermodel turned pop princess. This would create some hype for the new track.

Pippa would keep the paps up to scratch where Chloe was hanging out.

As they left the airport Chloe watched the paparazzi through the tinted glass of the limo. A fleet of hungry Paparazzi were following them on motor bikes all desperate for a snap of Chloe and Tyrese.

Whilst Tyrese had been in Europe he had become quite a star in his home country, tracks from his album were played on all the major radio stations, downloads had gone crazy, people stopped him on the streets and plagued him for autographs and the record company had issued him two tall unfriendly security guards, they looked like Russian spies he joked. He kissed her passionately in back seat of the limo. Chloe felt uncomfortable with the two bodyguards watching. Tyrese told her she had better get used to the stiffs as they were there twenty-four hours a day.

Tyrese hadn't had the time to look for an apartment as he had been so busy recording, he had taken up residence at a newly built five star hotel, his suite was sumptuous, he thought that it was crazy to rush into buying something when he was going on a five month tour after the launch of the single.

Chloe marveled at America, everything seemed so big, tall buildings, wide roads, no one walked, everyone travelled by car. In Thailand if you were lucky one family in ten had a car, one car to serve them all here in America the whole family had cars even the teenage kids.

After a serious love session that exhausted them both, Chloe mentioned that she would like to go sightseeing. Tyrese hated to disappoint her, she was being picked up at seven am the following morning, they wanted her in the studio first thing. He snapped a disk in his walkman and flipped her the earphones, she had to learn her background vocals tonight.

It was not as scary as she thought the vocals were easier than she had imagined, there was a poetic spoken piece in the middle of the track, she had to do this and her broken English-Asian accent gave the piece an edge. They took his portable ghetto blaster into the marble bathroom, the acoustics were better there and Tyrese sang the song while she practised the background vocals. She was tired and jet-lagged, it was just as well that she had slept on the plane she thought as she stood under a cold shower, it was funny how westerners couldn't have cold showers, as a child in Cambodia they never had hot water, she had poured dishes of rainwater over herself, they collected the earthen pots of water in the rain season and used it to shower, cook, clean and wash their clothes.

At seven am the car arrived, Tyrese told her to get made-up in the car, they were late and time was money, if they ran over budget it was taken from his royalties and there were a dozen people in the studio waiting for them.

Chloe watched Tyrese in the sound booth, he had headphones and his body was animated as he sang his heart out. Chloe was nervous when she did her bit, they had her sing it over and over till she was exhausted. The spoken piece had been harder than she anticipated, at that point in the track there was no music only her voice, they wanted her to sound strong but soft, in the end they seemed satisfied. She was glad it was over and flopped in a chair sipping black coffee to keep awake. They spent the whole day recording one song and she found it weird that to record a three minute song took so long. The music business was indeed just as crazy as the fashion business.

She was secretly excited about appearing in the video, she had always dreamed of seeing herself on film, when she had seen Marisa's movie she had wondered how it must feel to watch yourself on screen. They had no time for sightseeing Tyrese was under high pressure and wherever he went, she went. There were meetings and interviews TV chat shows, television appearances where he lip synced the songs, it was three days till the video shoot and they had a late night appointment with the director to discuss the script.

Alex North was a new wonder child in the industry her videos had an edge that guaranteed airplay. She was a tiny woman who looked almost like a student, she flipped through the storyboards with Tyrese. The story line was a boy meets girl adventure, simple but not in this dimension, she intended using lots of computer animation. She was delighted with Chloe and scrutinized her flawless beauty shamelessly. There would be scenes where both she and Tyrese would be body painted like zebras, yes zebras, He would be half man half zebra, tomorrow they had made a three hour appointment for him with the hairdresser that created his leopard hairstyle and he was getting his done like a zebra. Tyrese was glad that he would be able to relax for three hours, after they had exhausted the plan, Alex introduced them to the stylist and they had to try on the video clothes, the stylist was cool for a Canadian. He had a purple Mohican and was wearing so many rings it was unbelievable.

Chloe tried on her outfit, she looked stunning and it fitted perfectly except the shoes were too big, she was after all Asian and they hadn't expected that she would have such small feet. Tyrese was not too enamored with his outfit but the stylist showed him a photo, explaining on film that it would look fabulous.

The ten dancers' costumes were uber cool, everyone had a different outfit the stylist Jay Jay assured them that it would be 'a styling trip'.
In the main scene both he and Chloe would be body painted, they showed him a test photo of the effect that it would give. Tyrese would be half man half beast. 'Suits him, very in character,' Chloe chirped in laughing. He was gonna be a unicorn they would add his beast bits by computer which meant that he would be wearing blue tights as they were working on blue screen for that part and his legs would have to temporarily disappear.

Chloe was to be filmed underwater as a mermaid, her tail would be also like a zebra.

A zebra mermaid very funky she thought coordinating her tail with Tyrese's hair.

Making a clip was expensive, these were big budget videos and the success of the track was usually dependent on the video. They would be shooting in film and the editing techniques and computerization made them into mini movies, sometimes even lousy tracks became hits because they had the fattest clips.

The night before the filming Chloe couldn't sleep, she woke up with big black circles under her eyes and cried, she had wanted to look her best, Tyrese laughed and assured her that they were having one of the best make-up artists in America there for her. He cost a fortune and would make her look stunning, he joked that they could always touch her up by computer and at this remark she threw her hairbrush at him the brush sailed through the air and hit him on the bum, 'Careful my love,' he joked, 'I am naked in this video.'

Everyone was in a panic, the final edited version of the song arrived late while they were in make-up. It sounded fantastic and Chloe couldn't believe the magical thing that they had done with her voice, she sounded so sexy.

The studio was alive, the lighting technicians were there and everything was in full swing at eight am two make-up artists had already started on the girls and the hair people were arriving soon.

Tyrese waved Chloe goodbye as they both were whisked into separate rooms to be transformed.

Two hours later Chloe emerged looking far better than she ever thought she could look, she put Marisa to shame. Tyrese wolf whistled at her and begged that she try to look like this every day. He had his stunning black and white zebra outfit and in his white destroyed shirt and pants he looked like something from a primeval planet. Chloe sashayed across the room mimicking the way that Marisa did, she was taller and looked like a wildcat the assistant director clocked her move immediately and told her, 'Yes girl, that's the look, that's definitely the LOOK'..

It was funny the make-up gave Chloe a new confidence she studied her reflection proudly and realized for the first time in her life that she was beautiful. The dancers were being shot separately, they were ready for Tyrese and Chloe, after lunch they would be body painted apparently their body painting would take about four hours.

Tyrese had made many videos he was photogenic and he knew his best angles, he was easy to shoot and did all his scenes in one take. Chloe was a trifle nervous at first as it seemed strange to be standing in the middle with a whole film crew round you, after a few minutes she relaxed forgot the cameras and gave her all.

Alex shot a lot of footage of her, Chloe presumed that this was because she was no good, it was however quite the contrary when they finished filming Alex invited her to look at the monitor. Chloe stared in disbelief at her image the camera had loved her.

They had a quick lunch and disappeared into Tyrese's dressing room where two other make-up artists skillfully and painstakingly body painted them for the blue screen scene. Chloe looked at Tyrese, in reality he looked ridiculous wearing coloured tights with his body painted like a zebra and the matching zebra hair, he laughed, her skin was painted silver with little metallic fish scales and she was squeezed into a skin tight ankle length skirt that she had to hobble around in, her tail would be added and his animal legs would be conceived in the editing room. Cute couple Alex joked as Chloe hobbled out hanging onto Tyrese's arm. The special effects team seemed pleased and they proceeded to film over and over again till Alex was satisfied.

They were glad when Alex shouted that's a wrap, filming on the blue screen had been weird no one knew what the edited finished product would look like except Miss North and she was tripping on the neon coloured dancers costumes. Alex's heart raced with excitement as they filmed. High as a kite she imagined the finished production on screen. Tyrese would be galloping through the clouds yes he would be a flying zebra and Chloe would be immersed in the sea her tail swirling.

Tyrese didn't understand the connection between a flying zebra and a mermaid but Alex assured him it was ART pure ART.

She would spend the next three weeks with the CGI and editing team in the basement of her studio surviving on a diet of sushi, vodka and joints till the clip was mastered.

Twenty-three days later the video was ready, they sat in Alex's editing office and when they were all seated and relaxed Alex pushed a remote, slowly the lights dimmed and a screen came down from the ceiling.

She had been right, the finished video was top-notch, everyone looked fantastic and the clever visual images made the song more intense you would never forget this clip.

Alex was a genius, Chloe held Tyrese's hand she was so excited, she looked stunning, perhaps, she thought better looking than Marisa. Tyrese as half man half beast was sensational.

Chloe's underwater mermaid dance was mesmerizing. Alex was worried about her bare breast for the American market she thought it was cool for Europe but that it was too much for the States. She said that if the American music channels had a problem with the tits she would re-edit that part, everyone was happy with that. In Thailand also the bare breasts could have been a problem, she was body painted but in some countries the slightest sign of a nipple was taboo.

They watched the clip five times and everyone thought it was awesome.

They gave them all copies of the disk so they could watch it at home back at the hotel.

Chloe watched it in slow motion for hours it was the first time she had seen herself on film.

Alex had been right, the Americans wanted her to lose the nipples, apart from that they loved it and the track was fantastic.

Pippa was radiant when she saw the video, she was glad she had used that expensive bitch Alex, this was cutting edge at its best maybe they would get nominated for best video she thought as she watched it for the second time. This clip spelled money she thought, lots of dollars lots of pounds, rupees and whatever, she was gonna put it out globally the Japanese would love it, it had number one written all over it.

She wished that she hadn't been so stupid and fallen out with him she was also impressed by this new girl, she would cut a single with her, she was a beauty. So she was the one that Tyrese was banging and he had actually got engaged she had seen the ring in the clip they had let her wear it the video. The diamond was huge like a piece of ice, she was real pretty and photogenic and had great tits, pity she thought that they would have to cut them out the Americans would never accept that.

She called Alex personally to compliment her then she called Chloe to ask her if she was interested in doing a single, she said she would have someone drop a demo to their hotel and asked her to congratulate Tyrese on their engagement.

Chloe had no idea that Tyrese had lived with Pippa and thought she was sweet to have said that.

To Tyrese it was pure sarcasm, he called the London record company he was eager to know if they were going to give him a contract he didn't want to commit to anything with Pippa.

They promised to email him within three days, he was happy with that. He was sure if they saw the new video and heard the track that they would snap him up. He decided he would ask Alex if she could play the clip on line to their London office, technology was a godsend.

Chloe and Tyrese had little time to celebrate their engagement, his agenda was full.

He advised Chloe to do the single he thought that at least she would get a start, he warned her not to sign anything unless he checked it out and told her to do a one off single contract.

He didn't want her to get tied up in Pippa's web.

Within a week the video was on TV it was so cool and the song rocketed to number one immediately in the US in the hit parade.

Tyrese got his email he had a deal, a bloody good deal. The new clip had clinched it and he was so looking forward to telling that bitch that he was out, there would be bitter hassles with Pippa of that he was sure. His lawyer had already forewarned him that she might hold him to do promotion tours of the single.

Pippa had been delighted that Tyrese had actually called her secretary to arrange an appointment, his contract was almost over and he was probably coming to crawl and sweet talk her. He was coming the following afternoon and Pippa hadn't seen him for six months, she had her hair done in the morning and dressed to perfection, she wanted him to see her looking her best and she asked her office to draw up a new contract for him and kept in her top drawer.

It was about time that he apologized she thought as her secretary buzzed her to say that Tyrese was waiting in the reception.

She greeted him warmly and stared at the tall well-dressed man who entered her office.

She studied him, she had forgotten how handsome he was, he turned something on in her and her stomach began to flutter and she thought that perhaps if he was very sweet she would let him fuck her right here on the table, she pressed the button that lit up the red do not enter light outside her room. She started to compliment him about the success of the new single and pulled the contract out of the drawer, before she could explain the draft of his new contact he took over the conversation, the last time he had seen her she was in handcuffs he mused.

Looking the woman who had controlled his life for almost two years he stared bitterly into her eyes and told her that she could stick her contract up her white saggy ass, he concluded that he had signed with her rival company and before she could speak he stood up told her she was one sad bitch and walked proudly out of her office. As she watched his broad shoulders and tight buns disappear out of her office she hurled the table lamp across the room.

As soon as he left she lined up three lines of Colombian coke and snorted them up greedily, she hated him. She was still in love with him although she had hidden her feelings and he was making her money. She thought that as his career went from strength to strength that he would come back to her, she had thought that this Asian kid was just a fling.

The blood sprayed all over his unsigned contract, shit she cursed ringing for her PA to bring her tissues. Another fucking nose bleed she cried, it was the coke her doctor had warned her that they would have to put a metal plate between her nostrils the cocaine had destroyed her nose, her new personal assistant arrived with tissues and she growled at him to get her some speed, her PA nodded and made her exit, she had asked for the drugs like she was asking for office stationery.

Pippa's and Tyrese's Lawyers had been having a bitter battle, she was holding him to do promotion and she wouldn't budge, the new record company were pressing him to start recording a new album and the stress was making him crazy.

Two months later she still had him by the balls and they were flying between Detroit and London every ten days.

Chloe's first single, an upbeat dance track was being mastered and she had made a video which would be released soon. It was to be released in Japan and Thailand first as Pippa wanted to test it in the Asian market.

Chloe knew that her single was being launched in Japan she didn't know that was also being released in Thailand.

Pippas's hate for Tyrese was reaching boiling point she had lost one of the biggest money-makers and he had gone to one of her competitors to make it worse she was madly in love with him.

She fully understood how in anger Rogillio had murdered that blonde tart's lover, she could stick a knife in Tyrese. She had the press office send photos and a biography of Chloe to the music channels and teen magazines in Tokyo and Thailand she hadn't planned a lot of promotion budget for Chloe but she looked great in the clip and wanted to have some buzz about her. The only upside of Chloe having a torrid romance with Tyrese was that their union guaranteed lots of press.

The tabloids were full of photos of the glossy good looking celebrity couple.

Whatever the duo wore was hot fashion news, the paparazzi hounded them, all hungry for the shot.

Chloe had been snapped in what was a Marilyn Monroe moment on the red carpet at a premiere, her dress had blown up exposing her nicely groomed lady parts. The paparazzi had a field day and made lots of dollars from the ultimate beaver shot. Chloe learned rule number one never leave home without your knickers. Her dress had been so flimsy and the stylist had advised that she remove her underwear. She would never work with that stylist again. She cringed the following day to learn that her exposed genitalia was on the cover of every smutty tabloid and newspaper worldwide.

CHAPTER 10

Thailand

Diederick was in the bar, it was low season and the bars were losing a fortune. Tourism had dried up and even the Americans and Europeans were not traveling anymore. September 11th had badly affected tourism and the boom that they had awaited when the Euro was introduced didn't come. Then there was bird flu, the tsunami, military coupes.

Diederick was deeply in debt, he had borrowed money from an underworld figure they were pressing him for repayments. Diederick had tried to sell up but no one was stupid enough to buy.

He clipped a girl on the ear she was reading a bloody magazine in the bar, he ripped the book out of her hand and told the mama-san to keep them in order, he was just about to throw the teen magazine in the bin when he looked and looked again at the cover. It was someone who looked like Chloe. Flicking through the magazine he found a double page spread, it was Chloe there were pictures of her all dressed up, in one she looked like a mermaid there was also three photos of her with a tall handsome black man. He screamed at the mama-san to tell the young girl to come to his office, the girl was pleased she thought that he was summoning for sex, she needed to pay her rent this week.

Lucy spoke perfect English and he wanted her to read him the whole story word for word as it was in the magazine. Lucy complained that it was difficult to read, when he slipped her a five hundred baht note she smiled, fucking whores he thought they were all the same he thought.

Diederick couldn't believe it Miss fucking lesbian whore. Lucy started translating Miss Chloe make single, 'A single, SINGLE WHAT?' he growled impatiently at the pretty young girl sitting across from him in her underwear, giving him a dirty look she proceeded, 'She make a record and is music star, she number one! she make big money... too much in America she Thai lady but come from Germany she discovered by Pippa Curtis big boss of Curtis Village Records she engage for marry to number one star a man name Tyrese, her record in shop now. Good music,' she added telling him that, 'The DJ had played her song three time already tonight,' she concluded, proud of her English. Diederick's face was scarlet he ordered her to go downstairs and get the CD from the bastard DJ, she tottered off in her platform shoes wondering what she had said wrong, she had never seen him so angry.

Diederick felt a pain rush up his arm, stress, he thought frightened that he would have a heart attack.

She eventually returned and threw a CD on his desk and scampered away. It was true, she warned all the girls downstairs, 'To watch out for the big boss he was angry too much.'

'Lying cow,' Diederick exclaimed as he studied the CD cover so she was marrying a pop star.

How the fuck did she get to America? Probably with Carla's fucking money, yes her money it should have been his if Carla had left him the money he wouldn't be in this mess now.

He scribbled down the telephone number on the CD cover of Curtis Village Records and at three in the afternoon American time he dialled the number and claiming he was a booking agent in Bangkok he demanded to speak to Pippa.

Pippa was on antidepressants, she wanted so much to destroy Tyrese he was making her look like an idiot in the industry. She was furious that the temp receptionist had put a booking agent on to her, she didn't talk to these people she had staff for that, the man was on the line and she was just about to transfer him to another extension when he started to talk.

The hair on Pippa's neck stood on end as she listened to the guttural German accent.

Yes! She thought, there was a God. She had a way to destroy Tyrese, she hoped that what Mr Diederick had told her was true, she said that she didn't want him to spend money calling her and offered to call him back at her expense. Fate, she thought as she scribbled down his number if the receptionist hadn't been sick this man would never have been put through to her, she switched on her tape to record his call and sat back and listened.

Diederick was angry, very angry, apparently Chloe had been a whore at his brothel she had run off with his sister, a German Lesbian called Carla Diederick. He claimed that she had bumped off Carla and inherited his money adding that he loved his sister. According to him she had a fake ID.

She was from Cambodia, Diedrick threatened to go to the press in Bangkok. Pippa prayed that this was true, he could have been a crazy and she warned him not to go to the press and said as president of the company she took this very seriously. She said that she would have to have proof as he was just a voice on the telephone and added that if it was the truth she would pay him a handsome retainer. Diederick offered to scan and email some photos of her with his sister in Phuket that they had sent him before she ran off. Also some naked photos of her dancing topless in his club and one of her being fucked by a customer, he added that he would have to cut the head off the customer, she understood fully and gave him her private email address.

Thirty minutes later Pippa opened Diederick's mail, it took forever to download the photos and they came on her screen one at a time. The first was of a smiling blonde woman with someone who could have been Chloe, the next was indeed absolutely Chloe she was wearing a thong dancing on a pole, she even spotted the little mole on her left breast, the third photo was a shocker Chloe having an orgasm scratching an old man's back as he penetrated her.

What a perfect pair they make she mused, both prostitutes, this would put the lid on Tyrese both professionally and emotionally. She called Diederick back right away and asked him if he would like to make a lot of money real quick, she told him to bring as much evidence as he had. It got better he had a video of her at an orgy being fucked by three guys in the private room upstairs, none of the girls knew that they were being filmed that night. He often filmed his girls in action with hidden cameras. Diederick sold the tapes to the sex tourists that frequented his establishment.

He was a voyeur he liked to watch his customers and Go-Go ladies in hardcore action.

Bring all the tapes she added, a first class ticket will be at the airport, she said that he was not to worry, he would be handsomely paid, all he had to do was turn up at the airport and bring as much dirt as he had to Detroit.

She would collect him personally at the airport and she told him she reckoned that the tabloids would pay him a hundred thousand dollars for his story. She would double it and that she would organize everything, she made it clear that as president of the company he would not be allowed to mention anything about her or their contact, if he failed to follow this rule he would not be paid.

Diederich thought she was a lovely lady, real honest and caring he rushed home and prepared to pack she had said that his flight details would be emailed to him from another email address. By the time he got home her email had arrived and he was to be at the airport in six hours. He scrambled through the drawers in his bedroom to find Chloe's tapes, they were his favorites, he had about twenty naughty pictures of her, also he figured that the four tapes and twenty hard core photos should be sufficient.

Pippa went personally to the airport to collect Diederick Schubel, she recognized him immediately, he looked every inch the brothel owner, overweight with a ghastly polyester printed shirt with rows of vulgar yellow gold chains round his neck. Pippa smiled her most dazzling smile at the pot-bellied man and opened the door of her new Mercedes sport for him. They went right back to her office where a buffet lunch was waiting for both of them, after she had locked her door and pressed the do not disturb light she sat back and listened to the man's story. He showed her the photos and popped a video band in her television. While Diederick wound back the first film she excused herself and went into her bathroom, she sprinkled the two lines out and snorted them greedily, what a buzz, she was so high she could fly, she could destroy not only both of their careers she mused but also their wedding plans. Their cosy little love nest would just explode when the press got this, she couldn't wait to call Philip Peterson it would be front cover scandal, global scandal now that Tyrese was an international hit. Shame she thought about Chloe's singing career, she did one more line and returned, it took all her composure to remain calm. She was so, so pleased that this piece of scum had crawled out from the woodwork, the videos were pure porn and the DVD disks were even better. It was great. Chloe indulged in all kinds of lewd things with absolutely gross men he had four tapes and disks she watched them all.

What a variety, a gang bang, some lesbian sex and lots of blow jobs, she was so photogenic and there was no mistaking that it was her, better still the piece de resistance, Diederick had discovered her Cambodian ID card, he had found it stitched into the lining of one of the handbags she had left when she had done her disappearing trick with his sister. He had gone through apartment with a fine toothcomb when she left, looking to see if there were any drugs stashed away, the flat was in his name and he couldn't afford any problems with the police.

Pippa imagined the headlines. Tyrese's mother had been a prostitute, he had started his career as one and now it just so happened that Miss-squeaky clean-butter wouldn't melt in her mouth – Chloe was also a whore herself, she imagined the headlines! Prostitute's son becomes prostitute then marries a prostitute it would shelve his career in Europe for sure. As far as Chloe was concerned she had put a clause in her contract too, a character clause saying that if for any reason her single was withdrawn that she would be responsible for Curtis Villages losses, Pippa made a rough calculation since her single was planned for release in ten countries she could sue her for loss of profits, 200000 dollars in sales times ten would be two million dollars, it would finish the slut. She emailed her lawyer to arrange a quick meeting, then Diederick her new best friend and her headed to Philip Peterson's office. Philip owned a tabloid empire his magazines had the highest circulation on the globe his speciality was celebrity gossip. Boy Oh Boy did she have a front page story for him.

He offered the hundred thousand dollars to Diederick for the exclusive rights to the story, he was really excited about it and was going to publish the juicy scandal in twenty magazines which were selling in all corners of the globe. Pippa wondered how Tyrese's new record company would take it, they were pumping a fortune in to his second album and had given him a ridiculous advance, the initial momentum of sales on his first album were slowing down and she had made her money out of him. Diederick and Philip signed a secret contract which stipulated that Pippa's name would be withheld, she put Diederick up at a five star hotel and asked him to send all the bills to her office.

Diederick celebrated with a Budweiser from the mini bar, this money would keep the heavies off his neck for a few months.

Pippa went back to her office, she had asked Philip to keep her copies of the tapes, she trusted him and had known him for years and he had never double-crossed her. After the initial scandal in the tabloids Pippa would ensure that all the sex tapes went viral, she anticipated having millions of people download the tapes. Tyrese and Chloe's lives would be hell and she would love watching their destruction from the wings.

She called her dealer and ordered a big bag of coke she was going to celebrate tonight and go to a club, she wanted to screw and she needed a man. The barman at the Dome Palace was hung like a horse he liked s and m and would do anything for two hundred dollars, she was going to the Dome Palace that was for sure.

When the club closed at three Pippa invited Sven to a private party at her place, he knew who she was and what her tastes were, he told her he would charge her 300 dollars, she agreed, she had had him on several occasions and it was worth it.

While she was in the shower Sven took a Viagra, he hated doing these old kinky birds he much preferred boys and thought that after he finished her he would go cruising for a nice muscle Mary.

Sven handcuffed her to the rings that were suspended on the wall and wearing nothing but a leather mask he teased her with a soft leather whip, Pippa reached orgasm before he made love to her, she screamed in pleasure as the young muscle man pumped into her flesh, in her mind she imagined that it was Tyrese on top of her.

She was disappointed that Sven was not going to stay the night and she grudgingly paid him the 300 dollars. Before he left he did some coke and asked her for the taxi fare, she threw the fifty dollar bill at him and he left.

The euphoria of the drugs had ebbed and she was feeling down, catching her naked reflection in the wall to wall mirrors that lined her bedroom walls she shrugged in disgust, she stared at the naked old woman in the mirror and decided right there and then that she was going away for two weeks holiday. It was long overdue but she would go now, the Botox had no effect any more she wanted a face lift, breast implants and a bum lift, she would call her surgeon in the morning she was tired of this old body the timing was perfect she would disappear while the heat was on Tyrese, she had competent staff and she could take her mobile and laptop to the clinic, she had piles of paperwork to do, she personally checked every account from her bookkeepers. In hospital she would have time to focus on the financial side of her business and get in condition. She wondered if they could put the metal plate between her nose too when she was in. Her nose was fucked up and the nose bleeds were persisting she made a list of all the things that she wanted done, eyes, chin, breasts, butt and added liposuction on her thighs she would look divine when she returned.

Philip did a real suicide job on Tyrese and Chloe, front page stuff with a six page editorial as starter.

He had found photos of Tyrese's junkie mother and had interviewed the neighbors, the woman, also a prostitute that did men for twenty-five dollars died in squalor whilst Tyrese was number one in the hit parade and lived in five star hotels. They had photos of him as a stripper and interviewed some of the guys that he had danced with. They had said that he used to screw the clients for a hundred dollars. They also featured the prostitute that he had been caught with in the car, she had said that he had paid her twenty dollars more to have sex without a condom, she claimed that he had forced her and that she had been glad to have been rescued by the police. His affair with Marisa had been exposed and they speculated that it was this affair that had made Rogillio become violent.

Then it was Chloe they sabotaged, they featured a photo of Tyrese and her smiling and flashing her huge vulgar diamond engagement ring. Her claims to be a model were rejected, Philip published a whole series of photos, her lap dancing on a pole, other censored photos of her in orgy scenes and lesbian encounters from the video were given a two page special. Diederick gave a personal interview of how she had slept with over 150 men and ran off with his lesbian sister, he hinted that he suspected that she had murdered her and he claimed that she had robbed him of his inheritance. They even printed her original ID card from Cambodia.

Pippa packed all the tabloid magazines in her bag she wanted to gloat over them in the clinic, she wondered how Tyrese and Chloe were, poor dears. She wondered how the president of Saviour Sunshine records was handling this dilemma. As her driver whisked her to the private clinic, she dialed her lawyer to start proceedings against Chloe, according to the morality character clause her single was to be recalled and would not be released, Pippa was suing her for three million dollars, she asked her PA to personally deliver some orchids to Diederik at his hotel she wished him a pleasant flight back to Thailand.

Chard sat in the business class compartment of a flight bound for Amsterdam it was a long flight from Bangkok and he hated flying, a hired assassin and hit man he was nicknamed The Hawk in the business, he worked freelance for different underworld organizations and prided himself as being the best. The sophisticated lady next to him had fallen asleep, he borrowed the pile of magazines that she had stuffed in the backrest of the chair, anything to pass the time. As he glanced through the American gossip magazines he froze and slowly read the article about a beautiful model and American singer he looked and looked again at the small photo of the Asian woman she wasn't Thai she was Cambodian and he recognized that face. Years ago he had been hired by the mother of a Cambodian drug Baron to track down a young girl, he had searched for her for four months without succeeding, he remembered her well because it was in his history the only job that he didn't finish. He couldn't wait for the plane to land he had to contact them, after years the bitch had surfaced successful and free, not bad for a cold blooded murderess. She had slit Po's throat with a mango knife and to everyone's horror dismembered her own husband. When they had discovered his body his throat had been slashed open from ear to ear and his dismembered penis was lying at the other end of the room.

She had been young when she did that, amazing that she had just walked out of Po's estate when there were dozens of armed security personnel there.

Po's mother would be particularly interested in knowing that he had discovered her identity.

The moment the plane landed at Schiphol airport he dialed the number, Madame Po was very, very excited to learn that the girl who had butchered her son and disgraced her family had been traced. She instructed Chard to finish the commission that she had given him and asked him to promise that he would make it painful, fifty percent of his retainer would be transferred within the hour to his Swiss account.

In the airport "The Hawk" looking like any other tourist purchased all the gossip and celebrity magazines, he wanted to know where the bitch was stationed so he could attack.

After reading every article and scribbling down some notes he made some phone calls canceling the appointments that he had come to Amsterdam for and booked a flight to London where Chloe was living with her pop star lover. Unfortunately she was lying low the dreadful press over the pair had created a media frenzy, dressed in a trench coat and carrying a camera he joined the other fifty paparazzi and camped outside their Mayfair apartment.

Looking at the elegant building he felt a rush of adrenaline his prey was inside, she couldn't stay inside forever.

Tyrese was broken when he discovered her background, they had had a bitter fight and he had discovered another side to her, did anyone know how it felt to discover that the woman that he loved and had promised to marry was a hard and callous whore she had slept with hundreds of men, she had been lesbian, her whole existence had been a lie.

Both grounded in the apartment hiding from the army of reporters that kept a twenty-four hour vigil on their love nest.

Tyrese was in a deep depression his world had been shattered, he had loved Chloe.

Saviour sunshine records was furious, they had shelved his album and suspended his contract, he had been requested to return the advanced retainer that they had given him. All costs of producing the album would be Tyrese's responsibility and the morality clause in his contract clearly stated that they could revoke his contract and hold him liable if any personal publicity damaged the record label's identity.

Chloe didn't seem bothered to hear that Pippa was suing her for the ridiculous amount of three million dollars, she seemed more obsessed that they had disclosed her real identity, when she learned that the papers had published her ID card she had been hysterical, she had not batted an eyelid at being called a whore or seeing the naked obscene photos of herself in uncompromising positions but she had screamed in horror when she saw that her ID card had been published. Tyrese suspected that there must be some dark dangerous secret from her past that she had hidden, an even darker secret than the ones that were spread over every magazine on the bookshelves.

Tyrese employed a young city lawyer called Mercedes Thomson. Miss Thomson was an attractive woman and looked much younger than her thirty years, she had an excellent reputation and Tyrese needed the best. Curtis Village Records were also suing him for a crazy amount and he desperately needed her to sort things out. He had moved out of the Mayfair apartment, he couldn't stand the sight of Chloe and she had thrown his engagement ring in his face. He had packed his bags and left, it had taken them almost a half hour to get away from the press that surrounded his car. His driver had panicked and almost drove over one which led to more bad publicity and yet another lawsuit. Tyrese holed himself up in a West End Hotel, the management were not too keen on having him as a guest and only agreed when he proposed renting a whole floor.

Chloe was like a rat in a trap, she was terrified when she saw that they had revealed her true identity, she couldn't believe that she had been so stupid as to have left the card in the apartment, that bastard Diederick had ruined her life, perhaps right now the Cambodian police were searching for her. She imagined that they wanted her for murder and had nightmares about spending life in a rat infested Cambodian Jail.

What she didn't know was that the police had taken nothing to do with the Drug Baron's death, the safest place for her on the planet would indeed have been a jail cell.

Chard had connections with hackers and for a few hundred dollars he got her private telephone number and email address. Posing as a representative from Curtis Village records he arranged an appointment with Chloe, explaining that Pippa had wanted him to speak to her personally hoping that they could come to an agreement and the charges could be dropped.

Chloe felt relieved that perhaps there was a solution, she agreed to meet him, he would come to her flat for a private talk the following day.

Chloe did her hair and applied make-up skilfully she wanted to impress Pippa's representative.

Chard shook her hand strongly and she found it odd that his palms were sweating as it was chilly outside. Perhaps she thought that the army of paparazzi camped outside her door had unnerved him they unnerved her.

She offered him coffee and he requested she put on Tyrese's new album, whilst she was pouring coffee she noticed that he had turned the volume up full.

Chloe tried to be charming and smiled at him sexily as he opened his briefcase, she stood frozen in her tracks when she saw the look on his face, his dark eyes stared at her, they were the eyes of the dead she thought and she had never seen anyone look at her like that. The glint of the blade made her scream, within seconds the beast was on top of her, his powerful body pinned her to the ground. He placed two dental clamps on her mouth, she struggled and kicked but he was too powerful, slowly and expertly with the fingers of a surgeon he cut out her tongue taking the time to carefully to wrap it in a plastic bag. He ignored her as she lay on the floor in a pool of her own blood, her eyes stared and her pupils followed him round the room, after tying her ankles and hands together he took the blade and slashed her clothes like ribbons, when she was naked he slowly slit her open like a piece of meat he left her lying on the floor letting her bleed to death. He snapped some photos with his phone and sent them to Po's mother and after cleaning himself up left her apartment and melted into the crowd of press that lined the avenue.

Madame Po was delighted with the tongue that the Hawk had delivered, at last her son's name was avenged. After seeing the gruesome photos he deleted them, she handed him an envelope with a nice bonus and they enjoyed tea together before he left.

Tyrese lost it completely, he had just ordered room service and was kneeling on the bed when the news flash appeared. 'Savage killing in serviced apartment' it was like watching a dream, Chloe had been brutally murdered they had cut out her tongue gutted her body like a fish. The woman that he had loved was dead. He had called the police and they had taken him to the scene, he had vomited when he saw the state of her body and collapsed in shock.

The police suspected that she had been murdered not by a psychopath, but by a hit man, they had found out through intelligence that she was wanted in Cambodia for slitting the throat and dismembering her husband. The words rung in Tyrese's head but didn't make any sense, how was it possible that he had shared his bed with a murderess.

Pippa was deadly depressed in her clinic, the operations had been painful and she looked like a mummy she had seen on TV that Chloe had been brutally murdered, 'You can't sue a dead girl,' she thought sulking.

His fans were angels, genuinely feeling sorry for him, he had lost his career and now this.

He had enough salt in the wound she thought, the guy had no one in the world to turn to.

Tyrese was sedated and attended Chloe's funeral looking like a zombie. Her coffin was covered in orchids his sobs echoed throughout the cemetery, the press clicked their cameras all through the ceremony and the photos of Tyrese's face awash with tears hit the front pages with headlines using the title of his last single, 'That's What Love Can Do.' It created a swing of sympathy towards him, the effect the photos had on the general public were tremendous and his album started selling at a record pace.

CHAPTER 11

Marisa

Marisa called out of the blue to tell him that she understood, she promised to visit him in London when she was next there and hung up without as much as a goodbye. She hadn't even mentioned where she was, she had been keeping a low profile but she had been photographed looking glamorous with a wealthy business Tycoon in the tabloids and had done a two minute cameo walk on in a television sitcom. Apart from those two public appearances she seemed to have vanished, she was probably hiding on some millionaire playboy's yacht Tyrese imagined.

The truth was that she was staying at the Count's villa in Tuscany. She was eight months pregnant and couldn't wait to get rid of the beastly lump, she hated the effect that the pregnancy was having on her both physically and emotionally and the moment the child was born she was going to dump it on Yoji's parents. She was sure that they would be delighted to have a piece of their son, she hoped that the beastly thing looked like him but she was worried that it would be black it could have been Tyrese's or even Rogillio's.

The old Count had been a darling to her, Count Vidal had spent a lot of time with her at the villa pampering and spoiling her like mad. When her waters broke he joined her in the delivery room and held her hand while she cursed and pushed trying to rid her body from this invader.

The infant screamed and the nurse held him up, thank God she thought it was Yoji's, he had Oriental features and later he would grow up to follow in his father's footsteps as a champion kick boxer, the only features he inherited from his mother were her bright blue eyes and golden hair. He would be an unusual young man the count exclaimed. Marisa insisted they give her a tummy tuck immediately after the child was born as she wanted to get her figure back instantly.

Marisa begged the Count to be a darling and employ a Japanese nanny, as soon as the child was ready to travel she wanted to send him to Tokyo to Yoji's parents. One hour after the birth she was sitting in bed having her hair done, she was wearing a huge Sapphire choker that the Count had given her as a gift. Vidal had also employed a personal trainer so she could get her figure back, the trainer was gorgeous, Italian and macho as could be she was looking forward to her work-outs. Marisa called Yoji's mother, she was elated to be a grandmother she agreed that she would fly to Milan to collect the child herself, the Count's office would arrange whatever paperwork was necessary. The starlet hoped that she would come and collect him quickly, the little brat made such a noise she would be glad to see the back of him. Vidal was a sweetie she thought, he had taken care of her for almost seven months and another plot came into her mind, he was a sweetie, impotent and seventy, if she married him she would get a title and surely in a year or so he might drop down dead. He was absolutely loaded, she put some blusher on her breasts and put a coat of thick lip gloss on her lips she wanted to seduce her Count into proposing marriage and hoped that he would be stupid enough to accept.

The shock of Chloe's death put another perspective on Tyrese's predicament, he didn't care about the music business he had made enough to start a small business he had never liked the fact that as a personality you had no privacy.

Mercedes had been trying to reach a settlement out of court with the record company and he was pleased with her, she was older than him but he felt drawn to her pale blonde looks.

She was smart, had won every case she had handled, she lived in a smart town house in Knightsbridge. Tyrese was lazing in his hotel room unshaven and wearing sweatpants when she called, Tyrese thought that something must have gone wrong that she had called him so late, it was eleven o clock and she told him to drop everything and gave him the address of her house she told him to jump in a taxi and get there quickly.

Within a half an hour he was ringing her bell, the paparazzi had followed his taxi and were grouping round him in the street sticking microphones in his face and asking the rudest questions about Chloe. He prayed that soon they would turn their attention to someone else, this was one part of the business that he would not miss it was like living in a goldfish bowl.

Mercedes answered the door wearing a pretty dress and a great big smile on her face. She invited him into the lounge, there were two glasses and an ice bucket with a bottle of champagne propped in it, she said before they had a celebration drink she needed a signature, she had just come from his record company. They were going to drop the lawsuit against him and they had reconsidered, they would release his album in six months, the retainer that he had received would be returned and he would receive a higher amount of royalties when the album was launched, Mercedes had done a wonderful job. They sat and chatted and he enjoyed watching her relax, normally she was dressed in severe tailored suits and without her glasses she looked rather sweet as he was leaving he gave her a spontaneous kiss on the cheek to his surprise she grabbed him close to her and kissed him passionately on the lips. Now that he had ceased being her client she thought that she could show him her feelings. Tyrese ended up staying the night, they made love slowly and intensely in front of her log fire he was lonely and now at a time in his life when he needed someone.

Mercedes filled the gap. Sooner or later he would have to pick up the pieces and get on with his life, he couldn't laze around hotel rooms for the rest of his life.

He saw Mercedes whenever she was free, being a high flying lawyer with international clients she travelled frequently, she had gone to Brussels for a court case. Tyrese had fallen asleep in his hotel suite when he woke with a start. Room service were banging his door, he was furious that they had made a mistake and opened the door to give them a piece of his mind. In the doorway looking absolutely stunning stood Marisa, fully made-up wearing an ankle length white fur coat, her neck ablaze with diamonds, she screamed, 'Surprise! Surprise!' Tyrese held his breath, this woman was the kiss of death, every time he saw her something disastrous happened.

He had read in the papers that she had married and snared a seventy-one year old Count, the same Count that had owned the fabulous villa in Tuscany. He joked that he should address her as Countessa, she barged into his room and threw off her fur, under the coat she was completely naked except for her high heeled silver shoes, diamond choker and emerald earrings.

Tyrese made love to her up against the door, for a moment time had stood still and they were still in the villa after a torrid sex session he lay in bed and watched her as she poured drinks.

Amazing he said, 'I've just fucked a Countess, you're my first aristocrat,'

'I hope you enjoyed it as much as I did,' she snapped. She explained that she was in London shopping, she had purposely booked the same hotel as him and she had a room along the corridor. The Count had taken her to Scotland, he had gone hunting, it was the pheasant season but she was too bored for words, she had been stuck all day with women who looked like horses, it was cold and draughty in the castle and she hated it so Vidal let her go to London to have a spending spree.

She sat down on the bed and drank the vodka martini in one go, she had four homes, a yacht and a private jet at her disposal an she was bored, she wanted to get back into movies at least then she would be traveling.

She was frank and open with Tyrese, she told him about her secret baby and he was horrified that she had dumped the kid, she hadn't an ounce of maternal instinct in her veins.

She admitted marrying the Count for money and said that she had had a torrid affair with her fitness trainer, the Count was impotent. She was waiting for him to die.

Her bright blue eyes misted with tears when he mentioned Yoji, 'He was the one for me,' she spoke, her voice trembling. The problem with Marisa was that she was such an acclaimed actress one never knew if her tears were real or for effect.

They spent the night together and she slept with her jewels on Tyrese looked disgusted.

'People are dying of starvation and you are sleeping with a half million dollars on your neck.'

'I am starving too,' she moaned, explaining that since she had that beastly child she had been on a starvation diet. In the morning she gave him the blow job of his dreams then disappeared to her suite leaving a cloud of perfume lingering in the hall.

No one could do it better he thought, Marisa made the perfect Contessa, the perfect showbiz Hollywood princess.

She visited him every night for three days and then disappeared without as much as a goodbye. That was Marisa, she had used him for company and a bit of black cock, just like she used everyone he hoped that the Count had plenty of money, at the rate she was spending it by the time he was dead there would be nothing left.

Marisa had no friends, women didn't like her for obvious reasons and to men she was a sex object.

Mercedes thought that something was wrong when she arrived back, he had gone to sleep complaining of a headache. He didn't want to make love, the truth was Marisa had burned him out, their sexual three day marathon had all but exhausted him and he felt guilty, Mercedes was so sweet, Marisa was just a bitch.

Pippa admired her tight butt, pert tits and wrinkle free face, she looked ten years younger.

The suffering had been worth it, they had inserted a steel plate in her nose and warned her that if she didn't kick the habit she would die. She was celebrating her new gorgeous body with a special treat, she was having a party and she had rented two escorts, they were 500 dollars apiece, expensive she mused hoping that they would be worth it. The doorbell rang and she let the two immaculately dressed muscle men in. They looked like something out of GQ magazine, a bit too well-groomed she thought, she preferred the rougher types, rougher like Tyrese.

The boys stayed the night, they fucked her in the Jacuzzi, on the sun deck and in bed, they earned every cent of the five hundred dollar fee, she would book them again.

Three nights later Pippa had gone with a new artist and her entourage to a club, she ran into the two boys there, they had obviously been working and were now spending their hard earned cash out on the town. They introduced her to one of their colleagues a stunning South American girl named Gina Sanchez, She was a stunner and charged the men she slept with 1000 dollars an evening, pity she was a high class hooker Pippa thought, she would have looked great in a video. The dazzling beauty oozed with sexuality half the men in the room had hard-ons already, she joked all of the men at her table wanted to mount her.

Pippa was high on a mixture of cocaine and Tequila, she went to the ladies room with Gina and as they fixed their make-up a really good idea came to her mind. She gave Gina her card and asked her to come to her office the following day as she had a job for her. Gina looked embarrassed explaining that she didn't do the lesbian thing, Pippa roared with laughter and told her that wasn't for her it was something else and something that would be well paid. The next day Gina walked into her office one hour late, Pippa made her an offer, she wanted her services for two whole weeks, she wanted her to go to New York and spy on Tyrese. She had heard that he was having an affair with a lawyer and she wanted Gina to use her sex appeal to wreck their relationship, she was to try and cast her spell on him and make him fall in love with her, she also was instructed to find out what had happened with his record contract. Pippa used her influence to arrange that Gina would be in the suite adjoining Tyrese's she was convinced that he would go for this Gina she was a knockout, she offered Gina a reasonable amount of money and added that perhaps she could make a single one day

The boys had told her that Gina dreamed of being a singer, she had no intention of offering a contract but wanted to make sure that she would do her best.

Tyrese had been in the reception when she had arrived, she arrived to check in wearing a floral georgette sheath that clung to her breasts, her golden skin was a smooth as Chloe's she glided through the reception with a flower behind one ear, every man in the room looked at her. She possessed that same animal sexuality that Marisa had. He jumped in the lift with her and the porter hoping to see which floor she was on, he couldn't believe it she was on the same floor as him, and better still in the suite next door. She must be an actress he thought, when the porter had put her luggage in her room she knocked on his door, he was surprised she told him that she was unsure of how to use the air-conditioning and she asked him if he could show her as reception was engaged, she told him that she was in New York for shopping.

She was alone and that she didn't know the city she asked if he could show her directions on the map his hands were trembling, he couldn't take his eyes of her breasts she was like a mixture of all the women he had adored rolled into one steaming Latino dream girl.

He presumed that she must have wealthy parents if she could afford a suite here he put his charm in full throttle and asked her if she would like to join him for dinner in the evening.

Gina hadn't imagined that it would have been so easy. Tyrese went back to his room feeling like he had won the lottery she hadn't even recognized him. Gina sent a text to Pippa saying contact had already been made. Man she is a fast mover Pippa thought, she must have just arrived in the hotel.

They ate a sumptuous dinner in the rooftop restaurant with the lights of the city shimmering beneath them, Gina wore a pomegranate coloured dress and red lips, sitting across from her was driving Tyrese wild, she was so hot he had had an erection all through dinner, he was glad that Mercedes was in Vienna for three days.

This creature Gina was there for two weeks his heart raced. The way she ate was erotic everything about her oozed sex, the dress was so slinky when she stood up to go to the toilet he noticed that she was naked underneath the flimsy fabric. Her eyes sparkled in the candlelight she was like a Latin version of Marisa.

After dinner they went to the club in the hotel and danced he could feel she was naked under the silk dress, for the first time since Chloe he felt a rumbling in his stomach, either the lobster was off or he was falling in lust again.

Just after midnight they retired to their rooms, in the lift she asked him innocently what kind of business he was in. He was glad she didn't recognize him he hated women falling all over him for his fame, he sheepishly admitted that he was a singer. Pretending not to know him she said that she only listened to classical music but found it interesting that he was musical she asked if she could hear his work and he invited her for a nightcap in his suite she looked so innocent and was reluctant he assured her that he would be the perfect gentleman and she agreed. In his room she stood

223

in front of the lamp sipping her drink knowing full well that he would be excited by the fact that she was naked under her dress. She listened to his album and looked unimpressed she said that she liked the ballads a lot and thanked him for dinner she left him with a raging hard on and he couldn't sleep knowing that she was right next door.

Gina was enjoying her vacation all expenses paid by Pippa. Of course she would tease him for one more night then move in for the kill, after she had fucked his brains out she knew that he would fall under her spell, men always did she thought their brains were in their dicks.

She did like his music she had danced to some of his songs when she had been a lap dancer, he looked quite cute in reality and she wondered why Pippa was so interested in him, perhaps she was trying to poach him, she had to make sure she destroyed his relationship he hadn't mentioned a relationship. Some yuppie Lawyer would be a walkover for her, once men had tried Gina they always got hooked she would have him eating out her hand in forty-eight hours.

Pippa was pleased with Gina's progress she didn't believe in wasting time, she had already successfully snared Tyrese. Pippa took a slug of the bourbon out of the open bottle that graced her desk, she felt a sudden pang of depression, since the day that she had lost Tyrese her sumptuous apartment had seemed so empty, she was growing impatient and hyper, Dino her pusher had been supposed to deliver her some coke, he was unusually late and hoped that he had not been picked up by the police.

Her head was filled with memories from the past, a kaleidoscope of images of her and Tyrese sprang to her mind, his smile, the sight of him as he slept spreadeagled on her bed naked skin glowing in the morning light, she slugged another gulp of bourbon, she asked herself what the motivation was to destroy his music career. She had been keen for him to succeed initially she remembered that she had been bored when he had thrown himself into the football career, she had argued with him bitterly to give up kicking a ball about a field and concentrate on music. He was always training going to bed early, too boring for words, one night she had had a call from a friend who was a police officer. Tyrese had been in the Jacuzzi when Damion had called to warn her that the following day at the game they were going to do random drug tests on the team. The moment that her informer had hung up she called her dealer, he had promptly delivered her a tasteless illegal performance enhancing drug. The following morning she had woke early and prepared her lover's breakfast before he went to the game. Her hand had trembled as she spiked his orange juice with a large measure of the substance. She had been bitterly disappointed when that evening Tyrese had returned grinning triumphantly, he had scored two goals and he mentioned that they had done random drug testing on a two thirds of the team, he had been in the category that had not been tested so he had no idea that she had laced his drink with enough performance enhancing crap to have him suspended. He had taken her for a slap-up celebration dinner at Gerald's top French restaurant, she had been positively grim the whole evening and had slipped to the toilet seven times during the course of the meal to do coke.

Pippa had eventually managed to wreck his football career, she had destroyed his proposed marriage to Chloe. Revenge was her goal and her obsession to shatter his relationship with Mercedes and ruin his new recording deal was a priority that was preoccupying her mind.

Loneliness was a driving force that encouraged her to destroy the one person on the planet that she deeply loved. She was used to getting everything that she wanted and wasn't prepared to accept being dumped by a two bit stripper.

She was drunk and looked out at the stars on her balcony she blamed God for making her fall in love with Tyrese. Love was the thing that we craved, love was the emotion that either made us feel euphoric or melancholic, love was the thing that had the power to make us feel good or bad, happy or sad. 'Fuck Love!' she screamed throwing a crystal glass over the edge of the railing LOVE was a four letter word, a sickness, a deficiency an emotion that destroyed us.

Between the sheets of his hotel bed Tyrese was making love to Gina, she was sensational and as she sat on his erect penis he watched her voluptuous breasts jingle jangle in the morning light he wondered where this fantasy would lead, exploding in orgasm he rolled over on top of her and proceeded to make love again doing it his way. He had only known her for two days but was fascinated by her. As he pumped expertly away driving her to ecstasy, he didn't hear Mercedes as she put her keycard in the door. She had arrived a day early from Vienna and had wanted to surprise her lover. Mercedes stood motionless in the doorway watching as his tight buns pumped away at the woman whose long golden legs were wrapped round his waist. The extremely beautiful girl screamed a carnal cry of delight exactly at the same time as Mercedes hurtled the gift that she had brought for Tyrese. The Viennese Porcelain antique vase hit the writhing bodies and smashed inside the wrapping paper as it hit Tyrese's buttocks. Mercedes ran so fast out of the room that Tyrese only saw the pained look on her face for a second. Gina smiled and covered her naked body with a sheet mission accomplished she thought as she watched Tyrese's naked body chase after the pale pasty, frumpy blonde that had made a hasty exit.

As Mercedes dived in the lift someone stepped out and looked disapprovingly at Tyrese's naked body, he returned to his room to find Gina sitting at the dressing table triumphantly applying a coat of glossy lip gloss. While Tyrese tried Mercedes' mobile Gina quietly dressed and left his apartment, mission accomplished she thought, no need to linger she thought she had all the information that Pippa wanted and had successfully destroyed his relationship with Mercedes. She had never thought that would have been so easy, she was being paid handsomely and the sex with Tyrese had been heavenly. After packing she called the airport but to her dismay she learned that all the flights were full, it looked like she would have to endure another day in this dreadful city. She called Pippa, she was so pleased with the news, she told Pippa that she would be flying in and she asked her to pick her up at the airport and reminded her to transfer her money immediately. The balance, Pippa promised would be transferred by telephone within the hour. She decided to go shopping to Greenwich Village and treat herself to a new dress she would also check her bank balance to make sure that Pippa had paid the amount as promised.

She was just leaving the hotel when he rushed up and grabbed her from behind. Gina was startled she thought it first that someone was going to steal her bag, she turned and stopped in her tracks Tyrese had grabbed her, the look in his eyes was that of a hunted animal, for a moment she thought that he was going to strike her however he grabbed her, lifted her in the air and kissed her for so long that she couldn't breathe.

Pippa arrived at the airport and had to drive round and round, Gina's flight was a half hour late and eventually she parked the car and waited at the arrival hall. All the passengers from New York had disembarked but Gina wasn't on the flight. Pippa was furious she had been waiting for ages she dialed Gina's mobile but it was dead.

Gina was completely naked except for the expensive high heeled boots that Tyrese had bought her, she was leaning over the balcony of their penthouse suite, holding the railing she screamed as Tyrese brought her to a supreme orgasm, the lights of Manhattan twinkled and the cool night air blew her hair. Tyrese made love to her again in the moonlight and they held each other in a strong embrace. Tyrese was not in love with Gina but she did do things to him that almost no other woman had done, he wanted her, their relationship was based on lust not love she craved sex and loved anal sex as much as he did.

Love and lust the two emotions that should never be confused, in reality lust has nothing to do with love. Tyrese had asked her to come with him to Europe to promote his album, Gina agreed, there were people that she was avoiding so where better to hide than in Europe.

Two days later as Tyrese and Gina left the hotel the paparazzi caught them and snapped avidly away, both Mercedes and Pippa were shocked when they opened their morning newspapers and were confronted on the third page with a photo of Tyrese and Gina holding on to each other in a passionate clinch.

Mercedes was not accustomed to losing, she was devastated, the image of Tyrese's naked buttocks bumping and grinding into Gina was stuck in her mind, she stayed off work for three days pretending to have flu, on the fourth day she resigned from her job and after packing the bare essentials she flew to Hawaii and went to see her old school friend Clifton Taylor.

He had his own office their and had offered her work a thousand times, he was delighted and surprised when she told him that she was coming to live in Oahu. He admired her talent as a lawyer, her reputation was flawless, also he was in love with her and had been since their schooldays the night he had lost his virginity to her in the back of a borrowed Cadillac was the night of his life and he had promised himself as an adolescent that one day he would have Mercedes. He hoped that she would warm to him and wanted to give her all the financial, emotional and spiritual support that she needed. He knew that she had been having an affair with the pop singer and he had seen yesterday's papers, reporting that the pop singer was running off to Europe with a South American beauty.

What better a time to seduce Mercedes than when she was on the rebound.

'Bitch, Fucking Whore.' Pippa screamed throwing a Chinese Ming vase across the room, she couldn't believe that Tyrese had gone to Europe with Gina, she had sent Gina to ruin his relationship with Mercedes and now they were having an affair and she had already transferred the money to the bitch's account. In a fit of temper she fired her secretary then called her dealer for some Quaaludes, she needed something to help her chill out. She also called the escort bureau and asked them to send a guy, any guy as long as he had muscle and a cock she didn't care what nationality she screamed at the girl on the other end of the phone.

Depressed she had an idea, she asked the girl to send Sven and three others she wanted to have an orgy. She wore a leather basque, a thong and a spiked dog collar.

Pippa was as high as a kite, she smeared on a slash of plum lipstick and tried to conceal the dark rings under her eyes with powder. The constant drug abuse was showing.

The Quaaludes and the escorts arrived simultaneously and Pippa over indulged in drugs and flesh after she had taken the pills she ordered all four men to fuck her one after the other, she hated men they were only good for her pleasure she mused as she humiliated the four handsome studs that were catering to her every whim. After two hours she went into the Jacuzzi with the men, there was one she liked, he was South American extremely handsome with a dashing smile she decided to keep him for the night and send the other three home.

Manuel masked his disappointment as his colleagues left the building he was not looking forward to spending the night, he was tired out already and wanted to get home to his lover, a blonde haired blue eyed surfer.

Fortunately Pippa fell asleep the combination of drugs and alcohol left her snoring. In the morning she handcuffed the Latin god to the bedposts and rode him like a horse. After he showered she threw 3000 dollars at him Manuel grabbed the money and walked out, he hated this job and wanted to go back to stripping he had worked at gay revues before and preferred it to sleeping with middle-aged bitches.

Pippa drank a bottle of vodka straight and swallowed a handful of pills, her maid found her on the bathroom floor, at first she had thought that she was dead but seeing that she was alive called paramedics and went with her to the emergency department of the hospital.

The emergency unit was busy with car crash victims, shootings and people that had been mugged.

The doctors looked disapprovingly at Pippa and treated her roughly as they forced the thick tubes down her throat and nose to pump her stomach. They knew who she was and found it frustrating that such a wealthy powerful woman as her would be so stupid as to overdose.

Pippa kicked and struggled as the nurses pumped her stomach, as soon as they had finished she sat up and screamed that she was going to slash her wrists next time. Her aggression towards the nurses and staff resulted in her being sedated and kept in a room for three days. It was a long three days for Pippa with no illegal drugs, no alcohol and no sex.

One of the hospital staff must have called the press, there were paparazzi positioned outside the building, she was furious when she read the newspapers they claimed that she had tried to commit suicide and that her body had been filled with sperm, when she left the hospital in a wheelchair sporting dark glasses the press were waiting like vultures.

Manuel the hooker had made quite a lot after reading in the evening papers that she had overdosed, he sold his story the headlines read 'Seventeen year old boy joins in wild orgy at Pippa Curtis's penthouse.'

The directors at head office suggested that she went on holiday, she had been overworked and they wanted peace to try and get the company back in shape. Recently Pippa had been impossible to work and with almost fifty percent of their artists were unhappy and twenty-five percent of her artists had signed up with other labels.

The directors booked a holiday for her in the Maldives, it was a paradise, far away from all the problems of the company.

Pippa only agreed to go if she could take Sven with her, there was no way she was going to go lie on a beach by herself. She wanted Sven for amusement, the directors knew he was an escort but agreed that she needed company they briefed Sven before they left to watch her and not let her do drugs and to regularly report to them how she was.

Tyrese's singles had been selling well in Europe and when Gina and him arrived at Heathrow airport the press were there waiting, there was little happening in London and they seemed to love the photographic good-looking couple, the fact that Tyrese had had bad press made the pair even more interesting.

Gina tagged along to all the promotion and chat shows where Tyrese charmed the interviewers with his ghetto wit. Whenever possible the young couple stole some free hours to sightsee, shop and make love.

They enjoyed London then moved on to Paris for three days, the paparazzi didn't seem interested which was relief they enjoyed a nice meal at the trendy Buddha bar, went to a great night club called Cabaret and shopped with a vengeance.

Paris was a massive, elegant city and the new lovers fell under its magical spell, eating in sidewalk cafes and drinking in the grandness of the architecture. Gina loved Europe it was her first visit, every country had its own personality and everywhere seemed so different they reluctantly moved on from Paris for quick visits to Munich, Brussels and Amsterdam.

Every city had its own character and Amsterdam was charming, the couple sailed down the narrow canals on a sightseeing voyage. The city was small and intimate there didn't seem to be any kind of quality nightclubs, the Dutch seemed to prefer simplicity and any show of wealth was regarded as vulgar. They did however manage to steal some hours between commitments to visit the Rijks Museum and admire the Rembrandt's. Holland was really laid back, there were drug cafes on almost every corner of the streets. The Netherlanders tolerance to drugs and sex surprised Gina, the city had its own red light area where gorgeous girls sat in their underwear in the windows, when the women had customers they simply closed the curtains. The sex workers paid tax and were treated with respect, sexually the Netherlanders were light years ahead of the English who seemed basically to be living in the dark ages when it came to all things carnal. Perhaps it was better to be liberated like the Dutch, in the UK the sex crimes, abduction, rape and assault were on the increase.

The downside of Holland was that the city was flooded with tourists who flocked here to enjoy the freedom of the drug culture, it seemed that half the population were stoned. Gina and Tyrese laughed as they studied the menu in a coffee shop. Colombian Hash and weed cultured in the Golden Triangle were favourites, Gina tried the space cake whilst Tyrese opted for an unusual joint. The Dutch recognized him but ignored him, they were not a race to be impressed by celebrity and their attitude left both Gina and him free to walk hand and hand through the city.

Their trip ended in Italy, Rome was a splendid place where they enjoyed an overdose of culture. America was going to seem bland in comparison to Europe for sure Gina groaned.

Florence was amazing and the couple spent three free days there at the end of their trip.

Tyrese called Pavel from their hotel, he was in Tuscany and demanded that they come for a few days to chill out, he was having a party and he would not take no for an answer.

Pavel had met a dancer from the Ballet, Tyrese was glad to see him look so jovial he had taken Chloe's death so badly. On the night after they arrived Pavel and his new lover, Sergio hosted a party, half of cultured Paris turned up, there was an array of dancers, opera singers, art dealers, sculptures, writers and poets.

Tyrese was the only pop star and he was surprised when very very late Marisa made a grand entrance accompanied by a fitness trainer, the Count was apparently in Monaco at their apartments. Tyrese was shocked at the transformation in Marisa, her flawless beauty had turned into a manufactured hardness, she drank too much and talked too loud and Tyrese was sure that she was coked out of her skull, her pupils were so dilated that she possessed a sinister expression and she didn't blink all night.

Ignoring Gina the stoned screen goddess flirted openly with Tyrese, overdressed in a haute couture creation and dripping with the most vulgar jewelry imaginable, most of the guests were laughing at her. Since her movie career had all but disappeared down the drain she had taken to drink and drugs and her faded beauty seemed tarnished.

Gina hated her immediately she sensed that Tyrese had had something with her and regarded her as a major threat. Tyrese felt sorry for the Count he must have regretted the moment that he had married this woman she was the kiss of death.

Gina was not pleased that Tyrese had accepted Marisa's offer to drive back to Milan with her, she wanted both him and this Gina to come to Milan to attend the premier of her latest film, she had only a supporting role but wanted to cause a stir by turning up with Tyrese.

His record was selling well in Italy and it would be good PR to have him there, the Count would be attending so she would be on her best behavior thought Tyrese as he accepted.

Gina argued with him in their room, she wanted to go back to London she had a strange sixth sense premonition that this faded starlet was nothing but trouble.

Tyrese promised to buy her the most expensive designer dress that he could find, this changed Gina's attitude and her depression turned to glee as she imagined herself being photographed on the red carpet. Gina wasn't used to media attention and she loved it, seeing her face in the paper on Tyrese's arm gave her a new status, not bad for a common whore from the back streets of Rio.

The journey to Milan had been unbearable, Marisa had drunk a whole bottle of gin on the way, she hurtled insults at her lover and driver and they had to stop the car three times as she was sick.

Gina tried to persuade Tyrese that they would stay at a hotel Marisa wanted them to stay at her penthouse apartment which was a palatial apartment in one of the city's oldest and most elegant buildings. The apartment was like a palazzo in the clouds, she had footmen, a butler and an army of maids and kitchen staff. It was like stepping back into a bygone era where she was queen of her own empire. Priceless paintings lined the walls of the penthouse and Gina wondered what it must be like living in a place like this, it was almost like living in a museum. In an environment like that Marisa's tendency to overdress was acceptable, Marisa dressed for dinner every night like a Hollywood star from a bygone age. Most of her staff were under thirty and extremely handsome she couldn't imagine why the Count allowed her to employ such men it was obvious that she had created a male harem, the looks they drew her made it obvious that she had enjoyed sexual encounters with them.

It seemed that Marisa lived in her own private world, dressed to the nines and drugged up to the eyeballs she was a shadow of the woman that she used to be.

The night of the premiere arrived, Marisa's make-up artist and hairdresser arrived four hours before they were due to leave, after they had preened Marisa to perfection they offered to make-up Gina. It was the first time that she had been professionally made-up and she looked superb. Marisa was not so pleased, she scowled as she looked at Gina thinking that she looked too beautiful. Gina wore the sexy long red dress that Tyrese had bought her in Paris, it was simple and she outshone Marisa in her overdone couture gown.

The limo arrived and when they reached the venue, Marisa grabbed Tyrese's arm and told Gina to walk in with the Count. The press seemed more interested in the stunning South American beauty in the slinky red dress than the coked up brash and showy actress, the next morning there would be more press coverage of Gina than Marisa.

The film was bad and Marisa's role was mediocre Tyrese could hardly believe that she was the same woman who had stirred his emotions on screen, her amateur performance was embarrassing and the revues were dreadful.

'Bastards!' she screamed throwing her shoe at a porcelain family heirloom as she read the revue. The Count was becoming tired of her outrageous spending and enormous ego.

What he had once found absolutely captivating he now found exhausting. Tyrese wished that he had stayed in Florence it had been a nightmare trip and Gina was looking upset. Marisa had been totally hostile towards her, the Count was at his wit's end and he was going back to Monaco. Marisa watched his car as it drove off towards the gates of the courtyard.

Tyrese wanted to speak to Marisa seriously, he gave Gina a wad of cash and asked her to go shopping for two hours as he wanted to have a serious talk with Marisa, he promised to meet her at a cafe in the centre near the cathedral. Gina was reluctant to leave him with her, she was a man-eater, however the large handful of money was tempting and she wanted to buy herself something special to wear from one of the hundreds of designer stores that were scattered all over the city.

She had just bought a lovely shirt for Tyrese and was coming out of the store, the car screeched to a halt and parked on the pavement Gina dropped the bag as the three men forced her into the back seat.

Gina screamed and kicked and scratched as the three men held her down, she bit one on the ear and he screamed in pain, the car with darkened windows sped towards the country and they forced a bag over her head. At first she thought that they were trying to kill her but then she realized that they were just preventing her from knowing where she was going.

She was guided into an old barn and as they ripped the bag off her head Gina trembled with fear, sitting in an armchair immaculately groomed was the most ruthless man in South America, the sound of his voice chilled her she had never expected to see him again. She hadn't seen him since the night she escaped from his hacienda in the back of a car along with a consignment of cocaine.

She had met Julio at the club where she lap danced he had tipped her handsomely when she table danced for him in a private room. That night when she had left the nightclub his bodyguards had waited for her, within seconds they had overpowered her and thrown her in the back of a limo, they had taken her to Julio's hacienda, a fortress in the middle of nowhere. Julio had kept her there as his sex slave for three months, when she objected he would beat her.

Her existence there was a nightmare sometimes when he was drunk he would assault her and after he had taken his pleasure he would invite his bodyguards to have her. One after the other the five guards would savagely fuck her whilst Julio watched. She planned her escape carefully and in the end escaped with a large bag of cocaine stuffed in a rucksack.

Julio's men had searched for her but she had dyed her hair and managed to keep a low profile. Julio had been in Rome and the moment that he had seen her photo in the paper he had flown to Milan especially to see her. For a moment she thought that he was going to kill her, however he walked up to her and drew his finger across her lips. His eyes were black as coal and he showed no emotion as he took out a gun and inserted it in her mouth. Gina closed her eyes and wished that he would pull the trigger she was shaking from top to bottom and he was laughing, eventually he removed the magnum from her mouth and she slumped to the ground, he told her to shut up and listen after promising her that he would never hurt her. He asked her questions about Marisa, at first she didn't know where the conversation was leading but she soon got the drift.

Marisa was rich, extremely rich she was always dripping in millions of dollars of jewels he had read in the papers that she spent every weekend in the country at the Count's summer house, he wanted to know everything about the house, which doors had alarms, which were locked, he wanted her to draw a map. They were going to kidnap Marisa the following weekend and hold her for ransom.

He wanted both her and Tyrese to stay at the villa and when it was quiet they wanted her to call them on the mobile and they would move in. Julio was pleased to hear that no one bothered to put the alarm or lock doors it would be easy after, she had signaled them they would move in through the French windows tie her and Tyrese up and race off with Marisa.

Gina had no option but to go along with their proposal they would have a twenty-four hour watch on her and if she double-crossed them then they would kill her. If everything ran to plan she would be free and her debt to Julio would be over.

The men dropped her in Milan near the Via Spiga, she trembled as she made her way to meet Tyrese he was waiting at the cafe and looked surprised that she had no bags with her.

She said that she had been just looking and that she would prefer to come back along with him. Tyrese was so busy ranting on about Marisa that he didn't notice the man in the dark suit at the next table. The car arrived and they headed for the Count's villa, Tyrese wondered why she was so quiet, perhaps she was tired.

The following weekend they were all in the drawing room drinking Martinis, Marisa dressed to the nines in a negligee with lilac marabou trimming and huge diamond and emerald earrings was reading a fashion magazine, Tyrese was sitting on a chaise lounge writing down lyrics for a song, Gina, at his feet was sitting cross-legged on the floor doing her yoga exercises.

The van sped up the drive and along the gardens at the side of the house, everyone was startled as the eight masked man with handguns spilled into the room through the open French windows.

Two of the large men held Tyrese while another tied his hands and feet together.

Marisa screamed a piercing scream as a huge brute of a man scooped her up and whisked her towards the car, another man tied Gina to a chair, a maid and the butler came rushing into the room, one of the masked men fired a shot hitting the servant in the leg.

It all happened within seconds, they were gone as quickly as they had entered. Tyrese's papers were scattered on the floor, pieces of furniture were overturned and the whole incident seemed like a scene from one of Marisa's films. The shocked maid cradled the butler in her arms, he had collapsed in shock when they hit his leg, blood spilled over the priceless Aubusson rug.

One of the staff had seen the men put Marisa in the black armored vehicle and had hit a panic button, the alarm system was rigged up to the police office ten miles away.

The police arrived quickly and seemed alarmed, nothing like this had ever happened in these parts. Marisa's kidnapping had been front page news. Tyrese had been frustrated that he had not been able to do anything, he was strong but they had completely taken him by surprise. Since the incident Gina had been very subdued, she spent most of her time in bed and sulked around refusing to make conversation with anyone. The Count was on his way back from Monaco and a whole team of experts had taken up in the formal dining room. Computers and telephones lined the Regency dining table and everyone in the house had been interviewed. The tension was gripping, Julio made no attempt to contact the Count for two days, he wanted them to suffer, he knew that there would be an army of special police there monitoring calls, on the third morning he sent an email demanding six million dollars for the return of Marisa.

In an isolated farmhouse on a vineyard outside Sienna Marisa was making her captors' lives hell. Julio himself had worn a mask and went to her room, he wanted to see this great beauty in the flesh. He was mesmerized by her sensuality, hair tousled and make-up smudged she looked every inch the screen goddess, her pale pink breasts peeped through the ripped silk of her negligee, as he approached her for a closer look she cursed him and spat at him. Julio laughed at her spirit and silenced her by slapping her hard on the face, she was tied to the bed and she struggled as he slowly ran his fingers across the flimsy fabric of her dressing gown, with one swift movement he ripped the dress from top to bottom the fabric fell away and exposed her naked body.

Marisa imagined that she would be raped, instead Julio sat across from her and watched her struggle enjoying the fear in her eyes, she was one of the most beautiful creatures he had ever seen he could understand why the old balding Count would pay so much for this girl she was special.

After a day Marisa learned that opposing her captors was getting her nowhere, she tried another technique the head man was male and like all other males he found her attractive she would use her sex appeal to trap him then perhaps she could escape, she would even fuck him she thought if it would help, he was after all a mere man.

Marisa managed to twist him round her finger, the handcuffs and ropes on her ankles were released and at every opportunity she had she flaunted herself at him. It was having an effect, she could see how he stared at her through the knitted mask, he had taken to bringing her tray of food personally every evening, she planned to make her move that night Julio had been so completely surprised when she had unzipped his pants, he exploded in orgasm minutes after she had performed fellatio on him whilst he was still holding the food tray as her dyed golden head bobbed up and down.

Marisa had developed a bond with her captors, she drove Julio wild with ecstasy as they made love, while they had rampant sex Julio's bodyguard would stand and watch Marisa enjoyed giving him a performance and would position herself so that he could get a good look.

She had been captive for five days, Julio was getting more and more irate.

The Count had point blank refused to pay the ransom, secretly he hoped that they would kill her she was well insured and was nothing but trouble. The Count was well aware of her indiscretions.

She was a slut and he had no intention of paying for her return, if he had divorced her she would claim millions, this situation was perfect hopefully they would bump her off.

One night after he had fucked her, Julio lay down and sighed, he ripped off his mask and Marisa stared at him surprised that he was so handsome, he stared at her, his dark eyes narrowing and told her that they had a problem.

Marisa was furious when he explained that the Count had made no effort to pay, she imagined that he was trying to get the cash amount together in unmarked bills. However Julio explained further that he had told them that under no circumstances would he pay even one dollar, in one telephone conversation he had actually stated that he was glad they had taken her. Marisa sobbed and her breasts heaved as huge crocodile tears ran down her cheeks removing the large diamond necklace and earrings she handed them to Julio and fell into his arms. Julio had grown very fond of this woman, she was extremely beautiful and hot as hell in bed he wondered where this situation was going. He looked like an idiot, he had kidnapped someone and was stuck with her, she had seen his face. His men thought that he had gone soft, normally he would just have shot her and sent her corpse in a body bag back to the Count, but she had touched a part in him that no one had. He held the sobbing girl in his strong arms and felt a desperate urge to protect her. He thought of the possibility of smuggling her back to his hacienda to be his mistress. He could feel droplets of her tears on his chest and the warm soft sensation of her naked body aroused him. Marisa was a great actress she was fully aware that she had a grip on this criminal bastard, she would deliver an Oscar winning performance and escape by hook or by crook. Each night she heard the men arguing with him, they were not happy and everyone was under severe pressure it couldn't go on much longer like this. It had been three weeks since they had taken her and even Julio was getting fatigued.

She missed the comforts of the villa, she had no clothes, no bath and even worse no make-up. The food was ghastly and she missed her daily intake of booze and drugs, over the past three weeks she had noticed that she had lost weight, her skin was clearer and she had dried out.

Julio had been her amusement, she had in a perverse sort of way enjoyed the sexual clinches with her captor, in bed the roles were reversed she possessed the power over him.

Day by day she had cast her magic spell over him and he was becoming submissive to her.

He had taken to sleeping with her at night his bodyguard was now stationed outside the door. Marisa imagined escaping she had no idea where she was but she dreamed of escape.

Each day to the disappointment of his men Julio spent more and more time with her. Nerves were at breaking point she knew they drank at night till midnight then Julio would come into her room and spend the night. He had joked with her that if the Count didn't pay that there were two alternatives, one kill her or two take her to his home to be his sex slave.

When the men were drinking they placed a guard in her room, that night she teased the young man, flaunted her breasts and stripped, at the sight of her lying spreadeagled on the bed, the young criminal couldn't resist he moved towards her and unzipped his pants, Marisa licked her lips provocatively and just as he pulled out his erect member she struck him hard on the head with the heavy bedside lamp, within seconds she had dressed in his sweater and pants and slowly she opened the window and jumped out, it was ground floor and she landed on the ground without hurting a limb.

It was dark she ran as fast as she could through the vine yards and down the valley, after twenty minutes she hit a road there were headlights in the distance she stood in the middle of the road waving frantically and hoping that it wasn't one of Julio's cars.

The female driver screeched to a halt and Marisa spoke in as good Italian as possible.

Ordering the lady to drive as fast as she could while the alarmed driver headed for the nearest village Marisa called the police, an hour later the guard had stirred. Julio had screamed when he retired to see the guard tied to the bed gagged with one of Marisa's stockings the open window told the story, she had escaped.

As quickly as they could they evacuated the farmhouse, their three cars were just driving out of the gates when the fleet of police cars approached from two angles, Julio and his men were caught after a ten minute gun battle that ended with two of Julio's men and one policeman being killed.

Marisa's photo was on the front pages of every newspaper the next day. She claimed that her husband was behind the kidnap plot, that he wouldn't pay the ransom and that he had been trying to claim insurance for her, she was intending taking the Count to the cleaners and was going to screw the bastard for every dollar that she could get. He would be sorry that he had ever met her and the public were on Marisa's side, fascinated as they read of her sex ordeal at the mercy of savage South American bandits.

Julio had evaded the police for years and he regarded himself as being beyond the law in his own country, now he was in prison and would face severe charges, if they returned him to his own country he would be tried for murder and drug trafficking charges, his life was ruined.

Marisa identified all the men that had been her captors in a police line-up, she refused to do it behind glass preferring to look them in the eye as she walked along the line. As she smiled and looked into Julio's eyes, he stared at her eyes filled with hate she smiled and disappeared out of the room feeling triumphant.

Marisa employed one of the world's best divorce lawyers to settle a deal for her. He worked on a straight twenty-five per cent and having him represent her almost guaranteed a huge retainer.

She would try and bankrupt the Count in a vicious public battle that the press would adore.

She would destroy the Count's aristocratic family name and drag his entire family to hell.

She was aiming for one billion dollars as a settlement.

Tyrese had gone back to London with the estranged Gina the day he saw on television news that Marisa was free and that the gang had been arrested, Gina seemed to lighten up.

Tyrese had also been shaken, he had been surprised to learn that the Count refused to pay the ransom demands there were lots of ugly articles in the gossip columns and he was delighted that Marisa had survived. As usual she was using the scandal for press coverage and public relations and had been offered to star in a film that was based on her ordeal.

Tyrese wanted to create a distance between Marisa and him she was nothing but trouble with a capitol ''T''.

Recently his relationship with Gina had been under strain, he had thrown himself into his job staying in London to record new tracks and work on his videos. Gina lazed around mostly at his hotel suite and had become very dull. Tyrese had a series of live gigs to do, he hated the live performances they seemed to drain him and his pre stage nerves were overwhelming he was king of the stage frightened performer. While he was on the road Gina stayed in London, he was drained after each show and was tired it was lonely in this business and they had grown so apart since the kidnapping that they didn't even call each other.

Tyrese had to honor his contract, he was tired and hated the circus that came with the gigs. Sometimes he would lip sync, sometimes he woke up and did not remember what city he was in.

In Birmingham he had his bodyguard bring him two groupies. The waifs gave him a blow job before he went on. After he came he felt disgusted, he was turning into a male version of Marisa he thought zipping up his pants.

He had a gig to do in Manchester, then another in London, as his sleek black limo sped to the venue to take him for a sound check he sat in the back of the luxurious car feeling sad and lonely. As they sped through the early morning traffic he didn't notice a young girl on the street, she was rushing to work, late and trying to catch a bus as she walked towards the bus stop Tyrese's limo cut the corner and splashed muddy water over the only coat she possessed, the eighteen year old girl muttered in a strange native tongue and headed for the bus, she was already a half hour late, she was an asylum seeker and worked as a cleaner, their paths would cross sooner than they thought, today she was going to the same venue as Tyrese.

Yarka was mopping the floor when the man returned from his sound check, someone shouted at her that she had no right being in the room she didn't understand too much English and thought they were asking her to clean quicker she splashed water on the floor, the PA was ushering her out when Tyrese looked at her, the girl dropped her mop and turned round and Tyrese's heart skipped a beat, the kid in the blue shapeless overall was so beautiful that it made him draw his breath in. He told the PA to stop shouting at the girl, he handed her her mop with a smile and told them to let her do her job. He studied her as she cleaned the floor, wondering what a beautiful creature like this was doing mopping a floor, she looked like a model. They called him to do another sound check before leaving he instructed his agent to find out who the girl was and what her name was and her employers' name.

He also requested that she be there tonight at the show to help backstage with drinks.

When he returned that night the pretty young girl was there in his dressing room, he was amused that she had no idea that he was the star she seemed so shy and sweet, he was disappointed that she didn't even ask him for his autograph, someone explained that she hardly spoke a word of English. When he went to perform he invited the girl to come to stand in the wings, she was soon to learn who he was.

The gig went well and the fans screamed forever, he did two encores and raced back to his dressing room to shower, as usual there were a dozen people in the room. Yarka was serving drinks to his entourage, Tyrese shot her a smile and she smiled back, the press arrived and the TV cameras, Tyrese had to do some interviews but he told his manager to find out about this girl and that he wanted her to work as part of his crew. The manager protested that she didn't speak English, Tyrese told him to get a translator, at first the manager thought that he was taking the piss, then he noticed the look in his eyes Tyrese, the star, the boss wanted this girl to be part of the team and entourage and on the pay roll tomorrow.

Yarka was delighted she had by accident landed a new job with a good salary. Her new boss was handsome, some kind of pop star, he was always rushing and surrounded by people but she liked him he was friendly and sweet.

The next evening whilst he changed for the second half of the concert he studied her as she laced his shoes, she was so so cute and she turned him on. She was a foreigner he had been told, a refugee, all alone with no family or friends and he was falling in love with her.

After the show he was taking her to dinner, he had hired a translator because he wanted to know all about her and she was surprised that he had shown a personal interest in her, she was dressed in an old grey pullover and worn jeans when they went for dinner with the translator, and somewhere between the tian of crab and the grande soufflé Tyrese found himself falling head over heels with this urchin.

She was eighteen, an orphan and her family had been killed when she was eight, she was a rare diamond waiting to be cut he thought, wondering what lay beneath the baggy rags she wore. The translator explained that the following day Tyrese's car would pick her up at one o'clock as they were going shopping. He invited the translator too. Tyrese was going on a shopping spree the following day and wanted to treat her to some proper clothes.

She lived in a room way outside the city in a block of flats for refugees, neighbors stared at the limo as they waited for her to emerge.

Yarka reluctantly took the armful of expensive clothes and disappeared into a fitting room, when she emerged Tyrese looked at her in awe, just as he had expected she had a great body, she looked surprised as she stared at her reflection in the mirrors. She looked fantastic in the little black dress with the large price ticket, the cut of the dress accentuated the fine lines of her body. She tried on seven outfits and Tyrese delighted in buying them all for her, today she was Cinderella, after shopping he dropped her at a hair salon in South Molton Street and instructed the stylist to give her a new image whilst he went shopping for himself. An hour and a half later when he returned to the salon he couldn't believe his eyes when he stared at the ravishing beauty that was waiting for him. She looked stunning, just stunning who would have thought that only two days ago his car had splashed water on her as she crossed the road. Since he had met Yarka he had forgotten all about his sour faced South American lover who was holed up in his London penthouse whilst he stayed in a hotel.

As Tyrese's album sales rocketed, his promotion campaign became more intense, the record company had him under extreme pressure. He had live performances, TV appearances, interviews, photo sessions and gigs all over Europe. The more he worked, the more they wanted, his entourage had expanded and his daily routine seemed to be growing into a circus, he now traveled with a small army of people, bodyguards, public relation officers, pluggers, DJs, managers, personal assistants, make-up artists, hairdressers, stylists, lighting men, sound technicians and dancers, sometimes he forget all of their names. In the beginning he tried to be polite to everyone, but the bigger his crew the harder it was, sometimes he was so tired he didn't know what city he woke up in. He seemed to spend more times on planes and in airports than anywhere else and as soon as they arrived and he did his thing he was whisked off again and rushed to another location. His fascination with Gina had been short-lived, he had returned to London to find that Gina had taken off. She had seen the tabloids and had left him to return to South America. She had a spicy Latin temper and as well as emptying the safe of all its contents, money, jewellery and all his valuables she had shredded all his clothes including his new video costume which had been flown in from Paris, his laptop had been destroyed and all of his music files deleted. 'Hell has no fury like a woman scorned' he thought as he sat in the middle of his trashed up living room he was glad to be rid of the Latino bitch.

The record company were not pleased with the lack of progress on his new album, he had hardly put pen to paper and they were disappointed in his attempts at writing, they wanted another album quickly and had hired some song writers to try and speed things up.

Will Fisher one of the executives was sure that Yarka was a bad influence, secretly he had frightened the shit out of the girl and arranged a visa for her to go to Canada where she had a cousin.

When Tyrese was in Munich for three days they paid her off and sent her packing.

Tyrese was devastated when he returned to find her gone, unlike Gina she had left everything that he had ever bought her and took only the clothes that she had arrived in,.

The record label thought that when she was gone he would work harder on the album but the incident had the opposite effect, Yarka had been his inspiration without her he felt numb.

Stardom wasn't all that it was cracked up to be and Tyrese started living on uppers and downers to get him through his daily commitments.

There were lots of parties but it all seemed so pointless, he missed being able to walk down the street and go see a movie. Now he realized why Marisa had become so reliant on drink and drugs, it was lonely under the spotlight and he had no friends. The people that surrounded him were like leeches, his intake of drugs increased and his arguments with the record label became more heated, the pressure they put him under was too much and they knew it but they wanted to squeeze as much out of him as possible before he dried up and the next hot property came along.

He got an offer to do a movie, the record company thought it would be excellent promotion for his unfinished album it was a small part and would require three weeks shooting.

Tyrese was excited he had always dreamed of being in a film and the three weeks on location would be like a holiday.

At first after Yarka had left he had spent weeks trying to find her, he wanted to know why she had disappeared, he knew he had been away a lot and that she had this insecure phobia, he missed her but didn't believe in love anymore, from now on he would never get emotionally involved, he would use pretty women for sex and sex only. When he felt like it they arranged for beautiful hookers to come to his room, there was no shortage of groupie pussy hanging around and he was happy with the set-up, his personal assistant arranged everything for him from condoms to coke, nothing was too much for a rising star.

Before he went filming he had to record six songs, to his management's surprise he did it effortlessly and efficiently, he was glad that he was off shooting. They were filming in Bangkok and an island in Thailand, sunshine, palm trees and no more music he longed to be away from the madness of the music industry.

CHAPTER 12

Bangkok

He stopped in Dubai for an overnight stay, the hotel was superb it had a fleet of Rolls Royce's, no one seemed to recognize him and he felt a new sense of freedom. It was a luxury indeed to be away from the screaming fans and autograph hunters and he was glad to have left the paparazzi behind.

He felt wide awake when the plane touched down at Don Muang airport. He was so used to flying he didn't get jet lag anymore. Bangkok was so different from anywhere he had been before, the streets were full of people and the traffic was horrendous. On every corner of every street someone was selling something and the city seemed alive twenty-four hours a day. He had been given a day to acclimatize and get over the jet lag that he didn't have which was a luxury in itself, a whole day with no commitments. They had put him into the Oriental the sumptuous hotel had a history of famous patrons.

Donning a baseball cap Tyrese sneaked out alone and became a tourist for the day. He went to the Royal Palace and saw the Emerald Buddha, then went to Chatumchak market which was an experience, this market was one of the biggest in the world and one could buy everything from a fighting chicken to diamonds, it was sweltering hot in the market and he got lost for hours as he searched for bargains and played tourist.

After a hot shower he felt invigorated and sported another cap, t shirt and jeans and took off to Patpong, it was nine pm and the traders were in full force selling copies of designer bags and watches. The area was full of tourists and he spent an hour marveling at the illegal copies of watches that were sold on the street, direct copies by the top designers being bargained for here for a few dollars.

Behind the market stalls were bars and pretty ladies lined the streets offering their services, the neon signs of the Go-Go bars and massage parlors lined the streets and ones senses were titillated with a cocktail of odours spilling from the street vendors.

The aroma of shrimps, suckling pig, duck and spicy Thai noodles floated through the air.

Tyrese bought some illegal DVDs which he was sure wouldn't work as they were so cheap, then he stopped at Go Go bar for a drink.

Inside the bar was not as bad as he had expected, he sat with the other tourists at the oval bar and watched twenty beautiful smooth skinned girls dancing on poles. They were perfectly made-up, were topless and wore skimpy G-strings with ridiculous high heels, all of them sported numbers and as the music played the girls changed it was fun to look at the girls most of them were quite flat chested but some had what he suspected were silicone boobs.

Deciding to go on a pub crawl and enjoying the freedom of being a faceless man in the crowd he ventured into the brightly lit neon alleys and tried some of the other bars, the Thai's were so friendly it was a pleasure to be here he thought smiling at a bevy of beer bar girls that were trying to lure him in to their establishment. His next stop was a rather classy establishment with lots of doormen and elegantly dressed hostesses, the place had class but the formula was the same there must have been about eighty gorgeous girls, there were two stages and on each were thirty girls, here they were all beautiful a different class from the other three bars he had visited, he had two drinks and sat mesmerized looking at the women as they danced, each one special in her own right. In Europe many of them could have been models, suddenly Tyrese sat frozen in his seat he was shocked, they were playing his song. The reality struck him of how famous he was, here in a brothel on the other side of the world the DJ was playing his disk he marveled at the girls as they gyrated to his voice, smiling to himself as he left he wondered how they would have reacted if they had known who he was. Generally as a rule the Thai women didn't like black men, the Thai's liked white skin, the darker the baby the lower the class, most of the women used bleaching agents and the soap had whitening agents in it. Sad really as the most beautiful Thai women were indeed the dark skinned ones.

Tyrese had noticed in the hotel on the television channels that all the women were a ghostly white shade, this was a sign of beauty in Thailand he preferred like most men the golden honey coloured ones.

A tout had lured him into a samlom and took him to an area full of dingy back streets.

Here in a nasty bar he watched the ping pong show. Some unattractive older women were sucking up ping pong balls and doing tricks with their pussy. Another was smoking a cigarette with her clit, a tiny woman was shooting darts with her vagina and busting balloons. The floor show was sleazy and Tyrese felt sickened. They ripped him off with a fat bar bill. They pestered him to take a massage in a sleazy room upstairs, he escaped.

The toothless rickshaw driver took him to a bar filled with scantily dressed girls, Tyrese ordered a beer then realized that the hookers were in fact all Ladyboys. He sobered up and decided to get back to the hotel. Thailand was notorious for its transgender sex trade and some of the ladyboys were better looking than real women. He had had enough adventure for one night. He had cringed imagining the shock that he would have got if he had woke up with a chick with a dick.

Tyrese was enjoying the freedom of being a mere mortal, he had drunk a lot and tiredness was kicking in, he had contemplated taking one of the girls back to the hotel but had decided against it he didn't need any negative publicity and he was exhausted.

When he got back to his hotel suite he found himself scribbling down some lyrics for his new album, one night in Bangkok had made him feel alive, no wonder someone had written a song about that. Bangkok was amazing its vibe, the atmosphere its people the smells had indeed awakened his senses, that night he dreamed of the pretty young Go Go girl number thirteen he woke up with an erection to a wake-up call.

He ordered room service and shaved and showered trying to look cool for his meeting with the director, he was a little nervous he had never acted before and his film experience was limited to his video shootings. He had read the script, his part had little dialogue, he was a villain and would be shot in a scene by an undercover cop, seemed simple enough. They were going to film in Phuket it was off season and apparently quite quiet there. The director and his coach arrived and they had a relaxed chat about the role, it was an American/Asian production and the Japanese director wanted as much violence as possible in the movie.

Recently there had been a trend for Asian movies and Tyrese was glad that he had the part.

They had chosen him after seeing one of his video clips he had the face and the look that they wanted. The fact that he hadn't acted before was irrelevant they knew that they could pull the performance out of him he was tall and handsome and could look real mean on film.

They were teaming him up with a blonde Russian secret agent a new face from Moscow.

This would also be her first major film, her milky skin and white hair would be a striking contrast to Tyrese's ebony skin, they would look stunning on screen the producers had added a love scene just to add a bit of sex to the plot. Tyrese grinned from ear to ear when they introduced the sexy six foot Russian, it was gonna be fun to make love to her on film and get paid a lot of money for it too.

Unknown to Tyrese his record company had proposed that they use one of his new songs as the film theme. In the end they would choose a romantic ballad and their steamy love scene would be used in the promotion trailers, having him in the film was a big plus especially now that they were going to use one of his songs. Now that they were extending his part he would have to stay on another two weeks, they had chosen a ballad that was being mastered and when the track was finished he would also shoot the video there in Phuket. Secretly Tyrese was pleased to have to stay another couple of weeks he loved the island and the Thai people and the filming was fun too, most of the time they spent a lot of time hanging about it was rainy season and sometimes the light was not favorable. Making movies was different from the music industry he was amazed how many people were involved.

The part he played was easy enough, most of his scenes made no sense he imagined that everything would gel together when it was edited. For the dangerous scenes he had a body double and stunt man, sometimes he would have to do his scene over and over and he wondered if that was because he was so inexperienced and it worried him, however the director seemed to be pleased and apparently they were running to schedule, if they hadn't been pleased with him they wouldn't have extended his role. Anna the six foot blonde Russian was not enamored by the addition of the love scene, she hadn't liked Tyrese right from the start. Tyrese had thought that there would be some on screen fireworks between them but there was no chemistry between them and he was dreading the love scene.

On the day of their scene she arrived an hour late and in a foul mood, she had been eating garlic and raw onion and her breath was disgusting, Tyrese knew that she had done it to piss him off, he insisted that she use a mouthwash before they proceeded. At first he was afraid that he would get carried away and get a hard on while they filmed, however Anna was as cold as ice and the dozen crew, lighting and cameras made him nervous and his member remained fortunately flaccid and shriveled,.

Filming with Anna was a major headache she did everything possible to throw him off balance and he was glad when their scenes had finished. While shooting the love scene she had been a real bitch. Tyrese had joked that he could do this for as long as she wanted. On screen they made a striking combination, his black skin and her pale complexion, it took hours to film their sex scene and when the director announced it was a wrap Tyrese walked off the set mumbling that he could understand why men became gay.

His action scenes were easy he had been a sports man and he enjoyed the fight scenes. On screen he looked good and his performance was compelling, Anna looked great on screen but her personality left a lot to be desired.

Phuket was beautiful, the island was green with foliage and the sea was a pale blue, Tyrese wanted to see more of the island but their shooting schedule started early in the morning and dragged on till midnight, he would appreciate from now on how hard the people in this industry worked it was even more strenuous than the music business.

There was an electricity between Tyrese and Anna in their fight sequence, he looked at her with pure hate as he slapped her hard on the face, she kneed him in the balls with sheer aggression the director was delighted they shot it in one take, little did he know that they were not acting they simply hated each other.

After completing the shooting the whole crew had a party it was fun and on his last day on the island he chartered a speed boat to take him to Phang Ag the landscape was beautiful with surrealistic rock formations popping out of the sea. They enjoyed a sea food lunch of fresh lobster and squid in a restaurant that was built on stilts in the middle of the ocean. They returned home at sunset, the sky turned a thousand shades of orange as the sun dipped into the horizon. For the first time in weeks the pressure was off and he was alone. The next day they had to film some video scenes then he was really free. He lay by the infinity pool surrounded by candles. The fragrance of jasmine filled the air and the sky seemed filled with stars. Tyrese sipped the coconut milk and for a moment the world was a private paradise. The crack of thunder rocketed through the heavens and lightning danced in the sky. Tyrese lay on the sun lounger letting the rain lash off his body. It was rainy season and the weather was unpredictable. Thailand was indeed a paradise, the people were charming, no wonder it was called the land of the smiles.

Tyrese was sorry that he had to fly back to Bangkok, he had a night in the city before returning to London and he wanted to go out and have some fun.

He decided to go to a massage parlor, inside the sleazy decor was exactly what one would have imagined, the peeling 70's floral wallpaper clashed with the cheap lino on the floor. He ordered a Singha beer and looked through the glass there were around forty young girls wearing red dresses they were sitting on benches looking at a TV he studied the girls they looked so young they all had numbers on their dresses after his second beer he asked the mama-san for two girls, he told her the numbers and they came from behind the glass wall, they looked smaller in stature and he dwarfed them as they led him up the narrow staircase to the private rooms where he was to experience a body to body oil massage. The two girls were sweet they giggled as they led him to the room.

The room was dark with a single red light bulb, in one corner of the room was a mattress with worn looking clean sheets, on the other side of the room was a cracked bathtub, in the centre of the room was an inflatable air bed with floral design. One girl filled the bathtub the other prepared the towels.

Within seconds the girls had stripped naked and they were peeling his clothes off, one removed his clothes while the other neatly folded them, they giggled at the size of his penis looking surprised at how large he was. The girls led him to the tub and started to soap his body with a soft perfumed soap, their nimble fingers washed him carefully. After he was clean they dried him with large soft towels, the girls signaled that he should lie on the plastic air bed he lay on his belly and listened to the music on the loudspeaker, the girls poured some jasmine oil over his naked body both ladies poured oil over themselves then with expert skill and coordination they massaged his wet naked body with their oily naked bodies. Like a ballet they danced over his body their breasts massaging his back, legs and buttocks. After a half hour of a teasing erotic massage they turned him over and repeated the process, his erect penis throbbed in excitement as their silky golden bodies teased him.

It was the most sensuous experience that he had ever known he was almost coming with excitement for an hour the girls teased him their slender bodies slipping and sliding over every inch of his flesh at one point one girl walked on his body, his senses stirred as both girls tongues darted along his groin and skilfully licked at his cock in unison. Tyrese exploded in orgasm and lay on the tacky plastic mat his heart beating, the dilapidated decor only added another dimension to the experience. After his orgasm they led him to the bathtub and showered and soaped his body again he dressed and tipped them 1500 baht each it had been a wild experience and he was glad that he had dared try it, his heart was still racing as he left the establishment. He stumbled onto the bustling pavement and a flashbulb blinded him, he heard the click of cameras, he had been too late to cover his face two days later the photo hit the tabloids. Clear as a bell he was captured with a guilty look on his face making an exit from "The sexy Cat Massage Parlour" the photo depicted him standing in the doorway with the neon sign above.

Tyrese was devastated but the studio didn't mind, the Bad Boy image was perfect for the role he had played in the film, the tabloids were kind stating him as the enfant terrible of the silver screen his record company didn't mind as long as the film studio didn't he had got the theme track and it was almost guaranteed to race up the charts, the video was hot, filmed in the exotic location of Phang Ah bay, the surrealistic rock formations made a dazzling backdrop for the clip.

Since Yarka had left him he had been writing a lot and doing as much touring as possible, the record label were delighted and the new album was almost in the can.

One morning Tyrese got a letter from Canada in his mail, it was written in Yarka's native tongue.

He still had the translator's number in his telephone so he called the man and asked him to pass by the following day to decipher her letter. Tyrese had tears of rage in his eyes, he couldn't believe what the man was telling him. Yarka's letter had been angry and aggressive she told him that since he had dumped her she had found a new life and a new man, not a rich famous man but an honest hard working laborer one that loved her. She told him she was getting married and that she hated him for not having the guts to tell her face to face that he didn't love her.

Tyrese was confused, he asked the translator why she was so angry with him, the translator told him he thought she had a right to be angry after the way he had treated her. Tyrese was infuriated when he learned that his manager had asked the translator to explain to the girl that she had to leave that she was given a visa and a lump sum to go to Canada. The translator had thought that it was Tyrese that had given the instructions to do this, he was paid by the record company an extra month's salary to do this and the girl had left in tears the same day while Tyrese was in Birmingham.

Tyrese sat alone in the room and thought of Yarka, he had loved her, his fucking record company had sent her packing, they had gone behind his back and eliminated her just like that, controlling his life just like Pippa had done. There was return address and for a moment he felt like flying to Heathrow and taking the next flight to Toronto, he missed her but she was in love with someone else and he didn't want to ruin her happiness. He called his lawyer he asked him to trace the girl through the visa office he requested that they send her 20,000 dollars as a wedding gift.

He had asked the translator to fax him a copy of the letter that the record company had sent him and a copy of the bill that they had paid him to get rid of his lover. The next morning at nine am he walked through the doors of the record company, walked past his manager's secretary and burst in the door, he threw the two pieces of paper in his face and without saying a word he walked out of the office leaving another envelope on the secretary's desk. He was quitting, he was finished, they could fuck off he wasn't going to finish the album or be their puppet anymore, they could sue him or throw him in jail if they liked he was through with this business, he was tired of being controlled and manipulated.

Every day for a month he got threatening letters legal papers, bills he tossed them in the bin without reading them he asked his lawyer to handle everything and refused to have any contact with the record company.

The producer that he had done the film with called him to tell him that the editing had gone real good, he was offering Tyrese a major role in a big budget Hollywood movie. They wanted him to fly immediately to Los Angeles for a screen test. There is a god after all Tyrese thought as he rushed to pack a bag, he had to leave for the West Coast in two hours, he was looking forward to getting away from Europe he had had enough here. He called a cab to take him to the airport.

As the car crawled through the crowded streets Tyrese watched as the rain lashed against the windscreen thinking that yet again another chapter in his life had closed.

CHAPTER 13

Hollywood

Pippa had driven Sven crazy in the Maldives, he had returned after a week and since then Pippa had been in a famous rehabilitation clinic for months. She hated the basic room that she shared with a one-time drug addict and had been appalled that she had to clean her own room and participate in housekeeping duties, discipline was not her strongest virtue.

After she had been labelled cured she returned to her penthouse apartment and went in to her office two or three days a week. She was off drugs and booze but had become addicted to something else, she had an addiction to sex, without the coke and the booze she couldn't help thinking about sex, she thought about it day and night and her appetite was insatiable, each night she combed the singles bars and clubs picking up men whose names she didn't even bother to ask. In the day time she would pick up men in the Park or supermarket and if she didn't find one she went on line she used a webcam to show herself on screen and surfed the net to find sex crazed partners like herself.

The more men she had, the more she needed, sometimes three men a day would pass through her bed sometimes she would have threesomes with young men she met jogging in the park, she never slept and had lost all interest in her business, she was fortunate enough to have good managers that were running a tight ship for her. In some ways without her they were doing a better job, fewer artists were straying away and there were less clashes of personality without her fiery presence.

Feeling unwanted and alone she lived every sexual fantasy that she had, often when she made love to these nameless faceless creatures of the night she would think of Tyrese and pretend that it was him on top of her, she wondered where he was and wondered if he ever thought of her. The last time she had seen a photo in a tabloid he had been with another young beauty she had been pleased that he had thrown Gina out already she hated Gina with a vengeance she had double-crossed her.

She had been beaten and robbed twice by strange men who she had taken home, they had taken her jewel box and credit cards, the second time it had happened she didn't even call the police the first time they had warned her to be careful.

There was a young Latino in her shower, he had fucked her three times and she didn't know his name, names were not important anymore kicks were important she liked the hunting more than the act of sex itself, hunting in the bars, on the net, in the park, the danger and thrill of the unexpected gave her a kick and she had a rule that she never went back for second helpings.

She had long lost count of the men with whom she slept she had no idea how many there had been.

The young stallion admired himself in the mirror, he was feeling smug he had dipped her purse while she had been asleep and he had stolen four hundred dollars he didn't feel guilty, he had banged the old bag three times, his dick was sore. While she was in the shower he would make his exit, he contemplated taking the DVD player but was scared that the concierge might raise the alarm, he dressed quickly in the bathroom wanting to put on his clothes in case she wanted more.

Pippa was disappointed to see him dressed, she was hoping for another session before she threw him out, the moment she went into the shower he pocketed her Swiss watch and left, his heart raced as he walked past the doorman.

The moment he was in the street he hailed a cab and jumped in, it took Pippa three hours to notice that the watch and her money were gone, she was angry, they were vermin these lads.

She went online checking to see if there were any new messages for her. She went into the chat room and a pervert came on private chat with her. He was a pilot, forty and rather good-looking, he was in the city at a hotel room and available now. Within ten minutes she was dressed and made-up and was sitting in the back of a taxi speeding towards his hotel. Another day, another man she thought applying red lip gloss as she went up in the elevator.

He answered the door wearing only his captain's hat and boots just as she had ordered him to do she mused slipping out of her coat.

She accepted his offer to so some coke, Pippa ripped of her coat, she was wearing stockings and a dog collar with six inch designer heels. The pilot liked her, she was mature and dominating. He had taken two Viagra. She had taken a few uppers.

The flight to L. A. was uneventful, Tyrese had been pestered by some fans at the airport and he had had to sign a half dozen autographs, the security checks had taken forever and the flight had suffered a two hour delay, he had been so upset that he had been unable to sleep and arrived in the States feeling disgruntled and tired.

He had only four hours to freshen up and catch some sleep before his meeting at the film studios. They had arranged a car to pick him up at the hotel, as he waited in reception he felt uncomfortable in the sharply cut Armani suit, perhaps he was overdressed.

Tyrese had wanted to make a good impression at the meeting, he wanted this film deal more than anything.

The meeting went well, the only drawback was that they wanted him to finish his album, he had no credibility in the movie business they were backing him on his music career and popularity to give his name credibility, the release of a hit album coordinated with the film release would generate a buzz of excitement. He dreaded finishing the album in London but understood their point, he would go back to Europe and finish the videos and last three tracks then finish his contract with the recording company for good.

The next morning they picked him up at the unearthly hour of five am for a screen test, he suspected that they were testing his discipline and had gone to bed early anticipating their motive. They had explained the script, it was a big budget blockbuster set in the civil war.

A dramatic costume drama with mind-blowing battle sequences and emotional love scenes.

He would have the starring role and there were major Hollywood stars queuing up begging for the part, really they were taking a chance offering him the role, he had only had a minor part in his recent film. He however did have the face, spirit and charisma of the character they wanted to play. He was nervous as he entered the sound stage he had been in make-up for two hours, they had dressed him in rags. He was to be chained on a sinking slave ship and had they expected this screen test to be strong enough to persuade the director that he was the one for the roll.

As the cameras rolled Tyrese slipped effortlessly into character. They filmed the scene three times and that was that, as he walked nervously off the set he wondered if he had played his role right or wrong. Two days later he got the call, he had the part, they had been moved by his performance and on-screen presence, they wanted him to come to the studio for further talks to discuss the role and his retainer.

Using Tyrese was cheaper than using a major star, it was more risky but they actually saved millions of dollars by deciding to use him, a major star would have however guaranteed a box office pull. Tyrese was a pop star, he had sold millions of albums as a singer, as a football player he had also had millions of fans, the studio were banking on the fact that he was a household name and that his presence would create a stir. He had been excellent in his first movie performance although his role had been small he had delivered an excellent on-screen presence.

Tyrese was just happy to get the part, he knew they were offering him buttons but if he scored in this movie doors would fly open in the future. The part would be demanding and there would be tremendous pressure on him to deliver, he would be working side by side with two famous supporting actors and a red hot young newcomer from Ireland. The young girl with the red fiery hair would also snare the leading female role in the movie, their on screen charisma would prove to be electrifying and their forbidden on screen romance would touch the hearts of audiences worldwide. The passionate tale of a plantation slave and an aristocrat's daughter would be a dramatic old-fashioned love story and Tyrese would be the hero. The filming schedule would take almost a year it would be heavy going, they had already given him a script and introduced him to a voice coach. The movie was to be shot in The South and on location in some remote part of Eastern Europe.

Tyrese threw himself to work studying the script with a fine toothcomb, he wanted this to be perfect, his whole film career was hanging on this and he was grateful to have had the chance. There were people in Hollywood laughing at the fact that he had been chosen for the role, half of Hollywood were expecting him not to deliver.

There were three months before filming began, Tyrese headed back to dreary dismal London to complete the album. He had made it clear that he would only do the minimum of promotions and that a tour was out of the question, on the strength of his last album they were releasing this one globally, they wanted to press as much out of him as possible in the two months that he had agreed to work. They reckoned that he would calm down and rethink the situation once the album began to sell, they had planned three singles to be released at six week intervals then the album would be released a month later. By the time the album hit the stores Tyrese would be well into the filming of the movie and the hype of the movie would be getting circulated at the same time that the album would be getting released the overlapping of the projects were exactly what the studios wanted.

Tyrese had offered to write a heart-rending ballad as a film theme but the film studio had other people in mind for the theme song, they didn't want to risk too much on a newcomer, however they had given him the green light to come up with an idea and if it was better than what they had in mind they would consider it.

Tyrese was sitting late at night reading the script for the hundredth time, he knew most of his lines already and had played every scene out in his mind's eye. It was late and he was so tired he was almost drifting into sleep. Suddenly without warning he heard music in his head, he grabbed a pen and scribbled lyrics on the back of the script, a song flowed through his head and in his mind's eye he visualized a video, that night he didn't go to bed he stayed up all night composing the tune which would in actual fact become the haunting movie theme.

At five am he was still awake, he had a recording appointment in the studio at eight, he was supposed to be singing in the last track for his album. He decided that he would try this one instead the song was so clear in his mind that he couldn't wait to record it. An hour earlier than planned Tyrese appeared at the studio and by the time the technicians and musicians arrived he had it all down on paper, everyone was surprised at the melancholic song, it was different from anything else that he had done however by late that evening they had recording of an amazing track.

Tyrese was excited, they sent the raw recording to be mastered and remixed, everyone who heard the track was excited and everyone added their piece of individual magic to the track and it became a masterpiece in its own right.

The people at the film studio had expected a pop song, they sat speechless round the table as Tyrese played them the demo. The room filled with the velvety rasp of his voice, the producer and director felt a race of excitement the song made the hair on the back of his neck stand on end, without a doubt this was the theme tune, the haunting lyrics depicted the essence of the film. The producer closed his eyes and could see the video. Tyrese on a slave ship being beaten and lashed, the rough seas, his passion for the young virgin redhead, the dramatic story, the tragic end, the song was perfect.

Tyrese had taken them off guard, there was more to the man than they had imagined, his talents seemed multifaceted they would shoot a video at the same time as the film. Tyrese made a hard deal on the musical part, if he wasn't earning from his acting role he was going to earn from his musical involvement.

For the next eight months Tyrese ceased being Tyrese, he forced himself into character and became Abu the African slave captured and brought halfway across the world to work on a plantation. Tyrese ate, breathed and slept Abu no one knew where the character stopped and Tyrese begun, the emotional role was exhausting and Tyrese felt the mental anguish of being in character.

Sometimes after a long days shooting Tyrese would be reduced to tears, it was hard for him to get out of character, he was delivering a stunning performance and the directors were awed at his screen presence they had made the right decision by choosing him. The tall well-dressed pop star had indeed became Abu, body beaten and bruised on the outside, mentally scarred on the inside. Tyrese had learned to dig deep into his emotional pockets and use all the pain from his past to make Abu seem more real. The chemistry between Kristy O'Donal and him was electrifying, when they had their first screen kiss her ginger hair seemed luminescent against his black sweaty skin, pure screen magic a feast for the eyes.

The way they filmed the movie was amazing, they had used excellent lighting, almost like a Rembrandt, from start to finish the whole film seemed a collage of golden hues. The filming was an art form with breathtaking landscapes, even the battle scenes had a streak of beauty in them, the wide camera angles and golden colour was scintillating to the eye.

The forbidden love scene where Tyrese, having received thirty lashes from the overseer, bruised and beaten left dying in a barn is saved by the virginal aristocratic Southern Belle, the shocking red hair against the bleeding welts of his skin, As the slave in rags stripped her of her pearls and fine laces the contrast was visually stunning, their torrid forbidden love affair and tragic end would propel them both to fame, making them synonymous with great screen legends like Anthony and Cleopatra, Heathcliff and Cathy and Scarlet and Rhett.

Abu and Jade would electrify and captivate audiences globally, everyone who saw the movie would be touched and silent as they left the theatres.

Tyrese had developed a close friendship with Katie O'Donal she was twenty-one from Dublin.

She had been chosen from thousands of girls to play Jade, she had done several television plays but nothing big. Their on-screen presence was electrifying, off screen had developed a deep friendship, she was a lesbian, it was her greatest secret the studios didn't want anyone to know that her make-up artist was her lover, they thought that it would be bad for publicity. She had confided in Tyrese right from the start because she could feel his attraction for her and wanted to be straight with him. Her career like his was banking on this movie and she was in for it heart and soul.

Like Tyrese she had a problem getting out of character, she had been transformed into the Southern Belle, they spent a lot of time together, after filming they would eat together and stay up till all hours rehearsing the following day's scenes. Katie's lover, a rather unattractive dyke seemed jealous of Tyrese's friendship. He couldn't understand what a beautiful talented young woman like Katie saw in the frumpy dyke, he guessed that she like him was lonely. It was such a waste he mused admiring her great body in the candlelight, remembering that she was gay had she been straight he would have loved to have given her a good banging himself.

Katie had become his best friend, he adored her and she had believed in him when no one else had, and he had believed in her. Attitudes towards them in the beginning had been quite hostile but the tables had turned now that they had seen what they were doing, they were treated with more respect than at the beginning, they were going to make this movie a blockbuster.

They had been in Croatia filming for three months, everything seemed so primitive, the crew were getting tired, the days were long and everyone was missing their families and friends. It had been seven days a week for months and Tyrese and Katie were jubilant, they had enjoyed every moment it was the perfect escapism for Tyrese he had no personal life right now and he would be sorry when the filming stopped he would miss the acting and his friendship with Katie she had become like a sister.

On the set tempers often frayed and they were returning to Hollywood to shoot some location scenes. It would be a pleasure to be in the studio again, limos and parties Katie screamed as they filmed the last shot in the plantation sequence.

Five star hotels and room service Tyrese joked, they had missed their luxuries as they packed and headed for the airport.

Tyrese soaked in a bubble bath in his hotel suite, it was heaven he thought, he had missed a bathtub on location they only had showers and he liked to relax in the tub, play some music and chill out, he could spend hours in the tub. Katie was staying at the same hotel. It was cool, sometimes the studio arranged for them to attend functions and parties, Katie's lover was livid she hated being scraped aside and left in the hotel suite to watch videos while they partied. However this was Hollywood and it would have created a bad vibe if the public knew that their new screen goddess was a lesbian. They wanted the world to think that Tyrese and her were having an off-screen romance it would add excitement to the publicity and hype around the film.

Tyrese had finished his last album quickly but they had thought that twelve tracks were too few and added a remix, they also suggested that he added a cover version of a seventies hit. He had been reluctant to record the cover, he had hated the track, however he had been keen to get started with the film and had recorded the track. He was actually shocked that the single had raced up the charts to a number one position in five countries, the video had been thrown together at the last minute and on a low budget, it was weird that sometimes in life the things that one put the least effort in were the things that would bring the greatest achievement.

Katie and Tyrese attended the premiere, arriving together in a long limo, she looked stunning in a lemon coloured couture creation that had been borrowed from the Paris catwalks, he wore a lemon dinner suit, they made a dashing couple and the paparazzi went wild snapping away photos.

Rumour had it that they were an item, no one had caught onto the fact that Katie had been living with her female partner for two years. Alex was her make-up artist, hairdresser and personal assistant, she was unattractive and dull and it amazed Tyrese that they were connected, he just couldn't imagine them together in bed.

Alex stayed in the shadows and sneered jealously at Katie on the arm of Tyrese, she suspected that one day she would lose her movie star lover to a man, she was bisexual and she seemed over friendly with her tall black co-star. The night before the premiere Alex had a raging fight with Katie, she had repeatedly accused her that she suspected that she was sleeping with Tyrese, the argument had gotten out of hand when Alex had threatened to slit her wrists and Katie had punched her so hard that she had nearly knocked her unconscious.

The frumpy frustrated woman waited in the wings wearing dark glasses to cover her black eye as the two stunning stars walked slowly up the red carpet towards the theatre.

Alex was sick of hiding in the shadows it had been her who had gotten Katie started in the film business she had been working as a make-up artist on a minor movie with an underground lesbian director called Shirley, the girl chosen for the role had been in a car accident two days before shooting and she had a broken hip and they were distraught at the thought of finding a new actress for the leading role it seemed an impossible dream.

She hadn't broke the news to the crew as she was afraid that she would lose them, she had had a grant for this film and she didn't want to forfeit it. She postponed shooting and Alex and the whole crew were put on hold while she held castings to find a new last minute chance.

Alex had been depressed, she had gone out to a popular lesbian venue and was focusing on getting drunk when the door opened and a girl walked in, she was young and looked nervous she was wearing a tweed coat, a rucksack and a knitted hat with a scarf round her mouth to protect her from the fierce winter weather that was raging outside. The club was quiet, most people hadn't dared the roads, the girl removed her hat and scarf and Alex sobered up. This girl had something special it wasn't just her perfect bone structure and good skin it was something else, she had a striking charisma that shone, she was too small for modeling which was a pity because her face was sensational.

Alex had approached her and bought her a drink, one drink led to two and Katie burst into tears as she told the sympathetic stranger that she had ran off from her father who had tried to force her to have sex with him. The girl was homeless and that night Alex took her home and fell in love with her. In the morning, Jonathan a friend of Alex's turned up on their doorstep and they shared breakfast. Jonathan was a struggling young photographer with dreams of being the best fashion photographer in Europe, his eyes nearly popped out of his head when Alex's new bed partner stepped out of the bedroom, hair tousled and wearing a man's shirt, she was the most sensational girl he had ever seen.

After breakfast Alex made her up and Jonathan enthusiastically shot two rolls of film of the stranger. After shooting he raced home to develop and hand print the photos, he turned up at nine in the evening with some grass and an envelope, Katie was stunning, the camera loved her from every angle. Alex called Shirley, she wanted to pass by with some photos of Katie, she was hoping that Shirley would cast her as an extra as the girl was penniless.

Alex had no idea that the leading lady had been hospitalized as soon as Shirley looked at the photo she had a vision this girl would turn her mediocre film into an award winning low budget movie. Strange she thought, as she studied the ten photographs carefully one by one, how one person's bad luck could change another's fortune. She demanded that Alex bring Katie to her office immediately and as soon as they were introduced she knew that this was the face that would launch her film career as a director. The fact that she had never acted and had zero experience didn't seem to disturb her she could smell success with this girl and even if she couldn't act now she would by the end of the shooting, hence Katie's film career had begun from being a nothing to becoming a somebody had been a short road.

Her inexperience and naiveté had been difficult in the early stages of the shooting but with Alex by her side she had survived it all and delivered an extraordinary performance.

The super low budget film was a small masterpiece in itself and had a cult following.

Katie made two other films with Shirley before getting a Hollywood deal. Her role as Jade with Abu would be the biggest movie she made, Alex was confused, this was the day she had longed for and she knew she should be proud however she was obsessed with jealousy just watching all the attention that Katie was getting, stardom had changed her and she was afraid of losing her.

At first she had relied on Alex for everything, she had given her strength and confidence to pull the thing off, by the end of the filming Katie had blossomed, she was a quick learner and was fascinated by the sight of her own image on film.

Sitting in the darkness of the theatre Katie held on to Tyrese's hand, the film was moving and Katie could hardly believe that it was her own image that filled the screen. Lost in their roles Tyrese and Kate had dug into the pockets of their souls to become Abu and Jade, there was an eerie silence as the film ended. The credits rolled on the screen and for a moment they both wondered what the audience attending had thought, it had taken the audience a minute to compose themselves, most of the women had tears in their eyes, after the deathly silence in the darkened theatre the whole audience rose to their feet, the roaring standing ovation was clearly a sign of success they clapped and cheered for what seemed like infinity, that night two new stars were born.

It would be one of Katie's many future screen appearances the roles of Abu and Jade seemed to have been written for them and they fitted into their moulds like no one else could have.

Alex disappeared into a yellow cab, Katie didn't even notice that she had disappeared, she was too busy signing autographs, giving press interviews and dazed to have been aware of anything.

There was an ocean of Champagne at the after party, Tyrese didn't want the night to end he had danced all night with Katie, she had gone to the ladies room to freshen up her make-up.

Tyrese had gone to the bar for a refill and it was there that he first laid eyes on the Brewster Twins. The twenty-one year old identical twins were heirs to a global hotel and shipping network, they had inherited the family fortune when their parents had died. Their private plane had crashed mysteriously off the coast of the Gulf of Mexico. Clarrisa and Penelope had changed their names to Destiny and Paris, abandoned their Swiss finishing school uniforms and to the horror of the Empire's directors had taken over the business together with their crippled brother Wesley. In just one year they had transformed their stiff and somewhat dated hotel chain completely, using the hottest interior designers in the world they had transformed their mediocre hotels into swinging Boutique hotels, the minimalistic design and Feng Shui inspired concept and been a great success with the Hip and the In Crowd. The rooms had been transformed into spacious lofts, the coffee shops to sushi bars, the addition of holistic health spas swinging night-clubs, chill out lounge areas and art galleries had made the hotel group's profits soar and the concept had been an overnight success.

The girls were the companies own PR department they were young, beautiful and ambitious. Wesley ran the business side from the confines of his wheelchair whilst his sisters attended every film premiere, concert and party on the planet.

Tyrese was fascinated by the long leggy totally extrovert twins, rumor had it they did everything together, before he had a chance to introduce himself they walked up to him and grabbing his hands they dragged him to the dance floor.

Around four am Tyrese was whisked off in the back of a pale pink stretch limo, sandwiched between the two twins they drank another bottle of Rosé Champagne in the back of the car.

They arrived at one of their Boutique Hotels. The reception staff discretely pretended not to notice as the girls entered the private elevator that took them to their penthouse duplex.

Tyrese was drunk but he was indeed impressed by the sheer grandeur of the apartments, like a glass box perched high on top of a slender building, the panoramic view of the city was breathtaking. The sun was coming up and the sky seemed ablaze, Tyrese thought that he was dreaming the two girls had stripped him naked and were skillfully licking his body from top to bottom, the double sensation of two tongues and twenty fingers manipulating the zones of his body that were about to explode at any moment were driving him crazy. Destiny and Paris took control and he submitted to their capture lost in total ecstasy, he licked Paris's pussy while Destiny sat on his cock they changed positions mechanically and drank the pleasure from his loins like two thirsty animals till Tyrese exploded in orgasm.

They all fell asleep in a massive circular bed, it was morning Destiny pushed a button and the music grinded to a halt as the electric curtains closed and the room became dark. Drunk and high with elation Tyrese fell into a deep sleep the twins curled around his body like snakes, they had not made love to Tyrese it was Abu that they had desired. To the Brewster Twins Tyrese had been a fantasy, they held on to the tall slave as he lay snoring in their mink clad bed that was large enough for a dozen people.

When Tyrese wasn't promoting his film he spent all of his time either partying or screwing with the Brewster Twins they were a hot trio and the press had a field day.

Tyrese had found himself falling in love with the two racy twins, for the first time in his life he had taken Viagra just to keep up with their sexual demands. He wondered how the two had found the time to build up the hotel chain they seemed to spend most of their time partying, shopping and getting laid. In the three weeks that Tyrese had joined forces with them they had never mentioned the word work, the whole idea seemed so alien, they had agreed to join Tyrese to promote the movie in Europe, they were going to go on the family jet and the first stop was Paris, the girls were ecstatic. The premiere there coincided with the fashion shows and one of France's hottest designers had begged them to be in his show they always caused a riot on the catwalk and spent a fortune on clothes.

They had decided to stay at the Intercontinental, the Hotel was lavish and grand, right in the hub of the city near the designers, the best restaurants and clubs.

The first night they went to the Buddha Bar where they relaxed to the music, after an excellent meal they moved on to Manray, the street was lined outside with hopefuls desperately trying to get in, within seconds they were shuffled in the entrance. It was fashion week, the place was full to the gunnels and the fashion set were out in force. Tyrese and the twins were accompanied to a table with their bodyguards, every head turned as the two twins made their entrance wearing identical designer creations and Tiffany jewels.

The atmosphere was electric, the music throbbed and they polished off several bottles of vintage champagne, the Twins danced with Tyrese and cameras flashed. The Twins loved being in the celebrity set, they flaunted their wealth with unashamed abandon. Tyrese was wearing a white suit with white bandana and a diamond dog tag that the girls had given him, together they danced the night away and it was almost daylight when they arrived back at their suite. The girls had invited three designers and six models back for a nightcap, the group had landed up having an orgy which the girls had instigated. Tyrese hoped that no one had photographed him as he had switched from partner to partner, all of the people were quite famous, two of the designers had been gay so he and one other guy had been left to service all the women, the twins and the six pretty young models, they had had sex in every conceivable position and Tyrese was exhausted when he had fallen asleep. The twins were having sex together, totally insatiable they had so much energy he wondered what kind of medication they were on to sustain such a lifestyle. In the shower he stood under the steamy water for a half hour, trying to wash off the scent of all the women he had had sex with, the smell of their perfumes seemed sickening now, he was tired and shattered.

Tyrese slept the sleep of the dead, he woke at three in the afternoon and ordered a large room service late breakfast, he was ravenous and was surprised that they had delivered it so quickly wearing a towel round his waist he answered the door, it was not however room service it was Katie almost unrecognizable in dark glasses and a fedora. She bounded into his room and fell into his arms her body trembled and tears were rolling down her cheeks, she had been filming in London but had taken a week off, it took around ten minutes for her to stop sobbing and Tyrese was beside himself with worry.

Katie sat curled up in the antique sofa, slowly she contained herself and told him what had happened. His breakfast had arrived it lay cold on the table that the waiter had wheeled into his room. Katie had been filming, her schedule had been frantic and shooting had been dragging on till the early hours almost every night. The Director had had a tiff with Alex and had banned her from the site as she was interfering and had been interrupting the shooting schedule. They had complained that Alex's make-up had been poor and did not comply with the desired look for the costume drama, so she had stormed off the set screaming and shouting at Katie. That night when the studio closed Mercedes had dropped her at her Mayfair hotel suite and she found Alex in bed, the sheets were red with blood, she had slit both wrists. Katie had panicked and called reception they had called an ambulance. Alex had died before they arrived. Katie was beside herself she was so upset, the Valium had calmed her but she still was devastated about Alex. If it hadn't been for her she would have been working as a waitress, she felt indebted in a strange sort of way and Alex had been her rock, without her she had felt so alone and useless, being a successful movie star was one thing but fame had its price, it didn't keep you warm at night and no one seemed to be interested in the real Katie everyone now saw only the screen goddess.

Tyrese sympathized with her and sat quietly in the chair while she slept for a few hours in his bed, he felt heart sorry for the lonely talented woman that lay near him. He knew what loneliness was himself, she had run to him simply because there was no one else to run to.

He was going to fly back to London with her to attend the funeral, she needed support.

Tyrese cancelled all his appointments and packed a smart black suit, he had never been close to the tight-lipped lesbian that lingered in the background like a strange dark shadow.

They arrived at Heathrow early in the morning and just as he had dreaded there was an army of Paparazzi waiting on them like vultures. They had gotten hold of the story and Katie's cover was blown. The headlines screamed in bold letters of Alex's death, Katie's lesbian affair was suddenly world news they had dug up every little detail about the suicide, being a celebrity was like living in a goldfish bowl, privacy didn't exist. Katie nestled her head in Tyrese's winter coat as they walked the gauntlet out of the building and into the BMW with darkened glass windows. The flash of the cameras had a strobe effect and time seemed to stand still as Katie walked to her car. At the films studios in London, the board of directors were holding a meeting, they were worried about the negative publicity, concerned about how she would finish the film and angry that they were behind schedule. In Hollywood her agent sat with his hands on his head, angry that her lesbian relationship had been exposed and he was convinced that her award nominations would be canceled. No one except for Tyrese gave a damn about the shattered, fragile little lady in his arms everything in the end boiled down to money.

The funeral was in Dublin, it was a dreary cold grey autumn morning in the small village outside the city, Alex's family didn't even make a show they were ashamed about the newspaper stories, there were only a half dozen people at the cemetery and as soon as formalities were over Tyrese and Katie drove back to the airport to fly back to London in the private jet that the film studios had put at their disposal.

They were eager to get Katie back on the set, every day that she stayed away cost money and they had been trying to shoot around her. Tyrese stayed for three days, to everyone's surprise she returned to work as promised on time, showing no emotion, she was a professional and gave the camera her best even though her heart was breaking and she cried herself to sleep almost every night.

CHAPTER 14

Pippa

Pippa had dried out, no booze no drugs she had had a dreadful time at the private clinic but had survived, she was looking good and had returned to the record company to take the reins again. In her absence there had been changes, they had stumbled on a seventeen year old genius he didn't drink, didn't do drugs, didn't smoke he was a grade A student, fresh and wholesome with a passion for music and the talent of a genius. Pippa had almost been dragged by a talent scout to a gig in a school hall, she had been reluctant to attend the school concert but when the kid and his group took the stage Pippa's dreadlocks almost stood on end, she had heard so many people over the years, this one made her tingle, it was the million dollar tingle she felt as she listened. He was the sound of the future, he had the face and the sound designed for the next generation. He was like a diamond, uncut and Pippa had planned to polish him up and make big profits for the future. After the performance she went backstage to meet the teen offering her hand and smiled a dazzling smile, Pippa's first words to him were, 'Romeo my man I am gonna make you richer than you ever dreamed!' The next day she had him in her office at nine to sign a five year contract, she had taken the kid under her own wing. As the excited teenager signed the paper Pippa felt her heart beat, he was gonna be a big star, right in front of her was a lad that would sell millions of albums, he wrote his own material and had told her that he had written eighty songs, he had been writing since he was ten years old. His poor parents had taken two jobs to support his career. Pippa had drawn up an awful contract, in a year he would regret ever having signed the deal, she took a cheque book out of the drawer and wrote a cheque for a large amount, she handed it to the kid and his eyes widened. He was impressed, she wanted to keep the kid happy he was working as a waiter earning a few dollars a day and he had never seen so much money. He had just signed a paper making her joint owner of all his material for five years, she called her assistant Jeremy she wanted him to arrange a stylist, the best of course, a hairdresser, a make-up artist, a driver and bodyguard. She wanted him put in an apartment, and she wanted him to start recording immediately in a studio.

She wanted three producers to start mastering his work and she wanted a guy with a video to start making a film of everything the kid did, like a "the making of" film, she wanted to groom the lad and prepare him for the future and wanted Jeremy to arrange a photo session for the following Friday, everyone involved with Romeo had to be the best, he was going to be one of her most important money making products. She wasn't sure if she wanted the rest of his group they were a spotty talentless lot she would let them hang around for a week till he settled in. Pippa arranged an appointment with his parents, a plain couple they were ecstatic that their son had been given a chance, his father had remarried when s Romeo's maternal mother had died of cancer when he was six. They looked at Pippa in amazement studying her rainbow dreadlocks and eccentric clothes, they were delighted that their son had been given an advance and saw the woman in the leather seat as some kid of Fairy Godmother.

Romeo was so fresh he had talent written all over him, Pippa was excited she wanted to oversee every little detail of his career.

The first day he had been taken to the studio to record his first track, he had told Pippa that he hadn't slept all night he had been so excited he claimed that new songs were just springing into his head. After a couple of hours she had a call from his producer, Pippa had a meeting with an attorney and she had taken the call thinking that something must have gone wrong, J.J. was excited, he told her that the kid had delivered the track in one take, even in its raw unmastered version it sounded incredible. He wanted her to come down to hear the track. Pippa got rid of the boring attorney and drove in her vintage Cadillac to the recording studio.

Romeo had more than delivered, he had sung two versions of 'Ghetto Boy Blues', both were amazing, she listened to the tracks and got lost in the vibe, it was the 'fattest' track she had heard. He had done a blues version and a rock version of the song, she tried to look unimpressed but couldn't, he was a piece of magic in the making. They had some lunch and listened to the two versions over and over again.

Romeo was glad to see Pippa, he was so high with natural excitement that he thought he was going to burst, excitedly he begged her to listen to a song that he had written at four in the morning, the lyrics had jumped into his head like a message from the gods.

Romeo's brain seemed to work overtime he always seemed to be doing two things at once.

He had written 'Message to the Gods' on a scrap piece of paper and he wanted to do two versions. Pippa sat and listened as the pint-sized boy with acne went into the recording booth, he coughed and cleared his throat and then something happened, he sang the song and Pippa had that tingling feeling, she could hardly believe the magic that was streaming through her headphones, the song was fucking amazing J. J. glanced at her and gave a thumbs up sign. Once in a decade a kid like this was discovered, she was almost speechless when he stopped singing he looked at her questioningly wondering if she had been disappointed. It wasn't often she was lost for words, the song was Fucking Amazing, it had number one written all over it, she smiled at the kid and asked if he any more like that one. He looked at her sheepishly and replied that he had around thirty other tracks as strong as that. At first she thought that he was being sarcastic, he wasn't, he started singing again another song and she sat there gobsmacked with dollar signs in her eyes.

While Romeo was recording she called Jeremy and ordered him to get his ass over there to take charge of Romeo she wanted him to be watched twenty-four hours a day.

A week later a dozen people sat in her office listening to the seven tracks that had been quickly mastered and remixed, all of the material was hit material, not only was it good for the American market it was hit material for the global market, Europe, Asia they would all eat up little Romeo, she knew that the little spotty boy was megastar material, he would go to the top and surpass all their expectations.

Jeremy had been bitching all day, Romeo loved to sing, to write, to record but the visual thing was not for him, he hated posing for photographers, refused to be revamped by the stylists and had point blank refused to have his hair dyed The make-up artist was at her wit's end, in most of the photos he had blinked and crossed his eyes. It was time for Pippa to explain to him that the music business today was very visual, clips and photos were part of the package, she herself went shopping with him and the stylist, they spent a small fortune on designer clothes and Romeo backed down and agreed to let Pippa's crew create an image for him.

They had cleansed his skin, straightened and whitened his teeth, dyed his mousy hair blond and had it cut in a wild Japanese style, he had moaned as they tinted his eyelashes and had groaned as they forced him to wear clothes that looked fit for the circus.

When he saw the results of the photos he grinned and promised never to complain again he looked 200 per cent different. The spotty nondescript school boy had been transformed into a sexy hot looking young pop idol. They had made a series of photos of him in black and white wearing only jeans, his naked torso had been covered in oil and they had tinted the photo, colouring the jeans and his eyes in blue and shaded his hair in a golden colour. Cheating by computer they had enhanced his muscles, trimmed his waist and shaded in a six pack, the Photoshop result was stunning. Pippa had a mock album cover and poster made. He looked wide-eyed thinking that it didn't look like him at all, the image was compelling, this would be the album cover young girls all over the globe would buy the album just for the cover and gay men would freak out. Pippa arranged a home gym to be constructed in his apartment and hired a personal trainer, she wanted him to develop a real six pack before he went on tour.

Romeo was tired his days started at six am he was writing recording and preparing for an album release and tour. She had employed a choreographer to teach him how to move, they were going to shoot three videos for the singles. She was investing a small fortune in him and he hadn't even had a hit. Romeo hated the dancing lessons he had two left feet, he was ultra-negative about the lessons till a couple of leggy dancers turned up, suddenly his interest in choreography became more intense. Pippa had purposely put the girls with him, she had a method in her madness. Young Romeo lost his virginity to the long leggy dancer Gemma, her silicone breasts had fascinated him, his sexual escapade had lasted no longer than seven minutes he had been so excited that he had almost came before he entered the willing blonde bombshell.

Romeo didn't know that Pippa was paying Gemma triple the fee to have regular sex with the boy wonder, the sexual capers had worked wonders he had suddenly learned to dance and looked forward to his dance classes.

The first video they shot in a warehouse, the usual ripped jeans and leather, some scantily clad gorgeous babes showing an abundance of flesh, Romeo clad only in his low cut jeans covered in oil surrounded by babes in bikinis dancing in the rain. Romeo had been so nervous on the day of the shoot she thought that he would collapse, they had done his solo scenes over and over and it wasn't easy. Pippa was glad that Gemma had been on the set, Pippa had suggested that she give him a blow job to calm him down they had disappeared for ten minutes into his make-up room and he had returned to the set with a whole new attitude, Gemma had promised him another blow job at the end of the shoot. Romeo's hormones were raging and after her promise he seemed keen to get it right quicker, his on film performance improved instantaneously and Gemma stood in the wings giving him moral support.

Romeo had it seemed, fallen in love with the dumb blonde dancer, Pippa promised him that when they went on tour they would take Gemma on the road. Romeo looked pleased, blow jobs every night he thought.

The video turned out well even though it had been shot with a relatively low budget, the next one was planned to be shot in Europe in Amsterdam. They would release the first single worldwide, they would do some European television shows and shoot the video, she had planned visits to Amsterdam, London, Brussels, Munich and they would be gone for ten days. Sweden, Moscow and Prague would have to wait for the next trip.

Perhaps after Europe they would try a mini tour, New York, San Francisco, Tokyo and Bangkok.

Normally she would make him do small gigs, students unions, private parties to get experience, with Romeo she didn't want that she wanted him to major live TV chat shows, music channels would play his video and the pluggers would ensure that the radio DJs would give him maximum airplay. After that she wanted him to do a world tour, major arenas, big venues, football stadiums and the like, she wanted to launch him as something special, no starting at the bottom he would start at the top.

As expected the first single 'Ghetto Boy Blues' raced up the charts within days of release.

It came as no surprise that Romeo had achieved overnight success. Pippa protected him and treated him with kid gloves she didn't want him to be burned out before he had begun.

She encouraged him to work on new tracks for a second album and kept him under a rigorous guard. He was shocked at the stir he had created and was surprised that his first single had hit the charts in ten countries. This lad was on the money.

Pippa arranged a meeting for all the staff who were on Romeo's team, they had been bitching and complaining and she had called them all to her boardroom at head office, over coffee she warned them that anyone who rocked the boat would be dismissed, she added that one day they would all be proud to have had the honor of working with Romeo, that they should be proud to be have been a part of pop history anyone who upset the kid was out, full stop. Finish, end of debate.

Romeo was never tired, he loved the attention, his days started at six am he worked out for an hour, wrote then went to the studio around midday, he recorded new tracks with enthusiasm and often in the evenings performed on TV shows.

Pippa had a gig arranged at a baseball stadium, it was a charity event and they added Romeo at the last minute, she wondered how he would fare doing such a large gig. She had kept it secret and told him the day before the concert he would be sharing the stage with major artists and megastars, Pippa prayed to all the gods that he wouldn't freak out, there would be 70,000 people there, it was a test for him and a challenge.

Romeo had diarrhoea, they gave him pills in the dressing room and Pippa was for the first time worried. He had freaked out at the idea of taking the stage with his pop heroes. They had brought him in by helicopter, the stadium was full and as he looked out of the helicopter he had thrown up. There were 70,000 people in the stadium. He had never seen so many people in his life and the idea of entertaining them live frightened the shit out of him. Someone knocked on the door and shouted. 'Five minutes,' Pippa was sick, she wondered if perhaps springing it on him had been clever. He looked so small and fragile, his face was white and the make-up looked like a mask. The second knock came and broke the silence, 'FUCK!' Romeo mumbled wishing he could disappear.

The bodyguards surrounded him and Pippa wrapped her arm around him as he was ushered to the stage, it seemed to take forever to get to the entrance. His ten dancers climbed the stairs in front of him and Pippa slapped his back he was hyper ventilating and sweat was breaking out on his forehead. Pippa dried his forehead with a sleeve of her Dolce and Gabbana blouse, he looked like Bambi she thought staring at his large brown eyes. Suddenly he heard his intro, the intro he had written when he was eleven, the dancers disappeared through a slash in the curtain and he walked out on stage, the music played and he jumped on the podium. The pyrotechnic fireworks went off behind him and his heart thumped in the tight snakeskin shirt. A million things raced through his head, the smell of the fireworks the sheer size of the stage, the audience roared and screamed and as they did the whole stage trembled, the dancers were around him the audience hadn't seen him perform they were hungry for him and as the intro faded he was blinded by light. Suddenly as if by magic he forgot where he was. He sang his song like he never had before pouring his soul into the lyrics, forgot the audience and Pippa wept as she watched him on the large screen monitors, she could see his heart beating through the tight shirt, his eyes were glazed with emotion as he emptied his lungs to the crowd. Within seconds he had cast a magical spell over the audience, he had them all in the palm of his hands. The two off key notes went unnoticed and at the end of his performance he held his hands up in the air and the whole stadium went crazy, their cheers and applause was deafening, the light blinding, the stage trembled beneath his feet and time seemed to freeze as he drank in the adulation of the crowd.

Basking in the spotlight he bowed and the crowd went wild, they wouldn't let him leave the stage. He had been only expected to do one song, they had asked Pippa to bring two pieces of music and she asked him if he could do 'Message to the Gods', they had not rehearsed it and the dancers had no choreography but he was high as a kite with emotion and was up for anything. The sound of 70,000 people screaming his name was deafening. They signaled that he music was prepared, the attendant with the earpiece signaled to Pippa and when he heard his cue he walked slowly with his dancers back on stage. The audience roared in anticipation and his heart raced as he burst into song. The haunting lyrics of the second song touched the very souls of the people in the stadium and at the end of the performance the applause seemed to last forever. Romeo stood in the centre of the podium surrounded with scantily dressed dancers, he stood bathed in light, his hands held up to the fans.

He wished this moment could last forever, never in his life had he expected to feel such elation he basked in the spotlight and drank in the sound of the applause, this was what he had been searching for, this one moment in time was what he had dreamed of, looking up at the blinding white light he imagined that his mother was watching down from heaven. Tears ran down his face and he left the stage into the darkness and chaos of backstage. Surrounded by guards and his crew he was ushered to his dressing room to shower. Pippa was talking but he couldn't hear what she was saying, she was crying he had never seen her show such emotion. In the shower he could still the applause he dried himself and dressed, the make-up girl touched him up, the hairdresser did his hair while the stylist buttoned his shirt. He was eager to get to the V.VIP area, he wanted to watch the other stars perform, he wanted to sample their magic. Pippa was bursting with pride this was a night to remember.

Everyone in the stadium would remember this performance for the rest of their lives. This kid would make her a fortune. He was destined to become one of the greatest stars in the history of the music industry. She had his team retouch her make-up and slipped into a sparkling designer dress.

There was a party after the show, most of the stars didn't attend they were whisked off in their limos after their performances. Pippa took Romeo and his entourage to the party.

It was time to introduce him to the press, blinded again by the flash of flashbulbs Pippa was surprised that he stopped and posed quite confidently for them.

Something happened that night to Romeo. Artists whom he had saved his pocket money to buy their albums came to compliment him and have photos taken with him. The boy that hated dancing danced all night till even Pippa was exhausted, like a male Cinderella he didn't want the night to stop. Pippa hugged him and told him just to focus on being himself and keep on doing what he had done that night.

Romeo was a quick learner, now he understood the need for the showmanship, this was show business and that required style. He knew now how important make-up and costumes were, it was another world up there. Romeo had his first taste of champagne that night and was tiddly after two glasses. They slipped into a dark stretch limo and as the car left the compound he spotted about sixty fans waiting at the gate, they were waiting there in the rain and when they saw him in the car they went mad, screaming his name and chasing the car. Pippa was beside him sipping a crystal goblet of Dom Pérignon, his head felt light.

The car sped along the road and the streetlights seemed to shine brighter than he had ever noticed, Pippa signaled something to Gemma, then pretended to be looking out of the window. Gemma kneeled and unzipped his pants, he closed his eyes as he felt her soft red painted lips on his cock, at first he was flaccid and he was embarrassed that Pippa was there but after a minute of her expert teasing he grew hard and exploded in orgasm to the sound of his own voice on the stereo. Gemma smiled licking her lips she swallowed his load while Pippa grinned.

The morning papers were full of Romeo the new Boy Wonder had kicked all the other megastars off the front page, he looked at the paper in disbelief truly believing that his mama was up there somewhere helping him.

He became an overnight sensation. Pippa doubled the amount of staff working in his department, suddenly everyone wanted to have him. After their planned European stint she wanted to do a tour, Big Cities, Big Venues, Big Bucks!

Pippa called the stylist, she was asleep, she wanted her to get her fat ass over to the studio. They were going on a shopping spree and she wanted a look put together for Romeo immediately, she wanted teenage girls to wet their knickers when they saw him and teenage boys to copy his look.

By the time his entourage arrived in London he had that slick bad boy look that Pippa had desired. Selling music was all about sex, artists had to have sex appeal and she had hired a team to preen and groom her protégé, his success had put a different look in his eye, he seemed to be suddenly more grown up and possessed a new charisma, the spotty boy had disappeared forever and a handsome pop prince had emerged.

There were thousands of fans waiting at Heathrow airport, Pippa was pleased the UK was an important country for music if he was big here he would be big elsewhere.

She booked them into Blakes, the hotel was divine she had stayed there for years she liked style, screw all this minimalism she thought, new minimalistic boutique hotels were not for her.

In London he did several television shows, did a photo shoot for a pop magazine and at night they went to some clubs. They went on a club crawl, she wanted to investigate what the DJs were plugging there, they went to Rouge, a Gothic Monthly Bash and a gay disco, the latter frightened the shit out of Romeo he wasn't into the gay scene at all.

They met up with a producer he was a hot new talent and had a string of chart successes.

The fact that he was permanently stoned was worrying but his work was good, Pippa wanted him to remix two of Romeo's new tracks.

Pippa spoiled him shopping at the designer shops in Sloane Street and they spent forever in Harrods. 'Enjoy this,' she joked, 'next time you come you'll be so famous baby you won't be able to walk on the street,' she knew it was true and sad, in a way fame and celebrity would strip his freedom but right now he was relatively unknown in Europe, that was all about to change in a few months he would be a product that was sold globally. It would be lonely up there but that was the price of fame.

Romeo embraced every experience with gusto and wonder. Pippa was his rock and Gemma was always there in the background.

Inspired with everything he saw in Europe, Romeo scribbled constant lyrics on scraps of paper, these scribbles Pippa learned would soon be transformed into bestselling singles and platinum selling albums. His inspiration gushed like a waterfall, sometimes in the middle of the night he would wake with ideas running through his mind.

They flew to Brussels then on to Munich for two nights before arriving in Amsterdam.

Pippa loved the vibe, Amsterdam was so cosmopolitan, so laid back she had arranged that Romeo go remix some tracks in Hilversum and shoot a video. She had planned to have her hair done at the Hair Police. She wanted to have green dreadlocks, it was a long process but the effect was worth it and she wanted to look hot, while her protégé was working. She combed the coffee shops smoking Colombian grass, these cafes had menus that had every conceivable kind of weed from the Golden Triangle to Timbuktu. It was a trip.

Quite by accident she stumbled on an amazing boutique, the stylist who was working on the video had recommended it. On a canal in the centre of the city, Webers was an experience in itself, the shop boasted a superb collection from young designers and the joint owners were superb. Teun, a style Guru helped her try some of his business partner's exclusive creations. Most of the designs were by his business partner Desiree Webers, she had an amazing talent Pippa thought as she tried on dozens of individual creations. Each design was better than the next, it was an Aladdin's cave of red-hot ideas. Pippa bought lots of items, she was surprised at the prices they were so reasonable, they would cost five times more in New York she mused but creations like these couldn't be found in the States they were exclusive to Amsterdam, each piece she made was a masterpiece. Pippa was honored to meet the designer, she had popped into the store with a new creation, she was like a breath of fresh air and rather eccentric.

Pippa thought she was amazing, absolutely gorgeous with a warm persona, finding a shop like this was a miracle she could have spent all day there admiring the large stock of superb creations.

It was like discovering an Aladdin's cage of fashion. She wanted Romeo to come here to look for a video outfit, apparently Desiree had made many exclusive outfits for many stars.

She purchased seven outfits for herself and two for Romeo, there were lots of cool things for the dancers too she would send the stylist here.

Amsterdam had lots of little ateliers where young designers made clothes but Desiree Webers was the one that had the real talent, her success lay in her ability to keep coming up with new designs, she had a handwriting that was her own but she diversified.

Pippa popped into the studio, it was in Hilversun miles from Amsterdam, she stopped in the hall, she could hear

Romeo he was singing a new song that stopped her in her tracks it sounded amazing, "Fuck!" she thought it's even better than his hit single.

God bless the day I laid eyes on him she thought waving at him, he was in a booth, earphones on and singing his lungs out. She marveled at the transformation that came over him when he sang. Off stage he seemed so small and insignificant, when he sang something happened, when he stepped on stage something happened, he became suddenly ten feet tall, even now in the confined space of the booth he radiated energy and when he sang it came from his soul.

Pippa remarked that he wasn't there to do a new track, he looked at her and explained that that had finished the other two tracks. Hank the producer was amazed, this kid turned up in a shapeless sweatshirt, he stepped in the booth and hey something happened. This pint-sized kid had this big voice, it just gripped and haunted you, he sang it and it was cool in one take, he was amazed, he had never worked with anyone like this, the kid was multi-faceted he could do a heavy rock song, a heart rending ballad or a cool pop tune, from rap to blues it all worked.

Pippa showed him the two shirts and pants she had bought at Webers, Romeo loved them and waltzed around the studio wearing them on top of his own clothes.

'Keep them clean for the video,' she screamed as he gorged at a takeaway Chinese.

'When's the video?' Romeo asked casually,

'Tomorrow,' she retorted and Romeo dropped the Chinese suddenly losing his attitude, she just loved springing things on him. Freaked him out.

Romeo, Pippa, Jeremy and the rest of his entourage arrived at the studio at eight am, the American producer was famous for making hot video clips, over coffee he explained quickly with story boards what was happening. It was a one day shoot and it was gonna be tough, the video for 'Message to the Gods' was medium budget, they would shoot on blue screen in the studio, then go on location to a small deserted park that apparently had this mysterious vibe, they would move on to a gypsy camp then do a dance sequence in a disused factory. The place was a hive of activity already with pretty girls being body painted in one room, lighting men setting up lights in one set.

Other members of the crew were preparing a harness on the blue screen area, apparently Romeo would be flying in one scene. After being introduced to twenty people whose names he had already forgotten he was whisked into hair and make-up.

He stood on a box because all the dancers were a head taller than him, he was wearing a metallic shirt and pants from Desiree, she had shortened them and delivered them personally, Romeo had been quite intrigued by her and was disappointed when she left the set he had hoped that she would have stayed.

The girls were almost naked, painted silver and looked like elegant sensual aliens. Romeo would do a dance sequence with them, their naked silver bodies entwined with his and after a strenuous dance routine he would drift upwards and fly above them they would jump and with the careful use of editing and computers he would fly like a god through the suspended dancers who would be frozen in midair. The scene took forever to shoot the harness dug into his crotch and he felt like a Charlie flying through the air. The shooting of the girls was delicate too, the music channels didn't like nipples or too much exposed flesh so they had to keep it tame and commercial.

After lunch they changed his hair and make-up and they went in three vans to a cold dreary location twenty miles outside Amsterdam. There was a wild landscape a mound of earth and a single tree, it looked kind of unimpressive however Romeo saw that on film it looked like an alien landscape, cool what filters and lighting could do.

It was three am when they finished the last shots in the studio, everyone had bags under their eyes. They had played his song at least two hundred times and his jaws were tired from lip syncing, they had been drinking coffee by the gallon and taking overdoses of high caffeine soda. Romeo hoped that he had looked ok in the close ups as he was real tired. Most people thought that making a clip was glamorous but his bones ached, he had sore feet and his stomach ached from the pressure and junk food.

It would take ten days to edit and add the computer effects to the clip the next morning.

Romeo had an eight o'clock call to do a morning TV program he was tired and would only have three hours in bed. Pippa thought that he was under too much pressure, she barked at Jeremy for arranging such a tight schedule. After the TV special they were off to Paris for more promotion. Romeo woke up after three hours sleep with a chill, a fever and a sore throat, he felt like he had swallowed a razor blade, his performance on TV would have to be playback he hated that. As he stood with the camera in his face the sweat ran down his back. Pippa had arranged for a doctor to meet them at the airport, they were off to Paris he couldn't be sick he had to do a show. Feeling more miserable than he could ever remember he was whisked to Schiphol Airport with a blanket round him. That night in Paris his make-up artist tried to cover up his red nose, he felt that he would pass out at any minute he did a three minute performance it seemed like an eternity and his eyes were watering, how he got through it god knows but as soon as he hit his dressing room he collapsed.

A doctor rushed to his bedside at the George Sanc he was confide to his bed for three days Pippa was furious that all their appointments were cancelled, pop sensations ceased to be human they couldn't get sick like mere mortals. Being sick cost money perhaps Romeo thought as he lay almost delirious in bed with a dangerously high temperature this was God's way of telling him that he was a mere mortal after all.

Pippa was infuriated that the schedule had been disrupted, Romeo was ill the doctor in Paris had strictly forbidden him to sing for at least a week they had cancelled all his interviews and appearances and she had made the decision to go ahead with the shooting of Romeo's video without him. The plan was that she would go to Amsterdam cast a two young models they would shoot the clip with the models and then later when Romeo was better they would shoot a half day with him in the studio, his image would be edited with the other shooting and hopefully it would be released on time the director Jan had persuaded Pippa to go along these lines and she had left Romeo in bed in Paris with an I pod and a new apple notepad that she had bought to amuse him. Hopefully she thought he would use the time in bed to be productive and write some new material.

She arrived in Amsterdam late in the afternoon the flight had been delayed because of fog in Paris and she was picked up at Schiphol airport, the casting was in progress and they were all waiting for her decision. When she arrived at the hotel the director and stylist had whittled the applicants down to four, three had arrived and were drinking coffee in the hotel room. The moment Pippa walked into the suite where the casting was being held she had made her mind up almost instantaneously, with one glance at the beautiful red-haired girl caught her attention, she was perfect for the clip, she was tall and elegant with classical bone structure, her face had graced many fashion magazine covers, Pippa recognized Yvonne immediately. Her unusual beauty would be perfect. Jan was pleased with her choice, this girl was famous in her own right and although she cost three times what the other models did she was worth it, she sent the other girls, two mousy blondes, home.

Pippa had still the male models to cast, she felt butterflies in her tummy as she looked through one of the boys' book, Jan had cut the option down to a handsome German blond model who had a lot of experience and another Surinamese black dancer who was merely passing through Amsterdam. The German fashion model had a great book he was handsome in a rugged sense and was extremely photogenic. The other boy had actually not turned up he had apparently called to say that his cab was stuck in traffic and there were only a few photos of him.

Ten minutes later a tall dark man dashed through the door, Pippa lifted her head and her heart skipped a beat.

Standing in the doorway was an absolute god he had been caught in the rain and his shirt was wet, sticking to his skin. Pippa could hardly believe that the lad was only eighteen, he was six foot tall and had the most perfect body she had ever seen. The combination of Yvonne with her pale skin and red locks and this absolute Adonis with his rippling dark muscles and mane of dreadlocks would be visually amazing, the fact that the boy had little or no experience was irrelevant, on film he would look great. Pippa asked the boy to dance.

Jan slipped on a copy Romeo's new song and Denzel started moving with expert precision, he may have had no modeling experience but his dancing was fantastic. Pippa sat transfixed as she marveled at his performance, he was a dream come true and she found it amusing that she had the hots for him.

They planned to shoot the clip in three days, till then Pippa was free, she had no immediate plans, the only things on her horizon were, shopping, getting stoned, partying and getting laid by young Denzel. When Jan went to the toilet she smiled brightly at the Surinamese god and asked him to join her for dinner. Later that evening they shared a magnificent Indonesian meal at one of the city's most famous restaurants, then after getting stoned in a coffee shop they returned to her hotel suite where Denzel made love to her in seven different positions, all his possessions were in his rucksack he didn't have a hotel so she invited him to share her lavish suite.

The next day after a hearty room service breakfast of caviar and champagne she soaped up his perfect body in the marble shower, she was so happy it had been weeks since she had sex and she was going to wear the kid out.

After breakfast they went to see the Rembrandts at the Rijkes Museum then went on a shopping spree. Pippa found all the clothes in the elegant P. C, Hoofstraat too tame and landed up going back to the superb little designer shop Webers, the store was set in a monumental building on a canal near the red light area, the area was one of the most trendy spots in Amsterdam, lots of writers and artists lived there it was hip. The following day there was a party called Wasteland it was supposed to be one of the best happenings, in the Agenda a special venue for the ultra-hip and totally uninhibited, Pippa couldn't wait, she had heard it was wild and she was in the mood for Wild since she met Denzel.

She treated her well hung toy boy to two great outfits, he looked so cool in the leather shirt and long army skirt, she had to buy it for him, he really liked a funky fake fur coat so she treated him to that for the event, she bought him a sexy thong and skin-tight vest to wear at the party. She herself opted for a slightly kinky neon green punk inspired dress that left little to the imagination, they bought matching metal spiked dog collars to complete the look. Pippa was so glad she had come to Amsterdam she loved the city.

The party was the next night and she had an appointment with The Hair Police in the morning, she wanted to look spectacular at the party and wanted to have some hair extensions. She was glad that Romeo had been sick, fate had taken its turn and here she was.

They made a stunning couple, Pippa with her green dreadlocks and fetish outfit and her toy boy in his sexy almost transparent garb, both exhibitionists by heart they ignored the looks of the people in the hotel reception as they paraded through the foyer to go to their limo, Pippa dripping in metal jewellery which jangled as she walked.

While they had been dressing they had drunk some wine and taken a little artificial energy in pill form, Pippa wanted to dance all night and she had encouraged Denzel to take an ecstasy pill.

All heads turned as they stepped out of the limo at the venue. When they arrived the party was in full swing, lesbians, leathermen and all kinds, freaked out on the dance floor she was introduced to a young Baron, the man of aristocratic background was only wearing boots and a dog leash he was being dragged through the room by a tall dominatrix clad in black wet look PVC.

It was a night where everything was too cool and every kink was regarded as normal. They danced erotically for hours their bodies were wet with sweat. Pippa was high as a kite she hadn't done coke for months but she decided that it was ok to have a little, she met a songwriter she knew from L. A. At first she hadn't recognized him as he was wearing a leather mask, however when he spoke she recognized the voice and they danced together. Vince had written two hits for her in the past and it was an absolute trip to meet him here. In the early hours of the morning they were invited to go to a private party in an old loft, Pippa was enjoying herself she didn't want the night to end she was glad to accept Vince's invite and together with Denzel and ten of Vince's friends they squeezed into her limo to go to the next party.

They arrived at the disused warehouse in the early hours of the morning, inside the venue it was so dark you hardly could see, bodies were pressed so close to each other that it was impossible to dance, the air was heavy with a cocktail of odors, marihuana, poppers and sweat it was just like the eighties Pippa thought as she started to dance with one of Vince's gay friends, he was over six foot tall and covered in tattoos. The tattoos were a work of art, his whole torso and arms were covered in intricate designs she found herself tripping on the lights, she was happy and danced for an hour losing herself in the music. The DJ was cool and the vibe was hot, unexpectedly she felt tired and slipped away from the tattooed monster, suddenly she noticed that she had lost Denzel and she wandered through a maze of dark corridors that led off the main dance area. The corridors led to rooms, everything was pitch black, in the dark rooms she was aware of bodies bumping and grinding, hands groped her body as she squeezed through the maze of corridors.

The drugs and the music were affecting her as she felt breasts and cocks rub against her. Suddenly she was grabbed by two men, in the darkness she felt powerless, one stripped her and within minutes she felt him penetrate her from behind, the other pulled her head and stuck his erect penis in her mouth almost choking her, something in her head was resisting but something else was fighting not to resist. Was this lust? Was this rape? She didn't know, she was beyond rationality, both men came and swopped positions, she felt another woman's lips on her nipples and reached orgasm as the second man pumped her from behind. The smell of his sweat turned her on, suddenly they were gone and she staggered down the corridor, a few steps further another man pressed against her, the feel of his fingers inside her turned her on and this time she sat on top of him. While she rode the stranger another man emerged he kissed her lips she grabbed his neck it was Denzel she recognized the dreadlocks and the dog collar they switched partners again and she was left alone as Denzel fucked the man that she had ridden. Suddenly she felt dirty and wanted to leave, she pulled down her dress, it was so dark and she had lost her knickers.

The first two men had ripped open her dress and she felt self-conscious as she fought her way through the crowd that were dancing. It had got busier and her head was spinning, for a moment she thought that she was going to collapse, the music, the pressure of the people, the mix of drink and drugs, the room was spinning and Denzel staggered out of the dark room and spotted her in the crowd. She was glad he had found her and he lifted her up and carried her to the exit to her Limo. Her driver had fallen asleep and Denzel had to bang on the widow to rouse him. When they arrived at their deluxe hotel, guests were going for breakfast and as they entered the lift, people frowned in disapproval at the middle-aged woman with her ripped dress and the young stud who was only wearing a thong and t shirt.

Pippa and her black super stud crashed and slept for almost twenty-four hours. They were just beginning to feel

298

human again when Jan called, it was the day of the shoot, he had no idea that Pippa was with Denzel they turned up together at the studio two hours late. Their late arrival together resulted in raised eyebrows from the crew.

They had started shooting the video, Yvonne had been made-up and looked stunning. Pippa felt old and haggard next to the lovely young thing as she was lying on a bed between silk sheets waiting on the arrival of her lover who was played by Denzel.

The young black stud looked no worse for the wear, Pippa had suffered a bad hangover but he looked just great, youth, Pippa sneered, she hated it.

The shooting went well and they finished at seven, the crew all went for dinner. Pippa wanted to go to sleep but felt obliged to join them as they went to a nice Italian by a canal, after a few glasses of wine Pippa had a new lease of life and had tried to encourage everyone to go and party. Denzel had persuaded her to go back to the hotel he had suddenly crashed and needed sleep.

In Paris, Romeo was feeling better he had been given the ok from the doctor and wanted to join Pippa in Amsterdam he wanted to shoot his part of the video and get it over with.

He had enjoyed his week in bed he had been physically exhausted and had needed the rest.

Pippa had been reluctant to tell him about the plans for a mini world tour she had booked him for.

A tour playing in Detroit, New York, San Francisco, London, Paris, Tokyo, Bangkok and Singapore, one show in each city in one month. She suspected that he would freak out but the sponsors were keen.

She had been lucky to get the venues. An aging star had died unexpectedly and she had been offered all the venues the deceased had planned.

Pippa broke the news to Romeo gently and to her surprise he was excited about the tour.

They planned to do a rehearsal by having a concert in a small city a month later.

For three weeks in America Romeo worked on the show, he had a problem with the choreographer and hated the dancing lessons, fans seemed to follow him everywhere he went and he was usually very accommodating to the fans and signed autographs and chatted to them regularly. He was usually accompanied by four bodyguards but the night of the trial show for some reason there were only two. That night his relationship with the fans would change forever. They did the show which went down well but there had been some technical hitches and Romeo had been upset about it. As they left the stadium there was an unexpected number of fans at the back stage entrance. Romeo was shocked at the amount of fans, they seemed almost hostile, waving he walked down the stairs. The limo was only ten steps away and the whole incident happened so quickly that they didn't expect it. As they headed for the car he was blinded with the flashing lights of the paparazzi.

As the crowd surged forward one of his two bodyguards slipped, the other turned and in the space of a second Romeo was swept up by the crowd and dragged ten meters down the street, more fans crashed through the barriers and he was surrounded by screaming hysterical fans. His hat and sunglasses were ripped of his face and the crowds were tearing at his clothes, for the first time in his career he felt frightened, after a few terrifying moments his bodyguards arrived with police and they managed to pry him free and get him in the car.

Once in the car Romeo was hyperventilating, the car was surrounded on all sides by the hungry fans who were rocking the car. Suddenly the crowd lunged forward again and a young girl was thrown forward, with a thump her head hit the car, she had been screaming his name and her teeth were knocked out with the impact. The blood ran down the windows, people were screaming, they didn't stop, more people on the other side were crushed against the vehicle.

His bodyguards were being punched and the driver couldn't move as there were fans on the bonnet and at the rear the excited expressions on their faces turned to a look of fear as their heads were crushed. Romeo put up the hood on his jacket and held his head in his hands for what seemed like ages. Outside a fight broke out, angry fans threw bottles at the car windows and blood seemed to splatter everywhere, the sound of police sirens sounded in the distance and after a few moments the crowds dispersed and the driver crept away.

Romeo felt sick, the incident had terrified him and the next morning the papers were full of photos. So many fans had been hurt and Pippa instructed the management to beef up his security measures, she was furious that something like this had been allowed to happen.

From that day on Romeo refused to mix with his fans, when the crowd had swept him away he had been genuinely scared, he had almost been trampled over.

The first stop of the tour was New York, it was there at the sound check he met for the first time his support act, The Bastille Brothers, he didn't like them from the first moment he saw them. Five Europeans that had been formed to join a Euro boy band, they had three things in common all of them were deadly handsome, each of them could dance and none of them could sing, they did a lip sync playback performance, one English, one Irish, one French a Belgian and a Dutch.

Romeo was furious at the promoters for giving this newfound boy band the opportunity to be on his tour and he had a vicious argument with Pippa and the promoters and he point blank refused to share the stage with the good-looking lads.

Romeo's jealousy was intensified when on the opening night the boys had a double standing ovation, the fans loved the good-looking wholesome Europeans and after one night he demanded that they annulled their contracts and found a replacement for the world tour.

They had to pay the boy band the full amount of their contract and the young newcomers benefited from a burst of publicity when the press did a feature on Romeo's jealousy. Getting rid of them had actually backfired, they got more media attention than they would have if they had merely done the tour.

Pippa was beside herself trying to find someone that could be a support act, she was delighted when the London office called to suggest a young Indonesian girl might be of use to them.

Amber was lovely, she was young and sexy, could dance and sing and Romeo thought that she would be perfect. Her first single, an up tempo dance song was good and due to be released in a week or so.

Pippa had her audition and after Romeo approved she gave the sweet little thing a contract to do the whole tour, the backers were pleased, she was eighteen with long legs and a perfect pair of boobs she would add sex appeal to the show.

Somewhere along the line Romeo had become a superstar with an ego to match, he was no longer hungry for success and easy to work with. His demands became greater and he was turning into a pain in the ass, he demanded two dressing rooms to be at his disposal one for him and one for his friends, even though he didn't have any. These dressing rooms had to be laid out to the approval of his feng shui master, he insisted on having Russian caviar, champagne, peppermint tea, fresh jasmine and orchids, as well as a make-up artist, hairdresser, stylist, masseur and chef on duty. Romeo didn't realize that he himself was to be billed for all the costs incurred so Pippa let him make his demands. She had seen this a hundred times, they started off with nothing and landed up with an attitude, the love of the public had transformed him into a demanding spoiled brat with a super ego.

Pippa was bored with Romeo, she was also bored with Denzel, she had persuaded Romeo to let Denzel join their group on tour he was a good dancer but Romeo had been jealous he was too good-looking and too tall. It had taken her a week to persuade him and in the end she had had to let him know that Denzel was her temporary lover.

Sometimes she would wake up in the middle of the night and think that it was Tyrese that was lying in her bed, they had similar skin colours and magnificent physiques but there the similarity ended she had loved Tyrese, he had took her places she had never been. Sex with Denzel was great he was young and hung and vigorous but she missed the love aspect, she had had deep emotions for Tyrese she had been in love with him and she was in "lust" with Denzel not in love.

One night they went to see Tyrese's new movie, it felt weird to watch him up on screen.

He looked like a demigod, after the film Pippa had been so haunted by memories she had turned silent, she hadn't dared tell Denzel that the guy that had played the heartthrob had been a stripper that she had discovered, instead she feigned a headache. That night as she lay in bed she had to admit to herself that Denzel was second best, all he was was a body to curl up against, he didn't fill the emotional void that she felt. She wished that she had never ever seen the movie with Tyrese, it had only awakened feelings that she thought were gone.

The next morning when Denzel rolled on top of her she pretended that it was Tyrese, sooner or later she would dump this stud she knew but what else was there in her life, at least he hadn't tried to get her to make a record. He seemed quite happy living with her and dancing on the tour, they paid him a pittance but he didn't complain he stayed with her she bought his clothes and spoiled him when she felt like it. She knew he was ac /dc and slept with everything that moved and she had accepted his bisexuality, he had an overactive sex drive and as long as he kept her satisfied she didn't care what he got up to in the daytime. He was always horny, always ready for sex, he would have made an excellent escort she mused he could have made a fortune.

Pippa couldn't sleep she was so mentally busy with the fucking world tour, the thing had disaster written all over it she had ignored all her other stars and was handling only Romeo.

Over the last few months his records had sold even more, his success had only made him become more difficult. It was weird how they all changed, the loneliness, the pressure it destroyed them all.

He was still talented, he was not at the burnt-out stage yet, she imagined he would keep producing music till he was eighty it was in his genes.

She wondered what Romeo did for sex, in the beginning she had paid people like Gemma to service him, now he handled his own sexual encounters. Rumor had it he liked groupies and was also having an affair with the stylist, a buxom blonde with silicone mammaries. Pippa had often questioned her bills, she seemed to get paid double the normal fee and she had noticed an expensive diamond ring on her finger, she guessed that he also had the hots for Amber, she wouldn't have been surprised if Romeo was also sleeping with Denzel she had seen the way they looked at each other.

Romeo had even fired the choreographer and requested that Denzel give him private lessons, she had caught them once in the shower together in the dressing room after a lesson.

Denzel had downright denied any relationship with Romeo, he was a perfect liar and Pippa knew that he would have slept with anyone to climb up the ladder of success. The truth was she didn't give a shit, as far as she was concerned Denzel could screw whoever he liked, their open relationship suited her she didn't want any emotional bonds with anyone at this point. She was dreading this tour, Romeo had turned into a rattlesnake and after the tour she planned on letting someone else handle him, she was going to handle other artists perhaps she would take Amber under her wing, she had a raw uncultivated talent that would work in the States.

The first stop of the tour was in London, there had been a hundred and one problems and the tour management had been replaced at the last minute. Pippa was anticipating teething problems there had been problems with the sound system and the sound technicians had been working through the night.

Quite unexpectedly Romeo turned up early he was not supposed to do a soundcheck till late afternoon, the dancers were in early too do a rehearsal and Amber was there to rehearse.

Amber had never done a live gig, she had recorded an album and made a low budget video which was expected to be released within weeks. The leggy fragile girl with the huge amber coloured almond shaped eyes was eager to perform for a live audience and Pippa had arrived just to check how things were progressing. If they had a good revue in London they were laughing, Romeo was releasing two singles one after the other in conjunction with the concert.

Romeo sat silently in the middle of the hall, Pippa sat a few seats away from him, they had become like strangers to each other, he had changed so much in the last six months. She had preferred his attitude at the beginning of his career, after the dancers had finished their three routines Amber walked on stage, it was early morning everyone was dressed casually in sweatpants with no make-up, at rehearsals it didn't matter all the glitter and glamour was saved for the show that's how it was in show business.

Amber however had gone to great pains to look good, it was ten am but she was immaculately made-up and was wearing a stunning outfit that sparkled on stage. She was of mixed blood, her father had been American and her mother Indonesian she was incredibly beautiful with perfect bone structure and a mane of shiny waist length hair, her golden skin was smooth as silk and her lips were large and sensuous and for an Asian her breasts were large, she was only twenty but looked very grown up as she took her place on the stage, she walked like a panther. They played her intro and she broke in to song.

To Pippa's amazement she sounded even better live than on disk, she had obviously put a lot of thought into the performance, her dance routine was superb and Pippa thought that they had been lucky to have got her. She was a lot better than the good-looking boy band that Romeo had demanded to be fired, She was young sexy and a fresh face, the boys would love her and the young female fans would all want to copy her, Pippa was pleased but made a note to talk to the stylist, she didn't want her to look too sophisticated she wanted to keep her young and sexy the clothes she was wearing now were too sophisticated for her and she needed to funk it up a bit.

Pippa asked four of the male dancers to come on stage, they rehearsed a routine with Amber and Pippa was happy with the direction, she was amazed that Romeo had sat through the whole morning without complaining. It was cold in the auditorium and normally he would have be making demands, today for some unknown reason he had left his ego in the hotel room and was behaving quite normally, when Amber was finished Romeo went on stage and introduced himself, he lavished her with compliments and invited her for a drink coffee with him in his dressing room. Amber blushed and appeared modest, to have been given so many compliments from a major artist had been flattering and they seemed to be getting on famously so famously that Romeo had suggested that she join him for a duet at the end of the performance.

Pippa couldn't believe her ears, she didn't know how they were going to pull that off, they would have to rehearse the song over and over to get it right. Amber hadn't even heard the track, Pippa tried to dissuade Romeo but he insisted that his new young support act would indeed join him on stage later, he like the idea of a duet, their voices would blend perfectly. Pippa shrugged and went off. She asked them to call her when it was perfected and she promised that she would return to hear the finished result. Later that afternoon the producer called her and requested that she come round to hear the finished result.

Romeo had been functioning on automatic pilot for months and although he sounded incredible he had in his heart lost his mojo. Watching Amber had inspired him. She possessed that naive hunger that he once did. Singing with her had rejuvenated his thirst for life.

The duet was incredible it was amazing as he thought that Amber had mastered it so quickly.

The combination of their voices was interesting and the audience would love it, it might be an idea to cut a single of this live she suggested a sort of unplugged live version could be released as a single.

They only had a few hours till the performance, Romeo took off in his Hummer he wanted to meditate and have a holistic massage before the performance. Pippa went to her hotel suite with a clip board and a pile of notes. Denzel fucked her in the shower twice, it was his way of avoiding the pre-show nerves, Pippa didn't complain, she enjoyed the unexpected spontaneous raw sex sessions with her ebony Adonis.

Romeo hated big crowds since the incident with the fans weeks before, his security had been revamped, six guards built like battleships were placed in charge of his security and he no longer stopped to linger with fans to sign autographs, he insisted that there was a distance between the fans and his car and tried to avoid being near the public.

Romeo snapped at the make-up artist and hairdresser ordering them out of the room, at the last moment he decided that he didn't like the outfit planned for the show and demanded that the stylist prepare some other choices, he complained bitterly that the shoes were too tight and that he wouldn't be able to dance in them. Emma the stylist had tears in her eyes as she dressed him, Mandy sprayed some gel in his hair and Jade the make-up artist sulked as she powdered his face. Romeo had been ignoring her for days, they hadn't had sex for a week and she was afraid that she would lose her job, the thump on his dressing room door signaled that his was his curtain call. Cursing he waved all the staff away and checked quickly his appearance, too much make-up and he hated his hair, he sneered at his reflection wondering if the clothes were all right, then surrounded by his bodyguards and Pippa he was led to the entrance of the stage. This was the moment he hated most, that single moment before he stepped on stage he was surrounded with staff, but he was the one who when it came to the crunch had to go out there and do it. He was trembling and sweating, Jade handed him a towel he wiped his forehead then ran on to the stage. The moment he stepped on stage and heard the roar of the crowd he forgot his stage fright, under the lights he pretended that his mama was watching from above and he sang his heart out, it was weird but on stage was the only place on earth he really felt alive he had this stage fright just before a show, he didn't want to go on stage but once on he didn't want to come off.

He danced with precision and performed like he never had before, the crowd loved him and he gave them his all.

The duet with Amber went down well when she stepped on stage in a sheer red dress on his heart raced, he sang the love song with heartfelt emotion staring right into her eyes, at the end of the song he surprised her by grabbing her and kissing her on the lips, she surprised him back by sticking her moist tongue down his throat.

The gig had gone down well and Pippa had heard that the music journalists were going to give them rave revues. Pippa was a little angry that both Romeo and Amber had not appeared at the lavish after party arranged by the record company, while she tried to make excuses for her star he was lying on his back in bed in his hotel suite, Amber totally naked on top of him. Romeo was so satisfied she looked so innocent but certainly knew how to turn him on. After the third time he came he wanted to sleep, he had to fight her off, she was as wild as a vixen between the sheets. He woke in the morning with her lips on his cock, he was glad she was on tour with him she had more class than Jade he thought as he came in her mouth, he would sack Jade later he thought, he never did like her make-up anyway he mused as he burst to climax.

They did get rave revues and it was off to Paris, in three days they would be doing the same show there and then it would be back to the states for the San Francisco leg of the journey.

In Paris Romeo wore a wig and hat and together he and Amber ditched the bodyguards and went up the Eiffel tower, they had lunch at a little cafe on the left bank and went shopping, raiding the designer boutiques. Their day ended when an army of fans recognized him and they had to escape in a taxi back to their hotel.

Pippa was so furious that he had sneaked out without his guards that she refused to join their party at Cabaret that night. What was the use of beefing up his security if he was going to take off by himself, these concerts were sold out, what would happen if he went out alone and was kidnapped or hurt, he would be responsible for the loss of the ticket sales and he would have to refund the money to the sponsors and fans. 'Sightseeing and shopping,' Pippa screamed, 'fucking asshole,' she added as she slammed the door of his suite.

That night they ate at the Buddha bar, grabbed a cocktail at Barfly then went to Cabaret to dance, Pippa went with Denzel to Manray, she thought that he was going to have whiplash of the neck, there were so many good-looking girls there that Denzel was just about creaming his jeans. She got drunk and argued with him, eventually they went back to the hotel and Pippa threw up in the toilet she had been mixing her drinks and had had one too many.

Amber was sharing a room with Romeo, Pippa found it ridiculous that she had to pay for the empty room that Amber had not even slept in. The paparazzi had had a field day, they had been following Romeo and Amber, the record company had been tipping the paparazzi off as they thought that the more publicity Romeo got the better his single would sell.

They had snaps of him shopping, eating, dancing and even kissing Amber, their photos were in every newspaper and magazine in Paris, Pippa was pleased till the shit hit the fan.

One rather tacky tabloid run a four page feature on Romeo and Amber, the world exclusive almost made Pippa's dreadlocks stand on end as she read the story. She wondered how Romeo would react when he saw the tabloid. She was sure that he was going to be livid, the show was planned for that night and tickets had been totally sold out.

The story claimed that Romeo's new "Juliet" Miss Amber was in fact not a woman but a man. Apparently Amber's ex-lover had been duped and had sold his story to the tabloid.

Amber was indeed a half blood, her mother had worked in a sex massage salon and her father had been an American GI, Amber had been born in a slum in Indonesia.

The child was called Chang, Amber had been born male, was raised in a rural village and then at thirteen had gone to stay with an aunt in Thailand and worked in a brothel in Bangkok serving men, at sixteen a wealthy German had fallen in love with the boy and paid for him to have the operation of his dreams, a sex change.

All his life young Chang had had two dreams, one was to be a woman and the other was to be a pop singer. Kurt the wealthy German lawyer had helped him achieve the first dream. He had undergone a series of operations at a clinic in Thailand with one of the world's leading sex change surgeons. The operations had taken some time, first the breasts then the final one, the removal of his penis had been a physiological experience, physically he had been transformed into a woman he could be penetrated like any other woman, they had created a vagina that could fool anyone. The operations were complex and successful. As a woman he had performed in a transsexual revue, his talent and beauty were noticed by a Dutch record producer, and Chang had moved to Europe, he had a woman's passport as he was now technically a woman. One thing had led to another, one door had opened another here. Amber was singing as support act for Romeo and warming his bed at night. Pippa wondered how Romeo would be reacting to this piece of news. In Asia transsexuals, transvestites and Ladyboys were treated as normal, some of Thailand's leading fashion models were transsexuals, it was no big deal.

She wondered if Romeo would be performing the duet with Amber after this. Romeo was so macho he didn't really approve of gays she wondered how he would take this.

Pippa arrived at his hotel suite, the bodyguard outside the room told her that Mr Romeo was still sleeping and that Amber was still in the room. Obviously he hadn't heard about this she thought as she rapped on his door. Romeo was not pleased at being woke up he had a hellish hangover and was still mad at Pippa for not attending the dinner the previous evening. Romeo was in bed with Amber wrapped around him, without speaking Pippa handed him the front page and he read it silently, then he turned to the four page article with photos of Amber as a man, it was then that Romeo exploded and punched Amber so hard he hurt his fist. The girl awoke with a start and cowered in the bed as Romeo hurtled a string of abuse, she had never seen him so angry and Pippa had to call the guards to separate them.

Amber had kneed him in the balls and was tearing his hair out he was screaming at her and punching her. The two guards received a few blows themselves as they tried to peel the two angry naked bodies apart. The hotel manager was at the door, other guests had complained about the noise, a guard wrapped a sheet round Amber and dragged her off to her room. Romeo had tears of anger in his eyes, he was humiliated he had been making love to a fucking geezer, he screamed at Pippa blaming her for everything, he would be the laughing stock of the planet, he was afraid to go on stage they would laugh at him they would call him a fucking faggot, he had been fucking a guy with a chopped of dick and he hadn't even noticed the difference, he had licked her fucking pussy just a few hours before and enjoyed it.

It was too much for him to handle. Pippa made the mistake about mentioning that night's gig, he freaked out how the fuck did she expect him to get up there in front of 100000 people and be able to fucking sing, Pippa raked through her handbag and produced a valium, Romeo swallowed it and swished it down with some flat champagne from the night before. The sticky liquid was warm and tasted awful without the bubbles. He felt like a sucker, a complete idiot, he had been made into a laughing stock, suddenly repulsed he ran to the bathroom and threw up he had been shagging a man it was too much to swallow.

Pippa stayed with Romeo all day, she didn't want him to be alone and for the first time in months he was grateful of her company. She arranged that The Bastille Boys fly in to do back up, Romeo was happy with that, he didn't want to see that con woman ever again.

The Euro Boy Band were delighted to be called back they were arriving by private jet in Paris at four in the afternoon and would do the same songs as on their first night.

Pippa kept Romeo calm with valium then about an hour before the show she gave him an upper and for the first time in his career he had decided to do playback, he was afraid if he sang live he would lose it. That night he was extra nervous to walk out on stage, he was terrified that they would all laugh. On stage he switched on to automatic pilot, his performance was robotic the moment he had finished the last song he raced back to his suite in his limo.

He locked his hotel doors and took the two sleeping pills that Pippa had left him, all he wanted to do was escape till the morning. He was traveling to New York the following day.

When they arrived there were lots of photographers at the airport the scandal had indeed hit the press there and he was a laughing stock, as they drove towards the city Romeo openly cried.

Pippa had an idea, she thought the longer that you hid from the press the more that they would hound you, she suggested he go on a live TV chat show and make a joke of the whole thing, he didn't fancy the idea but took her advice, That night the whole of America watched as he sat on live TV confidently chatting about the experience of falling in love with a transsexual, Pippa had had someone prompt him on how to answer and act and he had successfully pulled it off. The nation were no longer hostile, they were sympathetic towards him. Romeo had been nervous but he knew that Pippa had been right, this way it would all die down hopefully in a few days.

The press had not affected Amber's career, if anything it had given her a boost she had had lots of press and was featured in all the glossy magazines and in fashion shoots. Her single had been released amidst all the controversy and she had just signed a record deal with a major company every gay, lesbian, transgender and minority group on the globe would buy her single.

Romeo hoped that the curvy temptress would remain in Europe, he was happy that there was an ocean between them. Taking things to the extreme he had Pippa arrange an appointment with a shrink, the shock had indeed affected him more than anyone had expected.

The more he thought of it there had been odd signs, Amber had looked every inch the woman but sexually always taken the lead like a man, he had always been amazed that she knew what a guy liked, sometimes Romeo had nightmares that he was sleeping with Amber and she had this whopping great dick it was crazy he knew, but it freaked him out.

Pippa had roared with laughter when Romeo had confessed his nightmares, over the last few days Romeo and Pippa had developed a bond that they had missed for months.

Basically Romeo was homophobic, Pippa had swung both ways for her it was no big deal.

In the eighties everyone was bisexual.

Pippa was so tired, she was living on pills, the stress of Romeo's tour had been too much for both of them. The demand for tickets had made the promoters book extra dates, record sales were rocketing and when they were on the road Romeo was writing songs for the next album, even though he was under extreme stress he was disciplined. He tried to get a decent night's sleep and keep in good condition, he had filmed a video in Tokyo which looked real hot and he was just as popular in Asia as in Europe, he had received lots of awards but had never actually attended an award ceremony he was always traveling. One night as they travelled on the luxury tour bus that had been converted to fulfill his needs he confided in Pippa that he had wanted to cram as much into his career as possible, his star had risen so high he knew that it couldn't last forever.

The money was rolling in and he was responsible for twenty percent of her turnover, since the incident with Amber, Pippa and he had developed a bond and they actually laughed now about the affair.

Denzel had dropped out of the tour, he had taken Pippa by surprise in San Francisco telling her that his grandfather had died and left him a bar in Curacao, he was tired of traveling and wanted to go there and run it.

One day he was there dancing on stage, the next he was packing his bags. Pippa dropped him off at the airport with a heavy heart, she would miss her toy boy, as his tall frame passed through the passport control she thought there's plenty more where that came from.

The tracks that Romeo was working on were quite different from anything he had done before, Pippa was excited she was sure his fans would like the new sound.

They were on the last leg of the tour they had two gigs in Bangkok, the whole crew were exhausted and were dying to get back home, they had been on the road for several months and missed their families and friends. Pippa had given Romeo a three day break in the concert schedule, she wanted him to rest so they went to Phuket to spend three days there. It was August and the monsoon season was lingering, they had been invited to go to the Phi Phi islands on one of her friend's yachts, Pippa had declined, she had an awful hangover and Romeo had decided to go by himself he was eager to see the unspoiled island.

At this time of year the seas were rough and the coast guard recommended not to travel.

When they had left the sea was as calm as could be. Romeo was inspired, the sun was shining on him as he lay on the deck and the scenery was spectacular. They had gone first to Phang Ah the surrealistic rock formations that jutted out of the sea were incredible and after a superb seafood lunch they headed in the other direction towards The Phi Phi Islands. A few years ago the islands were remote and beautiful, a Hollywood studio had made a major film there and since that the island had been bombarded by tourists. Romeo scuba dived in the turquoise sea marveling at the coral reefs and the marine life that populated the crystal clear waters. He was glad that he had gone, the day had been perfect. When they decided to head home things changed, they were in the middle of the sea when the tropical storm started, the sky turned black and fork lightning darted all over the horizon. Suddenly their boat became like a piece of paper, the sleek white yacht was being tossed around the ocean as huge waves filled the boat with sea water. Romeo held on to a handle to prevent him from being tossed overboard, crew members vomited and their sick shot through the air. For over an hour the small craft was tossed around the ocean like a toy, everyone feared for their lives.

Back on shore Pippa had feared for their lives too, there hadn't been such a fierce tropical storm for years. Romeo was badly shaken and when he eventually did get back to shore, the experience had chilled him he would never go on a boat again as long as he lived. His passion for diving had diminished. That night he was deeply shaken and retired early.

The two concerts went well considering that he had been badly shaken up, he had been sexually connected with a Thai television soap star, she had taken him to a superb restaurant called, The Supper Club the interior was white and futuristic and they were served dinner in bed, afterwards they had danced at The Ministry of Sound the DJ had played two of his songs, it was a cool night no one recognized him and he had enjoyed the animosity of being lost in the crowd.

They had a great after party for the crew in Bangkok with fire-eaters and naked Thai dancers who were painted with neon paint that lit up in the dark. The dancers performed an awesome neon ballet, Pippa had wished that they had been on tour with them they were spectacular.

Everyone finished the tour in high spirits Romeo had the hots for the female dancer that had performed the illuminated ballet for them in Bangkok. The dark haired beauty was called Capricorn, he asked Pippa to have a visa arranged so that she could travel back with them to the states.

Pippa wondered if Romeo thought that she had a magic wand, the record company could pull strings but they were leaving the following day.

Pippa thought that Romeo would explode when she told him that it would take another week to prepare the visa, he shrugged and to her surprise announced that he would stay till her visa was ready, she wanted to show him the real Thailand and take him sightseeing up north.

Pippa had to organize two bodyguards to stay with them, she didn't want Romeo walking about the streets, his fear of the fans seemed to be ebbing but she didn't want any more incidents.

Traveling in limos with bodyguards only attracted attention especially in Thailand, Romeo wanted to be free to go to the markets and temples and walk in the streets like a normal person. Capricorn went shopping to a market, she returned triumphant with a surprise, she had bought him a cheap checked shirt, pants, sandals and a tasteless hat and sunglasses. Romeo frowned as he tried them on reluctantly, the fabric felt so cheap and there was nothing designer about them, 'Like that,' Capricorn promised, 'you will melt in to the crowd.'

Pippa was doubtful but let him go out with her to try, they caught the sky train near the hotel and went to the royal palace with a rucksack on his back and a camera he looked like just another tourist.

When they returned Romeo looked so happy, they had taken in a movie, eaten popcorn and even ate in a fast food restaurant, no one had recognized him and he felt secure with the idea of being a mere mortal for a week. Pippa was reluctant, his concert was finished he could release his bodyguards if he chose, they checked out of the five star hotel and moved into a make shift apartment that Capricorn had rented. Romeo had never been happier, Pippa was so worried about him but that week was the best week of his life, they rented a car and drove everywhere, they ate with the Thai's in the cheap corner restaurants.

Capricorn introduced him to her family and friends telling them that he was a history student.

Romeo saw life through other eyes, at night they went to karaoke bars and Thai clubs, he was amazed at the talent in some of these venues they had like so many stars here and they were singing in clip joints for a pittance.

The Thai's loved to drink whisky and Capricorn introduced him to the taste of Black label. At the clubs the Thai's ordered it by the bottle and for the first time for what seemed like an eternity Romeo could be himself and enjoy himself, The Thai's were fun loving people and laughed all the time.

On the last day they went to a market and he bought lots of things that reminded him of Thailand. On the Friday they spent the whole day at the Embassies and Consulates organizing the visa. Deep in his heart he could have stayed longer and he was hoping that the visa was not ready, the idea of going back home and being a prisoner in your own home made him cringe. He had indeed enjoyed being a mere mortal for a week, it felt great to go to the supermarket or go jogging alone, recently when he jogged he had bodyguards with him it felt kind of weird even when he had gone to the toilet they waited outside, it was embarrassing to say the least.

They flew from Don Muang airport first class to New York, Capricorn had never flown before and was sick with nerves, she closed her eyes tight and fell asleep before take-off, she had no idea just how famous that he was or how rich, she was so naïve. When she went to see her family once a year in the north she traveled on a bus, flying was a big deal for her.

He smiled at her, her head on his shoulder she was a beauty. While she slept, inspired by the week of freedom he wrote three songs as the plane headed through the clouds towards the land where he would never be free.

There was an army of paparazzi waiting for him at the airport, the record company had tipped them off no doubt. Capricorn covered her face at the assault of flashbulbs and gasped as she entered the mile long limo it was disgusting she thought to have such an ostentatious car.

Capricorn gaped open-mouthed when she entered his penthouse duplex, 'You live here alone?' she exclaimed as she wandered through the rooms. Romeo thought how different this must be for her, he had loved the week in the tiny studio with her it had been nice being a mere mortal. He thought it was best now to explain who he was, he showed her his albums and press map then flicked on the massive plasma screen TV and played some of his videos, 'Oh My Buddha!' she exclaimed. 'You look same, it's the same you,' realizing that it was indeed him up there on the stage, she looked shocked. She knew he was a singer but hadn't envisaged that he was a megastar. They were only in the apartment ten minutes when the concierge called to say Pippa was on her way up.

Pippa arrived with his PR man and secretary, there were papers to sign and plans to make she growled, 'No time for jet lag sweetie,' she purred as she kissed him on both cheeks. There was something different about the way he looked but she couldn't put her finger on it, it was like all the stress and aggression had been drained out of him, he looked wholesome hearty and what's more he had this look in his eyes. My God she thought amused, he is in love, that was it, he was in love with this what's her name miss zodiac sign the girl from the neon ballet. She did dance well, probably great in bed Pippa thought. After he signed all the papers he sat Pippa down and showed her all the photos of where he had been in Thailand. The temples, karaoke, Pippa couldn't believe this was Romeo, this girl had like put a spell on him he was almost a human being again the super ego had been shelved.

Pippa rattled on there, was a very important party that night, she wanted Romeo to get some sleep because he had to attend, she looked at plain Jane disapprovingly and whispered in Romeo's ear that she would have the stylist drop off some clothes for her, she asked Capricorn her dress and shoe size and disappeared in a cloud of Dior perfume.

The young couple slept the sleep of the dead, woke around seven at night made love then lay in the Jacuzzi, there were no curtains in the bathing area and she could see the lights of the city glitter like diamonds. At eight the concierge brought a rail of clothes and boxes of shoes for Capricorn, Romeo explained that they were going to a big party with lots of stars and that Pippa had arranged some clothes for her. Capricorn marveled at the creations, she had never seen clothes like it, she couldn't believe the dress she selected was 3ooo dollars and the shoes 600 dollars, you could live for a year on that in Thailand she claimed.

When Capricorn emerged from the dressing room Romeo sucked in his breath, in the Versace dress she looked like a movie star, she had applied her make-up carefully and piled her hair high on her head. There's going to be a lot of jealous guys there tonight he joked, Capricorn looked at the three large diamond rings and vulgar diamond cross he wore.

For added bling. 'Copies?' she remarked, 'Yes' he lied, embarrassed to admit they were worth hundreds of thousands of dollars. He made a mental note to buy her something wildly expensive and sparkly she would be the only jewelless woman at the party tonight for sure.

She certainly scrubs up well, Pippa thought raising her eyebrows in approval as Capricorn made her entrance.

Pippa was glad Romeo had found love. Fame and fortune were pointless without love.

Perhaps this Asian lovely would bring him back down to earth, they made a perfect couple on the dance floor and

Capricorn was intrigued by all the famous faces that she recognized but didn't recognize, she felt like Cinderella and nicknamed Romeo, Prince Charming.

The concert tour had been a success, Romeo's album was selling well all over the globe.

He was working on some terrific new material and taking time to chill out with Capricorn.

Pippa was giving more attention to the other artists her company had signed up, she wanted to give Romeo some space till he had enough material for the next album.

The wedding invitation arrived in her mail, the perfumed invitation took her by surprise she had no idea that Romeo had been so serious she presumed that Capricorn had been a flash in the pan so to speak. She was invited to attend a lavish private reception at a castle in Scotland in a month.

Pippa dialed Romeo's number and congratulated him, she couldn't believe that he was settling down, perhaps it was time and Capricorn had brought him back down to earth. To the whole world he was a megastar but to the simple Thai girl with the pearly smile he was merely a man, his success didn't impress her, his wealth of fame did not attract her she had fell in love with the boy whom she met in Bangkok. She was the best thing that had happened to him. Romeo had brought his family a sprawling villa on South Beach in Miami they had gone to stay with his parents at the lavish villa. Romeo loved Miami it had become so hip and trendy, lots of celebrities and Europeans had homes there and there were always lots of parties. One of their neighbors was a well-known European fashion designer and he had promised to create a special gown for Capricorn to wear at the wedding. She had already seen the sketch and was excited, they had already started work on the creation at their headquarters in Paris.

Romeo spent his days lazing by the pool, jogging on South Beach, the afternoons were set apart for song writing and the evenings were earmarked for eating out, visiting the fashionable clubs and attending the array of cocktail parties at the jet set styled homes of his new celebrity friends.

At a dinner one night at a computer chip tycoon's home they met a lovely actress called Katie she was with a handsome man called Tyrese, apparently he had actually been with Pippa's label before he launched his film career. He was in Miami looking for a holiday home and he had dragged Katie along for female companionship. Romeo had read somewhere that the actress was a dyke, he didn't believe it, she was one of the hottest looking chicks that he had ever seen. When he had mentioned on the phone that the previous evening at a dinner party he had bumped into one of her old singers called Tyrese, Pippa had gone strangely quiet and had changed the subject almost instantly, to her horror she learned that he had invited Tyrese and an actress to the wedding.

One hundred guests flew in on private Lear jets to Scotland to attend their wedding, they were staying two nights at a huge country estate with excellent security.

The first evening all the guests dressed for dinner and gathered in the main dining room.

Pippa's eyes darted eagerly around the room till she spotted Tyrese, she had forgotten just how handsome he was, almost everyone was in pairs and she felt like the odd one out.

Fortunately she was seated at the head of the table beside Romeo's parents.

All through dinner she found herself staring to where Tyrese was seated, he looked almost captivated by the actress at his side, he was eating every word she said and had not even noticed that Pippa was in the room.

After dinner she tried to catch his attention but he ignored her. On the dance floor she positioned herself next to him, Tyrese looked right through her like he had never seen her before, her heart bled.

Being in such close proximity to the man she loved was painful, she hated the elegant young actress that was dancing with him, she had seen her films she was young beautiful and rich, Pippa went to the ladies room and stared at her ageing reflection in the mirror. She felt consumed with jealousy and couldn't wait for the wedding to end.

The ceremony the next morning was lovely she had never seen so many flowers in her life.

Romeo had flown in literally millions of Thai orchids and the young couple said their vows under an arc of fragrant orchids, Capricorn looked stunning in a couture creation that was nothing less than spectacular. Pippa felt suddenly alone and sad, she was forty-five, successful and alone.

As the young couple said their vows Pippa felt tears well up in her eyes, tears of happiness or jealousy she didn't understand what they were, she had made a decision she didn't need a man, didn't need to marry. Men she used for sex and sex alone, she decided right then and there that she was going to get pregnant, all her money, all that she had worked for, where would it go? She wanted a baby that was her dream.

She had never seen Romeo so happy as he danced with his bride, his eyes shone and he looked at her with such total devotion it was moving. Her whole family had been flown in from Thailand and they were all enjoying themselves to the hilt.

Totally pissed on champagne Pippa disappeared to her room, she called room service and ordered a bottle of champagne, a young man wheeled in the trolley with the champagne and as he opened the bottle she slipped out of her dressing gown and pressed her body against his, the boy was taken by surprise. He made love to her and within moments had ejaculated she hoped that this would be the seed to impregnate her.

In the morning at ten there had been a farewell brunch planned, Pippa had stayed in her room she hadn't even said goodbye to the bride and groom., The sound of the helicopter taking off woke her up, it was too late now, that was Romeo and his new bride leaving the estate they were off on honeymoon to a secret location for two weeks.

It took several hours for the guests to leave, streams of limousines and security guards transported the celebrity guests to the nearby airport. Pippa was the last to leave, the same waiter had delivered her breakfast and she had sex with him again just for the hell of it even though he was hopeless.

She had popped a hundred dollar bill in his top pocket as he left.

While Romeo and Capricorn enjoyed an idyllic honeymoon at a private villa on a remote island in Greece Pippa returned to Detroit and took up on her old habits. She called a few numbers and had lots of drugs delivered, for a week solid she partied every night, did coke, speed and went to singles bars and clubs in the course of a week she had slept with eleven men. She met them mostly in the clubs, one she met whilst she was at the gym and she had sex with them all and only two used condoms. She had sex in toilets, dark rooms and in the back of cars belonging to strangers. By the end of the week she was wasted and her cleaning lady raised the alarm and contacted her PA at the record company. The more sex she had the more she craved. She hooked up with nameless guys she met online and became addicted to perverse sex acts. One night in a bar a guy had put a date rape tablet in her bourbon. He and his three friends proceeded to rape her in the back of a truck. It was the weirdest experience, her mind and head seemed to function but the rest of her body was paralyzed.

Her promiscuity persisted and for three months she binged on drugs alcohol and overdoses of sex, she frequented swinger nights and orgies indulging in group sex.

One night at a dinner party of a famous film director, the host put a tab of LSD in her apple strudel.

Pippa had the worst trip, the experience shocked her as she had attempted to jump from her penthouse balcony. The maid had fortunately been there and grabbed her as she stood on the ledge.

Romeo had flown in with Capricorn and he was eager to let Pippa hear the demo of his new tracks. He wanted to see her reaction face to face as he hadn't seen her for months and he had missed her. Both Capricorn and he were shocked when they walked into her office she had lost so much weight and was so thin she looked ill, it was almost like she had aged ten years, her skin was pale and she had dark circles under her eyes. While she listened to his new tracks she did three lines of coke.

It was ten am and she was wasted, as high as a kite. Romeo watched as she threw up in the wastepaper basket, they left her to listen to the demo she had asked them to meet her at Fabians that night for dinner.

Romeo and Capricorn sat for an hour waiting for Pippa, she arrived absolutely stoned and while they ate she drank a whole bottle of champagne. Romeo was sad he didn't know this side of her, she looked terrible and it was impossible to talk business to her in this condition, she told them that there was a new club open and that she had arranged a drink with some of the guys from the record company, they were all curious to meet the girl that had stolen Romeo's heart.

After a dinner they moved on to a new hot private club. Pippa disappeared to the bathroom and was there forever, he sent Capricorn to check up on her she was sitting in a toilet shooting a needle into her veins when Capricorn opened the door. Capricorn helped her back to their table. Romeo asked her to dance and Pippa freaked out to the music and she wouldn't stop. Romeo was sweating and returned to their table to join his wife, it was Capricorn that noticed Pippa collapse, as she fell to the floor blood spurted between legs turning the cream silk of her dress to a deep red. Within seconds security had lifted her limp body up, the ambulance arrived twenty minutes later, and took them to a private clinic. She had been doing coke, crack and heroine.

Romeo sat holding his wife's hand it seemed like an eternity till the doctor reappeared.

Pippa had taken too many drugs and had mixed them with a large amount of alcohol.

She had heart palpitations and had had a miscarriage on the dance floor. The mess between her legs had indeed been a two month male foetus.

The doctors had sedated her and Romeo returned alone the next morning to visit her, he wanted to talk. Pippa looked deathly, she was a shadow of the woman he had known and her face looked almost birdlike she had been on an alcohol diet for three months and had lost so much weight.

Obviously she had withdrawal symptoms, she looked nervous and hyper. When she saw Romeo she broke down, she had lost her baby. She had wanted a baby suddenly everything blurted out and he sat listening in horror as she told him how she had loved Tyrese and how lonely she was.

Romeo stayed a few days longer than planned and he went every day to visit Pippa, she had made a remarkable recovery and very quickly was looking ten times better. On the last day when they arrived with flowers he found her just lying and staring at the ceiling, there was a strange look on her face that he had never seen before.

Pippa asked Capricorn to leave them alone for a moment, when she left the room Pippa told him that the doctors had done blood tests and discovered that she had full blown aids.

The words hit him like a blow and he broke down and sobbed, Capricorn heard his sobs from the hallway and entered the room to find them clasped in each other's arms with one glance she knew that something awful was going to happen.

Romeo left and promised to return at the end of the month, Pippa kissed him and thanked him but the way she had said her goodbyes had unnerved him, it was almost as if she was saying farewell forever.

Pippa was released from the clinic a week later and she spent every evening till deep in the night in her office and had endless meetings with her lawyers. On the last Friday of the month she arrived late in the office dressed and groomed immaculately, everyone thought that she looked great she spent the whole afternoon walking through each department and spoke to almost every member of staff she announced that they could all leave an hour early and thanked them for their hard work.

After the staff had all left she walked from room to room examining the photos on the walls.

Most of her life had been spent between these walls.

She had had a lot of good times here she mused running her fingers over the oval boardroom table, this was the table where many stars' careers had started, their contracts were signed on this table funny how a table could be so symbolic. She had made all her acts sign this very table for good luck. She smiled recognizing all the famous names whose names had been scribbled eagerly.

This was also the table on which Tyrese had made love to her time and time again, she closed her eyes and thought of him, his tall athletic body and dazzling smile if one had only one soulmate in one's life then he was hers. She had loved him and only him. She opened her handbag and left four letters on the desk then switched the light off for the last time.

Her office was the penthouse of the building, she opened the two doors and walked onto the roof garden where she had entertained some of the music businesses most famous faces, Tyrese had made love to her here also she thought, twenty-five stories high right on this very spot.

It was almost sunset and the sky was ablaze with pink fluffy clouds, everything seemed so tranquil up here, strange that she had never noticed that before. Down below the evening rush hour had begun.

She drank in the beauty of the moment, the city sparkled like a jewel in the setting sun.

Pippa thought of Tyrese kissing her as she climbed up on the railing she softly said his name as she sprang from the twenty-fifth floor. Her life flashed before her like a video clip. Her childhood, her teen years and a sea of faces, family and friends blinded her and a few seconds later with a crashing sound she landed in the empty car parking lot.

People screamed as they witnessed the incident. The woman had landed with a crashing sound and was lying in a sea of blood.

As her body torpedoed to ground level she thought of Tyrese, he was smiling at her, she was tumbling down a tunnel of clear white light. Friends she had loved and lost were waiting for her. The pain was gone, she left her body, she marveled as she floated above the scene watching as the paramedics and police arrived. She continued to fly upwards above the rooftops and through the clouds and through the universe. As her soul left her body she was overwhelmed by a sense of knowledge and understanding. She looked back at the body that had been the temple to her soul then was lost in a tunnel of light and peace. Death was not the end, it was a new beginning she had moved on to the next phase in the journey of life.

Chapter 15

Romeo

Pippa's funeral was quite a happening for someone who was lonely and had no friends, it was a surprise that almost 1000 people flew in from all over the world. Pippa in a sense had been Pop Royalty in the record industry she had opened doors for many years for many stars and even though some of them had parted on bad terms her death had shaken them deeply. Stars and producers flocked to Detroit to pay their last respects to the Queen of pop, famous faces and simple people who had worked with her on video shoots doing cleaning and catering all turned up en masse.

Romeo had covered her casket in the same Thai orchids that she had admired so much only months before at his wedding. Romeo wept openly like a child as he helped carry her coffin to the waiting hearse he wished that he had stayed longer he had felt her goodbyes were final and he had a lump in his throat as he attempted to sing a song that he had written for her.

She had been a real bitch sometimes but she had also been his fairy godmother and now that she was gone he and hundreds of other famous artists had suddenly realized that without Pippa they probably would never have achieved such success.

She had left four envelopes before she had jumped off the rooftop of her headquarters.

One was a copy of her will, another was for her Lawyer the third was for Romeo and fourth was for Tyrese.

Pippa had stated that after her burial she wanted everyone to go and have a party, she had selected a DJ and wanted him to play all of the hits that she had promoted over the years, she added that she loved everyone and thanked them for their service and all employees would receive a year's salary. Pippa being Pippa right to the end had tied up all the knots and left her orders.

She had left a long lovely letter for Romeo and her words made him cry and laugh all at once, she asked him for a final favour she wanted him to organize and sing at a charity benefit concert to raise money for a foundation that she had set up, she added further instructions would be revealed after her will had been read.

Tyrese was surprised that she had left him a letter he read the words in disbelief.

'Tyrese you were the only one for me, the one who opened my soul, let's hope that we meet again somewhere in time, thanks for being my greatest love and soulmate, you and only you were the one who made my heart sing, thank you for your music love you Pippa.'

Tyrese was choked with emotion, for as long as he could remember Pippa had been trying to destroy him, he had no idea that she had loved him.

After a sumptuous meal at a lavish location Pippa's lawyer requested that Tyrese and Romeo joined him for a private discussion.

Pippa had left her multimillion record company and all its assets to Tyrese, She wanted him to build it up as she had done and make sure that everyone was treated well, she was also giving him six million dollars to start a music foundation for underprivileged children, he had tears in his eyes he had always secretly dreamed of doing that but never had the time, trust Pippa to give him a kick in the ass from the grave. She wanted Romeo to be the co-founder with

Tyrese and she wanted Romeo to organize a charity event to raise more money for the projects. She asked them to round up every star that she had ever helped and get them to cut an album and do a huge charity show.

Romeo was ordered to write a hit single so they could all do a song together, she warned them that it better be a hot night because she would be watching from up there with his mum.

Romeo wept she had left him her beach house in Hawaii, her London apartment and a villa in Tuscany. Let's call it a belated wedding gift she joked.

The lawyer rambled on and on Tyrese sat mystified, he had no idea that Pippa had really loved him he had thought all along that she had used him. As a rightful beneficiary he would be president of one of the biggest record companies on the planet, he was speechless. Both men studied the papers before they signed making Tyrese president and Romeo under president. Shares were to be split on a 50/50 basis, Tyrese was to be president but Romeo had to have equal shares.

They would both have to stay on in Detroit for a week to sort out all the legalities, it was one hell of a responsibility and Tyrese was glad that Romeo was sharing the burden. As they shook hands they vowed to each other and to Pippa, wherever she was now, that they were going to double her empire and run it as she would have. The name Pippa Curtis would never be forgotten.

The day Pippa had died Romeo had woken with a start, she had been standing at the bottom of his bunk on the tour bus she smiled then vanished. Although the experience had freaked him out he felt an inner peace, it was as if she had come to say goodbye to him.

Tyrese was glad that he had no major commitments at this point in his life as he had made the decision to give up his movie career and move to Detroit to run Pippa's recording empire. He had been shocked that Pippa had left fifty per cent of her business to him. The main board of directors had been bitterly disappointed that both he and Romeo had been chosen to run the show.

Tyrese liked Romeo he had major talent and like himself was streetwise, all his life Tyrese had relied on his gut feeling, and he had this gut feeling now to put his heart and soul into pulling the strings of Pippa's global empire.

The first month was a nightmare, he moved to Detroit and stayed at a hotel, every day he woke at six am and drove to the twenty-five story building that housed the newly named TRGRC building which stood for Thy-Rom Global Recording Co. he had taken up camp together with Romeo in Pippa's penthouse office and every day from morning till midnight they combed through every piece of paperwork, contract and legal paper that held the company together. They both wanted to know every single detail, its strengths and weaknesses. Together the men worked hard, they had an army of good staff at the headquarters and international connections all over the globe it took them almost all of two months to get the grip of the place and they had decided to rule the empire with kid gloves.

Both of them had been artists Romeo was indeed still responsible for twenty per cent of the turnover, they knew the inside ways of the business, both men hired personal assistants and secretaries, they headhunted them from other major companies because they wanted to introduce fresh blood to the company.

Tyrese hired a hotshot black guy called Jay-d as his PA and a real sexy looking secretary called Pam. Romeo employed a personal assistant called Tammy she was about forty and had years of experience working at a major label in Europe his secretary was male with an outstanding CV.

Capricorn would have freaked out if he had employed a buxom secretary, Romeo's eyes popped when Tyrese introduced him to the stunning blonde secretary, 'Hey man,' he joked, 'can she type?'

The leggy blonde had a great background Tyrese joked that if he was stuck in the office till midnight at least he would have something hot to look at. Actually from the ten candidates he had interviewed she had been the most professional and Tyrese warned Romeo not to be fooled by the sexy figure and long legs.

Pam was one hundred per cent lesbian and had been living with her Lawyer over for seven years. Capricorn sighed a sigh of relief when she heard this.

There was a mountain of work to be done to reorganize things at the company, Tyrese focused on this while Romeo finished his album and continued with a tour that he had already started.

Romeo was worried about Capricorn she had been totally stressed while he travelled she had been house hunting for both themselves and Tyrese, they had both bought two superb penthouses a block from each other and she had been overseeing the renovations. Pippa had left Romeo her penthouse but Capricorn wanted her own place the renovations were proving difficult and the costs were way above the quotation, she had flown on the company Lear jet to join Romeo in New York, he was doing several television performances there.

When she entered his dressing room he looked at her in disbelief, she looked dreadful. After the performance they went back to the hotel and at five am Romeo woke up, she was not lying next to him. Romeo went to the bathroom and found Capricorn caressing the toilet, she was throwing up violently. Romeo called reception and accused the duty manager of poisoning her, they had a seafood diner from room service and he was sure that the lobster had been off, Romeo demanded that they send a doctor immediately. Twenty minutes later a doctor appeared and Romeo sat huddled in his dressing gown whilst the doctor gave Capricorn a lengthy examination. After ten minutes the doctor approached Romeo he explained that there was nothing seriously wrong with Capricorn and that food poisoning was definitely out of the question.

Romeo's eyes widened in disbelief, tears of joy glazed his eyes and he hugged the doctor repeating, 'Are you sure? Are you really sure!'

Romeo would never forget the look on her face as she lay in the hotel bed, he kissed her and held her in his arms then put his ear to her belly and listened for any sounds.

It was only six am Romeo ordered strawberries and champagne from room service he telephoned Tyrese and woke him up, then he called Capricorn's parents in Thailand and half a dozen friends in Europe, some of whom were sleeping and confused.

She had never seen him so happy he sat scribbling a design for the nursery and wanted to go shopping as soon as the stores opened, he looked like an excited school kid himself. Every two minutes he was asking her if she was ok, he was treating her like a cross between a queen and an invalid, he ordered her a healthy breakfast with fresh fruit and orange juice and was driving her crazy.

That afternoon he insisted in going shopping with her, wearing a new almost ridiculous disguise, an afro wig and raincoat with ancient gold rimmed glasses they went to every baby store in town he spent a shocking amount on baby clothes and accessories and enjoyed every minute.

After a shopping marathon, to her absolute surprise outside a hotel in Manhattan, Romeo actually approached a group of Paparazzi that were stalking some poor victim who was probably having lunch inside. He tapped the man on the shoulder and ripped off his wig, the photographers turned round and recognizing Romeo started firing away, flashbulbs popped and he even put back on his afro to give them some funny shots and let them take some of him and Capricorn, 'We are having a baby he grinned to the reporters.'

The press were amazed, usually he kept a low profile and within seconds they were on their mobiles giving the story back to head office. Suddenly a photographer screamed and a Hollywood starlet appeared in the doorway of the hotel, it was Marisa Duval, she had recently split up with her shipping tycoon lover and was just out of rehab, perfectly made-up she paused in the doorway of the hotel and lifted her head upwards to ensure that the press got a good shot before she scrambled into the waiting limo. While the press were busy with the racy starlet Romeo and Capricorn jumped in a yellow cab and headed back to the hotel. That night Romeo was on a chat show, he was supposed to be promoting his new album and had to sing two songs, Capricorn was snuggled up in bed watching the show, he surprised her by dedicating the song to his wife and their expected child, instead of promoting his record he spent all of ten minutes talking about how excited he was at becoming a father. He looked like a little kid she thought proudly as she watched the interview and when he did his performance he sang from his heart, arms outstretched like a proud peacock a look in his eyes that told only her that he loved her. She smiled recognizing the glint in his eye when they made love, that is what he was doing he was making love to her right there on live TV she mused. She had noticed that look the first night that he had made love to her, she had watched him in amazement the first time he had made love to her he had stared right in to her eyes compelling her to look into his just before he had climaxed. She saw a look in his eyes like their souls had connected, then they shone and his left eye seemed to twinkle, she adored the way his eyes crossed when he made love to her and that indeed was what he was doing now in the TV studio, he was making love to her knowing that she was lying in bed watching his performance. At that moment she felt the luckiest women in the whole world, she couldn't wait for the baby to arrive to share that love, she wanted to have two or three, perhaps five or six little Romeo's she thought as she drifted off to sleep holding her belly.

Romeo arrived home an hour later, he didn't want to wake her as she looked so serene and peaceful sleeping. He poured a drink and sat down, he looked at his wife nestled between the creamy sheets and thought that he had never been so happy he wished that his mother had been there to share this newfound happiness, in the glow of the firelight she looked like an angel he lifted a pen and inspired and started to write the song "Faces of Angels"

Romeo had never known such happiness, his career was going from strength to strength, financially he had more money than he could ever spend in a lifetime, the record company was blossoming under Tyrese's and his management and Capricorn was expecting his child.

Tyrese and he were putting the plans together for a concert. Thirty-five major recording artists had agreed to sing at the charity event that Pippa had asked them to organize. The money raised by phone in and record sales were to be put to the Pippa Curtis Foundation, her last wish had been to start up a foundation to encourage poor kids from dysfunctional families all over the world to embrace the power of music, many of the artists she had discovered like Tyrese had begun their live in the gutter. Hopefully her project would help open schools and create scholarships for many talented children, the poster campaign 'Shun Violence Embrace Music' had been Pippa's idea, for years she had dreamt of starting a foundation and she had written in her last letter to Tyrese that in the beginning she didn't have the cash and at the end she didn't have the time, she knew that the money the concert and album sales generated would be enough. I'll be watching the concert from the clouds guys, she had written.

The date was arranged and the artists lined up. Twenty of them were to pre-record a song for Pippa. Tyrese had written the track 'Power of Music' for her, to commemorate her life, They had commissioned a life-sized bronze statue to be made by one of the world's leading sculptors, the objective being that a cast of the statue would stand in each one of the music schools that they opened.

They had already employed a whole network of people to organize and run the project. Recording the track was a trip, it was an almost historic event to have so much talent in one studio at one moment in time, each one sang a verse and stamped their own special stamp into the track, both Tyrese and Romeo were honored to have taken part in the recording, with names like that it was sure to be number one in every country on the planet and all profits were going to the foundation.

The live concert was being televised in countries all over the world and people would be encouraged to make donations for the project. Every country that donated would benefit from the project as they intended opening music centers all over the world, they would groom talented students from poor families and help street kids and the homeless and if by chance they was real talent amongst them they would be groomed and trained and then be given contracts with TRGRC they would surely discover the stars of the future amongst their protégés.

By the time the concert date arrived Capricorn was indeed nine months pregnant and the child was due at any moment. She was constantly irritated and her belly was so swollen she had imagined that it was triplets but she had been determined to attend Pippa's benefit soiree.

Romeo would have been happier if she had stayed at home but she was adamant. Romeo had arranged a small seating area tucked behind a partitioned area adjacent to the stage, a handful of VIPs would enjoy the performances from there.

Capricorn was so excited at watching the show that she had ignored the piercing pains she was experiencing, she imagined that she had eaten too quickly at the buffet and sat back to watch the array of international talent that graced the stage. She was filled with pride when her husband took the stage and the 200,000 fans screamed so loud that no one heard her screams, water gushed between her legs and she fell off her seat in panic, her waters had broken, people gathered round her in horror and a security man called for an ambulance. Because of the concert the traffic was horrendous the roads were blocked and she was dismayed to hear that it could take up to an hour to get an ambulance there, they were trying to get an emergency helicopter.

One of the on-site doctors arrived at the scene and two nurses appeared at her side and they asked the men to screen her off from the stage. On stage Romeo was singing a medley of five of his songs out of the corner of his eye he had noticed that they had screened off the VIP area, he found it odd but had no idea that at that very moment his daughter's head had just peeped out between Capricorn's legs. Security guards scampered off to find towels and hot water as Capricorn screamed and pushed with vigor. Just as Romeo took his bow and the public roared in appreciation his daughter cried as she entered the world. After his encore Romeo ran sweating towards VIP area he wanted to know if she had enjoyed his performance, before the six security men could explain he had peeled back the screen it was like a mirage and he shook his head to see if his eyes were deceiving him, in the space of the twenty minutes he had been on stage his daughter had been born, ironically she had been born on stage.

Within the confines of the screen Capricorn lay on a pile of blankets cradling a little bundle, she was flanked by two doctors and three nurses that tried to talk to him, at that moment he couldn't hear what they were saying, another group had taken the stage and the roar of the crowd was deafening. He walked towards Capricorn, Romeo dropped his microphone and in what seemed like slow motion and she handed him the infant who was still red with blood and wrapped in a towel.

Romeo was so overcome with emotion he wept openly, the child was so small and fragile and looked so helpless he cradled her in his arms and drank in every detail of her being, above an air ambulance helicopter was approaching, the doctors helped Capricorn to board and together they were whisked off to a private clinic.

Three doctors were waiting at the heliport and Capricorn was taken on a bed to the clinic.

After a check-up the doctors confirmed that both mother and daughter were in tip-top condition.

While the doctors were attending to Capricorn and his newborn child, he had been requested to wait in the waiting room, the shock of what had happened had finally hit him and he prayed to God that the baby was ok, he was sick with worry, perhaps something had gone wrong it must have been an ordeal giving birth in front of 200,000 people. The truth was Capricorn was so glad that the baby was coming that she hadn't given a shit about the roar of the crowd, it had been weird listening to her husband singing while she had been pushing. For months Romeo had been preparing himself for the birth he had read a dozen books and even had classes, perhaps she mused it was better that he had been on stage. When he walked into her private room three quarters of an hour later he was still dressed in his metallic silver stage costume, his wife was propped up in bed looking radiant wearing a dressing gown with the clinic's emblem on it and in her arms was a tiny sleepy bundle. Romeo sat on the bed and looked in awe at his daughter, it was the most beautiful sight that he had ever seen. The time that they had kept him in the waiting room had seemed like an eternity, never before had he felt such emotion, he was engulfed with love, it was so weird he had this rush of emotion. Twin emotions which split his love down the middle, he loved Capricorn and he loved this beautiful tiny bundle.

Capricorn opened the baby's towel and he marveled at the perfection, carefully he counted every little finger and every little toe with a great big smile. This was he mused, God's perfection.

That night the clinic arranged an extra bed to be wheeled in to the room and he slept beside the two women he loved. Whilst Capricorn slept he lay awake watching every breath that the child made. They had agreed to call the child Pippa.

A nurse wheeled in two breakfast trays, opened the curtains and took the child away to clean and feed, Capricorn switched on the television just in time to catch the news, the concert had raised an absolute fortune, literally millions of dollars had been raised already and the cash was still flowing in. They both laughed at the footage of them being whisked off in the helicopter ambulance.

"Born on Stage" had been the headlines. The news of Pippa's onstage birth shielded from the 200,000 fans by a paper screen had been the talk of the day. Flowers were arriving by the truck load, Tyrese appeared at the clinic with a big pink teddy bear, he was so pleased to hear that they had called the kid Pippa and he voted to be her godfather. Unknown to Capricorn, the proud father had contacted her family in Thailand and right at this minute the whole clan were on a flight heading towards New York. Later that evening as they sat watching a video of the concert together there was a gentle knock on the door, Romeo opened it and smiled as her mother, father, six brothers and sisters, grandparents and aunt streamed into the room. They cackled away in Thai while Romeo made a video and took dozens of photos, Capricorn looked at him across the room, she didn't have to say a word, the look in her eyes was enough, Lord Buddha she thought thank you for this man. This was a quality moment beyond all moments she thought silently.

Romeo had built a house in Thailand for her family, they had promised to visit them but her surprise pregnancy had prevented them from travel and he knew that she must miss them and so had arranged for the whole gang to come over, the next month he had commitments, tours and shows and he wanted her to be surrounded with family, they had seven bedrooms in the apartment and they were welcome.

Since he had been successful he had cut all ties with his own family, they had been greedy and like leeches had tried to bleed him dry. One day he had rounded them up and one by one handed them a cheque, to his horror his father had asked for more, he was disgusted with them. They had even sold stories to tabloids and magazines, in his eyes now Capricorn's family were his too, they were a simple lot with their feet on the ground and to them he wasn't a superstar he was their son-in-law, when he had tried to surprise them by building a house they had opted for one less than half the price that he had offered to pay, they were simple working class honest people and he adored them.

Romeo recorded every living moment of the baby on film he had literally hundreds of photos, disks and videos of the kid as he called her. She was indeed his princess. He had gone shopping one day with her mother and he had bought almost a whole toy shop the teddy bears were spilling into their rooms as the nursery was full, 'You are a sicko.' she joked, 'you have a teddy bear fetish.'

Capricorn was glad to be surrounded by her family it was a Thai thing to be close to your family. One evening Romeo was doing a gig, there would be more than seventy thousand fans going, he decided to drag his in-laws along, they had never seen him perform live and had no idea just how famous he was. As their helicopters landed Capricorn's mother looked at the crowd and didn't believe that they were all there to see Romeo, 'People, too much,' she mumbled, she had totally no conception just how famous he was.

Capricorn's family stood open-mouthed as Romeo was whisked off with his crew, he had arranged a seating area again at the side of the stage and they took their seats and watched the support act. Twenty minutes later their son-in-law appeared wearing a silver suit, when he walked on stage the audience roared so loud that their seats vibrated and when the screams died down he grabbed the microphone and turned towards them holding out his arms, he announced that tonight, 'His whole family were here,' the lighting man shone a purple light on them and he walked towards them and sang a wonderful ballad, the audience loved the song and the emotional impact was mind blowing. His father-in-law sat in disbelief as he completed the rest of his awesome performance. His face was ten foot tall on the screens around the arena, he performed for his family that night and they were captivated like everyone else in the stadium. Romeo was at home on the stage and he shone like a true superstar.

The next morning Capricorn laughed when her mother scolded him for not getting up early.

She prodded him in the ribs, handed him coffee and retorted in broken English, 'You sleep too much, too much, no good, have to take Grandma look Statue of Liberty.' Romeo put the covers over his head and grunted, 'No like get up, I Superstar work too much.' They all laughed when Capricorn's mother brought Pippa into the room and dumped her on the bed, she gurgled and smiled at the sight of her father, he picked her up and smiled she looked so pretty all pink and frilly.

That day they enjoyed a day sightseeing, Romeo in one of his crazy disguise outfits, 'How are you going to explain these photos to your kid when she grows up?' Every day Romeo had a new disguise and Capricorn laughed, he did look ridiculous in the photos.

After a month sadly her family had to leave, Romeo was going to miss them, the apartment had been alive when they were there and they all went to the airport in one of the record company's stretch limos. Capricorn cried as they disappeared through passport control she promised that they would visit this year to see the house.

Romeo had employed an artist to paint murals on the nursery, it was painstaking and seemed to take forever, he wanted Pippa's room to be like a cartoon movie.

Tyrese had little time for a social life, he had thrown himself into the business and he was grateful that he had Romeo to turn to when things got tough. Running a major record company was not easy, he realized now the kind of pressure that had driven Pippa to excesses. He had experienced lots of sleepless nights since she left him at the helm, sometimes he missed acting, he seemed to spend all of his time behind the huge desk with mountains of paper work to deal with, or hassling with lawyers and legal experts. Dealing with artists was a real a pain in the ass, these kids walked in the door penniless with a dream of becoming a star. He would invest millions in helping them realize that dream, and when they did they suddenly would turn into snakes. He tried to groom the young artists he signed to be able to handle fame, it was not all it was cracked up to be. They all walked in the door wanting to sing, then after a few hits and the pressure they didn't want to sing any more.

Not everyone they signed up had success there were hundreds that just didn't make it. Every year millions of dollars were wasted on flops, in a way it was a gamble and talent didn't always guarantee success, sometimes the least likely ones were winners Lady Luck had a lot to do with it. A handful of the young hopefuls became megastars, some others were one hit wonders but the majority were losers, however the profit margin on the winners was high.

The music business was having a tough time, pirate CDs and downloads were flooding the market. All over the globe people were illegally downloading music and copying it on their home computers cd sales had plummeted and at the same time all the artists wanted bigger budgets for their tours and video clips. Music now was a visual media and even the most mediocre of songs could score if the video was cool. A good video was part of the package now, the better the clip the more airplay on the music channels. Good videos didn't come on the cheap the editing and computerized effects were extortionate.

Tours now had to be spectacular, lots of dancers, pyrotechnics, costumes, crew, transport cost a fortune and even with the sponsors it still was a lot compared to ten years ago.

Artists had armies of staff, stylists, make-up artists, hairdressers, choreographers, masseurs, chefs, dancers, designers, lighting technicians, sound technicians, managers, personal assistants, voice coaches, pluggers, valets, bodyguards and chauffeurs, the list was endless and it all cost big bucks. Fortunately for the ones who made it, the rewards were also incredible. The market had changed the live shows, tours and merchandising were where the big bucks were made.

Tyrese had no time for relationships, he had sex with escorts that he hired when he felt the urge. Most of the time he was too tired even to think about sex but he missed companionship and female company. It was crazy but sometimes when he went to Romeo's home for dinner he envied him, he had it all, success, money, a loving wife and a great kid and unlike most other artists he left his ego in the dressing room and in the environment of his home he lived a reasonably normal life. Tyrese had often been shocked watching him washing dishes or changing his child's diapers, perhaps that's why his marriage had been so successful perhaps that's why he hadn't turned like many other artists to drugs or excesses. Romeo had his family he wasn't lonely. He had been trying to persuade Tyrese to join them for two weeks in Thailand. They were going to visit Capricorn's parents and thought that the change of atmosphere would do him good and they were desperate to introduce him to Capricorn's nineteen year old sister.

It had been five years since they had taken the reins of Pippa's company and the time had flown, they had almost doubled the turnover since they had taken over.

Tyrese had to attend a party for an artist, he was extremely wealthy and had donated several pieces of priceless work to Pippa's youth foundation, they had raised millions and had opened seven schools in seven countries as well as three in America, the projects were proving successful and Tyrese had made it his personal mission to oversee every detail.

He was desperate that Pippa's dream would be successful so her dream had become his dream, indeed two of their top grossing artists had been at the foundation schools, the project was delivering already. Their schools were full of talent studying rock, pop, jazz, hip hop and classic music.

They trained the kids so that when they did get a contract they would know the ropes.

Tyrese stopped signing the mountain of cheques on his desk and looked at the clock he was really not in the mood for the party but felt obliged to attend, he had ten minutes to shower and get dressed. It was nine pm and everyone had gone home except the security. Tyrese looked at the worn leather desk, the one that Pippa had used, he remembered that he had made love to her right there on that desk, she had scratched his back and groaned as he brought her to climax, perhaps it was he thought on that desk that she had fallen madly in love with him, he had been a young man then, a stripper, gigolo, football hero, model, pop singer and actor, it all seemed so long ago and so far away it was ironic he had done it all and yet had done nothing at all.

He dressed quickly in a designer suit with sports shoes, he never liked to get too dressed up even when he attended galas, he would wear baseball sneakers with his tuxedo it was like his trademark.

He passed the life size bronze that graced the reception it had cost an absolute fortune, the likeness to Pippa was incredible he glanced up at her image and smiled she had been a terrific woman so full of energy and spirit he winked at the statue and said goodnight to the security men then stepped into the waiting Rolls Royce. The smell of the leather intrigued him it was only months old, who would have thought that one day a kid from the ghetto would be sitting in a car like this he mused, for some reason his mind had turned to thoughts of the past, his mother, the slum where he was brought up.

The gleaming car drew up at the brightly lit gallery. A small museum in its own right, the grounds of the traditional building were filled with clowns, acrobats and jugglers, trust Jason to create a spectacle he mused. Inside the building the place had been filled with large butterflies that were suspended from the ceiling, all the waiters and waitresses were dressed like Adam and Eve.

The place was jam-packed with celebrities, artists, authors, movie stars, aristocrats, patrons of the arts, Wall street wizards, plastic surgeons, Silicon Valley tycoons, sport stars and pop idols, as he squeezed his way through the salons looking for Romeo, he had been invited too, he acknowledged some of the artists that he knew were signed up with his company and continued to look for Romeo.

She was standing at the top of the stairs sipping expertly, applying lip gloss and checking her reflection in a diamond studded compact, he couldn't believe his eyes it was Marisa Duval it was as if time had stood still. He hadn't seen her for seven years but she still looked the same, she hadn't made any movies for years, she had received an enormous divorce settlement from the old Count that she had married and rumor had it that her Greek shipping tycoon lover was ready to drop dead at any moment.

Looking every inch the Hollywood diva she slowly walked down the stairs making sure that everyone in the room had seen her before she headed for the bar, secretly she was desperate to get back into the movie business she missed the attention and worship of the fans.

She was wearing a dress that had taken months to produce, it was encrusted with semi-precious stones and had cost her husband a fortune, Marisa only wore clothes once, she would discard her couture creation after this evening and not even think that more than twenty women had spent months creating it for her. She was wearing two of the largest sapphires Tyrese had ever seen they were encircled with rows of diamonds and hung from her ears, the matching bracelet looked so heavy that she could hardy lift her champagne, the sheer ostentatiousness of the set was blinding to say in the least, vulgar was an understatement but then again nothing was too big for Marisa and only she could get away with that dress and jewels.

Tyrese tapped her on the shoulder she raised her eyebrow and turned round lifting her head she smiled as he leant forward to kiss her, she still smelled the same, she had a certain smell, it was something unique and he remembered that smell, she had an old Parisian perfumer create the fragrance for her, she bathed in it and had her underwear rinsed in it.

'You should bottle that fragrance,' Tyrese joked knowing that she never would. She was still a striking woman but up close she looked older and under the perfectly painted, very professionally made-up face she looked tired, her body was still as voluptuous as it always had been and like for like she knocked spots off all the young girls in the room.

Marisa had that magical animal sexuality combined with an innocence that made you stop and stare, she had that special something that Monroe had, that secret magic ingredient that made her like a magnet for attention. She had sex appeal and even if she had been wearing rags she would have turned heads, sipping a glass of champagne or eating a cherry was an erotic experience for her and whatever she did, wherever she went, heads turned, she had that old-fashioned Hollywood charisma that no longer existed, indeed he mused she belonged on the screen.

She joked with Tyrese that she wore the heavy jeweled armband to prevent her drinking so quickly, he laughed. They talked about the good old days and for the first time in years he thought of Chloe.

Marisa told him about her dreadful divorce and how her Greek billionaire had rescued her from the evil old Count who only gave her a million dollar settlement, she added that her clothing bill alone came to more than that, Tyrese couldn't help but laugh she was a fruitcake he thought. They exchanged numbers and agreed to meet for lunch, Marisa joked that they would have to wait till her hubby kicked the bucket, he apparently was terminally ill and she herself was terminally bored, she added that she hadn't had a good screw for a year.

She warned him that her two security men were the absolute ugliest in the business. Tyrese laughed, she hadn't changed a bit, her mood subdued as two extremely tall men approached, they told her that it was time to leave, she finished her drink and whispered to Tyrese that she had to return to the prison, her husband was ill and he didn't like her to stay out late, the two mean looking bodyguards walked behind her as she made her exit leaving a cloud of perfume in the salon. After she left the room seemed so bland and empty.

Tyrese discovered Romeo and Capricorn and they sat round a table while Tyrese told them stories about Marisa. Capricorn had never seen a Hollywood Screen Queen and she was completely fascinated to hear that those rocks were all real. They were both really surprised to learn that Tyrese had had a torrid affair with the starlet. Romeo said, 'My God how could you get it up for her?' Women like Marisa frightened him, he preferred his lovely Thai wife.

Romeo and Capricorn complained that Tyrese was always alone and they joked with him that he was impotent and tried to suggest suitable partners for him, they warned him that if he didn't find a woman before they returned from Thailand that they would set him up.

Often they had planned dinner parties and invited a single girl for him and he had always cancelled at the last minute.

Capricorn and Romeo went home early, they were off to sunny Thailand to visit her family in two days and had 101 things to do. Romeo had a television performance so he left Capricorn to pack and while she was packing she noticed that the new nanny had bought three pairs of shoes for Pippa in the wrong size. She dressed her daughter and decided to take them back, she called her driver and decided to go to buy some last minute things. Normally Romeo wouldn't let her go out without one of the security men, but by the time they returned the store would be closed so she decided to go quickly and not tell him. The driver dropped Capricorn and Pippa junior at the entrance of the store, she ordered him to circle the block. The moment the car drove away two men pushed Capricorn, at first she thought that they were after her handbag. The men threw Pippa into a white jeep, one man had his hand over her mouth, passers-by looked stunned as the car took off at top speed. A man helped her up and she was surrounded by people, the reality of what had just happened struck her she broke into tears and screamed Pippa's name before fainting.

The moment that Romeo stepped of stage he was approached by two officials as he saw the men walk towards him he knew something was wrong. By the time he arrived at their penthouse it was swimming with cops, there was a whole crew setting up computers and attaching cables to their home telephone. In the lounge he could see Capricorn she was almost hysterical, he was devastated Pippa had been kidnapped.

He was so angry he screamed at his wife for the first time, she wept bitterly as he swore at her.

'How Fucking stupid can you be?' he screamed. 'No fucking bodyguards, I have repeatedly warned you!' he screamed at the top of his voice.

The shouting didn't help, he explained to the police that his wife thought that he was a normal guy, he wasn't, he was a pop star, a megastar. Megastars' wives couldn't just go shopping like other women, he had made it quite clear that she was never to go out with Pippa without security, she screamed back that she had done it lots of times, that she had gone to Central Park, that she hated bodyguards and was sick and tired of people breathing down her neck. Her answer only made him even angrier he couldn't believe that she had risked going out alone.

Romeo called Tyrese. Tyrese was on his way over, Romeo went into the toilet and kneeled down on the marble floor and cried, his sobs were so loud that Capricorn heard them in the lounge and she went to the bathroom and knelt down beside him. He was broken and his sobs tore at her heart, she was cradling him in her arms like a baby when Tyrese appeared. Looking at them both on the floor he felt a lump in his throat, his goddaughter had been kidnapped in broad daylight it seemed too much like something from a Hollywood movie.

The police said that the kidnappers would call, they sat without speaking. It was three hours before the phone rang it was indeed the kidnappers, Romeo answered and warned them if they harmed his child he would kill them, the evil voice on the phone laughed and hung up.

They were still arguing an hour later when the phone rang again, this time Capricorn answered and the police recorded the call, they demanded three million dollars within twenty-four hours in unmarked hundred dollar bills.

Romeo paced the room helplessly, he wished for the first time in his life that he was just a plumber or a painter or an ordinary man, he was afraid that they were sick that they would harm her, there was so much publicity about pedophiles and the idea of anyone harming Pippa was driving him crazy. He became so frantic that Tyrese called a doctor they gave him some valium to ebb his anger.

No one slept, they sat up all night in the lounge drinking coffee to stay awake waiting on further instructions from the beasts that had taken his daughter.

In the early hours of the morning another call came in, they wanted to know if he could deliver the money the following night. Capricorn kept them on the line while the police traced the call they obviously weren't professionals the police chief was convinced that they were amateurs. They wanted them to wait at the heliport on Pippa's building at midnight the following night and they would drop the girl and pick up the suitcase.

Tyrese made the necessary calls to arrange the cash, Romeo wanted the police to leave, he was happy to pay the three million ransom he would have paid ten million if they had asked.

Romeo couldn't sleep. Tyrese went home to organize things. Capricorn cried all night she was beside herself with worry. That night Tyrese put on some old clothes he took a wad of money out of the safe and went downtown to some seedy bars that he hadn't been to for years. By luck he bumped into one of Pippa's dealers called Mango who was a hard case, he had spent most of his time in prison and had escaped recently he tipped the guy 1000 dollars and got some information. Mango introduced him to one of Detroit's most wanted criminals who had been a real friend of Pippa's, he was a mean looking man with one eye, the black eye patch gave him a sinister look. Tyrese remembered that he used to drop by her apartment from time to time. When to Tyrese's surprise the guy with the black eye patch claimed that he knew who had done it and where they were. Tyrese asked him how much it would cost to get her back. The fierce man growled and looked at him with the one eye, 'Cost!' he roared. 'This kid is called after Pippa right?' Tyrese nodded and was amazed to hear that they would do it for free, well not for free, for Pippa. The mean man sighed and told Tyrese that it was Pippa that had set him up, bailed him out and had paid people on the inside to help him escape, he told Tyrese to stay there with Mango and assured him that within one hour Pippa junior would be there.

It was the longest hour that Tyrese had ever known, he watched the clock on the wall and as the hands crept round Mango offered him a hit, he refused, Mango assured him that the Patch wouldn't let him down, he added that nothing came free and that one day there would be a price tag on this. Tyrese didn't care about tomorrow he wanted Pippa back.

After fifty-five minutes Tyrese heard the screech of cars drawing up and seven men came in to the room behind them The Patch walked in he was holding Pippa's hand and she was clutching a bear.

'Uncle Tyrese,' she screamed throwing her arms round his neck, her voice was the sweetest music that he had ever heard.

The Patch was glad to have been of service, Pippa Curtis and he had been lovers way back in the day. Now they had to come up with an idea of how to return her without involving The Patch or his boys or making the police suspicious. Tyrese was relieved to hear that no one had been killed, what he had done was tie up the three men and leave them locked in a van in the farmhouse where they had held Pippa, he suggested that he have someone call the police and say that the bastards were locked in the van and that Pippa had been delivered to her Uncle Tyrese, he had some men escort him and the child home. When they had deposited them safely at their apartment they would alert the police. The Patch himself called the police department.

Romeo and Capricorn arrived a half hour later with a fleet of police cars and six bodyguards of their own.

Romeo's heart leaped as he looked at his daughter curled up with her teddy bear on Tyrese's sofa. The police arrested the three men, they had been gagged and bound and The Patch had been delighted to help, these were the bastards that had double crossed him in a drug deal they were amateurs.

After the police had left, Tyrese told them the real story of what had happened and Mango had told him that if they had paid that they would probably have killed the kid anyway.

Romeo felt indebted to Tyrese, he wanted to pay The Patch, Mango and the seven men.

He wanted to thank them personally, a week later Tyrese went downtown again and he asked Mango to take him to see The Patch, Romeo had put 100,000 dollars in an envelope for The Patch, and also had given him eight envelopes with 10,000 in each for Mango and the boys.

It was Romeo's way of saying thanks to some men whom he never would hopefully have to meet.

The Patch counted the wad of money and smiled, Pippa had been his friend a long time ago, she had had an affair with him, he would have done it for free, 'Remember Man,' he said to Tyrese. 'Anytime you gotta problem let me know!'

Tyrese let Mango drop him off at a taxi rank, all he wanted to do was go home and sleep, the last three days had been a nightmare, Thank God, he thought that Pippa was all right it would have killed Romeo if anything had happened.

Romeo had been shattered by the events of the last few days and he became so security conscious that he had a phobia about it, he didn't want to do tours or concerts, he hated large crowds and as for shopping he never wanted to go out in public again. He had hired some real estate agents to find him a secure property outwith the city and he had cancelled the trip to Thailand and instead had asked all Capricorn's family to come over.

Tyrese understood that he needed some time alone he cancelled all his concerts and gigs.

He was happy to spend his time at home with Pippa. Capricorn wondered if they would ever lead a normal existence again. Within days the estate agents had found him a lavish fortress with a huge price tag, he purchased the property without batting an eyelid and when they went to see it he went with seven bodyguards and a fleet of armored cars, this is the price you pay for fame he thought as the convoy drove him to see his new fortress.

The impregnable home was superb Capricorn was surprised that she actually liked it. He wanted to move in immediately and hired three designers to restyle the rooms, he wanted Pippa's family to stay with them for three months and employed round the clock security teams to ensure their safety. Pippa he decided, would have private tutors, it would be a sheltered existence Capricorn thought as she packed the boxes getting ready for the removal men.

The house was surrounded by an imposing wall with dozens of cameras. The bedroom had an escape route and panic room. Everything was alarmed.

The shock of the kidnapping had left Romeo quite paranoid, he blamed Capricorn for the whole situation and had taken to living like a recluse in his family fortress, he rarely came to the office to help Tyrese and when he did he was surrounded by guards. Since the incident he had not been writing, his creativity seemed blocked and Tyrese was concerned about his forthcoming album.

Tyrese spent most of his time in the office, he arrived around eight and stayed usually till midnight, he had his head buried in a pile of legal contracts one morning when Pam interrupted him, she looked nervous as she spoke and informed him that there was a lady with a child in reception who was demanding to see him.

Tyrese checked his diary and informed his secretary that if it was the lady with the wonder child who was looking for a scholarship her appointment was the following day at ten. His secretary seemed embarrassed and explained that it was not the same lady, just as they were talking a tall blonde woman barged in the door and approached Tyrese, she looked vaguely familiar but Tyrese couldn't place her. The steam was literally coming out of her eyes and she screamed at him in German then in English demanding to know why he hadn't reacted to the ten emails that she had sent him. Tyrese wondered if she was signed up, she didn't look like a singer. Puzzled he dismissed his secretary and asked her to sit down, the tall mysterious blonde burst into tears and he could make no sense of what she was trying to tell him. 'As president of one of the major record labels in the world madam,' he said sternly, 'do not think that you can barge into my office and just get an appointment.' at his outburst she sobbed even harder.

He sat back and listened as she explained, she was Mercedes' sister from Munich, she claimed that she had emailed him ten times, she was at her wit's end and had flown half way across the world to see him. Mercedes was at this moment in an intensive care unit in Munich.

She had literally hours or days to live, Tyrese was saddened to hear that she was dying of Leukaemia, her sister explained that she had been holding on till he reacted. Tyrese learned that his secretary had deleted the emails thinking that they were merely junk mails. Mercedes sister Tara pulled out her mobile and called Germany, she asked the nurse to set up the webcam as they had planned and she told Tyrese that Mercedes had something to tell him before she died and that she wanted to do it face to face,. Tyrese asked Pam to come in to set up his laptop she connected a webcam for him so they could see each other.

Five minutes later he saw Mercedes, she looked much older than he had remembered, she was propped up in bed and had almost no hair, the sight of her like this saddened and shocked him. She had dark rings under her eyes and she was so thin that she looked like a skeleton, at first her voice was so low he could hardly hear her and he turned up the volume and plugged in his earpiece, the frail dying woman had tears in her eyes, she told him that she had loved him and had forgiven him and demanded that he promise her something. Tyrese was speechless as she told him that after she had left him she had given birth to his son, Gunther was almost seven now and if she hadn't been dying she wouldn't have told him, she added that he could do DNA tests to confirm that he was his son if he wanted to but she added that he was his and that she was dying. She didn't want the child to suffer seeing her die, and didn't want the child to have to go to her funeral. She wanted Tyrese to look after him now, typical lawyer she added that since he had missed so many years that she had given Tara a video diary of him as he had grown. Tyrese was speechless in shock, Tara added that she had brought the boy here and he was in his secretary's office. Mercedes asked if she could say goodbye to him online but wanted to switch the camera off so he wouldn't see her like this. Tara wept as she watched her sister's image disappear from the screen, she walked towards the secretary's office to bring the child in, he had come straight from the airport he was tired and disheveled. Tyrese almost cried when he saw the kid there would be a DNA test needed but the boy was like a miniature version of Tyrese, it was the weirdest thing in the world to look at a child that you didn't know that you had. He was the image of his father, the same lips, nose and eyes. Tyrese sat motionless as Tara introduced Gunther to his father, the boy approached the tall dark man with the same face as his own and studied him closely it was uncanny, like staring in a mirror. Tyrese lifted the boy up on to his knees and told him that if he put the earphones on he could talk to mummy. The boys eyes lit up and he spoke to her for ten minutes about flying on the plane, he told her America was big and said that Aunt Tara had introduced him to a man who had the same face. Mercedes wept as she heard his word she said goodbye, then asked to speak to Tyrese, she asked him to take care of their son and the connection went dead.

That night at four am Mercedes died peacefully in her sleep, Tara got the call and headed for the airport leaving young Gunther at Tyrese's office. Tyrese went to the toilet, he stood staring at himself in the mirror, for years he had been secretly envious of Romeo's kid and here he was, a father. He had watched the video diary that night that Mercedes had compiled, her in the hospital with Gunther all red and sleepy after the birth, his first steps, his first words she had them all on film. Tyrese had watched it twice, six birthday cakes, six and three quarter missing years.

He called in Pam and formally introduced his son, she was shocked but not surprised, the kid was the living image of him and he announced to Pam that she would have to cancel all his appointments for a week, that he was taking the week off and he asked her to arrange two flights to Florida and reserve a hotel suite in Disney World. He was going on vacation with his son. So quite unexpectedly Tyrese had at last a vacation, he called Romeo from the airport and tried to explain the situation, Romeo sounded confused.

The week they spent in Orlando was fun, Tyrese became a kid again and Gunther's eyes just about popped out of his head. They woke up at seven every morning and went to the park early staying to see the late night illuminated parade, they swam with Dolphins and enjoyed all the magic of the theme parks, secretly Tyrese had always wanted to see Disney World but he had been too poor as a kid to have gone there. Gunther had taken to him fortunately, sometimes he asked about his mum and Tyrese told him that she was flying with the angels, 'Just like a magic fairy?' he asked wide-eyed,

'Just like the magic fairy,' Tyrese assured him with tears in his eyes.

Tyrese was having such a wonderful time bonding with his son that he called Pam to cancel his commitments for another week they were staying longer. On the last evening they were there Gunther had fallen asleep, Tyrese had scooped him up in his arms and carried him to the hotel shuttle buses, the child buried his head in his lap and for a moment he opened his sleepy eyes and stared at Tyrese he said in a little voice, 'Thanks Daddy,' it was the first time that the child had called him Daddy and Tyrese felt a lump in his throat,.

They called Aunt Tara every day in Germany, Gunther told her everything that they had done in great detail, the sound of the excitement in his voice was music to her ears. She had just buried her sister, she was so depressed. Tyrese explained that he would have to get back to work and he asked Tara if she could join them in Florida, she could stay for a week or two with Gunther and he would return and get back to running his business and try to organize a school and nanny for the child.

He was delighted when she agreed, he would actually have liked her to pick the nanny and have a say in the selection of his school.

Gunther was delighted to be marooned at Disney world with his aunt for two weeks, He had a long list prepared before she arrived of everything they were going to do for the two weeks. Every day he asked for his mother, he just didn't understand why she didn't want to come. Tyrese hoped that his aunt would comfort him.

When he arrived at his office he called in Jay-D he instructed him to employ a designer immediately and requested that they transform one of the guest bedrooms in his penthouse into a boys room, they had one week and an unlimited budget to finish the project, he also wanted him to call the real estate agent and ask for some information on properties in Orlando, he was interested in buying a home with at least seven bedrooms, a pool, a tennis court and separate staff apartments, he wanted a secure property in a good location. Jay D scuffled off excited at the idea that he would probably have to go to Florida to check out the properties.

Little Gunther called his father every night, he interrupted his board meetings, business appointments and important meetings, Pam had been instructed that no matter what he was doing if Gunther called he would take the call, Pam liked the new Tyrese.

When Gunther walked into his new room at Tyrese's penthouse his eyes popped.

The designers had created a dream room with a bed in the centre of the room built into a Ferrari, the walls were painted like a jungle with realistic palm trees with monkeys hanging from their branches, there were zebras and buffalos and crocodiles and a host of cartoon characters, the ceiling was dark blue and was sprinkled with stars that lit up at night. The designers had created his own personal fantasy land. Tyrese had hid the boy's eyes and when he had opened the door of the room he was so excited he screamed for joy and ran to the authentic tree house in the corner of the room. Tomorrow he promised the overexcited boy they would go to one of the biggest toy shops in the world and buy all the toys he needed to fill the spaces and places in his room.

Tara stayed with Gunther till he fell fast asleep in the shiny Ferrari, she had to admit that it was a stunning room but warned Tyrese over dinner not to spoil him.

She was amazed, Tyrese was completely different from what she had expected, he was clever, witty and extremely polite. After dinner they went into the massive lounge and drank wine she told him that since the day Mercedes had walked away from him she had never had another lover, Gunther had been her love.

Tyrese felt like a heel that he had been unfaithful to her and she had been so wonderful to him.

Tara was divorced, she had a florist shop in Munich, her husband had been a pilot, she hardly ever saw him, he had, she claimed a girl in every port and when she had discovered that her sister had a terminal illness she had employed someone to run the florist shop and moved into Mercedes' apartment to nurse her and look after Gunther. The child spoke English and German and had been attending an International school. In the end she couldn't handle looking after her sister she had had to put her in a private clinic, and after she had lost her hair and became quite fragile she had forbidden Tara to bring Gunther to visit, she had wanted her son to remember her when she was wholesome. Tara cried as she described how the illness had taken over her body. Tyrese was glad that he had asked her to go to Disney it perhaps had taken her mind off all the horrors she had been through.

That week they interviewed nannies that had been recommended from one of the best agencies. They all seemed so stiff and colourless and at the end of the day they looked at each other, disappointed that there hadn't been one that they liked. Tyrese asked if she would consider staying on for six months to look after Gunther, he offered her a ridiculous salary with which she could well afford to pay staff in her shop, see it like a long vacation he laughed. He was delighted when she agreed he worked long hours as president of his company, she understood this and promised to stay for as long as Gunther needed her.

Together they employed, a driver, a bodyguard and a tutor to teach him more English, after he settled down they would have him put into a good school.

Tyrese asked the same designer to transform another room for Tara, he hoped that if she had her own room perhaps that she would stay longer. Tara enjoyed selecting the fabrics and furnishings for her room, he wanted her to have her own environment, he also employed another maid and cook.

Romeo, Capricorn and Pippa accepted Tyrese's offer of dinner, they were dying to see this mystery son that had surfaced out of the blue. They arrived at seven in the evening with a fleet of cars and an army of bodyguards. It was unusual for them to drift away from their fortress, they lived like hermits behind the high walls of their impregnable estate.

As soon as they saw Gunther they knew he was indeed Tyrese's son, he even walked with that cocky swagger. Pippa and Gunther were almost the same age and she was wildly jealous when she saw his room and demanded that she wanted exactly the same room.

Romeo cringed when he heard how much that it had cost he really was quite mean sometimes.

Pippa didn't mix well with other kids she had never been allowed to go to school, she had a string of private tutors and spent most of her time in the company of grown-ups. Tyrese didn't want his son to be brought up like that he wanted him to go to school, make friends and have a life like other kids.

Tyrese organized some popcorn and soft drinks for the kids and put them in the screening room to watch a Disney film while he sat caught up with Romeo and Capricorn. Romeo had brought over a demo to let him hear some new tracks, Tyrese didn't say but he was disappointed, there was no more soul in his music.

He had business things to discuss with him so Capricorn went into the library with Tara to have a chat. Tara felt heart sorry for Capricorn she was so screwed up. It was the first time that she had met Tara but as soon as they were in the library together she opened up to her.

Since the kidnapping, Romeo had blamed her and they slept in separate rooms, they lived in a beautiful stately home filled with antiques and to the whole world it seemed like a dream home, to Capricorn it was like a prison. Romeo didn't communicate with her, he only spoke to his daughter. The only communication she had were with the bodyguards, the drivers and the maids. The loneliness was killing her, when he wasn't writing he was sleeping, each night she would hear him lock the door to his bedroom he had shut her out of his life like she didn't exist. Their sex life was finished, once she had spoken of divorce when she had attempted to take the discussion further he had beat her so badly that she had been bruised for weeks, her parents had been ill and didn't want to travel she missed them too.

Romeo doted on his daughter but Capricorn was worried about her she had no friends to play with and no contact with other children they had twenty-four hour security guards at the house, one was positioned outside Pippa's room, even when she went to the bathroom a guard had to wait outside. Romeo's obsession with security was driving her crazy the bodyguards watched them eat, watched them sleep they were forever lingering like shadows in the background.

Their presence in her home unnerved her. Each night she had to dress for dinner and she felt so unwanted and unloved that she had started to take anti-depressants. Romeo was getting stale, he had writer's block and when nothing was turning out properly he would go into a black rage and lash out at both her and the staff, the only living creature he warmed to was Pippa, she was the apple of his eye.

She knew his new material was bad but how could he be inspired living like a recluse.

He had no idea what was happening outside his estate.

She wanted badly to have a party or invite guests but he would not permit it, they had a dining room that sat fifty guests the ballroom in their home they had transformed into a night club and the expensively designed and renovated guest bedrooms had never been used, .the Olympic sized pool was never used either. The days seemed so long for Capricorn and the strain was getting to her. She begged Tara to talk to Tyrese to see if he could persuade him to get out more.

Tara suggested that Pippa came to play or watch a movie with Gunther once a week.

She also promised that they would they would visit. Capricorn told her that all guests had to walk through a metal detector in the hall, even the staff were monitored as they came and went, every room had security cameras linked up to a main security room. In both Romeo's and Pippa's bedroom there were surveillance cameras. It was more like a high security prison than a home.

As Tara waved goodbye to Tyrese's friends she felt sorry for them as they disappeared into the night in their fleet of long limousines, a family that was not a family. She was glad that she was a mere mortal and not famous if that was the price of fame she would rather stay a florist. She had no idea how rich that Tyrese was but she hoped that little Gunther would lead a normal life and made a mental note to check out the schools that Jay-d had recommended. The sooner the boy was out in the world and made friends the better.

Marisa made her come back with a trilogy of flops. The critics panned her for her wooden performance in a costume drama then slaughtered her attempt at comedy, her final attempt at being a cartoon heroine was meant to be serious but the film bombed and the studio released her from her five year contract in a public bitter battle. All of her box office disasters had cost the studio their reputation and millions of dollars.

Marisa disappeared from the public eye and the limelight and virtually disappeared into thin air with her shipping Tycoon. The glossy but tarnished couple spent most of their time entertaining on their yacht at various ports around the globe, they had docked at Puerto Banus for the summer and were enjoying a glittering existence with members of the jet set, Marisa purposely avoided the movie set, she preferred now to mix with the real jet set.

Royalty, diplomats, bankers and global tycoons, her fading beauty still impressed this public.

Her billionaire boyfriend adored the very ground she walked on and the air she breathed.

Her failure in a business that had once embraced her now embarrassed her, the last three films she had made had been nothing less than disasters and she had disagreed bitterly that the failing of the movies had been entirely her fault. Each one had been badly directed, badly edited and canned right from the start, for an award winning screen legend to have made three successive flops was unheard of.

Marisa was on the yacht her tycoon lover Vidal had purchased for her as a birthday surprise he had called it after her and her name graced the ship in solid gold letters. The vessel was one of the most expensive and exclusive ones to grace the seas, its gleaming streamlined aero dynamic form was unique. The vessel had its own helipad and their vintage white Bentley graced the deck, the crew wore white suits with gold epaulettes and gloves, the decor of the cabins was ostentatious and decadent beyond conception. The main dining area seated fifty and was accessible by a sweeping gold plated staircase, beyond the dining salon two gilt doors led you through to a formal ballroom with Regency furnishings and sparkling Venetian glass chandeliers.

The guests' suites were individually designed by some of Europe's leading designers each one was different and possessed its own character. Marisa's bedroom was a lavishly designed cabin at the helm with panoramic windows that overlooked the ocean, her marble bathroom had chandeliers and adjacent to her bedroom she had dressing chambers with floor to ceiling mirrors and specially designed wardrobes to house her several hundred pairs of shoes and rows of designer dresses.

The vessel was more like a Palazzo on sea than a ship, everyone who came on board was intimidated by its grandeur.

The ship's designer had created an indoor and on deck pool, a screening room, theatre, night-club, snooker room, library, gymnasium, spa, meditation chill out lounge an on deck breakfast area with gazebo, a roof garden and greenhouse, state of the art kitchens on all seven levels, four reception rooms, a formal dining salon and grand ballroom. The stunning ship was nicknamed the Empress of the ocean it had taken years to build and had cost Vidal an absolute fortune. It had taken months and they had combed the world to furnish the vessel with antiques, priceless paintings and pieces of art were scattered throughout the ship.

Marisa loved to entertain and Vidal adored showing off the masterpiece of the seas with its solar energy system and high tech engine.

In Puerto Banus there was a constant flow of VIPs, the jet set came in droves to see and be seen. Vidal's ship was by far the most breathtaking one in the port and the envy of everyone.

Marisa felt like a queen in this environment and was in her element when she entertained. When life got too boring they would dock and take off to some restaurant in the gleaming vintage Bentley convertible or go on adventures in the state of the art helicopter. It was breathtaking to fly over the whitewashed Spanish Villages like Mijas. Their guests were collected at the airport by helicopter and flown on board, the constant flow of guests made the pilot one of the busiest members of the crew.

Sometimes they would visit the small clubs and restaurants on the port, here the jet set gathered nightly wearing designer clothes with lashings of jewels, here the nouveau rich came to spend their money, there was no shortage of beautiful people and Marisa preferred it here to San Tropez, Cap Feratt or Monte Carlo, the energy and vibrance of the small port was electric. Here everything was about showmanship but for the aristocratic and old money set it was too vulgar.

One night after a magnificent seafood banquet on board The Marisa they all docked and went to a popular little club which was so exclusive that the guest list was like a who's who.

Politicians, princes and princesses, megastars and corporate magnates mingled with movie stars and squeezed themselves into the cosy but exclusive night club.

Marisa was centre stage dancing on the dance floor with one of Vidal's best friends who had made a fortune in Silicon Valley she looked magnificent in the 50,000 dollar designer dress that had been flown in from Paris that morning. In the strobe light the large diamond choker looked almost like a fake it was so large it was hard to imagine that anyone could possible buy it. Vidal loved to see her wearing priceless things it was a way for him to display his wealth. Marisa adored him and she gracefully accepted his lavish gifts with glee, it delighted her to wear the large pieces of jewelry that he surprised her with. It was not unusual for Marisa to turn up for breakfast wearing 300,000 dollars worth of precious jewels. With her green swimsuit she would wear strands of emeralds, with her Bordeaux bikini she would wear huge ruby and diamond drop earrings with her black swimsuit she would wear strand upon strand of priceless black pearls, she adored dressing up and he adored watching her dress up as well as he enjoyed watching her undressing.

He was particularly turned on when they had sex and she only wore her jewels and high heels, the staff had seen them often on deck making love in the moonlight, her totally naked except for millions of dollars of jewels and six inch heels. Marisa knew that the crew on duty took turns of watching them, it kind of turned her on. She always positioned herself so they could get a good view.

One night when he had fucked her doggy style against the railing she lost one of her hundred thousand dollar earrings, ten of the crew had searched for three hours without recovering it, they suspected that it had gone overboard. Vidal had been so excited that he hadn't cared and she joked that it was the most expensive fuck in the world, unfortunately that piece had not been registered with the insurance and Vidal had promised to have another one made for her.

There was a small army of staff working on board and all of them were extremely good-looking, well-mannered and experienced, sometimes when she was having sex with Vidal she fantasised about some of the men who worked in the engine room, there was an Argentinean black skinned one that she was particularly fascinated by, he was over six foot tall and had dazzling white teeth and unusual light blue eyes.

Vidal noticed her interest in him, he had watched her stare at him as he cleaned the deck, he made a mental note to have him fired at the next port.

When Marisa inquired where he was Vidal lied and said that he had quit. Any member of the crew that she became too familiar with seemed to mysteriously disappear, the staff turnover was high.

Vidal never allowed her to be alone on the ship, he didn't trust the young handsome men that they employed and had actually told the agency that employed his staff that gay men would have a preference when applying. Around seventy percent of his crew were homosexual, they looked good, worked well and didn't try to lay his beloved.

Marisa was totally oblivious to the fact that he preferred to employ gays he was clever enough to restrict the heterosexual ones without her noticing it.

One night when after an evening at a club they had returned and she had crept out of bed, Vidal had drunk too much and was snoring like an ox, the sound irritated her so she pulled on her robe and went outside on deck. It was a starry moonlight night and everyone was asleep, she had heard a noise coming from a lifeboat on the lower deck, creeping towards the sound in her bare feet she was shocked to discover two of the crew making love, she froze in her steps and watched, the sight of their powerful sun-tanned muscled bodies writhing together turned her on.

The young men were so engrossed in what they were doing they didn't notice her.

She was really disappointed, she recognized one of the young men to be the same one that only two days earlier had been watching her being taken doggy style on deck, she had thought that he had been watching her, now she knew that it had been Vidal that he had been watching. What a world she chuckled, all the best ones were gay, she coughed lightly just loud enough to disturb the two men then walked past them and said, 'Nice night,' she beamed winking at the two men, their faces turned beetroot red and their erections shriveled.

As she glided back to her room with a big smile on her face, lying spreadeagled naked on the silk sheets, Vidal lay his protrusive belly heaving as he snored like a buffalo.

Marisa fell asleep and dreamt of the two young sailors, she had been sad when the blue-eyed stud had left. Vidal hadn't known that one afternoon whilst he had been playing pool with Marcus that she had sex with the tall Argentinean stud in the engine room.

She had thoroughly enjoyed the experience with the primitive giant and still could remember that he smelled of oil and sweat, she was beginning to think that Vidal purposely employed homosexual staff, she could smell them a mile off, the movie business had been full of gays.

He was so jealous she thought as she drifted back to sleep.

The next morning she scolded him for snoring all night and took off to the spa to have a massage, she hoped that he suffered a nasty hangover and would stay off the alcohol. It was always the same, one drink too many and he turned into a bullfrog.

After brunch he approached her on deck and tossed a small velvet box on her lap. Inside was a magnificent sapphire bracelet, his way of saying sorry for keeping you from sleeping, she kissed him on the cheek and snapped the bracelet on her wrist, it was heavy and the baguette cut stones sparkled in the sun. He must keep a whole supply of presents for me she mused locked away in his private safe. She would have loved to have known the combination code, she was sure that he had her birthday gift locked away in there and was dying to see it. In three weeks it was her birthday, forty guests would be flying in and twenty would reside on board. Vidal was secretly planning a magnificent party for her and he had employed a well-known party planner to arrange a night that she would never forget, with her favourite opera singer, fire eaters, ballet dancers, tigers and a fireworks extravaganza that would illuminate the whole port.

The theme of the party would be "Harem" the whole deck would be transformed into a harem with both male and female belly dancers. A dancer dressed as Aladdin would be rolled out of a magic Persian carpet and present her with her birthday gift, male lap dancers dressed as genies would entertain her. It would be a lavish extravaganza and a night to remember. He had checked every little detail personally, as usual when he had a party it was a spectacle that no one would forget, the invitations had been delivered in small brass magic lamps by veiled eastern princesses.

Vidal just loved decadence and perfection, all his parties had themes and he adored conjuring up concepts. All of the food was being prepared by chefs from her favourite restaurants in Paris, Milan and London, the buffet they planned would be magnificent, a Chinese ice sculptor was being flown in from Hong Kong to create an exotic ice sculpture for the centrepiece of the table.

Marisa and himself would fly north by helicopter and spend a day together, when they returned to the dock in the evening the vessel would have been transformed into a harem their guests would be on board and he and Marisa would arrive on an elephant, it would be an absolute trip she would be an Eastern Princess, he had already ordered a designer creation that was being made in Paris the costume would be beaded and flown in by courier.

The party was in full swing, the yacht was docked near the port, Marisa and Vidal arrived at the port sitting on an Indian elephant then they dressed in exotic Arabian costumes and transferred to a shuttle speed boat that would transfer them to the yacht, the security arrangements were very strict all staff were vetted before being employed.

Marisa looked stunning in the expensive couture creation with lashings of rubies, emeralds and sapphires at her throat, they enjoyed a wonderful buffet and the guests moved from room to room enjoying the entertainment that had been carefully arranged, all of the guests wore skilfuly created costumes it was A Ball Masque and everyone was dressed in Arabian clothing, the women with Yashmaks and the men in Turbans with eye masks.

Vidal had disappeared to dance with the wife of a diplomat, Marisa had drunk too much champagne and she wanted to go to her cabin to change her shoes, the jeweled sandals that had been specially made were crippling her, as she made her way down the corridors of the ship she smiled to herself.

Vidal had presented her with a pair of diamond earrings, she had never seen such big stones, they were hundreds of years old and had belonged to a Czarina, they were uncomfortably heavy but rather stunning and they were worth over a million dollars, the matching necklace was just as uncomfortable but she reveled in the idea that several hundred years before these had been crafted for the wife of a Russian Czar. It was a pleasure to wear such enchanting pieces, she threw off the sandals and made her way to her dressing room, she was looking for the ruby encrusted slippers when two masked men came into the dressing room, at first she thought that it was two stray guests till the taller man extracted a magnum and pressed it to her temples. As the short stubby man in the gold brocade waistcoat attempted to put masking tape over her mouth she kneed him in the balls and scratched his face her initial screams were stopped as they empowered her and tied her arms and legs, she kicked and punched in every direction, bruising her captors. Once she was gagged and tied they ripped the two diamond earrings from her ears, tearing her ear lobes open, the blood ran down her neck then they snatched the necklace from her bloody neck and left her on the floor of the dressing room tied firmly to a pillar. She could hear them open her safe, she shivered thinking that there were millions dollars of uninsured jewels there, wriggling helplessly she struggled till she had no more energy then she slumped on the floor helplessly.

No one had missed Marisa for an hour, Vidal concerned that she had drunk too much sent three of the staff to go looking for her. When they reported that she was not in the night-club or theatre he went to her room thinking that perhaps she had been be sick. The moment he opened the door he knew something was wrong the painting that hid her safe lay on the floor, the door lay open and the sight of empty safe unnerved him, suddenly he noticed the blood stains on the floor, he panicked and was relieved to see that Marisa was alive. For a few moments he had thought perhaps that she had been murdered. After untying her he called the security. The coastguard arrived promptly on the scene, none of the guests enjoying the festivities were aware of what had happened below, several guests had been taxied to shore and the whole evening people had been coming to and fro.

Marisa had been robbed of the things that she adored most, she always had travelled with her favourite jewels and that night eighty per cent of her collection had been in the safe. Literally millions of dollars of jewels had been stolen. The chief officer ordered the guests to assemble in the main salon and they seemed shocked as he explained what had recently happened, one of the speed boats was missing obviously the thieves had escaped on it.

Marisa had been tied up for more than an hour, they could have been anywhere by now.

A fleet of officers searched the ship and took fingerprint tests on her apartments. Marisa still dressed in the genie outfit lay huddled up in bed too shocked to move. The police had interrogated her for an hour and a doctor had sewn up her earlobes, they were ripped literally open and she would have to have cosmetic surgery to reconstruct them.

This would be one birthday that she would never forget, the following morning she flew on the helicopter to the airport, she wanted to return to their Chateau in France she felt so violated that she didn't want to spend one more day on the ship.

Marisa had called everyone to tell them the dreadful story, when she called Tyrese he had been short on the telephone, apparently he had family problems, she was surprised as she had never heard him mention a son before.

Tyrese had been quick to finish his conversation with the spoiled brat Marisa, he had too many problems of his own to solve without listening to her whining that her jewels had been stolen. He had seen a report on the news of the incident and had been glad that he had declined the offer to fly to Spain for the party.

Gunther had been a sweet kid. So sweet that was till he reached the age of twelve, Tyrese had had little time to look after his son, as president of a major record label he had little or no time. The lad had been a problem, he seemed to be in constant trouble, he had employed a string of nannies, bodyguards and minders but no one stayed longer than a week. He had already been expelled from three schools. Tyrese was at his wit's end. He had asked Tara to come to look after the boy, he had paid her triple the amount that her business was worth to sell up and come back to Detroit, after three months she had nearly suffered a nervous breakdown. At fifteen he had been arrested for being in possession of drugs, at sixteen he was arrested for being in possession of an illegal fire arm. Just before Tara left he had been grounded on house arrest for dealing drugs.

Tyrese had been in an important business meeting when the police had interrupted him to inform him that Gunther had set the penthouse on fire, there had been 300,000 dollars worth of damage. Tyrese blamed himself for not having the time to bond with his son sometimes he thought that it must be genetic. Tara had bought him a kitten when he was ten, the Siamese cat had a litter and she had been shocked when she walked on to the terrace and saw the then eleven year old Gunther on the balcony of the penthouse throwing the furry little new born creatures one by one over the balcony. The child was evil incarnated and she had left Detroit in floods of tears.

Tyrese had spent a fortune on psychiatrists and doctors, the lad was spoiled and wanted for nothing. In the end he sent him to England to one of the best schools in Europe, he was sure that the change would be good for him. After a week the sixteen year old disappeared. He had emptied his bank balance and forged cheques for a formidable amount.

Tyrese had thought that he had mixed with the wrong kids he had been drug addicted since he was fifteen, he had taken cannabis at fifteen then moved on to harder drugs, ecstasy, coke and eventually heroin.

Tyrese had gone berserk when he returned home from business trip one day and found him in the toilet shooting up a needle in his arm, the boy had been a headache for Tyrese for years and his hair had turned white with worry.

After he had disappeared in England, Tyrese had flown there and spent three weeks searching for him, he hired detectives and top agents but the boy had vanished from the planet, several years later one night when Tyrese was watching the news he was shocked to see a feature about a young boy that had been arrested for drug dealing in Thailand.

Tyrese had looked at the news flash in disbelief the unshaven scraggy youth was indeed his son.

He had been sentenced to life in a maximum security prison and his existence had been a living hell. The conditions in the Thai prisons were horrific, prisoners were shackled in irons and forced to exist in cage like cells with fifty prisoners in each cell. They survived on meagre rations, Aids and other diseases were rampant. Tyrese had flown there with two of the best lawyers on the planet, however there was no appeal for his crime, he would never ever be released, they were making an example of foreigners charged with drug convictions and his outlook was grim, no amount of money could help him. Tyrese had went almost mad as he saw how bad the conditions were. There was nothing to be done. They could request and appeal a thousand times and it wouldn't help. For a time Tyrese thought that money could buy everything but he had now accepted the fact that this was not true in his son's case he was doomed. When Tyrese returned from Bangkok he seemed to have aged ten years and for months he found it impossible to sleep. He blamed himself for his son's failings and he hoped that Mercedes was not looking down from heaven at him. He felt that he had failed as a father, she had trusted him to raise the boy and he had failed miserably. Romeo kept trying to convince him that it was not his fault Gunther had driven everyone crazy for years and had had a self-destructive streak for as far back as they could remember.

At the lowest point of his life just when he thought that it couldn't get any worse it did.

His business was losing money at an alarming rate, they had lost a lawsuit with a major recording artist and were being sued for 60 million dollars, the court case had been horrific, like a soap series the whole shebang had been televised. What was worse is that the artist won the case and he would have to fork out sixty million dollars plus legal costs which were in their millions, also the saga was crippling for the company, sales in the music industry had plummeted.

They say what goes up must come down, his world was crashing by the moment and there was no one that he could confide in.

There had been a scandal over the Pippa Curtis Foundation, their project had been described as a scam, millions of dollars that had been collected had been creamed off, directors had pocketed funds and everyone was pointing their fingers at Tyrese.

Romeo had been living like a recluse, Tyrese had a violent telephone battle with him he hadn't given him any support, their friendship was under pressure.

Pippa junior had been an excellent scholar she had been a model student and had graduated with flying colours, she was a promising young artist and her talent was amazing. She had already at seventeen had two major exhibitions and sold lots of paintings she had little or no interest in the music business and had attended an expensive Swiss school. Romeo adored her she was the apple of his eye, no man was good enough for his daughter and she travelled everywhere with two security guards.

Capricorn lived a sad existence in the home that had become her prison, Romeo lived in the West wing and had decorators design for her in the East wing. She led a lonely life and was swallowing daily amounts of valium to help her survive. Tyrese wondered why Romeo didn't divorce her and set her free, she was a lovely woman. Tyrese couldn't stand to see the pain in her eyes, her parents had died and she seemed alone in the world.

Tyrese had a bitter battle with Romeo, he had wanted to withdraw from the annual benefit concert for the foundation. Tyrese knew that if Romeo pulled out as a major shareholder then all the other artists would pull out and if that happened then the whole foundation would collapse, no wonder he thought that Pippa had taken her own life.

In the end Tyrese convinced Romeo to perform at the New Year benefit which was going to be in New York. Romeo hated performing live, crowds frightened him, Capricorn was spending her summer holidays at their fortress in Florida, preferring the sunshine in Miami to the bitter snow in New York. Romeo had not had a hit record for years. His extravagant lifestyle was expensive and he was in millions of dollars in debt. He needed to perform to make money but had a phobia of crowds.

Romeo had flown to the Big Apple two days before the big event. His daughter and Capricorn were to fly in on the afternoon of the event and return to Miami the same evening on their private Lear jet. That night the weather had been so horrific in New York that half the audience hadn't turned up, many ticket holders had been stranded in the worst weather conditions that the East Coast had experienced in a decade, the fierce storms had grounded the city to a halt.

Pippa had called her father to say that because of the weather they would be late, she hoped both her and her mother would arrive for his performance. Miami had no snow but there had been a tornado. Romeo was on stage almost ready to perform, he glanced to the left of the stage and saw both Pippa and Capricorn standing at the back behind Tyrese they were dressed rather casually and were smiling at him. Forgetting that he was on stage he automatically waved at them. He was glad they were there, they had never missed a performance in ten years. This was to be his last big stadium gig and he was glad they had made it. Tyrese was nervous about Romeo's performance he wondered why he had waved at him it was an odd gesture. As he had watched Romeo's mediocre performance Tyrese had felt as though someone was behind him he had felt a strange chill in the air. After the two songs Romeo walked over to Tyrese and asked where his daughter had gone, Tyrese was just trying to explain that they hadn't arrived yet when the police officers approached.

To their horror they learned that both Pippa and Capricorn's bodies lay at the bottom of the ocean somewhere near the Bermuda triangle the Lear jet had exploded in the sky off the coast of Florida half an hour ago.

Tyrese watched as Romeo collapsed in a heap on the wooden stage, he had not said a word but the look in his eyes had said more than a thousand words. That night Romeo had died inside.

The air ambulance transported him to the hospital, once inside they had to sedate him, he was a man possessed with grief.

Tyrese slept in an armchair beside his friend's bed, visions of Pippa and Capricorn haunted his dreams, he wanted to be there when Romeo awoke.

That night in the dimly lit private hospital room Tyrese had talked to God it had been a long time since he had thought of God, he thought that God had deserted him, he asked why they had had to be taken he would have gladly died in their place. Pippa had only been a teenager she had so much to do and see, and poor Capricorn she had suffered loneliness like no one ever, to be alone is bad but to be alone within a relationship is dreadful how she suffered he thought.

To Tyrese's surprise when Romeo came round he was quite quiet, he had been hysterical when he had been admitted the sedatives had calmed him but they didn't mask the haunted look in his eyes. Tyrese wept as he observed his pain. Pippa had been his love, his life, his pleasure. He had been super protective over them but it hadn't saved them.

He told Tyrese that just as he went on stage he had seen them, they had smiled at him.

Tyrese thought that he was hallucinating perhaps but then he remembered that he too had an odd feeling, he remembered that he had thought it odd that Romeo had waved, the hairs on his neck had stood up, 'They didn't miss my last performance,' he choked, tears running down his cheeks, 'they were there, they came to say goodbye,' he cried.

The saddest thing of all was that there were no bodies recovered, the pilots, the crew, the security guards, his wife and precious daughter had gone to the bottom of the ocean.

Witnesses on a nearby fishing boat had seen the plane implode in the lightning storm then torpedo into the sea.

They held a magnificent memorial service at a cathedral, Tyrese had to support Romeo, it was as if he had doubled in age his shoulders slouched in the black coat. He dragged his legs into the cathedral as if he was eighty, Tyrese found it hard to mask his tears he cried openly through the service lost in emotion he cried for Pippa, for her mother, for Romeo, for Mercedes, for his own son who was at this very moment rotting away in a prison camp on the other side of the world.

He was glad that Tara had flown in to pay her respects he had not seen her for years and needed someone, it was ironic he employed almost seven hundred people but had no one to confide in, for the first time in his life he was lost for words what could he say to Romeo, what could he say to anyone.

After the service Tyrese had arranged that the Thai family brought some doves in cages.

One by one they opened the cages and set fifty doves free, the white birds disappeared into the clouds, Romeo looked at the birds as they vanished into the fluffy white clouds, he remembered how he and Capricorn had performed the tradition of setting birds free near the temple grounds they said that it brought good luck. He was grateful and enjoyed the symbolism of the event.

After the memorial service they went for a light lunch to a leading hotel. Tara noticed that no one ate a thing, the only thing that was keeping Romeo sane was that he had been sure that he had seen them. It comforted him and made him realize that there must be something after death he had seen them not once but twice, the first time on stage which coincided with the time of the crash and once again in the hospital, he hadn't told anyone but that night around three am he had woke up. Tyrese was asleep in a chair, he had felt a presence in the room like someone was sitting on both sides of the bed when he had opened his eyes he saw Pippa and Capricorn one on either side, they were smiling and it seemed like he could read their thoughts, they were saying goodbye and telling him that they would meet again, they seemed illuminated from within and surrounded by a golden light. He had rubbed his eyes thinking that it was a dream they had stayed for a second then kissed his forehead and vanished, after experiencing this he had felt stronger he had wanted to tell Tyrese but felt that it was better not to, it was his secret.

Romeo led the life of a recluse taking no pleasure in anything or anyone. He lived to die, his interest in the afterlife and spiritualism increased and he became increasingly obsessed with the paranormal.

He lived in Miami at their summer house he liked the climate and the blue skies, with the exception of security guards and maids he never had guests the only person he kept in close contact was Tyrese.

Tyrese threw himself into his work, he was desperately trying to turn things around and make the company profitable again. The whole industry had changed with the introduction of new technology there were hundreds of new developments in technology but talent ruled the roost, he had imagined that the Pippa Curtis Foundation schools that had opened world-wide would supply his record label with fresh talent. From the thousand or so pupils that had scholarships only a handful had become stars another dozen were one hit wonders that disappeared as soon almost as soon as they had surfaced.

Tyrese employed new staff in new departments he attempted to revive his business by employing young high flying executives, in the end he re-employed some golden oldies, he had realized that experience was achieved by years of hard work and that the more experienced his crew were, the more successful his company would become.

Tyrese was lonely he had little or no friends apart from the weekly long telephone calls to Romeo. Marisa called on average once every two months since her jewels had been stolen she had resorted to staying within the confines of her villa where she felt secure. Tyrese was sure that her relationship with the high flying shipping Tycoon was coming to an end, he had seen several photos of him with other young attractive women.

Marisa's passion for large expensive jewels had been replaced for a love of helping with charities, she had been working closely with several charities from the comfort of her home. Her attitude had changed, the shock of the robbery had driven her to look at life from another perspective.

She had undergone surgery to correct her ear lobes and she was preparing an auction of her once worn designer couture creations and planned to donate the money to charities.

Vidal was bored, he was sick of staying at the French villa and had strayed to his yacht and summer houses. He did not like the new homely Marisa, he had fallen in love with the blonde bombshell and had been perfectly happy with her parading around wearing expensive clothes and jewels, he had recently been seen entertaining several young beautiful celebrities and he seemed to be permanently in the gossip magazines.

Marisa didn't care she had never loved him she had connected with him because of his wealth, sexually and emotionally she was not attracted to him, in her lover's absence she had employed a handsome male secretary and her blatant affair with the handsome young man was no secret to the servants. She was sure that one of the butlers was reporting her every move to Vidal but she was beyond caring, he was never around and had been dating starlets for months, their relationship was diminishing and it was only a matter of time till they split.

One morning she was lying by the pool sipping Mango nectar when the butler brought her a letter on a letter tray, it was from Vidal he had enclosed the deeds of a Paris apartment that he had bought for her. There was a cheque for ten million dollars and a short letter thanking her for being so wonderful and wishing her farewell. It took Marisa two days to pack she was driven to Paris in Vidal's gold Rolls Royce, it was funny but she felt relieved, she had never loved the man and was at a stage in her life when she wanted some space. All her life she had been a man's plaything, she had rolled from one relationship to another since she had been a teenager, she was looking forward to living in the apartment that Vidal had given her it was elegant and secure and she planned to enjoy her life again and was looking forward to the freedom of being single for the first time in her life.

The first thing she did was hire an extremely handsome valet personal trainer, she told Tyrese that it was a whole new world, that she was free and she joked that operation toy boy had been set into motion she didn't want a heavy relationship anymore she had been a decorative bimbo for long enough now it was her time to use and abuse.

The years drifted by, Tyrese had hired a fleet of enigmatic executives to run the corporation.

Every year he travelled to Bangkok to visit his son, it was soul destroying to watch his son fade away behind the bars of the primitive Thai prison. He looked gaunt and skeletal and seemed to deteriorate every year. Tyrese had accepted the fact that his son had committed a criminal offence but his sentence seemed so harsh. Frustrated that all his money could not help he had wasted hundreds of thousands of dollars employing expensive lawyers to try and get him an appeal but it had been ten years now and no one had succeeded. Tyrese was not used to losing battles he had been a winner all his life he felt helpless now.

Tyrese had forgotten what being in love had felt like, he had had no one in his life romantically for so long he couldn't remember what a relationship felt like, when he felt the animal urge he called an expensive escort bureau and after he had relieved himself with a half hour of passion at a motel he would return home alone, his television had indeed become his best friend.

Chapter 16

Thailand

It was September, he had gone to Bangkok to visit his son, he was disturbed to hear that his son was in solitary confinement for stabbing an inmate, there would be no visitation allowed.

For three days he had returned to the prison only to be told the same story, disappointed he returned to the hotel. Bangkok was a dreary place in the rainy season, he had thought of going to the islands but a friend had warned him to stay clear, this was the worst time of year to visit. The rains had flooded the island and making trips to the other islands out of the question as the seas were too rough. He lay in his hotel bed thoroughly depressed, he had tried to re schedule his flight but the flights were all full and the waiting list was a mile long.

A taxi driver that he had booked for the day had suggested he go to Pattaya it was a small town on the sea. Years before it had been a sleepy fishing village but after the Vietnam War the soldiers had been sent there to recuperate, now the place was a thriving tourist destination, with lots of hotels, bars, restaurants and condominiums. The place had a bad reputation for its brothels, massage parlours and Go-Go bars, Tyrese was reluctant to go there, he had seen all there was to see in Bangkok, the bright lights of Patpong had been fun for a night and he didn't fancy going to Pattaya at all but the taxi driver with the cheeky grin persuaded him,.

Tyrese went for two days to Pattaya and ended up staying for a month. He loved the place, it was a melting pot, there were lots of expats living there and the seaside town had a thriving population.

At first he found it chaotic but after two nights he had learned how to laugh again and he learned to love the Thai people they were wonderful.

At first he had stayed at a trendy hotel, it was right on the seafront, had a busy bar and it seemed like a cool place to stay for someone in his business. After a few nights he decided that he was going to extend his holiday and he rented an apartment at Jomtien Beach, after a week in the apartment he put an offer in to buy the property, for the first time in years he learned to relax, he had fallen in love with the spacious apartment with panoramic views of the ocean. At night he would sit on the balcony around six thirty and watch the sun set, it was paradise on earth, he threw away his watch, slept till he woke up, ate when he was hungry and lost all track of time, he would fall asleep to the sound of the ocean and wake to the sound of the sea as it lapped on the shore. The apartment was a real find, in a top location right on the sea, when you walked through the garden you were on the beach. Sometimes he would wake up at three am, it would be raining and he would watch the fork lightning as it danced in the sky, the sea seemed full of fishing boats, at night their lights sparkled in the ocean like diamonds. The apartment had tennis courts, a sauna, gymnasium and there were several restaurants nearby it was like living in a seven star hotel. Most of the occupants were wealthy business men, there were Thai TV stars, diplomats and fashion designers living in the building, it was a gem of a place and although he only had two bedrooms he was happy for the first time in years.

He called the office every day and things seemed to be going well, the executives that he had employed were doing an excellent job, he cancelled his ticket and decided to stay an extra month to oversee the renovation of his condo.

Tyrese couldn't believe how cheap everything seemed to be, he was enthusiastic about the redesigning of his apartment. A crew of seventeen workmen were employed to complete the renovations he had redesigned the spare bedroom into an office and the first thing that he bought was a state of the art computer system with a webcam he wanted to communicate with his head office and had decided that with today's technology he was only the click of a switch away. Every day he would go on line and hold meetings with staff by webcam in his office in Detroit they watched their president on a huge plasma screen and they conducted weekly board meetings by cyber technology.

Tyrese was enjoying the sunsets and the evenings on the balcony, every day at six thirty he would steal an hour for himself just to sit and meditate whilst the sun set, the tranquility was invigorating and he made most of his major business decisions here over a gin and tonic.

Getting used to the Thai mentality was taking time, workmen were inexpensive but sometimes they simply didn't turn up, his electrical team had, so to speak, walked off the job.

He had planned to be finished in four weeks but the way things were going he suspected that it would take at least two months.

While the workmen knocked down walls and put in a new marble floor Tyrese went shopping for furniture, he had commissioned an artist to make some paintings for him and he was excited at being there.

He had little or no contact with the other people who lived in the building, sometimes in the early morning he would wake to the sound of the surf then go jogging on the beach. To access the beach he had to walk though the gardens down a jasmine and orchid lined path, the smell of flowers was so pungent it made one's head spin, it was strange being here in this other culture, he seemed more aware of everything, flowers smelled better, food tasted better, sunsets seemed more spectacular and the sky seemed more blue.

The truth of the matter was that he was exhausted, he had worked non-stop for years and needed a rest, it was great to be able to wake up when one wanted to and sleep when one felt like it.

The Thai climate and ambience was appealing to him he loved the friendly attitude of the Thai's they seemed to smile all the time and had a special kind of charm that was indeed infectious.

Most nights he would order from one of the restaurants in the complex and eat dinner in his room, it was rather like living in a luxury hotel. The first few weeks he was so busy with the builders that he flopped into bed every night early. One Friday he decided to go out by himself and he took one of the Thai Tuk Tuks, to the town, you waved the taxis down jumped on and rang a bell when you wanted off. He headed for the centre and had a nice meal at a popular Thai restaurant set in an exotic garden, the waitresses wore long silk traditional Thai silk evening dresses and one looked more elegant than the others.

Tyrese could understand why men from all over the world fell madly in love with Thai women, they were indeed strikingly beautiful and had amazing personalities. There were lots of foreigners in Pattaya, the seaside town was a popular destination with Japanese, Russians and Europeans alike, the climate here on the gulf coast was better, in the rainy season there was less rainfall and more sunshine. The other advantage was that one could drive from the airport here. Pattaya had a flood of tourists all year round and the town had cinemas, shopping centres, international restaurants, bars and clubs.

After a few drinks Tyrese found himself walking down the beach road looking at the dozens of stalls many of which sold bootleg CDs and DVDs, the beach road at night was full of tourists and at the end of the road there was a pedestrian street that Tyrese had never seen. The street was lined with beer bars and clubs, attracted by the neon lights Tyrese walked into the brightly lit area with its dozens of night clubs and go-go bars. Every few steps pretty young women in scanty outfits begged him to come inside for a drink Tyrese, decided to try one of the bars, just one drink he thought as two girls in tight sexy dresses led him. It was happy hour and the drinks cost absolutely nothing, inside there were few clients and he sat at a table and watched the twenty or so topless girl go-go gyrate on poles.

Tyrese looked at the immaculately groomed smooth skinned girls, some of them looked like high fashion models, most of them danced topless and had a number pinned on to their scanty G-strings, suddenly the disc jockey stopped the throbbing disco music and played a dramatic intro, every thirty minutes they had a show, nudity was illegal but they had security men on the door and if the police arrived they signaled to the DJ and the girls would scamper from the stage.

Tyrese wondered what kind of show they would have, the hostess explained that every half an hour they had a different show. Tyrese had nothing better to do, the place was nice and he decided to stay to watch two of the shows the first was a show performed by a totally naked girl, she danced in the dark with three candles dropping hot wax on her naked smooth skin, she tantalized the audience, the second show was a Hawaiian show, three Thai girls naked except for a garland of orchids on her head came out and performed a ballet to techno music the lights dimmed and switched to neon black light which illuminated the flowers on her head. Tyrese looked on in distaste as the pretty young girl started to pull a strand of illuminated orchids out of her pussy, she danced as gracefully as a ballerina, pulling out about fifteen meters of flowers from her vagina. Tyrese looked at the show, it was degrading to say in the least but he was amazed that the trio pulled it off with such grace.

He finished his drink and went to another bar, this had the same formula, the bar was circular and surrounded a stage with forty girls, every time the music changed the girls changed they moved up and three new dancers took the stage. In total they must have had around seventy beautiful young girls, all of them numbered and available, for the price of a meal in a restaurant you could purchase their services for the night. In Europe or America a night with one of these escorts would have cost ten times more, here the women, like everything else were cheap. Thousands of beautiful young girls entered the prostitution game they all wanted security and dreamed of marrying a rich foreigner, he felt sorry for them, most of them were country girls that came from the poor rural northern provinces and they flocked in droves to work in the massage parlors and go-go bars seeking fame, fortune and security.

In this bar they also had a show, seven absolutely stunning girls took the stage wearing only stockings and high heels and performed a lesbian ballet, Tyrese watched entranced as their bodies entwined in graceful explicit sexual formations, one girl was so beautiful he thought of Marisa.

In America this kid could have been a movie star and here she was performing in an obscene show for dirty old men.

Actually in the bars there were lots of young men and women too, foreigners regarded the go-go bars as merely a form of entertainment. Buses of Japanese tourists came to see the raunchy shows, they even had male go-go bars for women and gay men and being a go-go dancer was regarded as a good profession, up north in the rice fields they earned a few dollars a day, in the go-go bars they could earn two months' salary in two days.

The Thai's loved status, it was not degrading to earn money like this they respected money and money alone. The poor villagers that moved to the city and worked in the sex industry usually were respected by the locals as they earned a lot of cash and after a few years they would usually earn enough to return home start a business and build a home.

Some of the girls married rich foreigners, some made a fortune whilst others turned to drugs and died of aids, it was a gamble and the youth flocked to the cities to jump on the bandwagon.

Sometimes husbands and wives worked in the sex trade, the wives worked as go-go girls sleeping with dozens of tourists while their husbands worked as go-go boys sleeping with gay men. Most of the go-go boys were heterosexual but slept with men for money they seriously regarded their job as a profession, they lived in nice apartments had choppers and flashy motorbikes and usually pretty wives or girlfriends. At night after the go-go girls had slept with their customers and the go-go boys had slept with their customers they would meet up at one of the thriving night-clubs. The Thai's had no taboos about sex, they treated sex as a commodity and were extremely tolerant. Straight, gay, lesbian, transgender and every kink and fantasy was cool, whatever your taste, whatever your fantasy your dreams could be fulfilled. The Thai's had thousands of beautiful ladyboys and it was accepted in Thailand that many western men fell head over heels with these exotic creatures.

The bar system worked like this, if you saw a girl dancing who you liked, you asked the mama-san for her to join you for a drink, the girl would walk off the stage and come sit with you, if you liked her and it clicked you could Off by paying a 500 baht bar fine, she would hand in her numbered badge and dress then you could take her for short time or long time, short time meant that you could have two hours with her and long time meant that she would sleep with you. Some girls preferred to do short time that meant that after she finished with you she could go back to the bar to look for the next customer or go to meet her boyfriend at one of the clubs. If you took the lady for a long time she would stay the night and you could fuck her as many times as you wanted and then have breakfast together.

The most beautiful girls danced in the upmarket go-go bars, the less pretty ones with good personalities worked in the beer bars, plainer girls worked in the massage salons and the older women that were burned-out or sick walked on the beach road offering their services for the same price as a hamburger at a fast food chain.

Pattaya had four really big hot night clubs and every night after the go-go girls and boys fucked their clients they would go clubbing, many of them would blow their earnings the same night. The country girls liked to party, up north they didn't have entertainment everyone got up at five am worked in the fields and slept at nine pm, here in Pattaya it was twenty-four hour party land and most Thai's in the sex industry partied all night and slept all day they would wake at seven in the evening shower and rush to the bars where they worked each one immaculately groomed.

The Thai's were vain, not only the women but the men would spend hours looking at their reflection and grooming themselves, even the poorest people wanted to look good.

Tyrese got caught up in the nightlife scene, each night he would comb the bars, then move on to the clubs, each club had live acts and he was amazed how much real talent they possessed.

He was on a pub crawl one night in a go-go bar when he saw her. She was sitting in a corner looking like a frightened pup, the mama-san explained that she had just arrived that day from up north, her sister was one of the clubs top girls and her family had sent her to start work, she was twenty and had worked on a farm since she was eleven.

Kay had just arrived from the bus station and she was waiting for her sister to arrive. Tyrese inspected the girl, he couldn't imagine that they expected her to become a dancer she looked like a student with long shiny hair, a white school shirt and gold rimmed glasses.

The next night he went back to the club and to his surprise the prim and proper school kid type had been transformed, in her skimpy bikini and cowboy books she looked extremely sexy.

She spoke English and when Tyrese offered her a drink she accepted readily, explaining to him that it was her first night and that she was terrified. Her sister had been teaching her lap dancing all day and she was nervous, she told him that without her glasses she was half blind, she sipped her drink and told Tyrese about her family, she had six sisters, her father had died and her mother was ill she and her sister were the oldest and had to earn the living, she had studied and had wanted to be a doctor but because of their predicament she and her sister Lucy, would have to work in the sex industry, up till now Lucy had been the only earner in the family she was one of the top dancers at the club and was supporting her whole family. She was frightened of all the diseases that she had read about in school and told Tyrese that she was a virgin, he noticed a glazed look in her eyes as she talked about her life, she was eighteen but they had faked her ID card so that she could work in the club.

The Mama-san approached their table, she asked Tyrese if he was going to off her, if not the German at the end of the bar wanted to take her, she was a virgin and in high demand.

The girl looked at the obese German at the other side of the bar and clasped Tyrese's hand.

She had heard all sorts of stories about him, he was nasty to the girls and didn't pay well, Tyrese caught the look of panic in her eyes and produced a role of notes from his wallet, 'Yes! I'll off young Kay,' he said, 'for a month.' he added paying the bar fine for thirty days. Surprised Kay went to put her clothes on while the disappointed lecherous German sneered at him.

'Good choice mister,' the mama-san exclaimed snatching the wad of Baht.

Tyrese didn't know why he had been so spontaneous he had taken this girl for a month and he didn't even know if he liked her. She was radiant when she returned, 'THANK YOU too much,' she beamed. 'I don't like the German.' she added. She was finding it hard to walk in the ridiculous high-heeled boots her sister had let her borrow and she felt self-conscious in the skimpy halter dress. Tyrese actually preferred her in the simple white shirt and with glasses.

He didn't like the bright red lipstick and heavy make-up that she had been told to wear.

It started to rain so they dived into the shopping centre and decided to go to see a movie, it was a comedy and her laughter felt like music to his soul. Around one am the film finished and they caught a Tuk Tuk he took her to a hotel as his apartment was like a building site.

In the bedroom she looked nervous, it was her first time and he sensed that for her this was a big issue, just yesterday she had been up north working the fields, tonight she was in a strange hotel room with a strange man, he felt sorry for her he showered first then went to bed.

Kay had cried in the shower, she sobbed for her it was a traumatic experience to be a prostitute. Tyrese heard her soft sobs and pretended that he was asleep. He was excited he hadn't had sex for months but the young girl trembled as she lay beside him, he grunted and pretended to be fast asleep, he rolled over on his stomach to try and kill the raging hard on, she smelled like Marisa, like jasmine.

He had enjoyed the evening and was as horny as hell, however tonight he just couldn't, he felt so sorry for her. He didn't look at her like a bar girl she wasn't just a hooker she was a nice kid and he would play it cool with her and take it nice and slow, after all she was with him for a month.

When he woke Kay had her arms wrapped around him when he opened his eyes she was staring into his, studying him intently.

'Why you no like me?' she pouted, seriously disappointed. Then she gave him a traditional Thai sniff-kiss. Tyrese pressed his lips against hers and slowly slowly made love to her, when he finished he looked at her, a single tear ran down her cheek, when she went to the bathroom he noticed the blood on the sheets, she had been a virgin after all he thought.

That day they went to the beach, lazed around, went shopping and at five pm he took her to show her the apartment, he had bought her a nice wardrobe of simple clothes the type that upper class Thai's wore, with no make-up and her glasses on she looked like a secretary. He had only known her for twenty-four hours but felt that he had known her forever. She fed him from her spoon, teased him constantly and made him laugh. Through Kay, perhaps he felt alive again, she made him feel things that he hadn't felt for years, they stayed at the apartment and made love between the boxes and cement bags. Kay refused to let him pay a hotel as she didn't want to waste money, she had moved in with him the first day. He had gone with her to her sister's apartment to collect the rucksack that she had left there. Her sister wasn't pleased that she had moved in with a man, she had wanted her to work at the bar and have three customers a day, she screamed at her and threw the rucksack out of the window. In the harsh light of day Tyrese was shocked how bad the sister looked, she had dark rings under her eyes and she looked sick.

Kay never went back to the bar she became Tyrese's lover, friend and companion, he sent her back to school to finish the studies that she had dreamed of completing and every month Tyrese put money in a bank account that he had opened for her the first week that they met. Every month she went to the post office and transferred money up north. Tyrese wanted her to be independent. She had never expected it to happen, but she had fallen in love with the tall dark skinned American he treated her with respect and like a lady.

Tyrese hated to admit it but he too had fallen in love with her, she had given him a new lease of life, till he had met her he had felt disenchanted with life. It was funny he mused how you turn one corner and your life changes, if he hadn't come to Thailand to visit his son then he would never have met this enchanting creature. One night in bed Tyrese told her his life story, about Gunther, about everything. She sat propped up on one elbow listening as he poured his heart out, it was morning when they fell asleep and for so so long he had needed someone to listen. Kay was the one.

Tyrese bought a jeep and they went sightseeing to a Chinese Temple outside Pattaya, it was a lovely day with blue skies and they drank cold coconut milk fresh from the tree. Every day while the workmen completed the transformation of the apartment they would go and explore the tourist haunts, Tiger Zoo, The Crocodile Farm., Tyrese couldn't believe that he was doing all the things that tourists did and he enjoyed every moment. It wasn't actually the tourist attractions that he enjoyed it was being with Kay and seeing her reaction to everything, for most of her life she had been stuck in a village up north, he promised her that one day that he would take her to America and take her to Disneyland. One night they were in a bar having a drink and a music channel was on the screen and they played one of Tyrese's old videos. Kay was amazed, he hadn't told her that he used to be a singer and she sat open-mouthed watching his image on screen. At first she just thought that the sultry singer resembled him, then touching the scar on his arm she looked again and was so surprised she couldn't sleep,. The next day they went to the music store and they still had one of his albums, she was proud her lover was a superstar. She demanded that Tyrese buy all the copies she wanted to send her mother one.

Tyrese hadn't really told Kay who he was, he was enjoying the anonymity of his existence, the last thing that he wanted was to blow his cover, he liked being just a guy in a baggy t shirt here.

Suddenly the apartment was finished, it had cost a third more than budgeted and was perfect, together they enjoyed the sunsets and sound of the sea.

Tyrese had instructed his office to arrange a visa for Kay, he had got her a passport and wanted to take her for three months to the States, they would return to Thailand for Loy Krathong.

Kay was so excited that she was going to America, she had never flown before and was sick at the thought of being in a plane for so long. Before they went they drove up north and Tyrese was been introduced to her family, the whole village had turned out to meet the megastar, they had made him feel so welcome and he had adored the visit. He had had no conception of just how poor they were and it amazed them that they had nothing but seemed happier than most of the people that he knew. He opened a bank account and made sure that they had enough to live on when they were gone.

When they returned he decided that he would buy a house for her family, up north the prices were so cheap and he thought that it would be an excellent birthday gift for her.

When the company stretch limo arrived at the airport to pick them up Kay made Tyrese pose for a photo to show mum.

She had no idea that Tyrese was so powerful or rich and every day she seemed to learn something new about him and she wondered what on earth he saw in her. One night on TV they were showing one of Marisa's old movies. Tyrese confided in her that Marisa was an ex-lover. Kay couldn't believe it, that she was living with the same man that had been romantically involved with a screen goddess.

The first time she went with him to the record company she was awe that he was the president, she had never asked him what he did. She had seen him on line and presumed he did something with computers, she studied the photos that lined his office walls recognizing some of the famous faces.

The first week they were there he hosted a big party to introduce her to his friends and colleagues and she was really impressed when she accompanied him to a music awards benefit, it was a real trip to meet all these famous artists and she wanted photos of them all.

Tyrese had bought her lots of expensive clothes and she looked quite stunning, he was happier than he had been in twenty years and she was the secret, since he had met her he looked at life from another perspective and it felt cool.

Kay was so wrapped up in America that she didn't miss Thailand at all, whereas Tyrese longed to return.

Tyresse watched Kay as she slept. She possessed an innocence and haunting inner beauty.

Her beauty was not a manipulated beauty like Marisa's, it was pure.

Kay was so wrapped up with everything in America that she couldn't sleep at night. The idea of having a rich foreigner had been a delight. America was so different, everything seemed larger than life.

They went house-hunting and he bought a beautiful home on the outskirts of the city. The structure had been designed by one of Europe's leading architects and was stunning. Kay had fallen in love with the home the moment she entered, when Tyrese saw her face he had signed the contract immediately.

Whilst he worked and tried to restructure the company to make it run more smoothly she settled into the seven bedroomed mansion.

One afternoon he surprised her by coming home early, when she heard his car on the drive she rushed to the door thinking that something was wrong. Tyrese burst into the room carrying a huge bunch of red roses and dropping to his knees he produced a small box from the pocket of his Bermuda shorts. Kay couldn't believe her eyes as he slipped the diamond ring on her finger, two weeks after they celebrated their wedding day at a lavish reception in a Marquee in the garden of their new home. She felt like a princess in the expensive wedding dress that he had bought her, she wished that her family had been there to witness what seemed the most perfect day of her life.

The couple said their vows under an arch of Thai orchids, the dazzling purple flowers seemed almost luminous in the bright afternoon sunshine.

They had a lovely lunch with caviar, shrimp and Thai chicken followed by baked Alaska. Their four tier wedding cake was shaped like a Thai temple, it was a day that Kay would always remember, she had never been so happy and they danced together for hours then disappeared in a pink limousine.

The honeymoon in Florida was sensational, Kay felt like a child again as she visited the theme parks and hand in hand they watched the midnight fireworks display. The sky seemed filled with colour and she thought that her heart would burst with happiness as they made love in their luxury hotel suite. It was on that steamy evening filled with passion that their child was conceived. Tyrese had made love to her three times that night, he too was filled with happiness. He lay on the bed drinking in the beauty of her smile and realized that he had at last arrived in the place had dreamed of. Kay felt complete in his arms he was her prince charming and soulmate.

The honeymoon seemed all too short and they returned to Detroit with heavy hearts. Tyrese had promised her that they would go back to Thailand to celebrate their wedding with her family. For Loy Krathong, Tyrese was planning to buy a piece of land and build a larger home for her family as a wedding gift, she was so excited about this.

Tyrese worked late almost every day, Kay was lonely and had been feeling sick recently, she hadn't told Tyrese because she had presumed it was the excitement and change of climate.

He noticed that she had grown pale and that her appetite had diminished and insisted that she visit the doctor, that night when he arrived home she looked radiant she had prepared a candlelit dinner for both of them and over a glass of chilled rosé she told him that she had seen the doctor and that she was two months pregnant.

Tyrese's heart skipped a beat, he had secretly dreamed of having a family, he desperately wanted an heir, he was getting on a bit and wanted someone to hand the business on to when he passed on.

They flew to Thailand for Loy Krathong it was a festival in February that the Thai's celebrated with glee. At night everyone would go to the sea and place an offering of a beautifully made floral tribute in the sea. The people toiled for hours to create the stunning floral decorations with banana leaves, orchids and jasmine, it was the tradition to paddle into the water and light candles on your floral tribute and place it in the water. It was a sight to behold, the ocean was filled with floating flowers their candles flickering in the moonlight as they drifted out to sea, the ritual would bring you good luck and fortune, barefoot with their trousers rolled up to their knees Tyrese and Kay waded through the cool rippling waves and set their offerings to the sea. They watched as the flowers drifted off then bought two air balloons from a vendor on the beach, they lit the balloons and set them free into the moonlit sky and laughed as they drifted towards the heavens together. That night they watched the Thai traditional dancers perform in a popular restaurant then went home and sat on the balcony watching the thousands of floating tributes in the sea it was a beautiful experience and Tyrese was glad that he had seen the ritual, it had been a Thai tradition for hundreds of years.

The following day they hired a car with a driver and headed up north to visit her family and in the rural northern village they took their vows again with a colourful Thai traditional wedding ceremony.

Tyrese and Kay found a plot of land and employed a contractor to commence building a five bedroomed bungalow for her family. The plot had acres of land with flourishing coconut and mango trees, her family were grateful that he had made such a gesture and the next time that would visit Tyrese promised that they would stay at their new home instead of the hotel.

Kay was reluctant to leave she had missed her family and like all Thai's she liked to be surrounded with people, family and friends. In America she missed the company of friends, she had forgotten how cosy things were back in Thailand.

Tyrese had lost two executives to a rival company in Europe and he was filling in for them and seemed to work till ten pm every night. Kay was heavily pregnant and her stomach was so swollen that she could hardly walk, they both had refused to check what sex the child would be, they wanted it to be a surprise. Her loneliness was killing her, she had made no friends in America and missed her family and recently Tyrese had been traveling a lot, in the beginning she had traveled with him now she lazed around their home feeling lonely and miserable.

Tyrese had flown to New York to sign up a new hot talent and she had been left alone as usual.

She had gone to bed at nine o clock she was so tired she couldn't be bothered to wait up for him he had called from the airport to say that because of fog all the flights had been delayed.

Her waters broke and she woke in panic wondering what to do, fortunately Tyrese's car pulled up just as she was calling the ambulance, he seemed more excited than her as they sped towards the hospital.

Two hours later the twins were born, Tyrese thought he was going to pass out when he saw the little girl's head pop out into this word and his heart raced as a second baby cried its lungs out and tears filled his eyes as he held his son, One daughter, one son, Tyrese felt like the luckiest man on the planet.

They called the boy Orlando he had been conceived in Florida and the girl they called Paris.

Kay had always dreamed of going to Paris, Tyrese hadn't been too keen on the name but let Kay choose.

While Kay had been in hospital Tyrese had reconverted the nursery to make it suitable for two children, he had bought two cots and doubled up on almost everything.

Having twins was fun, however when one cried the other cried, when one woke up the other woke up, it was lots of work and Tyrese had to persuade Kay to employ a nanny to assist her with the kids. She had no family or friends here and she needed help, Tyrese was traveling a lot and the pressure of twins was quite something for her.

The children seemed to be so demanding that she flopped into bed each night exhausted.

She didn't like the idea of someone else looking after her children and tried to do as much as possible.

Tyrese was expert at spoiling the twins every time that he returned from a trip, he arrived at the door laden with gifts, the nursery was filled with teddy bears and every conceivable toy you could think of. Suddenly their lives had changed the children ran the show, having twins was no joke everything was done in stereo. Sometimes she was up all night nursing them but she didn't mind, she slept when they slept, ate after they ate and was on call twenty-four hours a day, she used the nanny as backup to help to feed them or change their diapers. Tyrese argued that she should let them do more but she refused to let them, insisting that she would be the only mother that they would love.

Kay was exhausted, the twins were tiring her out and Tyrese always seemed to be traveling or working late in his office. He never saw the kids, they were asleep when he left in the morning and asleep when he came home at night. The music industry was suffering, record sales had plummeted and it seemed that half the world was illegally downloading music. Financially it never been so bad since Tyrese had taken over Pippa's business, he missed Romeo.

The new executives seemed to be hopeless and he had taken hold of the reins again.

Romeo lived in Florida like a recluse his weekly calls had ended and he called Tyrese only once every three months He had taken a keen interest in studying paranormal phenomenon and spent most of his time with his head buried in books.

Suddenly the twins were six, they had started school and Paris was the apple of her father's eye. He had surprised them on their birthday by giving Orlando a pair of Dalmatians, his son was trembling with glee having just seen the movie 101 Dalmatians and Kay was infuriated that he had bought a horse for Paris,. She didn't like the idea of her daughter riding, after he had presented the animal with a bright pink ribbon round its neck, Kay had had a bitter argument with him. Tyrese was angry at Kay and they didn't speak for a week. Tyrese moved into one of the spare bedrooms and spent even longer hours at the office. Kay was depressed most of the time, she was lonely and missed her friends and family, the initial wonder of living in America had subsided she had grown to hate the land.

Having money and being secure had seemed like a dream, however the reality was something else, her children were driven to school and collected by a driver and bodyguards and she missed the freedom of walking in the streets, shopping and going to the Thai markets. In America she had made no friends, she had not been to Thailand for two years it was impossible to visit when the kids were at school.

On the twins seventh birthday she was icing a cake, Tyrese was not there he was in London on business he had been supposed to return for the kids birthday party but had called to say that he had been held up in the UK

Orlando was hovering about the kitchen waiting to lick the spoon that she had prepared the icing with, twenty children would be arriving in about an hour's time and they had hired a Ferris wheel.

Kay felt a strange feeling and for no reason she dropped the bowl of icing, the glass dish smashed on the kitchen floor splashing icing and broken glass all over the marble floor. At the same time the bowl fell she heard a scream from the grounds she rushed outside.

Marco the stable master was running towards the clearing behind the gazebo, Miss Maria the South American maid was following him, Kay stood frozen in the kitchen door she had a strange feeling that something was wrong, something was awfully wrong. After a few seconds she ran in the direction of the clearing. Scaramouche the horse lay in a heap, legs broken. Maria was screaming and throwing her arms in the air. Marco was on top of Paris trying to pump air into her lungs. Kay slumped down and held her dead child's body in her arms, her eyes were staring, she had fallen from the horse and had broken her neck and spine, her twisted fragile frame lay lifeless on the grass, the world seemed to spin and Kay blacked out.

Tyrese had been in a bitter boardroom battle in their Mayfair offices when the telephone call interrupted his meeting, staring angrily at his new secretary he snatched the telephone from her hands and sneered that he had explicitly said, 'No calls'

At first he couldn't understand what the voice was saying and he was going to hang up till he heard that it was Kay, when she told him that their child was dead he broke down in the boardroom, fell on his knees. The executives looked at him wondering what had happened as he dropped the telephone and broke down into violent sobs.

Tyrese was at the airport within one hour, he didn't know when he would get a flight and didn't care what it cost. The only seat available was tourist class and as he sat huddled in the cramped seats memories flashed through his mind. Paris his daughter had died on her birthday on the horse that he had given her a year earlier, his world crashed around him as he remembered her sitting in his lap only days before.

Kay was so spaced out with valium she didn't even speak, the day they buried Paris it rained from the heavens. Kay cried a river when she saw the small pink coffin being lowered into the grave, her cries echoed throughout the cemetery and Tyrese couldn't get the sound out of his head. He threw some roses and her favourite pink teddy bear into his daughter's grave then dragged himself to the long black car that waited for them. Romeo sat with them in the back of the car, Orlando looked as white as a ghost he had been so close to his sister and was deeply upset.

Kay took to her bed and didn't surfaced for three days, Tyrese sat in his study in an old chair for twenty-four hours. Orlando was left with his nanny at a time when the child needed his parents' love, they had abandoned him. Miss Maria was infuriated and she stormed into Kay's bedroom on the fourth day, opened the curtains and windows and with her hands on her hips demanded that Kay get up and get on with her life, she told her that Orlando needed her and that Tyrese had deserted him also.

How could Tyrese and Kay live like they had before? How could he return to his business?

A week later he returned to work, just before he left Kay had verbally attacked him in the kitchen she had blamed him for buying the horse, she beat him on the chest and accused him of murdering her child. He had slapped her so hard that she had been thrown across the room. When he arrived home at eleven that night with a bunch of flowers the house had been in darkness, at first he thought that they were sleeping and he checked his son's room, the bed was empty he crept along the corridor to their bedroom expecting to find her and Orlando curled up in bed, since the funeral she had been letting him sleep in their bed. The room was empty there was a simple note of paper on the bed. Tyrese read the message, she had gone, they both had gone back to Thailand she had left the same day and without remorse. Tyrese sat helplessly on the empty bed, he cried for what seemed like forever, in the space of a few days he had lost everything that he had ever loved.

Paris, Orlando and Kay, he didn't know quite how to handle it.

Kay sent him an email two days later to say that they had arrived in Bangkok safely she requested him to start divorce proceedings and send money to her bank account.

Tyrese called Bangkok but she refused to speak to him, in Thailand finished meant finished as far as she was concerned. She didn't want to see him again, she had hated America and was glad to be back in the land of her birth.

Orlando missed his father but was fascinated by the exciting new world he had landed in, his mother spoiled him, taking him to see the Palace, the Floating Market, the Crocodile farm and Elephant Park, this would be their home now, she would send him to an international school where he could speak English and study Thai.

When Tyrese accepted the fact that she was serious and had no intention of returning he sent them a large chunk of money to start up a new life, he contacted his lawyer to arrange divorce proceedings and with a heavy heart threw himself into his work.

He tried to work long hours, he hated the big empty house, everywhere he looked were reminders of his family the only family that he had ever known and he missed them, at night his dreams were filled with nightmares.

He blamed himself for Paris' death, Kay was right he had murdered his own daughter.

At work he was impossible, most of his good staff had left and the others who had to work closely with him were desperately seeking other opportunities.

Now he knew how Romeo had felt, to love was something, but to lose something you loved was unbearable.

He called one of Pippa's old friends and ordered some coke, after doing several lines he looked at himself in the mirror and felt disgusted, he walked to the toilet and flushed the remaining three hundred dollars worth down the toilet. He wasn't going to be like Pippa, he wasn't going to give up, after a few months he would go to Bangkok check out Orlando and go see Gunther.

Ironic that both his sons were in Thailand. One rotting in a cell the other lost in a new world.

Whilst Orlando discovered the delights of Thailand and attended one of the best International schools in the land, Kay used half the money that Tyrese had sent her to buy a delightful penthouse duplex in a good building in the bustling heart of the city. With the remaining money she opened a small boutique, after several years of doing nothing she approached the running of her new successful business with vigor. She met Naret when she was on a buying mission at the wholesalers in Pratumnam. He was twenty-eight, young and good-looking. When his mother had died in a car accident he had inherited the family wholesale fashion business, he had a wholesale unit in Pratumnam and exported large quantities of goods made in both Thailand and Vietnam to large European retail groups. He had fallen in love with Kay the moment that she had walked into his showroom, together they planned to join forces and open a retail chain of women's boutiques. With the generous allowance she received from Tyrese, coupled with her keen fashion eye it seemed inevitable that together they were a recipe for success and within ten years both Naret and her would be joint owners of a Global retail operation with two hundred shops worldwide.

While she focused on building her retail empire, which sold women's, men's and children's fashion. Naret provided all the production and concentrated on developing new high-tech factories with excellent conditions in rural Thailand, Vietnam and Cambodia. Gone were the days of sweatshops and the use of child labour, Naret built amazingly modern factories with excellent facilities for his workers, providing accommodation and transport as well as good salaries and conditions, he would develop these projects in rural areas, train staff and provide them with comfortable living accommodation close by to his factories in the apartment complexes that were developed specially for the staff.

Together they made a small fortune which they reinvested in the property business, the money they made in fashion tripled as they invested in the property schemes using top designers to develop wonderful private homes, hotels, shopping complexes and stores.

Tyrese's generous divorce settlement coupled with Kay's shrewd business mind and Naret's dynamic business acumen made them a major force. Kay's years in America had not been wasted, the sense of style that she had developed there had been instrumental in her developments back in Thailand.

Tyrese had been impressed that his shy Thai ex-wife had achieved so much success. He had gone to the opening of her boutique in Manhattan and marveled at the designer collections she had introduced under the labels of Paris for the womenswear and Orlando for the menswear. He had seen her magnificent stores in London, Paris and Milan and he was glad that she had called the womenswear line Paris. It made him feel that his daughter's memory lived on. As if by magic Orlando had developed his creative talents and was desperate to become a fashion designer, he was already studying in London at one of the best colleges in the world.

Tyrese always went to visit them once a year, he was happy that Kay had success and he genuinely liked her new husband he was a strikingly handsome man with a keen sense of humor and vibrant personality.

One day after Thanksgiving, Tyrese received a telegram, he immediately had thought of bad news the moment it arrived, who in this day and age sent telegrams, it was from Bangkok. Gunther had committed suicide, he had slashed his wrists and as Tyrese read the words he couldn't help feeling relieved. The pain is over now he thought. It's all over now. Tyrese had fought for fifteen years he had spent hundreds of thousands of dollars on lawyers and no one had been able to get him a pardon or a transfer back to the states. The grueling conditions of the prison were unimaginable and Gunther's life had been a living hell.

Tyrese flew to Thailand and buried Gunther there, only Kay, Naret and Tyrese attended the ceremony the boy had been locked up for so long that he had never made friends. Three times already he had tried to commit suicide unsuccessfully. Tyrese hoped that his soul would rest in peace. Kay glanced at her ex-husband at the service in the temple, he looked so old and frail, she shivered noticing the dead almost a haunted pained look in his eyes.

Kay persuaded Tyrese to stay for a week, they were going to her house in Phuket she thought that the change would do him good and had a surprise. Orlando was flying in for a short holiday from London they hadn't seen their son for six month she thought that his visit would cheer her ex-husband up. Naret was going to Cambodia to oversee the opening of a new factory that would employ around a thousand people, they would have some time alone to spend with their son who was almost twenty now, how the years fly in she thought, it seemed just like yesterday that she had held him in her arms she thought, thinking about Orlando.

Tyrese loved the huge elegant house that was tucked away on a hillside overlooking the sea. The sunsets were even more spectacular than the ones that they had enjoyed so much in their apartment in Pattaya years before.

The second night they were there Tyrese wondered why there were three places set for dinner, Kay never explained as they sat enjoying fresh lobster and seafood caught only an hour before.

The servants never get it right she sighed staring at the extra setting trying to hide the joy she felt, her driver had left already and at any minute she expected Orlando to burst through the door, the flight obviously had been delayed and Tyrese had been so hungry that they had started dinner.

The maid had just served them a generous portion of Orlando's favorite desert crème brûlée.

Tyrese was just remarking that his son had loved it and used to steal their portions out of the giant freezer in Detroit. He was just laughing, reminiscing about the night that Tyrese had heard a sound in the apartment in Detroit and armed with a baseball club he had crept into the kitchen half expecting to find an intruder only to have found Orlando, then five, sitting in the dark at the kitchen table with six empty glass dishes of crème brûlée and pudding all over his face.

They were just enjoying the moment when a tall young man burst into the room. Kay jumped out of her seat and rushed to greet her son joking that he must have smelled the crème brûlée. Tyrese was so overcome with emotion that he cried, Orlando had never seen him portray such emotion and hugged him tightly.

Sitting between his parents he declined the lobster and polished off two portions of the delicious dessert, between spoonfuls of the pudding he talked nonstop about London, his school, his collection and his friends.

Tyrese and Kay soaked the information up and enjoyed just being close to their child, he was so tall and handsome he had inherited his father's dark good looks and his mother's wit and personality the combination was electric, he lit up the room like a shining star. Tyrese was glad that he had gone, glad to see Orlando and grateful that Kay had never let him down.

They talked and talked till the early hours of the morning. Orlando had insisted in showing them hundreds of photos of his collection and to his mother's surprise he had a commercial eye and she could see that there would be money to be made from his designs. She employed eight designers now and planned to let Orlando run the design departments when he graduated, after an initial year of working she had planned to make him design director. There were so many creative aspects that she didn't have time for, the PR and promotion, the photography, the control of the shop fits. She couldn't wait for her son to be involved, he had a sharp eye and innovative ideas. She however had no intention of letting him loose in the business like a spoiled rich kid. He would start at the bottom and do a one year apprenticeship in the design before he would be promoted.

She didn't want any animosity from the other staff, he like everyone who entered her domain would have to earn her respect, work in a team and progress slowly. Kay knew that Orlando wouldn't disappoint her it was in his genes, he had learned to draw before he could walk and had a good creative head on his shoulders, whilst other kids had played football he had painted, she had encouraged his exceptional talent and it was fate that his creativity had moved towards fashion. She was delighted that he was studying design, he would graduate the following year and both Tyrese and Kay were planning to go to London to see his show.

They swam in the sparkling blue sea, overdosed on fresh seafood and had generally a great time, sailing on Kay's Yacht to Phang Ah and the little islands that dotted the sea.

The week was flying by, after a few days Naret flew in and they enjoyed an evening at a wonderful show. Phuket Fantasy was a superb show with Las Vegas type appeal, Orlando had seen it dozens of times and still loved it.

At the end of the week Kay had another surprise, again there were another two extra places at the dinner table. She refused to tell any of her men who was coming to dinner, the boys were desperate to know but she wouldn't tell them, they were all enjoying Pina Colada cocktails served in large coconut shells when they heard the sound of a car draw up.

Tyrese smile as Marisa climbed out of the back seat, overdressed as she always was. Tyrese remembered her as she struggled to walk in the dangerously high-heeled magnificent Dior shoes.

At close range he couldn't believe it, she looked younger than she had twenty years ago, hands on her hips she stared at Tyrese and scolded him for staring, 'Don't be so rude.' she mocked, 'I have just had every kind of lift there was to have,' she admitted proudly, boasting that her Hollywood surgeon had taken thirty years off her life.

Tyrese thought that she looked good but on closer inspection thought she seemed like a wax image, the skin of her face seemed so stretched it didn't look natural she was in her late fifties but looked sixteen, she raised the crystal goblet of champagne and toasted her plastic surgeon, it was then that the young man walked into the room. Tyrese was disgusted, he looked no older than his son, a mere teenager surely he thought Marisa didn't have a toy boy.

The young man was unusually handsome, obviously Asian but had light blue eyes and a shock of thick spiky white hair, he looked like one of the men you seen in the international fashion magazines and had a perfectly sculptured physic that obviously took hours of training.

Marisa introduced her son Xenon and it was only then that Tyrese remembered how handsome his father had been. Xenon was of course the son of Marisa's husband the Asian kick-boxing sensation who had been brutally murdered years ago. The boy had inherited both his father's and mother's good looks and was unusually handsome. Later at dinner Marisa had announced that she wanted Tyrese to sign him up with a record deal, she produced a disk from her evening bag and handed it to Orlando to pop on the stereo.

Tyrese was impressed the boy had musical talent and his wicked good looks had pop star written all over them. She produced another video disk of a low budget video that she had paid to have made, Xenon was magnificent on film it was obviously in the genes, he had starred in a Japanese soap series but was desperate to get into music and there was no doubt that he had talent and Tyrese was impressed with what he had seen over dinner. They laughed and joked and it was over their coffee and liqueurs that Kay noticed something, she knew instinctively that her son was gay, over dinner he had not taken his eyes off the handsome young man across from him he sat mesmerized in awe of his looks. Kay sighed wondering how Tyrese would take it he was so homophobic. She decided to wait till they were alone to approach the subject.

Xenon had noticed Orlando staring at him and it had unnerved him. Orlando had asked him if he would consider being a model for him for his graduation collection photos. Xenon had agreed out of pure politeness wanting to impress Tyrese, his future in the music industry depended on this man who he was meeting for the first time.

The next day at the pool Xenon borrowed his mother's sarong, he couldn't stand Orlando staring at him in his swimming trunks. Marisa was perplexed at her son's homophobic attitude, gays buy CDs too she muttered, warning him that in the film and music business there were lots of gays.

Marisa had little or no contact with her son for years, one afternoon she had switched on her television in a hotel room and saw a young man that resembled her ex-lover Yoji, she had known instinctually that he was her son, he had the face and mannerisms of Yoji his image on screen had stopped her in her tracks and she had flown to Japan to reunite with him. At first the grandparents had been reluctant to let her meet him but she had used her charm to win them round.

Xenon didn't know quite what to expect and was quite stunned when she emerged from her car, she looked more like a young girl than his mother with her well made-up face and perfect body he was impressed and fascinated by her.

She had brought him a collection of her movies on video and he had watched them in awe, his mother was indeed one of the sexiest women in the world he could see why his father had fallen madly in love with her.

Marisa's heart had skipped a beat when she was introduced to Xenon, he was the double of Yoji only perhaps even more handsome she hugged him in her arms and caressed him much to the embarrassment of his grandparents who quite obviously disapproved of her.

Using her irresistible charm she had persuaded Yoji's mother and father to let her take Xenon on a world trip, he had been starring in a TV soap series and the program was finished for the season, she had promised to introduce him to one of the world's leading record company directors and lured him by promising him a record deal with her old friend Tyrese. She hoped that the world trip would reunite them and repair any emotional damage from the past. Xenon had studied kick-boxing like his father, he had spent hours in the gym since he was a child, developing the ultimate body had been his chief objective and like his father he had stumbled into acting and had been an instant hit with the teenage population, his passion was however singing and he dreamed of having a hit single. Marisa had paid for a demo and video clip so she could show Tyrese how talented he was, she had no doubt that with the right material that he would be a star, he could sing, dance and was dangerously good-looking, young girls would eat him up.

After dinner Kay, Naret and Tyrese retired, Marisa full of energy suggested they go to a night-club up on the hill called the Safari Club. As they entered the club every male in the room sucked in their breath when she entered hobbling as usual on her dangerously high stilettos and swinging her hips in her incredible expensive designer dress. She walked across the dance floor to a table with Orlando and Xenon, one on each arm.

Within seconds two gorgeous American blonde tourists had hijacked Xenon and while they were on the dance floor Marisa pulled closer to Orlando and had a heart to heart, at first he blushed a bright crimson colour when she questioned him about being gay. He was mortified that she had detected his secret but she just wanted him to be at ease, he was so paranoid that Tyrese found out she vowed to keep it a secret and warned him to be more discreet when ogling at Xenon.

They had fun and in the end the two young men had literally to drag Marisa home, she had pouted her lip and protested by stamping her feet like a petulant infant then sulked all the way home.

Tyrese had promised to arrange a recording session for Xenon, he would get him a good song and they would do a demo and a video, he arranged a date the following month and invited both Marisa and her son to Detroit.

It had been a sad time when he attended the funeral service for Gunther but thanks to Kay and Naret he had relaxed a bit and he had been so happy to meet up with his son. Orlando had grown so and he was obviously talented and he had been impressed how successful Kay had become.

Time flew by and before he knew it Marisa and Xenon had arrived, he had a great pop song for Xenon to record, it had hit written all over it and he was sure that it would be big.

Xenon recorded the song in a day and it was remixed and mastered in almost three days.

Tyrese had arranged a video shoot with a top director, the scene was set in a lap dancing club, on the day of the shoot one of the three exotic dancers hadn't turned up they were short of a girl and to Xenon's horror his mother had butted in and suggested that she be in the video she actually wanted to play a lap dancing role, the director looked at her and wondered if it would work.

When Marisa finished in hair and make-up the stylist gave her a long pair of cowboy boots and a fringed G-string and bra. When she walked on the set everyone stared in awe, she was in her fifties but made the two other young girls look bland, she had a better figure and boobs than both of them. Marisa was in her glory, dancing under the spotlight she played up to the camera and to Xenon's complete surprise she looked great on film. In the final cut they would focus on her and fade out the other two young dancers into the background. Tyrese thought that they were joking when they told him that Marisa had played a lap dancer in the video, he thought that they were pulling his leg till they showed him some footage of her almost naked swinging around a pole erotically. He had to admit that she looked sensational with her long legs and tiny waist, she still possessed that magic presence and sex appeal. Marisa had enjoyed the experience it had been a thrill to be back on film and she begged Tyrese to let her do a demo and make a single.

Xenon looked great with his naked torso oiled up, he did some kick boxing stunts which were phenomenal, the video had been fun and the director was enthusiastic and he had not believed Xenon when he had told him that Marisa was his mother he had thought that she was in her late twenties.

When they saw the finished edited result with the clever computer effects that had been painstakingly added, everyone thought that it was indeed unique. Marisa was delighted to see that she looked fantastic on film, they had airbrushed the close-ups of her slightly.

Within a week of the song being released it raced up the charts, Xenon was marketable material and the young girls loved his looks and the teenagers were all copying his haircut and dance style.

Tyrese offered him a three album deal Xenon was ecstatic. Marisa was going to be his manager and Tyrese let her record a song just for the sheer hell of it. She wrote the video script herself and everyone was shocked that she looked so sensational in the video and everyone was even more shocked when her song went into the top ten in England, France and Germany so she smiled to Xenon, 'I'm an old bird but still got it going on.'

Xenon thought that his mother was slightly mad, she was almost schizophrenic, on one side very serene and on the other wild as could be. She did however run his affairs excellently using her sex appeal and charm to get him better deals and more royalties.

After the success of his album he was offered several film deals, the first of which was a low budget teen movie, the film was so successful it achieved cult status.

One day a script arrived that touched his heart, it had been written by Marisa and it was the life story of his father and she had suggested that he play the role, at first he was unsure, it felt creepy to get into his father's skin but with Marisa's gentle persuasion he agreed to immortalize his father's being by playing the role. Marisa would be director's assistant.

It was scary when they shot the movie and it was strange for Marisa to see Xenon played the role, he reminded her so much of Yoji it was alarming sometimes she cried as they filmed some scenes.

The emotional impact of playing the role of his father did not hit him till they had to film the murder scene. Xenon had taken some coke before the shooting Marisa wept as she watched, reliving the gruesome scene and watching the young actress that was playing her role she felt almost as if she was reliving the event. After playing the scene Yoji disappeared into his dressing room, the fake blood on his clothes made him paranoid, it was the most difficult scene that he had ever played and for a moment as he lay dying in the arms of the actress who played his mother he thought how shocked his mother must have been.

As a manager Marisa was a godsend she knew the movie business inside out and every trick and every little game the studios played. Her experience was invaluable to Xenon as a mother she was well simply Marisa playing a maternal role in real life had never been her idea of having fun, she was more like a friend to her son than a mother. She usually was the one that drank too much and partied too often. He was the one that scolded her for coming in late when she had to work.

For the duration of the movie the studio had put them up in a hotel suite. Xenon was being coached by his mother, working eighteen hour days and living in the same space was proving difficult, shooting had been on set seven days a week for a month and on the only day off that he had, to his delight his mother announced that she was going on a shopping marathon and would be out all day.

Excited at being on his own Xenon showered and dialed the number of two hot blondes that he had met a month before at a record company party. They were European dancers with perfect figures and big boobs, they had played the role of the exotic dancers in his first video and he had fantasized and dreamt of having sex with them since the moment that he had laid eyes on them. After exchanging in polite conversation for ten minutes he invited them both for lunch, within an hour they knocked on his hotel suite knowing full well that lunch was not on the menu, the chemistry on the day of the video shoot between them had been amazing and he wasted no time when they arrived, after a glass of champagne the girls stripped him slowly and he explored their perfect bodies with ecstasy.

Both girls gave him a blow job, he had fucked one and after she had come he left her lying spreadeagled on the bed, face flushed he was just concentrating on reaching orgasm, he had turned the blonde upside down and was holding her legs in the air pumping with vigor when Marisa walked into the room, without batting an eyelid she announced that she had forgotten her credit card and as she walked over to retrieve her handbag from the wardrobe she mumbled that Yoji liked that position too. In total shock Xenon dropped the girl's legs and she slumped to the floor, he covered his flaccid cock with his hands, his face as red as a strawberry. The girls were in panic thinking that Marisa was perhaps his wife, they scampered like flies trying to find their clothing which had been scattered through the apartment. Marisa grinned and made an exit telling them to have fun.

Xenon hadn't had an orgasm and his cock was reduced to a shrivel, he was so angry that he couldn't get it up, the girls who were rushing to dress were furious, they did not believe that the leggy blonde that had been at the video shoot was his mother she looked like twenty-eight and they thought it ludicrous that his mother would be sharing his suite. Xenon was super frustrated as they stormed out of the hotel room leaving him alone and unsatisfied. His mother was incorrigible.

Four hours later totally unflustered Marisa returned laden with carrier bags filled with expensive clothes, shoes and bags, she made no comment of the incident which made Xenon even angrier. She ranted and raved and modeled her new clothes and presented him with a new designer suit to wear at the party they were having when the film was completed.

Secretly Marisa had been shocked to have found Xenon with two women, especially the two bland tarts from the video he could have done better than that she thought soaking in a bubble bath she smiled to herself thinking how much he resembled his father with his perfect physique and all those muscles she would have fancied him herself if he hadn't been her son.

Xenon didn't know that she had been screwing the chunky hunky lighting technician, they had been enjoying daily secret sexual encounters in Xenon's dressing room whilst he was on set.

Three days later Xenon was to have his revenge, he was filming some scenes that they had asked him to reshoot, the scenes had been shot quicker than expected and he returned to his trailer for a break. As he opened the door his lipped dropped as he discovered his mother's knickers at her ankles she was being fucked rotten by a huge man that he recognized, he gasped in surprise as his mother looked at him then reached orgasm while the stalky man continued till he exploded in orgasm. Xenon darted out of the trailer and slammed the door. He laughed, the vehicle was rocking and their cries of orgasm could be heard by the whole crew. His mother emerged twenty minutes later looking totally unperturbed, she winked at him as she passed and he had to laugh, she was too much for a mother. The lighting technician tried to avoid eye contact with Xenon, he looked quite embarrassed actually and even worse his fly was still open.

That night Xenon went to the "IT'S A WRAP" party with his mother, he watched her dancing at the club with some Italian Gigolo he was younger than Xenon and almost foaming at the mouth as Marisa rubbed her thighs against him. His mother emulated sex appeal, her raw undiluted sexuality was overwhelming she was one hell of a woman, now in her fifties she was still red hot and made most of the other girls on the floor look bland. She had drunk too much again and Xenon imagined that he would be babysitting his mother again. The Italian Stallion had his hands on her ass and it was irritating Xenon. She was not a normal woman she was Marisa Duval a sex symbol.

It was an after party to remember, fueled with rage Xenon walked on to the dance floor and took a swipe at the Italian, the bronze Adonis ducked skillfully and Xenon hit his mother almost knocking her out. Super enraged, Xenon let loose with some serious kick-boxing moves which left the Italian bleeding and bruised on the disco floor, patrons screamed as the security tried to separate them.

The paparazzi had a field day when the police arrived to arrest Xenon, they flashed their cameras getting great shots of Marisa with her badly blackened eye the headlines spurted.

KICK-BOXING SUPERSTAR BLOODBATH.

Xenon was kept in the jail overnight, the studio manager bailed him out, Marisa holed up in her hotel suite with Enrico the Italian Stallion. The Studio were pleased at the front page scandal it was perfect free publicity for the film. Yoji and Marisa's life had been a whirlwind the siege at the after party reflected that trouble was in the family genes.

Enrico was no gigolo he was the heir of a pasta empire and rather rich, he had it seemed fallen madly in love with Marisa and after three days of making mad passionate love to her in the hotel suite he agreed to drop charges, a week later Enrico, Marisa and Xenon were all photographed together dancing at a nightclub the reconciliation led to more front page editorial and free publicity.

At first it had been hard to accept that a man who was actually younger than himself was banging his mother. Xenon was still sharing the suite with his mother and was extremely irritated that most night he couldn't get to sleep for the sound of their sexcapades. He had taken to sleeping with ear plugs and found it embarrassing to be frequently woken up with the sound of his mother having multiple orgasms. Enrico the Italian Stallion seemed insatiable he decided that it was high time that he look for an apartment where he could chill out and do some serious screwing himself.

Sometimes when Marisa argued with Enrico or misbehaved, he would come to Xenon for advice, there were however no rules when it came to dealing with Marisa; she had a whole set of rules that applied to her and her alone. She was a bundle of fun on good days but she could also be as evil as a rattlesnake on others. A succession of wealthy adoring lovers had turned her into a spoiled brat and that came as part of the package. With Marisa there were no guarantees or instructions, every day had to be taken one day at a time. She was a grown woman, a screen diva and sex symbol, who could ever imagine that living with such an entity would be easy. She was a woman with many facets and not all of them were shiny and Xenon warned him to play it by ear, take one day at a time and not to spoil her. There had always been a string of men that would buy Marisa expensive jewels, homes, yachts. Lear jets and cars.

Enrico and Marisa had a crazy relationship, Xenon had been staying at her penthouse as he was decorating his own home and things were running behind schedule, one night he came back from a hard day in the studio, he had been recording a track that he had no feeling for it and had been an exasperating day and all he wanted was to have a shower and sleep. The moment he got out of the lift he could hear the argument and when he opened the door he saw his mother naked except for high-heeled gold sandals and a miniscule G-string she was completely out of control and had thrown a priceless Ming vase at Enrico, the ancient vase had been one of the Count's family heirlooms she missed Enrico and the priceless piece smashed into small pieces damaging the new plasma stretch television screen. Xenon was infuriated and he lashed out at Enrico punching him in the face.

Marisa hands on her hips watched them as they wrestled then put on her sable trench coat and disappeared, she went to the nearest five star hotel and propped herself up at the bar, naked under her sable she looked like a very upmarket hooker. She drank seven vodka martinis, she thought about the day, she had gone shopping and was just leaving a store when she spotted Enrico's Bentley, the roof was down and to her horror Candy Redford the page three girl and soft porno queen was driving. She was so infuriated that her live-in lover had given that slut his , she realized that all the rumors of their affair were true and she knew that he had been lying to her when he had gone on all these unexpected business trips. Overcome with emotion and feeling the worse for the drinks she proceeded home but to her surprise both the men in her life had packed their bags and left.

Xenon had checked in to a hotel and Enrico had moved into Candy's apartment. Marisa hated being alone and every time she picked up a magazine or watched TV she was confronted with images of Enrico accompanied by the page three slut.

Marisa was emotionally wounded, she couldn't believe that Enrico had just vanished from her life. For three days she took valium, sleeping pills and lots of coke she washed the pills down with vodka drunk neat straight from the bottle. Xenon was in the studio when the call came, they stopped his recording and he was furious that they had asked him to come out of the sound booth, at first he didn't recognize her voice, it was a few moments before he realized that it was his mother she was wailing and sounded either drunk or drugged up. She told him that she had done something stupid and said goodbye in a slurred sentence. When Xenon hung up he raced to his Porsche and drove through every red light till he reached her apartment, fortunately he still had the key. As soon as he entered he could hear her cries, he followed the sound till he reached the bathroom. His mother was standing over the sink wearing a white mink jacket and white silk dress, her make-up was smudged and she looked deathly pale, blood was spouting from her wrist and her fur was matted with the red sticky blood. Xenon grabbed a towel and ripped it into strips, he cried himself as he tried to bind the slashed wrists. As soon as he had wrapped the towel tightly round her wrist she slumped unconscious to the floor, he called an ambulance but it seemed that they were taking forever to come so he scooped his mother in his arms and took her down to the car park. He drove like a madman till he reached the nearest hospital. The surrealistic sight of his mother on the trolley in the white coat that was saturated with blood made him wince. He waited in the waiting room till the doctors attended her, eventually a doctor approached him telling him that she was in stable condition, when she fell she had broken a leg and if Xenon hadn't arrived when he did she would have bled to death.

He arranged a private room for her with a nurse with twenty-four hour surveillance.

The doctors thought that it was advisable if she stayed in the hospital for three weeks to a month, she was suicidal and they warned Xenon that it wasn't safe to leave her alone. She needed to do rehab, her drug taking and drinking was telling its toll.

She had been so jealous of Enrico's new love that she had tried to kill herself, even though she was beautiful and looked young on the surface on the inside she felt old and insecure.

She had spent hundreds of thousands of dollars on plastic surgery to make her look young but on the inside she was so mixed up.

Xenon and Tyrese visited her almost daily, it was her birthday on Saturday and they had planned to go to see

Xenon, he was playing that night at a huge charity concert in Pippa's honor.

Tyrese had never missed one of the benefit concerts but decided to make an exception this year he would stay with Marisa. She had been so looking forward to going it was the biggest gig he had ever done and would be televised globally. Tyrese promised to come on her birthday as a special surprise he arranged a huge cake and had a massive plasma screen installed in her room, together they would have a birthday party and would watch the three hour concert live.

Marisa had dressed up to the nines for her birthday she had had a make-up artist and hairdresser in to make her up. Tyrese thought that she was crazy but complimented her, in the harsh hospital light the professional make-up looked quite macabre. Together they watched the first hour with glee, soon Xenon would be on and when he appeared on stage with his dance troupe the audience roared so loud she had to lower the sound.

Xenon looked spectacular in a snakeskin shirt and tight pants, his dancers wore snakeskin bikinis and had the wildest hair Marisa had ever seen. Xenon sang his latest single dedicating it to his father who he hoped was watching his performance from heaven. To Tyrese's and Marisa's surprise he announced that he had another song to sing, a special one that he wrote specially for someone who meant so much to him. The song was called "Wild Child" the lights dimmed and the camera moved in cropping his face on the screen, Xenon looked right into the camera and announced. 'Mama, this one is for you, just to say I love you! And wish you a Happy Birthday.'

Marisa felt elated as she watched the screen. Behind him the film screens showed a series of black and white images from her films and modeling days. Xenon started singing the lyrics that he had specially written for her, "You gave me birth-gave me life. Loved you all my life!" at this point there was a burst of light and an explosion, the screen turned white and the cameras switched off leaving only sound. Tyrese thought perhaps that the pyrotechnics had gone off.

There was sound they could hear screaming and siren's then everything blacked out.

Tyrese tried to call all of the numbers of the crew that were with Xenon, all the telephones were not available. He dialed the last number of the lighting assistant and to his relief he answered the phone, it was hard to hear or understand, there was chaos in the background the only word he could understand was bomb. Bomb!

A terrorist group had left a bomb under the stage, they had detonated it when Xenon was performing the song that he had written for his mother's birthday he, his dancers and the band had been thrown thirty feet in the air as the huge stage exploded and sprayed out into the forum.

Marisa fearing the worst zipped from channel to channel looking for breaking news, at last she found a channel that had some information, there had been a bomb blast at the charity concert. A terrorist group had claimed responsibility, there was no more information. Tyrese held her hand and they sat silently watching the screen for further news. Marisa wept when they announced that hundreds of people had been killed in the blast, hundreds more had been injured and trampled in the rush. The bomb had been underneath the stage, there was no doubt that her son had been blown literally off the face of the planet, like his father so young, 'TOO YOUNG!' she cried, it took three nurses to calm her and hold her down while another gave her an injection.

Tyrese watched her tears, rolling down his face he wished that they could inject him too, put him to sleep so that he didn't have to face reality. His telephone was ringing but he didn't react he was lost in emotion. It rang continuously till he answered, it was Kay from Bangkok she had been watching the concert too live and had just heard the horrific news.

Tyrese sat unshaven in the hospital chair he wanted to be there when Marisa came round.

Eight house later he woke up with a start, she was awake she was lying in bed staring at the ceiling at first he thought she had died, her face was white and with the crying her mascara had run down her cheeks. A nurse approached and tried to make her clean her face, she told the staff to, 'FUCK OFF.' Tyrese held her hand, she was broken. Eventually when she spoke she asked Tyrese 'WHY?'

Why did they out live everyone else? Why hadn't they been taken? 'Why him?' she cried and his heart went out to her ˙he connected with her he understood all there was to know about pain and grief he knew what she was feeling.

There was nothing to bury, Xenon's body had been blown to bits and Marisa couldn't handle it.

She had had just about as much as she could take, each night as she lay in the hospital bed she spoke to God blaming him for all the pain. She had been blessed with looks, money and success but the one thing she desired was love. Why was it that her God stripped her of everyone and everything she loved. She wished that she had died she wished that Xenon had never saved her life, this world was too cruel, too empty she had no desire to live anymore in this world, she had loved Yoji and he had been taken, she had been reunited with her son and through him she had felt closer to Yoji, now they both were gone. She couldn't handle it and wanted to kill herself but the nurses guarded her twenty-four hours a day.

Tyrese had arranged a memorial service and they collected her from the hospital, she was in a wheelchair because of the broken leg, in her black lade outfit she looked like something from another era, the Victorian lace veil covered her face and masked her grief. She never wept during the service there were no tears left. She blamed God for her anger, this was his way of making her suffer. She thought she was suffering for being a wild child suffering for being the type she was.

Enrico came to the funeral he was shocked when he saw her under the fine veil, she looked like she had aged thirty years overnight, she had changed, there was no sparkle in her eyes, the persona, the glamour the sensuous sexuality had disappeared forever. Tyrese wheeled her back to the car and she returned to her hospital bed and remained there for six months.

Whilst Marisa convalesced in the clinic Tyrese set about the gruesome task of cleaning up all of Xenon's things, in amongst all the personal things he found his diary. Inside, scribbled in pencil were the words of the song that he had wanted to sing to his mother, he called the studio where he had been recording and to his amazement learned that Xenon indeed had recorded the song. It had not been mastered but he had finished recording it. Tyrese instructed them to master the track immediately, what better a legacy for Marisa than this. It had been the last track he had put down in the studio. Tyrese poured a stiff gin and tonic and sat down to read the words.

WILD CHILD

You gave me birth, you gave me life... Loved you all my life.
A movie Queen of the silver screen you were never there.
Loved you all my life.
So hard for a little boy to sleep at night.
Didn't sleep at all dreamt of you... All my life.
Did you dream of me, did you dream of me... loved you all my life.
Across an ocean so far away did you dream of me.
You're a Movie Queen as far as the eye can see.
but you were always simply mama to me.
You gave me birth gave me life, Loved you all my life.
Did you dream of me like I dreamt of you... All my Life.
All my life I dreamed of you... Loved you all my life.
Loved you all my life... Loved You All My Life.
All my Life and just a little more loved you anyway.
I watched your movies on video my Mama the Movie Queen.
As a child I would Kiss the screen.
Dad's with the Angels somewhere far away, makes me blue.

Watched his films kissed him too.
Loved you both in my dreams loved you anyway.
You're not a mother in the conventional sense.
but I am first to come to your defence... love you anyway.
you gave me life you gave me life love you anyway.

Tyrese cried, he felt so emotional when he read the words he wished that Gunther had written something to him Alone in Xenon's apartment he sensed the ghost of the boy, he imagined the ghost of Yoji, Gunther and Paris too. A week later he presented Marisa with Xenon's last album he popped it on the CD player and left her alone to listen to the voice of her son, there were eleven tracks on the album and the last was Wild Child.

Marisa wept as she heard the words, perhaps he had sensed that he didn't have long on this planet, perhaps this was his way of saying goodbye. She had never heard him say that he loved her till that night on stage. Marisa asked Tyrese to repeat the last song again and again. She hadn't dared tell anyone, but she had had a dream two days after her son had died, she had given up all will to live, she had been so depressed and down that she had felt like she was dying. She had been almost asleep when it happened, she had a vision, the room seemed chilly and she had seen them both it was Yoji and Xenon they had sat silently one on each side of her bed they had smiled at her and she had stared right into the depth of their souls. Without speaking they had communicated with her, they had told her that they were fine and that they would all meet up one day in the future then they had vanished into a golden liquid light, arms around each other. Since that night, that dream or vision she had felt no sadness, she knew that there was something more to death something perhaps an afterlife. However crazy it may seem Xenon had had his time in this dimension he was needed elsewhere now, ironically Marisa, the one who loved to Live suddenly desired to die, to be with the two men that she had loved most of all.

Xenon's last album raced up the charts in every land they released it. The studio had withheld his film, Marisa decided to give them permission to release the film. Xenon would be immortalized on the silver screen eternally. It would have been the way he had wanted it she told the press at the premiere. It was so moving on the night of the movie premiere everyone who attended wore black from head to toe, every guest brought a bunch of flowers and laid them outside the theatre at the foot of a modern bronze sculpture of Xenon.

The film was emotional, to see her son up there playing the role of Yoji was alarming she cried her eyes out in the ladies room after the film. When the film had ended with the actress who played Marisa crouched on the street holding Yoji's lifeless carcass in her arms it was so moving the whole audience cried and when the credits rolled up on the screen the theatre remained totally silent. Without applauding they stood and expressed their respect for the remarkable performance that had been played by Xenon.

The movie was a box office hit, the controversy surrounding Yoji and Xenon had stirred enormous public interest.

Marisa couldn't bear to watch the film again it was too painful an experience. Tyrese had sat next to her holding her hand to give her strength, she was right they were survivors, sometimes being a survivor was fun sometimes it was tough.

Naret, Kay and Orlando had flown in especially for the premiere. Tyrese hadn't seen or heard from his son since Thailand, Orlando had been desperately disappointed that his father had not flown to London to see him graduate and attend the fashion show that had secured him magnificent press revues.

After the premiere Marisa and fifteen privileged guests went for a quiet supper to a small intimate restaurant that Xenon had discovered. Orlando was accompanied by an extremely handsome companion. Kay and Naret had seated themselves at the other end of the table they too were disappointed that Tyrese had not attended his graduation they had sent him an invite and he had forgot.

After dinner they went back to Marisa's sprawling mansion for coffee and drinks.

Tyrese approached Kay, she seemed so uneasy it was Tyrese who approached the subject when he inquired who Orlando's companion was. Kay began to sweat, she knew that Tyrese was homophobic he had lost a daughter and a son she knew that if she told him he would be devastated he would see it like losing yet another son. Kay tried to avoid eye contact and stirred her martini. Tyrese laughed, she was a bad liar and he commented how handsome the young man was and to her surprise excused himself and walked towards him. By this time Kay was in a profound sweat she was desperately trying to signal to Naret but he was in deep conversation with Marisa.

Kay watched as Tyrese chatted to the young Brazilian man Ernesto she wondered what on earth they were chatting about. Later Tyrese returned to where Kay was, she didn't know what to say.

To her utter astonishment he told her that he had invited Ernesto and Orlando to stay with him for a few days before they returned to Thailand, Kay literally swooned in shock. She couldn't believe that he could be so naive and not have noticed. He shocked her by saying, 'they make such a good couple don't you think?' she was shocked that he knew and even more shocked that he accepted it.

'I am not as square as you think.' he smiled at his ex-wife.

'When did you find out?' she asked inquisitively.

'My God Kay!' he laughed, 'I have known all along.'

'WHEN!' She shrieked so loudly that everyone looked in their direction. 'Since he was about five,' he added leaving her speechless. He had known long before Kay had and although he hadn't mentioned it he had long accepted it He was glad that his son had found happiness and it didn't really matter to him whether it was a guy or a girl that he had fallen in love with. The only thing that mattered was that he had found love. Tyrese watched the pair, the way they looked at each other it reminded him of how he and Kay had been.

When Kay told Marisa about their conversation she was delighted,' GOOD,' she beamed thinking that she had had an influence on Tyrese. She had been grooming him for the shock for months even she hadn't known that he knew.

Marisa disappeared to Thailand, Kay had invited her to go for a month or so. She had to Kay's surprise left all the trappings of the screen Diva in America. No limousines, no movie star designer clothes, no make-up or jewelry. Naret had never ever seen Marisa without the mask of make-up that she wore. She had actually even wore make-up when she had gone swimming on her last trip to Thailand. She looked completely different without all the glamour. On the flight she sat between Orlando and Ernesto teasing them wickedly for hours, Orlando missed the glamourous image that she had sported all her life.

She promised them that perhaps one night she would take them to a great little club that she knew in Bangkok and that she would get dolled up just like she used to.

Orlando and Ernesto had stayed for three nights at Tyrese's home and he had not batted an eyelid when he brought them in breakfast in bed on their last day and caught them wrapped around each other. He had left the breakfast on two trays and banged the door to wake them, it was odd looking at his son entwined in an embrace with a naked stranger but he had accepted it. A few years ago he would have been enraged and would have disowned him. He had changed, it was odd how pain changed your life, he had changed so much.

Whilst Kay and her husband attended to their businesses Marisa went on tourist jaunts with the boys, they had a great time together. Usually at nights they would eat dinner on the terrace and Marisa would entertain them with shocking stories about her life and the famous people that she had known. Telling them about her past had in a way made her dig into the corners of her soul, she had had a great life, a little mad perhaps but not ordinary in any way.

Together they had developed a close bond and she extended her visit, adding another month to her stay. She had promised the boys that they would go on an adventure to Cambodia.

It was hot and sticky and there seemed to be millions of flying insects everywhere, she had screamed when she saw a green snake and almost died when a scorpion crossed the room inches from her feet.

On the last day in Cambodia the heavens opened and she slipped on the stairs of a temple that they had gone to visit. The boys hailed two Samlons which was the same as rickshaws and the two puny drivers raced through the streets to get her to a hospital.

'No! NO! NO!' she groaned looking at the primitive dilapidated hospital, the place was crowded, it was for the locals, fortunately they didn't make her wait she was probably the only westerner that had entered the place. All the babies and children stared at her like she was an alien. Her milky white skin and blonde hair was a source of fascination in these remote places.

She was led to a tiny waiting room with a bare light bulb and the boys stayed outside while she waited for a doctor. The door opened and when she turned round she drew in her breath, she found herself staring into the eyes of the most handsome man that she had ever seen. Suddenly she had butterflies in her stomach and she was staring at him so intently she was unable to speak. Dr Klaichan was Thai he had worked in Cambodia for three years he was about thirty-nine and had a smile that Hollywood Stars would die for. He skilfully attended personally to her swollen ankle, bandaged it neatly and administered her with some painkillers, when he had finished writing the prescription he looked at her sheepishly and asked her if she would sign an autograph for him. She was shocked that he had recognized her, till he announced that she had looked exactly like that in her first movie. She was surprised that someone like him on the other side of the world had actually seen that film. It had been a success in some countries but bombed at the box office in others. 'Like you better without all the paint on your face,' he added shyly.

When she limped out to the waiting room the boys looked at her suspiciously, she looked different they saw a spark in her eye that they thought had disappeared forever. 'You look like you've just seen an angel,' Orlando joked. Dr Klaichan approached from behind and both boys stared at him admiringly, he was a great looking man.

When Marisa had given him an autograph she scribbled down her number too. The doctor was finishing duty and offered them all a lift to the hotel, it was on his way he explained, lying. It was actually miles away in the other direction. When they reached the hotel the boys feigned a headache and disappeared to their rooms leaving Marisa in the hotel bar with a bandaged leg and handsome doctor. She blew them a kiss as they ascended the staircase and promised to kill them in the morning.

Suddenly the boys had plans to visit places that Marisa wouldn't be able to visit, she had a sprained ankle, suddenly the boys didn't join her for dinner in the evening forcing her to accept Dr Somporn Klaichan's invitations. The night that she had been left in the hotel bar had been an entertaining one, as well as being a skilled and interesting person and dashingly handsome, Somporn had a fantastic personality. Since her son had died she had been sad and had lost some of her sparkle. Somporn had changed all that, that night in the little makeshift hotel bar he had made her laugh again, she had laughed so much her ribs hurt, he helped he up the staircase to her room and that night she couldn't sleep. It was almost morning when he had left, the sun was coming up and the Cambodian skies were ablaze with colour, as she drew the curtains in her room to block out the morning sun she saw a double rainbow, it had been raining and Somporn had used the monsoon rains as an excuse to stay and talk to her further. She smiled in awe of the brilliant double rainbow sure that this was a sign that things were going to change.

That night she fell asleep with a smile on her face she dreamt of Somporn and her, they were in a garden filled with flowers there were lots of children playing in the garden.

When she surfaced at three in the afternoon the boys pretended to be angry with her then looked at her, wide-mouthed waiting to see how her rendezvous with the super looking doctor had gone. She didn't have to tell them anything they could see in her eyes that he had rekindled a spark that had been latent. They pretended to be sick with jealousy and teased her wickedly.

Dr Klaichan worked long hours and there were no weekends off, whenever he finished his shift he headed to the hotel to pick up Marisa, she enjoyed each stolen moment with him doing simple things, eating in cheap restaurants, going for long walks. Somporn opened a door in her heart and even the simplest things seemed like blessed treasures.

Crazy as it seemed, food tasted better, skies more blue, the flowers that he brought her daily seemed to smell better than any perfume that she had had, everything seemed brighter, clearer and she was happier than she could ever remember. Suddenly even the simplest pleasures were the bringer of great joy, silly things like being caught in the monsoon rainstorms suddenly were fun. She was having to admit that in fact everything was the same the only difference was that she was falling in love, lying in bed in the hospital after Xenon's death she had felt numb, she had vowed that she would never ever love again, love was a double-edged sword, the pain of losing was greater than the elation of loving. She had made a pact with her soul that she would never feel for anyone or dare to love again. Somporn had changed all that, after a week of eating in places where she never would have ventured he surprised her by inviting her to his apartment for dinner, it was to be her last evening and she was sad, he had invited the boys but they had made a feeble excuse and had left them alone.

She had no beautiful clothes with her and decided to surprise Somporn by turning up as 'The Screen Diva' that he had so admired. While he worked she went shopping to buy a glamourous outfit and some make-up, she hadn't missed the painstaking routine that transformed her from a mere mortal into a movie star, it took her two hours to do her make-up and dress her hair. The boys had laughed, she had joined them for lunch with a headful of large rollers in her hair, 'Special date?' they joked, glad she was back to her old self.

The boys waited downstairs with her till Somporn arrived, it had been so long since they had seen Marisa they had forgotten how beautiful she looked, as she slowly descended the hotel staircase the boys wolf-whistled, she looked stunning all the glamour and sex appeal was back and she looked sensational in the slinky black dress. She had been pleased with the transformation, it had been a long time since she had made the effort to look like this. The old man in the reception stared at her as she deposited her room key, 'Look Good Madam,' he chuckled, 'Same Same Movie Star.'

The boys laughed in unison at his comment he had no idea who she was.

When Somporn stormed into the reception ten minutes late his forehead was wet with perspiration from the grueling day's agenda. He froze open-mouthed in disbelief, Marisa looked so good just like she did in the movies looking like that made him feel inadequate and nervous.

Marisa felt overdressed when they arrived at his humble two roomed apartment, it was such a mess she couldn't believe it. He excused himself explaining that with his long hours he had no time to tidy. While he showered she wandered through the apartment drinking in all the details of his life, the photos on the wall of his family, his graduation and friends, his books and records all seemed of interest. She smiled discovering three videos of her old movies, she joked with him that he must have been the only person that had actually purchased one of the videos as the film had bombed it was truly the worst film she had ever made and she was embarrassed.

Somporn looked ridiculous wearing the checked apron, within literally moments he had rattled up a superb seafood starter and a wonderful chicken dish cooked in coconut milk, over dinner he had been rattling on at a terrible rate telling her his simple life story. Suddenly she realized that she hadn't heard a word that he had been saying, all the time that he had been talking she had been looking at his lips, he had these amazing white teeth and the best smile she had ever seen, his lips were full and sensual.

The colour fascinated her, the first time that she had seen him she had thought that he was wearing lipstick. He had these unusually coloured pinkish lips and she was intrigued by them since the day that she had laid eyes on him. She had been infatuated by his lips, she remembered when he had been putting on her bandage she had actually imagined stretching up and kissing him.

He had asked her a question twice and she hadn't answered he realized that she hadn't been listening and looked disappointed, he thought perhaps that he had been boring her, to cover his embarrassment he lifted their plates and started to clear the tables, she waited till his hands were full of dishes then when he was helpless she grabbed him by the tie and pulled his face close to hers. Somporn closed his eyes, she could feel him tremble as she kissed him and kissed him, he dropped the plates and held her in his arms he was so so nervous in the arms of this beautiful creature, with her Hollywood glamour and almost untouchable beauty he trembled and it was she who undressed him. When he made love to her on the old sofa in the cheap rented apartment he was so tender she cried. This was not sex she thought as he took her, this was love, she stared at his incredible lips and kissed him like she had never kissed anyone in her life. After they'd orgasmed he held her in his arms and for the first time in what seemed like a hundred years she felt safe and complete. He fell asleep in her arms and she studied his face, counting each eyelash and gentle imperfection, she stared at the ceiling fan and smelled his neck. She promised to remember the smell of the cheap soap that he had used in the shower forever.

At that moment she realized that she couldn't leave Somporn, this perhaps was the person that she had been waiting for. Odd how destiny worked she mused, sometimes disaster led one to another place and through pain another door was opened. If Xenon had not been killed she would never have met Somporn she would never have come to Thailand and never imagined of going to Cambodia. She stayed the night at his apartment and they made love in the old wooden carved bed under the mosquito net. That night neither of them slept between bouts of passionate love making they talked and talked, he wanted to know everything about her and she had spent two hours telling him about Yoji and Xenon.

The next morning when they arrived at the hotel, the boys were waiting in reception, horrified that Marisa hadn't packed, they all rushed to her room to help. There was only one flight and they had to get on it. It took them about three minutes to stuff everything into her bags and Somporn drove like a mad man to get to the airport. He had been silent all the way and Orlando and Ernesto had thought that perhaps that they had had an argument they rushed to the check-in desk, fortunately there was a half hour delay and there was still a queue of people waiting to check in.

Marisa missed the luxury of using private jets. Traveling en masse did not amuse her.

The boys checked in their bags while Marisa raked through her bags looking for her passport. Somporn stood behind them looking sadder than anyone could, they had spent their last night talking about their past, they had not mentioned their future. He thought perhaps that she had just used him for fun and had a heavy heart. She checked in her two bags and Somporn walked with them to the passport control. He said goodbye to the boys and leaned towards Marisa to kiss her goodbye. As she stared intently at the pinkish lips that were approaching she jumped back avoiding his kiss. 'I am not kissing you good-bye,' she shrieked to his astonishment, she added, 'I refuse to kiss you goodbye ever,' and announced to the surprised lads that she was staying that she was not leaving.

Somporn had thought that she was rejecting his farewell kiss because it was over, he smiled the widest brightest smile that seemed to light up the whole airport. They waved goodbye to the boys and went to the ticket desk to ask them to retrieve her luggage. This proved to be a real hassle and caused further delay. That day Marisa moved into the modest apartment, while Somporn worked she did something that she had not done for years, she cleaned and tidied up.

Dr Klaichan took three weeks vacation and together they travelled back to Thailand. Kay was delighted that Marisa was staying and had offered them to stay at the holiday home in Phuket, to her surprise they declined the offer. Somporn was taking her first up north to Kholat to meet his family and then they were going to Chang Mai, Chang Rai to do some sightseeing.

His family were super impressed that he had a movie star girlfriend they didn't even seem to notice the age difference. Somporn showed her a side of Thailand that she could never have seen, his family were wonderful they made her feel like family within days. They went on tours and stayed in simple hotels, the landscape in the north was beautiful she fell in love with the country, its people, its climate, its food, everything about Thailand invigorated her just walking through a market here made the senses tingle, the smell of the pineapple, the mangoes, the fish, everything here seemed to be richer, the smells the sights were intoxicating. She had fallen in love with Dr Klaichan and fallen in love with Thailand too she realized that this would be her home.

One night over dinner she announced to Somporn that she had always had one dream that she had never discussed with anyone. It was the only dream that she had never realized, she concluded that he could help her realize this dream. She had always wanted to help underprivileged children.

Tyrese had shared her desire, in Cambodia she had been shocked and moved by the extreme poverty. At the borders the street kids and beggars had unnerved her, also in Thailand there were so many poor kids some lived on the streets others were caught up in the prostitution racket. She explained to Somporn that she had earned a lot of money and had a large divorce settlement. She had always felt that God had been too good to her and had given her money too easily, she wanted to do some good with that money and suggested opening a children's hospital, orphanage or school.

She had more money than she could ever spend in a life time, she had lots of wealthy friends that would be glad to donate large amounts and she wanted Somporn to help her, to leave his job and set something up, she suggested that they would be fifty-fifty partners and concluded that she would finance the whole project. Somporn sat silently contemplating the offer that she had made. He was reluctant about her financing the whole project he had no idea just how rich she was, all of the royalties from Xenon's music career were paid to her and she wanted to transform this income to do some good. After a few moments Somporn surprised her, he would be her partner in the project if she would be his partner in marriage, if she married him he would agree. It didn't take Marisa long to agree, she had never been happier he was younger than her but most of her lovers had been too so it was no big deal to her.

The next day he handed in his notice at the small rural hospital where he had first met her, he left after only a week, at his farewell party Marisa donated a large cheque to the hospital which would be used to restore the building and buy new equipment.

Marisa enjoyed her new, she felt completely at home in Thailand she invested a large amount of money to open a children's hospital and a rehabilitation centre for street kids and abandoned babies. Somporn was chairman of the board, he had complete responsibility for the running of both the hospital and centre, they had been together for around six months during that time they had been so busy setting up things that they worked seven days a week. Marisa found it personally rewarding to be involved in this project she had always worked in the film and music industry and it seemed so superficial now, however the film business had gave her the money which gave her the power to open these facilities.

They rarely had time to see Kay and Naret they were so busy expanding their now global retail business, Orlando had started to make his own label, his first collection was to be launched any day. He was making a designer range together with his lover Ernesto, his mother was opening a store for his collection and they were having a big fashion show at a fashionable venue. Marisa had promised that they would go to see his show they had so little time but she wouldn't miss it for the world.

The fashion show was an extravagant affair, all of Thailand's film stars, entertainers and celebrities were there along with some foreign pop stars that Tyrese had flown out to generate a bit of International vibe.

Marisa and Somporn sat with Kay and Naret on the privileged front row along with some international press, a Thai superstar and an American rapper. Orlando and Ernesto were backstage, it was total chaos in the changing room, make-up artists, hairdressers and stylists rushed to put the finishing touches to the thirty fashion models that had been hired to wear the clothes. Enrico had never seen Orlando so nervous, someone popped back stage to announce that his father had just arrived from the airport, Orlando was glad that he had made it.

The models hit the catwalk and his collection got rave reviews, Marisa being Marisa ordered two thirds of the collection, she didn't do it because it was Orlando she ordered the pieces because she loved them, it was exciting for her to see the show, many of the ideas he had sketched when they were all in Cambodia. Flashbulbs popped as Marisa switched on her movie star magic.

Kay was relieved, the fashion world was so fickle she knew after reading the reviews that his range was going to be a hit, she was happy that Tyrese had made it on time she had been nervous that he would have missed the whole show. However he made it just at the last minute and she could see the pride on his face as he watched the stick thin surrealistically beautiful models parade up and down on the cat walk. At the end of the show Orlando and Ernesto walked on the stage to a burst of applause, he was proud of his son and he was happy that he had someone to share his life with.

After the show the boys went to The Ministry of Sound to dance and celebrate with all the models and VIPs. Tyrese went with Kay, Naret, Marisa and Somporn for a quiet dinner it was the first time that he had met Dr Klaichan and he liked him instinctively.

He listened as Marisa talked excitedly about her children's clinic he was happy that she was doing something worthwhile with all the royalties that she was receiving from Xenon's album sales. Since he died tragically they were selling more of his albums than when he was alive.

That night Tyrese handed Marisa an envelope with a cheque for half a million dollars for her project, she handed the cheque to Somporn and his eyes opened in disbelief it was not from the record company it was a personal gift from Tyrese to them.

The following afternoon they took him to see the construction of their rehabilitation centre.

Tyrese was impressed, when Somporn was in the office she confided in Tyrese that she was happier than she had ever been, somehow all the tragedy that she had endured had been leading her to this point in her life. Destiny she sighed was ruthless she wished that she could understand it, she added that she loved Somporn more than anything and that was what she was afraid of. In the past anyone and everything that she had loved had been taken away from her she loved him like no other but was terrified that their relationship would be doomed also.

Tyrese returned to America, he had enjoyed seeing his son and strangely enough felt closer to Kay than he had when he had been married to her, she had blossomed over the years.

Naret was the luckiest man on earth, he suddenly realized how meaningless and lonely his own existence was, he worked from morning to night making other people rich and famous, wheeling and dealing in an industry that was changing daily.

Everything in the music industry was carefully planned but no one could control the egos or destinies of the artists that the business depended on. Success in this business made people tremendously wealthy fantastically famous but usually made them crazy.

He admired Marisa, it was amazing how she had changed when she talked about the helpless street kids to whom she had become "mother" to, her eyes lit up. It was obvious that she loved the handsome doctor who had inspired her to give up her superficial lifestyle and do something worthwhile, she too had found her soulmate. For Tyrese every night was lonely, he ate dinner alone that had been prepared by his maid hours before, usually he slept around two am and was up at six, He had kept his physique in good condition, exercising every day and jogging whenever he could.

He had seen so many artists come and go, they were all a commodity to him, longevity in this business was a component that was rare the stars that he signed had usually a short lifespan either the public got bored with them or the star got bored with the music industry.

He was proud that the Pippa Curtis Foundation to help underprivileged children had been a success, they had projects now all over the world, although he had little to do with the running of the foundation it was proving successful. Thousands of street kids had turned their backs on violence and drugs and embraced music, he made a mental note in future to focus more on that arm of his business, perhaps he could link up with Marisa and develop a program in Bangkok too.

He was glad that Orlando had chosen fashion, at least it was something that he loved he knew sadly that because of his sons sexual preference that he would never be a grandfather, the Andrews' family name would stop after Orlando's generation it was sad. One day Orlando would inherit the global empire that Pippa had left him, he wondered if the lad could handle the burden of running a billion dollar business, he wondered if he would have the balls, drive and commitment to sit in Pippa's big leather seat and run the company.

Sometimes he wondered where it would all end, he had put his life and soul into running Pippa's empire, everyone seemed to benefit but him, he was tired, years of pressure were getting to him and life seemed so pointless when you had no one to share it with. It was on nights like these that his dreams were filled with ghosts of the past. In one horrifying dream that seemed endless he saw the faces of all the people that he had loved and lost, from his mother to Paris perhaps Marisa was right perhaps they both were doomed.

He woke in a sweat with the ringing of the telephone, it was three am and it was the private line that only a handful of people had, something was wrong.

He was surprised to hear Romeo's voice on the line, his calls had become less frequent over the years, his old friend had became an eccentric recluse. To his complete astonishment Romeo announced that he would be flying on the following day. Knowing that Romeo hated traveling he wondered what was wrong.

The next evening after work his old friend made his way to his home, the fleet of limos arrived promptly on time three stretch limos with blackened windows drove up the drive.

Romeo entered with his three bodyguards, a spiritual guru, a holistic healer, a tantric masseur and personal assistant. Tyrese was shocked at how frail he looked, he seemed to be half the size he had been before he was wearing a long white coat that drowned him, a white bandanna, sunglasses a white rucksack and with rings on every finger he still had retained his superstar image. His fashion sense and passion for style.

Tyrese showed his entourage into the library and told them to help themselves to drinks, then he and his old friend went into the lounge Tyrese was genuinely glad to see his old friend he had at one point been like a brother. Tyrese mixed two Pina Coladas, he remembered that it had been his old friend's favorite drink. They chatted about general things for an hour and Tyrese filled him in with all the details of the company that he still had fifty percent shares in.

Romeo seemed so nervous and agitated but at last he seemed to relax and started talking to Tyrese like he had years before. He told him that he lived alone but being male he sometimes felt the urge, he had a regular escort that he hired from time to time when he was horny. She was a tall beauty from the deep south who charged an arm and a leg.

A few weeks ago they were having fun and as he had been fucking her at the side of the pool she had ran her nails down his back. Tyrese wondered where this story was heading as Romeo never usually discussed his sexual encounters at all.

In the middle of their passionate lovemaking she had discovered a lump on his back, he seemed too excited to be bothered but as she clasped his neck she discovered yet a bigger lump. There were three lumps on his back and neck.

The following day he had gone to see a doctor and after a series of tests they had concluded that he had cancer, the ultra-scan showed that the cancer had spread through his body, quite simply his body was riddled with cancer. They had wanted to give him treatment immediately but he had refused.

Tyrese's eyes widened in disbelief, he couldn't understand why his friend didn't want to be treated, it was imperative that he had treatment quickly. Tyrese tried to persuade him that he should commence the radiotherapy as soon as possible. Romeo's face lit up as he explained that it was his time now that at last he could join Pippa and Capricorn and as far as he was concerned death couldn't come quick enough.

Romeo had thought of nothing but death since he had lost his daughter he was actually relieved that he was dying he believed strongly in the afterlife and thought that everyone had a time to leave this world, this was his time.

Tyrese continued to try and convince his good friend that he should have treatment but he would hear nothing of it, he produced a thick wad of paperwork for Tyrese to read.

Tyrese was to be executor of his will when the time came. His will surprised Tyrese he was leaving his shares in Pippa's company to Tyrese, a large amount of money which amounted to sixty percent of his wealth was to be donated to Pippa's foundation, he had made all of his money out of music now he wanted some of that money to go back to her foundation to help others. His home in Miami he had left to his spiritual guru and had to be turned into a spiritual healing centre, two million dollars were to be put in a foundation to run this project and half a million dollars had to be put in a bank account for Miss Pamela Barton, the long legged hooker from the deep South. He wanted Tyrese to inspect all the papers, there was also details of his funeral arrangements, he wanted to go with Tyrese to their lawyer in the morning to sign all the necessary papers, he was keen to tie up things before he became too weak to handle them.

After his friend left he watched as the long shiny cars disappeared out of the driveway feeling sad and confused.

Tyrese was suspicious of the spiritual guru he was glad that he was not leaving his complete fortune to him, he went into the lounge and poured a stiff drink, the strong whisky burned his lips, he was confused and upset, he hadn't expected to hear that Romeo was ready to leave the planet. He picked up the pile of paperwork, meticulous in every detail. There was also a box, it contained over seventy new songs that Romeo had written there were some disks in the box too, he popped one in the CD player, the sound of Romeo's voice filled the room. The song was a hit, one after one he listened to the new material, tears in his eyes as he listened to the raw unmastered original cuts of the new material with a simple piano backing. Tyrese cried like a baby at the thought of losing yet another close friend, soon there would be no one left. Marisa was right they were the ones that outlived everyone, the ones that had to survive sometimes it was harder to survive than to die he thought.

The next day they spent three long hours at their lawyer's attending to paperwork, then Romeo headed home they had already started renovating his South Beach Mansion into a spiritual healing centre and Romeo wanted to supervise the conversion.

Tyrese hugged the frail little man, he seemed like a bundle of bones under the oversized tracksuit he promised to visit him in Miami in two weeks.

Chapter 17

Supermodel

Two weeks later Tyrese flew to Miami to join Romeo for a weekend at his South Beach Mansion. Romeo had been excited and proudly showed him the new wing that would house the holistic healing department of his spiritual awareness centre.

They had a great weekend, the bright Miami sunshine and graceful palms made Tyrese feel free as they walked along South Beach watching the never ending parade of beautiful girls and handsome men. The pale pastel ice cream coloured buildings sparkled in the evening sunset.

On the Saturday evening Romeo broke the rules by hosting a pool party. As gorgeous young blondes splashed around with the handsome young muscle men in the pool Romeo joked with Tyrese to, 'Check out da pussy in da pool,' Romeo looked tired he retired to his room about midnight leaving the rest of his guests dancing round the poolside.

Tyrese was lost in contemplation when she approached, he was lying on a sunbed with his eyes closed when she tapped him lightly on the shoulder, he opened his eyes to see a tall amazing looking blonde in front of him. She was six foot tall with legs that seemed to go all the way up to her armpits. She was a Dutch fashion model in Miami to shoot a catalogue for an International fashion house, she introduced herself to Tyrese as Yvonne, her body glowed in the moonlight and he had to admit that he had never seen a miniskirt and bra look so good. She had that cool untouchable type of beauty that these spindly super models possessed. She had commanded a million dollars for a perfume campaign and her agency charged two hundred dollars a day for her shoots. She was the reigning Queen of the catwalk and the top designers adored her. She had earned five million dollars this year and was hungry to have her own clothing line. She knew full well that Tyrese's son had a global fashion empire and she hoped that Tyrese would be her stepping stone. She grabbed his hand and dragged him over to the dance area, before he could object she was dancing sensuously around him Tyrese hated dancing he hadn't danced for a year and felt rather awkward amongst the youthful well defined bodies that were gyrating all around him. The leggy Dutch blonde would have gone on all night if he hadn't dragged her off the dance floor and hustled her over to the bar area.

He was just about to introduce himself when she stopped him in his tracks she grinned and said, 'Tyrese Andrews, ex-football hero, pop idol, movie star and record company mogul,' she knew exactly who he was and where he came from. After a few drinks they retired to his room, the moment they closed the door she unzipped his pants threw him on the bed and sat on his throbbing cock, after some of the best sex he could remember she cuddled up to him wrapped her long legs round him like a spider.

In the morning he woke with the sensation of someone sucking his cock, she swept her silky blonde hair across his thighs and brought him to orgasm with an expert blow job.

After he came she pulled him out of bed and forced him into the shower she soaped up his body and made him so horny that he found himself erect throwing her up against the cold marble wall he fucked her again in the shower.

While she dressed he looked at his reflection in the ceiling to floor mirrors she had awakened something deep inside him, he had thought that his sex life was over that he was old and worn out, however this tall leggy stranger had made him orgasm five times since last night she was like human Viagra he thought as he admired his reflection.

When he entered the bathroom she was naked except for a tiny G-string and high heels she was expertly applying make-up and looked sensational with her long blonde hair piled high on her head, she slipped a long T shirt out of her designer bag and pulled it on. She looked almost indecent he mused inspecting her closely. In the harsh light of day she was even more beautiful than he had thought, she blew him a kiss and disappeared out of the room. Tyrese was mad for not asking for her number, he had thought about her all the way back to Detroit.

In his office at the main board meeting he found himself thinking about her, at night he would wake up with a hard on thinking about her pale milky skin as he had fucked her up against the bathroom wall.

He was surprised, this kid had made him crazy he was old enough to be her father but he just couldn't get her out of his mind. In desperation he had an idea, they were shooting a video with a new rap star called Softie he could use her in the clip. He had his assistant call all the model bureaus in Miami, there were three girls called Yvonne shooting there at the moment the agencies emailed the three photos of the girls for his inspection.

The first photo was a anorexic thin red-head from London, she looked more like a drug addict than a fashion model, the second was a buxom dark haired German model that specialized in Lingerie and swimwear, he was relieved when he clicked on the last photo and Yvonne the leggy blonde bombshell's image filled the screen of his Apple Mac.

He called the model agency himself to book her for the video, fortunately she was available on the day but he cringed at her day price, she was ten times more expensive than any of the other models.

The agency didn't know if she would want to do a video and they told him that they would have to get back to him. So he mused she wasn't just a mere model she was a super model and an expensive one too. The agency had warned him that if she agreed that they would have to pay her first class flight back to Europe and put her in a five star hotel.

When Yvonne heard that Tyrese was trying to book her she was delighted, she had wanted to get out of modeling and cut a record, she had fallen into the fashion world by accident when a scout had seen her in a supermarket two years earlier and in the twenty four months she had worked she and graced the cover of every major magazine and modeled for the best designers in the world, she had pocketed millions of dollars from perfume and beauty product campaigns.

She had hoped that their paths would cross again and she had purposely not given him her number as she wanted him to make the first move she knew how men's minds worked, especially powerful men like him. He was the Emperor of the music industry and she would have him twisted round her finger within a month, he would launch her music career and secure her a clothing line deal with his designer son sooner or later she was sure she would have it all.

When the agency hadn't called him back by six he thought that she was not up for but it at seven pm the e telephone rang it was Yvonne's private booker from London, she had agreed to do the video shoot and would arrive the following evening. The Agency had pre-booked a suite at a five star hotel and they wanted Tyrese's fax number so he could sign the contract before she arrived.

The video director was pleased that they were having a supermodel to appear in the video but was confused that Tyrese was prepared to pay her 30,000 dollars for a day's shooting this was a low budget video and they couldn't imagine why suddenly he was lashing out on extras.

Tyrese lied, saying that having a well-known ace in the clip would be good for PR in the UK and Europe.

Softie was a huge monster of a man from Philadelphia, his name was a joke really as he was so large and fierce looking that he frightened people. He was over the moon to have Yvonne in his clip, he had seen her on TV and in perfume campaigns in the glossy magazines his bitch read. Softie had been living with a dancer called Pearl for years, she had the best tits and the hottest booty in town she was not pleased at all that they had chosen this stick thin bitch to be in his clip, she would make sure that her man wouldn't be alone for a moment. She was havin' no motherfukin' supermodel gonna cream her dude.

Yvonne arrived at the airport at ten o'clock in the evening. Tyrese sent a large limo to pick her up, she was taken to her hotel and he had arranged flowers and champagne in her suite, he had been tempted to go to the hotel to have her again but decided to play hard to get. He had his assistant deliver a shooting schedule and script and let her brood alone in her room.

Yvonne was surprised that Tyrese hadn't turned up at the airport she thought that he would be waiting there with his tongue hanging out, usually she could twist men round her finger, this one perhaps was going to be difficult. After a light breakfast of fruit salad and juice Yvonne was collected and brought to the studio, as she entered she felt all the eyes looking at her. They were inspecting her and thinking is this what costs 30,000 dollars a day. It was kind of crazy she had to admit that while some people starved in underprivileged countries that she was being paid such ridiculous amounts for merely looking pretty. The whole crew stared at her jealously, she looked nondescript with no make-up and she could see the disappointment in their eyes, most of the real good models looked plain without make-up, their faces were blank canvasses for the talented make-up artists to use their skills.

Softie had been disappointed too when she walked in, six foot tall with long legs and not an ounce of meat on her bones he sulked. Pearl had been relieved, she had gone to great pains to dress that morning and had made herself up to perfection to compete with Yvonne.

Sadly in her gold high-heeled boots, pink hat and tangerine fur jacket she looked more like an upmarket hooker than anything else, she rolled another joint and slagged Yvonne, 'Hey man check out that skinny muther fukker Bitch, No tits. Flat as Olive Oil and white as an Alien Honey,' she grinned passing the joint to Softie. Softie pinched her ass and popped a pill in his mouth he wanted to get ready for the cameras it was early and he wanted to have some artificial energy to 'get it goin on'

When however two hours later Yvonne came out of make-up everyone looked at her in awe, the tall almost scraggy scarecrow that had arrived had been transformed into a tall goddess with the help of blonde hair extensions she had this mass of golden hair, her face immaculately made up was fantastic and in the sequinned bra and shorts she looked red hot.

Pearl looked at her in disbelief. "It's all fuckin make-up man," she sneered jealously as she looked at Yvonne the Supermodel.

The director was so horned up, Yvonne was a delight to film she loved the camera and on film she was awesome. She was used to people running her down, she knew herself that without make-up she was a plain Jane, it was always the same, last week they had her booked for a beauty cream and when she walked in the door the company director's face fell, the same man was amazed when he saw how she looked in the finished poster shots. Having her face on their product raised the sales by fifty per cent.

They were filming a scene when Tyrese arrived, he hovered in the wings and watched as Yvonne strutted her stuff making love to the lens in the special way she did. They were shooting her on a green screen, the director had the idea to clone her in the finished film so there would be twenty Yvonne's. Tyrese was so intrigued by her that he could have taken her right there on the studio floor. She did love the attention and did give the camera her all, the crew stood still as she danced. She was perfect from all angles and just having her on set added a special dimension to the clip.

Tyrese followed her into her dressing room while they changed her make-up he told her that after the shoot he would pick her up and take her to dinner then disappeared. Usually she washed off the make-up as soon as the shooting was finished this time she kept it on, the full theatrical mask with dark eyes and red glitter lips, she always carried a little black dress in her bag she slipped it on and asked the stylist if she could have the high heeled black boots from the shoot. The effect was stunning, the slinky backless mini dress clung to her naked body like a sheath. She had kept in the hair extensions and the hairdo looked like a metre high she looked like a wild lioness and she hoped that Tyrese would like the effect.

Tyrese picked her up in a stretch limo and as she stepped in the back he noticed that she was completely naked under the short black dress that hardly covered her body he had poured two glasses of champagne and they drank it quickly, as the car sped towards the city Yvonne unzipped his pants before he knew what was happening he was deep inside her, the idea that the driver was watching them only seemed to excite her when Tyrese tried to push the button to screen off the driver she stopped him. Tyrese was lost inside her, the smell of her perfume the taste of her cherry lip gloss made him crazy and they exploded in orgasm together just minutes from the restaurant that he had booked. They smiled at the concierge as he led them to their seats. As the waiter pushed in her seat he thought that she smelled distinctively of sex.

Everyone in the restaurant looked at Yvonne as she made her entrance provocatively naked under the slinky fabric, she looked stunning looking like this made having no tits not an issue Tyrese thought drinking in her beauty. It was ridiculous he thought but he was totally captivated by her, he hardly knew her but she had in that short time cast a spell over him completely.

They ordered oysters washed them down with champagne rosé he had duck, she skipped the main course then they devoured the house speciality dessert which was called floating islands in real terms it was a light warm meringue served on chilled vanilla custard which was laced with wild raspberry coulis.

Tyrese could still taste the bittersweet raspberry coulis on her lips as he kissed her in the back seat of the limo as they headed to his home.

He spend, the next two days and nights in bed with Yvonne, he gave his maid two days off so they could be alone in his home when they were hungry they ordered food from their favourite restaurant. Both of them had switched off their mobile phones. Yvonne knew that the agencies would be furious and that Armando her Dutch personal booker would be furious. She didn't care they were all earning plenty from her, without her Armando's job simply wouldn't exist, she had a personal booker in Amsterdam and one in London and as Tyrese made love to her she imagined how angry her bookers would be.

He had made love to her in every conceivable position and was exhausted it had been so long since he had slept with someone he almost had forgotten what it felt like.

He noticed how little she ate, usually she would order food then just play with, it have a few mouthfuls and toss it around the plate then leave it. He guessed that trying to retain her figure must be difficult she counted every mouthful of calories and had told him that if she had the choice to eat or drink she would rather drink. He had caught her once in the bathroom with her fingers down her throat trying to make herself sick. Realizing he had caught her, her face had reddened then she joked that it was an occupational hazard she had to keep thin to earn the huge amounts that she did, her body was her temple her main source of income and she had to keep it thin.

It rained and they lay in bed watching one of Tyrese's old movies he had been really handsome when he was young she mused watching him make love to a screen goddess.

Tyrese blushed with embarrassment he wasn't the best actor, you certainly did the love scenes without a problem she joked.

When the film finished she unzipped his pants and pulled him on top of her just as he was about to explode in orgasm she asked him the question that she had wanted to since she met him. She reckoned that at this point he would agree to anything. 'Tyrese darling,' she whispered in his ear, 'I want to cut a record deal.'

'Ooooh. Kay!' he screamed as he reached orgasm, she smiled and ran her longer fingernails down his sweaty back.

Tyrese didn't care if she was using him for a deal, he had signed a lot worse than her recently, she was beautiful, looked good on film and could sing moderately, better still she was red hot in the sack and for the first time in years he felt young again.

To his delight Yvonne cancelled all her modeling options for a month and stayed to record her single. The track sounded good and Tyrese decided to make a big budget video with one of New York's top directors. He flew up with Yvonne to shoot the video, everyone knew that they were an item and everyone struggled to make sure that everything went well for the boss's bird.

The video was nothing less than sensational, the music channels would love it. Yvonne had pulled all the strings with seven of Europe's top designers and her video had turned into a fashion extravaganza. She was fashion royalty and had millions of fans on Facebook and zillions on twitter.

Yvonne had never looked better, she wore seven stunning outfits in the clip and sported seven different looks. The song "Fashion Victim" was an instant hit and Tyrese advised her to start recording for an album, he was planning on using eight of Romeo's new tracks for her and was looking for five more, thirteen was Yvonne s lucky number. She reminded him that he had met her on the thirteenth and that she had been staying in room 1313 when he had made love to her when she came to shoot Softie's video.

Yvonne couldn't just stop her modeling all together she had contracts and commitments that she had to fulfill and she agreed to spend the next six months flying between Europe and Detroit modeling and recording simultaneously. Contracts had been signed, she had dozens of bookings.

It was going to be exhausting she knew to commute between America and Europe but she would have to do it. She was smart enough to know that she had around two years left in modeling and she wanted to stop at the top, she had seen other girls that were rejected, their careers abruptly halted when they were 26 she was not going to be one of them.

In the course of the next six months Yvonne professionally completed all major commitments, she did catwalk shows in New York, Milan, London and Paris. She did a perfume campaign and some commercials for beauty products. She did seven magazines covers and twelve fashion editorials for major magazines in between she jumped on planes and recorded eleven songs in studios in Detroit, London and Amsterdam.

Her Agents were sorry to see her retire from the fashion scene she was hot property and they were making millions out of her, they did everything to try and persuade her to rethink her decision to stop but she was adamant that this was the direction that she wanted to take.

Secretly she had always hated the world of fashion and modeling, she found the people shallow and the job boring.

One night after a glossy magazine shoot in Paris she had gone clubbing to Manray. She was dancing on the dance floor when suddenly the DJ played her disk 'Victim' he announced over the loud speaker that she was number one in the dance charts.

The whole club had gathered around her on the dance floor as she danced with Tommy the model that had been in a perfume campaign with her, she felt like she was flying, listening to her own single, she was number one in the Dance Charts it was a trip.

The agency in Amsterdam held a huge party in her honor, the day she left they had hired a club and everyone who was someone in Amsterdam was there along with the people from the London Agency. Tyrese had flown in for the party and he was proud to have her on his arm, when they arrived at the venue that night by boat they had lights outside the sixteenth century building, it looked like something from a film, inside huge screens had been set up and images of Yvonne's career were flashing from screen to screen. Large wonderful photos of her editorial shoots, perfume campaigns and fashion shows filled the screens the magical images of her unusual unique beauty were indeed awesome. Tyrese was proud to be with her it also gave him a chance to meet her parents and sister, her father had been a farmer and her mother a housewife, it was strange to think that these simple people could have created such a creature of perfection.

The girl who had been skinny and too tall was bullied at school because she was an outcast, look how her life had changed.

That night Yvonne was going to perform, it would be the first time that she had done a live show and she was going to sing three songs. Tyrese had arranged that Softie would do a pre-show then she was to take the stage with six handsome male dancers. After she had greeted her guests she went backstage to be made-up and transformed into a Dance Diva.

She introduced herself to the dancers they were gorgeous and she was sorry that Tyrese had come, she had taken a liking to one of the Surinamese dancers with dreadlocks to his waist.

Softie was having fun in Amsterdam, he was high as a kite and surrounded by groupies, he had left his fat assed Bitch of a girlfriend back in the states. She had a fractured hip which she had acquired when Softie had thrown her down a flight of stairs. Pity he hadn't killed her Yvonne thought as they applied a second pair false eyelashes to her eyes.

It was nice to be the centre of attention here in Amsterdam, she was a little nervous, she had never sung live. She knew all the people in her dressing room well they were like family to her, her stylist, make-up artist and hairdresser she planned using them on the shooting of her three videos that were scheduled to coincide with the album.

She could hear that Softie was finishing she would be on in a few moments she sprinkled some of the white powder on the dresser and sniffed it up greedily, the coke gave her a buzz she could feel the adrenaline kicking in, they announced her name and she stepped out onto the stage to a deafening applause, 'HEY GUYS!' she said in Dutch, 'I haven't done anything yet.'

Encircled with handsome muscle men in tight jeans she sang her song, it went down well with the audience even though she had started off key, once she got into it it was all right. The next two songs were even better and Tyresse applauded and cheered with the rest of the guests.

Yvonne was on a high when she came off stage this was what she wanted to do, she had no regrets at leaving her modeling behind this was her destiny.

She went to her room to change into her party dress, the place was crawling with press, almost every magazine and newspaper had photographers there, outside the paparazzi were lined up in droves she wanted to look her best.

While Tyrese was enjoying polite conversation with her parents, Yvonne was in the shower being fucked like an animal by the dancer with the dreadlocks, as soon as they came she tossed him his jeans and asked her make-up artist to continue with the painting of her face.

Twenty minutes later she emerged looking sensational in a long silver sheath made from what looked like chain mail she had borrowed the dress from a designer in Paris, it was superb and she looked great in photos but it was dreadfully uncomfortable.

The party lasted till four am, Tyrese and Yvonne left by water limo which was a luxurious ship that would drop them at their hotel.

Yvonne was on a personal high fuelled with cocaine and ego she kicked off her shoes and stripped off the expensive borrowed evening dress and reclined on the sofa. It took Tyrese three seconds to get out of his clothes, he had missed her so much, while he made love to her she thought of the young dark man with the dreadlocks, how tight his buns were and how powerful he had been. She made a mental note to book him for the tour that they had planned. Tyrese was not going to be able to come on the tour he had end of the year finances to control and a host of meetings with the executives, this was cool as she would be alone on tour with six handsome hunks, five band members and three security guards.

Yvonne moaned, pretending that Tyrese had driven her to the height of ecstasy she was glad that he was leaving tomorrow she was dying to make the three videos and longing for her album to be released so that she could dump him. Once her album hit the charts she could be her own boss, he wouldn't be stupid enough to break her contract if she had success and even if he did she would get another deal based on the success of her hit single she had used him to break into the business and her plan had worked she had no intention of banging the boss forever she liked young hunky men not middle-aged sugar daddies.

The next morning she crept out of bed before he woke she couldn't bear to make love to him again she was on a downer after all the coke and scrambled through her bag to see if there was any left.

It was finished. She switched off the alarm and woke him when his car arrived downstairs, he was late for the flight and furious that the alarm was broken, he didn't have time to shower or make love to his lover, apologetically he threw his things in a bag and kissed her on the cheek promising to call her every day, he raced off.

As soon as he left she dialed the number of Clifford he turned up with some Heroin half an hour later. She was angry, she hated that crap she had asked him for coke not this cheap shit. Eventually she took the needle out of her bag and injected it into her vein. The drug kicked in and she chilled out, everything seemed fuzzy and she felt so relaxed.

She was aware of someone else in the room, there were flashes of light it hurt her eyes, someone was penetrating her, she thought that Tyrese had left, the man was deep inside her the flashes hurt her eyes, she giggled Clifford had unzipped his pants he had his cock in her mouth she was choking on his dick and she was glad when he finished she fell fast asleep with his sperm running down her lips.

When she woke up it was dark, she crawled out of bed feeling shattered and switched on the light. 'Bastard!' she screamed, Clifford had emptied her handbag and taken all her credit cards, cash and the diamond earrings that Tyrese had given her. 'Motherfucker!' she cried remembering that he had sex with her also.

It took her an hour to cancel all the cards she didn't want to call the police, what could she say, that her heroin dealer had raped and robbed her.

She scraped together her belongings and headed for the airport, she had to record three songs in London and after they were completed she was going on location to Tokyo to film the video for Oriental Princess after which she would complete the other two in a studio in Detroit.

Fortunately Tyrese was not accompanying her to Tokyo. She drank three gin and tonics on the flight, the air hostesses recognized her and took great pleasure in discussing how plain she looked in reality. The photos of her party were splashed all over the front pages of every newspaper, the stewardesses were right she did look like shit she had forgotten that the photos would be everywhere. She had lost her dark glasses and hadn't even combed her hair. She had heard the air stewardesses whispering about her. She disappeared into the toilet with her make-up bag to try and paint on a face. She stayed in the toilet for twenty minutes and the other passengers complained that they couldn't use the toilet. She emerged looking quite reasonable and was ready to face any photographers that were waiting in London airport.

She was glad that she had made the effort because as soon as she went through customs she was greeted with an army of flashbulbs, the clicking of the cameras jolted her memory to the night before, she hoped that that Bastard Clifford hadn't taken any photos of her. She had been stoned and drugged out her mind.

Yvonne smiled and posed for the press telling them that she was there to record the last series of tracks for her album.

Tyrese called her on her mobile thank God! She thought that the Bastard hadn't stolen her phone, she was booked into a hotel and was expected at the studio, she would be in the studio for three consecutive days then she had a series of meetings with a publicist, her manager, personal assistant and she would also do a photo shoot for a music magazine.

On the Saturday morning a stylist would fly in with her video costumes and she would select which ones she wanted, also some clothing for the other two clips. Sunday she had another photo shoot for a teen magazine, a lunch with her pluggers and an audition with the choreographer of the video. Sunday evening she would have dinner with the head of their London office. Monday at five thirty am she would be at the airport heading for Detroit.

Fuck she thought looking at the grueling schedule being a pop star was worse than being a supermodel, on her trip to London she didn't have one free moment.

She also was having a problem with the security guard that was to accompany her everywhere, he was ugly as sin, had no sense of humor and followed her like a shadow even when she went to pee he was there. It was too much, when she had called Tyrese to complain he had simply said it was record company policy and that she had better get used to it. She traveled with her entourage in what was becoming a circus.

She recorded the songs as best she could, the photo shoots were the easiest but she didn't like the photos, in the fashion world the photographers created artistic images these so called pop mag photographers didn't have the same eye, their photos seemed ugly in comparison to what she had been used to.

Every night she flopped into bed, they had another guard posted outside her room, she felt like a prisoner this was only the beginning she thought it can surely only get worse she dreaded to think what her life would be like when she became a big star she had one hit now and that was bad enough.

One day she stole a half hour to go shopping, she had ditched her guard when he went to the toilet. She had taken a taxi to Oxford Street, it was scary when a crowd of teenagers recognized her and pursued her into a store, they pressed against her, mobbing her and fighting for autographs it was really scary, store security had to been called and they peeled the hungry teenagers off her. They arranged a car for her, just as she left the store a photographer clicked away, the next day the photo of her was in the papers free publicity for the store she thought. After that experience she never undermined the bodyguards again, she actually became friendly with them and even wished them good morning and good night. The security men were pleased that she had had a scary experience it had tamed her down she was a real bitch and any improvement was welcomed by them.

Yvonne was going to learn that life as a Pop Queen was not going to be easy the transition from supermodel to superstar was going to prove difficult.

The long flight to Tokyo was grueling she was glad that her bodyguard was in tourist class.

Tokyo was so so different from anywhere else in the world, they filmed her video at night, the director was young and it was difficult to understand him. The Japanese youth were really into fashion they had their own way of perceiving European ideas and their own way of developing trends, Yvonne was intrigued by the interesting cast of fashion victims that they had cast to appear in her video, one was more freakier than the rest, she looked like an amazon compared to them and in the high-heeled boots she seemed twice the height of the extras.

They filmed the video against a backdrop of Tokyo's brightly neon lit streets. Yvonne looked like a tough girl in her leather biker jacket, punk make-up and ripped fishnet tights. The video was all about bright lights, fast cars and freaky people. Because of her connection with the fashion world everyone expected her videos to be special.

Tyrese was excited when he saw the finished clip, it was wonderful, the extras were fantastic and they had added a kick-boxing scene that looked like it had been designed by computer graphics. Yvonne smiled as she admired her image on screen they had airbrushed her till she was perfect.

Tyrese was standing in the wings watching Yvonne on the blue screen they were shooting her third video for the track 13 Cyber Lovers when the call came, it was the call that he had never wanted to receive, Romeo had passed away in his sleep minutes before. Tyrese waited till Yvonne came off the set then took her into the kitchen to explain why he was leaving, acting disappointed and genuinely sad she kissed him on the forehead and wished him well. She told him to call her to tell her when the funeral was so she could fly out to be by his side. The moment he left she sighed with relief, he was driving her crazy. The quicker that she escaped form this relationship the better.

She waved goodbye to Tyrese then went back to the set this shoot was gonna be fun she thought as she watched Ray the Surinamese dancer with the dreadlocks and rock hard buns as he did a break dance routine for the camera.

At the end of the shooting she invited four male dancers including Ray and a tall blond boy called Justin back to her home with three female dancers, she had no intention of inviting the girls but she didn't want the bodyguards to be suspicious.

While the girls and the gay guy partied in her pool she Ray and Justin were engaged in a heavy sexual threesome, to her surprise Ray was just as into Justin as he was into her both men fucked her one after the other then she gave them both a blow job she orgasmed as Ray fucked her doggy style while she sucked Justin's juicy dick.

This time she made sure she had Ray's cell phone number, he was hot and up for everything with no strings attached. Fucking them in Tyrese's bed had been a mind blowing experience in the morning she ripped off the stained sheets and checked the bed, floor and shower for hairs or traces of other people, all the dancers left at sunrise.

Tyrese looked at the bird like features of the man who had once been his friend he looked so old and frail almost unrecognizable, the cancer had spread through his body at an alarming rate. He was at peace at last, he had suffered terribly in the end refusing to take pain killers he would be with Pippa and Capricorn now he thought looking up towards the sky.

Tyrese had arranged the funeral for the following Tuesday, Yvonne, Kay, Marisa and Orlando would be flying in for the funeral and half the music industry would be there.

Yvonne was glad she was going to the funeral everyone who was someone in the music business would be there and she would be the new star hanging on to Tyrese's arm. She saw the whole ceremony as a public relations stunt.

Tyrese hugged Marisa and Kay he missed them so, the ladies glanced at each other as he introduced Yvonne, they didn't like her they had read so much about her in the tabloids.

Orlando was excited to see his father he had missed him it had been ages since he had come to Bangkok. There had been a war in Iraq, serious deaths caused by SARS, who in their right mind wanted to travel these days. The funeral was a sad but stately affair, Romeo was indeed pop royalty, Tyrese wept at the service.

Somporn was in Cambodia running the hospital that they had just opened. Naret was in Berlin at the opening of their new store. Kay, Marisa and Orlando were in Florida for Romeo's funeral and they intended staying for a week, it had been ages since they had seen Tyrese and they wanted to give him some support at this bleak point in time.

Ernesto had been left alone in Bangkok, he was glad he was always stuck with Orlando and had no freedom, they worked every evening till deep into the night and he had been bored for months. Seizing the opportunity he went out on the town every night enjoying the sleazy bars and nightlife in Patpong, each night after work he would take a taxi to Suriwonge road and visit the bars, he drank a lot and enjoyed the sex shows in the gay bars that he had become regular patron. Each night he would take one or two of the go-go boys to a hotel where you could rent rooms by the hour. In a cheap hotel frequented by prostitutes he would have wild sex sessions with the handsome young men that worked in the go-go bars.

The hotel had mirrored walls and ceilings and he had almost jumped out of his skin when he was in the shower with two guys when a cockroach darted over his foot.

His nightly adventures became more frequent as he became addicted to the sensation of new flesh. Ninety percent of the men who worked in these bars were straight, the kick of sleeping with handsome straight macho men had become addictive to him, sometimes in the daytime he would leave the office and go to a massage parlour, his craving for flesh became more intense and on the night before Orlando arrived home he went early to the club and took seven men off, they rented a large suite in a hotel and had a sex orgy after they had done everything that he wanted he gave the men their money and asked one of them to sleep with him.

Orlando noticed a difference in Ernesto when he returned from America he seemed distant and irritated, sometimes he would leave the office in the afternoon and not come back for hours, other times in the evening he would go alone to the cinema while Orlando worked on the new collection.

Orlando didn't mind him going to the cinema he usually went around nine and was home at eleven thirty.

Little did he know that every night he said that he was going to the movies he lied. He would go to the sleazy bars and pick up a go-go boy take him to a room for two hours of short time sex then return home. Ernesto had become quite involved with one man that worked in a club as a go-go boy, he was a well hung twenty-six year old with a perfectly toned body and a criminal record. He was married to a prostitute, she worked in a Patpong go-go girl bar, both of them were on drugs and owed a lot of gambling debts, Jimee as he was known was one of the stars in the fucking show, he hated the men who he was forced to sleep with but had decided to work in that business as he had had no schooling and it was the quickest way to earn money. He was hoping to find a western man that would be stupid enough to set him up in his own business and buy a house for him. Many of the young men who worked as go-go boys had landed lucky they all had big cars, choppers and flashy apartments. His problem was that this mean guy named Ernesto was taking him every night, he paid him the minimum and he never had a chance to meet any of the other wealthy clients, the owner of the club had said that he had to go with Ernesto he was a good customer that bought a lot of drinks.

His wife was angry she was constantly nagging and making him crazy, she was mocking him that he must be turning gay, at night after he had slept with Ernesto he didn't have the power to fuck her. She complained and whined on one hand, but it had been her that had got him in this business in the first place, he had been a carpenter earning three thousand baht a month up north now as a go-go boy he was earning two thousand a night, he was heterosexual, sleeping with these men made him sick he took drugs to forget and had money lenders on his neck.

Taking drugs was risky in Thailand it was jail and when you were in there they threw away the key, he had been in before for a minor offence it was scary, thirty men in a small cell with a ball and chain on your feet.

One night Ernesto appeared at the club where he danced, they left and went to the same cheap hotel with the cockroaches. Jimee had had a vicious fight with his wife, she had thrown all his belongings out of the window of their flat.

He had taken a yabba pill to space himself out his pupils were like saucers.

In the grubby hotel room with its sperm stained sheets Ernesto had been angry that he couldn't get a hard on, yabba had that effect and in his profession it was crazy to take such a drug. Jimee pretended that he was tired out and offered to give him a massage he kneaded Ernesto's flesh and poured the oil over his naked body. Jimee suddenly felt such hate for the dirty homo underneath him that he wanted to kill him, he cursed and screamed at Ernesto and everything seemed to blackout, suddenly he realized that he was strangling Ernesto his strong hands were squeezing Ernesto's throat, his face was blue and he could hardly breathe. He would never forget the look of pure hate in his eyes as he tried to choke him.

Suddenly as if coming to his senses Jimee jumped of the bed releasing the client from his grip eyes staring like a mad man he pulled on his t shirt underpants and jeans then went through Ernesto's wallet and removed all the money he had in it then he ripped the gold chain of Ernesto's neck and kicked him in the stomach. He ran out the room and disappeared into the brightly lit streets leaving Ernesto doubled up in pain. The room boy found him two hours later naked and in shock, the boy helped him into his clothes and hailed him a cab.

Ernesto was glad that Orlando was working late, he showered and went to bed pretending to be fast asleep when Orlando arrived home an hour later.

The experience with his long time boy a go-go shook him so much that he didn't dare go near Patpong, he had become attached to Jimee and missed him. He had lied to Orlando that someone had ripped off his heavy gold chain in the street, there was a large gash on his neck where it had been ripped from his neck, he had not wanted to report it he claimed as it hadn't been insured any way.

Over the next few months he started to visit the bars again, he never ever saw Jimee again. One of the boys told him that he had gone back up north and was working as a joiner again another said that he had gone to Germany with a foreigner.

Ernesto made a rule never to take a boy twice, each time he went he would take another man, never going back for seconds no matter how good the lad was. He had read in the paper recently that a German tourist had been stabbed seven times by a go-go boy on yabba he had felt lucky that he had not been strangled. The drug was becoming a major problem in Thailand they were clamping down on it as most of the violent crimes were stimulated by these nasty little pills.

Kay had noticed that Ernesto had not been himself recently, they worked day and night and she wondered if they took the time to eat properly. He had lost so much weight and looked dreadful. Orlando was so submerged in his collection that he hadn't noticed how thin his lover had become, one day in the studio while they were doing fittings for a fashion show Ernesto collapsed, he was having difficulty breathing. They thought that it was stress till the result of the blood test arrived.

Orlando sat in the waiting room his head in his hands too afraid to call his mother, he called Somporn in Cambodia in tears. Ernesto had Aids. Somporn had called Kay on her mobile, she had been in a traffic jam in the city, she abandoned her car and hailed a cab she wanted to go to the hospital to see her son. He was surprised to see her and jumped into her arms.

Somporn had told her to get Orlando tested right away he was afraid. Kay marched him into the blood test department, little did he know she thought, that she was more nervous than him. They could have the results in four hours, while he was in giving a blood sample she called Tyrese. She didn't know what time it was in America she couldn't think straight, as soon as she heard his voice she burst out crying. Tyrese shot up in bed almost knocking Yvonne off the bed, it took her several minutes to calm down. Tyrese was beside himself, he thought that something had happened to Orlando. 'What is it?' he screamed repeatedly only to be answered with her sobs.

Tyrese put on a robe and went and sat in the den it was early morning and the sun was just coming up. It looked like it was going to be another lovely day, however it wasn't going to be lovely for him if Orlando had aids, if he died he would kill himself. He wept and prayed for the first time to God, he prayed so hard his knuckles turned white. When Yvonne surfaced she found him sitting in a foetal position crying like a child. He prayed over and over again that Orlando was safe, he asked God to take his soul to do anything but harm his only son.

It was the longest six hours he had ever known. Back in Thailand, Kay and Orlando had gone to see Ernesto he looked deathly ill with dark circles under his eyes and a drip in his wrist, he was wearing an oxygen mask and was asleep.

Actually he was awake he couldn't bear facing Kay and Orlando so he had pretended that he was fast asleep. Orlando touched his hand and he felt consumed with guilt. Almost choking at the sensation of his touch he prayed to God that he had not infected Orlando with this deadly illness. In moments of sheer lust he had unprotected sex with some of the boys that he had picked up in the bars, how foolish it all seemed now to risk a life for a moment's pleasure.

An elegantly dressed staff nurse approached them, the results were there and they had to go to see doctor. Kay's heart was beating so loudly as she took the elevator to the other floor, she thought that the buttons on her silk blouse would pop off. The doctor introduced himself with a smile then looked at his computer screen, as far as he could see Orlando had not been infected, however under the circumstances he advised that he should have a test every two to six months, the virus could be latent in his system. Further checks would have to be made, he asked Orlando about his sex life and his mother sat trembling as he answered.

As soon as she was out the doctor's office she tried to call Tyrese, she knew he would be waiting for her call her hands were shaking so much she couldn't dial the number. Orlando, eyes wet with tears, took her phone and dialed his

463

father he told him himself what the doctor had said and Tyrese cried with happiness. He wanted Orlando to fly immediately to Detroit.

He wanted to see him. Tyrese ended the call with words that he had found hard to say to his son, he told him that he loved him then hung up.

Tyrese was angry at the dirty South American Fairy that lay dying of aids they would be on tenterhooks for six months now.

The next day when Orlando arrived at the hospital Ernesto looked much better, the oxygen mask had disappeared and he was propped up in bed eating lunch.

Not one to beat about the bush he wanted to level with Orlando. As he listened to Ernesto's confession his eyes misted with tears, for almost a year he had been sleeping with literally dozens of prostitutes he could hardly believe his ears as he confessed about the massage parlours and go-go boys about the nightly adventures with faceless men whose names he didn't know.

Ernesto didn't want to hang around to let Orlando watch him die, he had only a few months to live and he wanted to sever the emotional ties so he lied to Orlando that he had fallen in love with a go-go boy. Orlando walked out of the hospital room devastated, the nurses watched as he walked down the corridor. In bed Ernesto covered his ears, he could hear the sound of Orlando's tears from his room the wailing echoed through the hallways of the clinic.

The next morning Kay's driver delivered four suitcases with all of Ernesto's belongings to his hospital room her chauffeur handed the sick man an envelope with a first class one-way ticket to his home town, Rio de Janeiro with the ticket she enclosed a cheque for a year's salary.

Marisa had been shocked when she had heard the news, she dropped everything and raced to see Orlando she couldn't bear the look on his face it was obvious that he was broken-hearted.

She was so relieved that his tests were clear she prayed that the following blood tests would be ok.

It was Marisa who persuaded him to go to see Tyrese.

Two weeks after the international release of her album and first video and the night before Orlando arrived Yvonne had packed her bags and walked out of Tyrese's house. At first he thought that she was joking, they had been getting on fabulously, with eyes as cold as ice she sat down and stared at him. He could hardly believe his ears, she was telling him that she had used him to get to where she was and now her album was released she wanted to keep it on a strictly business relationship. If he was smart he would keep on working with her, she had the ability to make him lots of money he would be crazy to dump her and if he did there were others who would snap her up in a jiffy.

Tyrese was in shock, he had heard rumors that she had been banging one of the dancers but had dismissed them as evil gossip. He was down and depressed, Orlando was arriving in the morning, he had an idea.

He was glad to see his son at the airport and he hugged him and had a surprise, he had charted a jet, they were going to Florida to Orlando for two weeks to do a bit of father and son bonding.

They stayed at a hotel in Lake Buena Vista and went to the theme parks and had fun, Orlando talked about Ernesto and Tyrese talked about Yvonne they shared their problems and after a week decided they were both blind and crazy to have been involved with such losers.

Both their lovers had been whores and liars that had cheated on them.

The holiday did them both the world of good, Tyrese was reluctant to return to Detroit. Orlando was reluctant to return to Bangkok.

Tyrese arranged a meeting with Yvonne, she had been so confident that she was going to be so big that he would beg her to extend her contract. He had a big surprise for the long legged bitch. He was suspending her and since he was the rightful owner of all of Romeo's songs he was withdrawing the right for her to sing them or release them.

She turned up at his office expecting him to be pleading for her to sign a fat juicy contract but she had a big surprise coming as he presented her with the bill for the recording, the video shoots, the stylists and hairdressers and dancers and tour expenses she would have to pay him a million dollars in expenses alone. The press were on his side and no one would touch her after he was finished. Just to make life even better this drug dealer in Amsterdam had sold his story about her to a tabloid, he had been waiting for her video to be released before he sold the sick series of photos of her having sex with two guys. The tabloid published the photos but blacked out their dicks, in Europe she was finished. He called one of Pippa's old friends he wanted them to trace that guy, he would be interested in buying some of these photos too. He would give them to a tabloid for free, he wanted to finish her off for good-globally.

Tyrese sent Clifford a first class ticket to come to see him in Detroit he had the scallywag picked up by a stretch limo, Clifford had saved the best for last, he had some great photos of her snorting coke, doing heroin and being fucked. Tyrese especially liked the one where the two guys were doing her together he paid Clifford handsomely for the negatives then sent him on a flight to Miami.

Yvonne cried in horror as she read the stories in the tabloids, she was a heroin shooting sex crazed junkie to the press, someone had put some shocking pictures of her on a website and it had been international news. Her singing and modeling career were finished, the only contract she would get was a porn film, she had cried when her agent had called and told her that the only offer she had had was from a dodgy American porn producer.

Tyrese was all smiles as he clicked on the website with the dirty photos of her. It had been worth the expense what was it Softies bitch had called her A flat chested scraggy ugly mother fucker and anorexic bitch with no booty, a birdbrain, perhaps he mused Pearl had been right after all.

Ernesto flew home to Rio, he had been an orphan, born in the backstreets in a favela and abandoned at birth he had no family that he knew of. He turned to the church for comfort and spent the last months of his life in a Catholic hospital, shortly before he died he wrote a letter begging forgiveness to Orlando, by the time the letter had arrived he was dead and buried. He had suffered horribly and had been blind at the end. HIV was a dreadful illness the stigma and shame connected with the disease was shocking. Ernesto left what money he had to the AIDS foundation. The hospital had informed Orlando of his death a month after he had been buried, every time Orlando tested he was nervous.

Kay prayed like she never had before that he was negative, the six month period passed and all his tests had been all right they hoped that he would be healthy.

Marisa had been busy with Somporn, their clinics had been a huge success and she was delighted with the personal satisfaction that she had from working with sick children.

She was successful too at raising money for her cause, her movie star status had been useful for attracting the right people, she could handle politicians, the police and all the authorities that she needed. Perhaps she thought that God had led her to this place.

She had grown so close to Orlando, since the death of his lover he had become more and more dependent on her.

Kay and her husband were doing well, there was a global depression and like all businesses theirs suffered too. It was all swings and roundabouts in the business world she had always said.

Marisa had been pressing Tyrese to host a charity event to raise money for children with problems. He had already contacted all of the artists he thought that would do it and they were having a meeting in New York soon. , Marisa was glad that she had sprained her ankle in Cambodia who knows what she would have become if she hadn't met Somporn.

He was her guiding light and pillar, he had been amazing at developing the children's hospitals over the years and together they made a great team.

Yvonne had become a real junkie, her career had plummeted after the web scandal and the last they had read about her was that she had used the last of her cash to open a drugs cafe in Amsterdam there they apparently called them coffee shops.

One evening Kay hosted a dinner for some friends, Marisa was there of course looking fabulous in one of Orlando's creations from next seasons collection. She really was a terrific sense of inspiration for him and over the years she had become his muse.

Somporn turned up late from the airport he had flown in from Cambodia and brought a bright young foreign student doctor with him.

Antoine was very shy and incredibly handsome, Marisa was jealous of his curly golden hair.

She remarked that over the years she had invested hundreds of thousands of dollars just to try and get that look. Kay watched her son as he nervously ate his starter and pretended not to look at the young handsome student with the bright green eyes.

Somporn suggested casually that Orlando show Antoine the temple of the Emerald Buddha the following day. Kay smiled, she knew exactly what he was up to, Antoine was obviously gay and Orlando had been alone ever since the dreadful news of Ernesto's illness.

The next day Orlando showed the student Bangkok they went to the Royal Palace and had lunch at the Oriental Hotel, their friendship blossomed and Somporn arranged for Antoine to be transferred to one of their units in Bangkok. Marisa did everything possible to make sure that they kept bumping into each other, she even invited them for a stay over at her new penthouse, after dinner she announced that she had to dash to her other home leaving them alone. The ploy worked they were inseparable after that night.

Tyrese wanted to come to Bangkok but he was up to his eyes in work but was desperate for a break he agreed to join Somporn, Marisa, Kay, Naret and Orlando and his new companion at Marisa's wonderful new holiday home in Phuket. It was off season and there was a chance of rain but he didn't care it would be great just to get away from the pressure of the record company.

He arrived amidst a violent storm, the rain was so heavy that it blocked the motorway, it took forever to get them to Marisa's new home where everyone was waiting for his arrival. Orlando hugged his father and introduced him to the clean cut blond handsome medical student. Tyrese spent a whole hour talking to Antoine and Orlando was proud of his father, he had sensed Antoine's nervousness and tried to make him feel comfortable.

Marisa feeling girlie slipped into her exhibitionist mode and insisted modeling all of the new samples that Orlando had designed, she wore all six creations and walked like a model on a catwalk. Tyrese had to admit she was a devil, she still had what it took, she insisted that everyone was going to dance and cleared the tables away so that her guests could have some fun.

Tyrese watched her dancing, in the candlelight for a moment she looked like twenty again.

Xenon had been right she was a Wild Child she was like a female version of Peter Pan she would stay young forever, her effervescence was infectious she had them all up doing a tribal dance routine that she had invented.

Orlando loved her, Antoine thought that she was crazy but crazy in the nicest sense, after hours of frivolous fun Orlando asked if Antoine and he could watch some of her old movies, she cringed at the thought and joked that he would chase the lad away if he had to suffer her old movies. Everyone went to bed and left the boys glued to the television screen.

Orlando had seen her films hundreds of times but he never tired of watching them again.

It was sunrise when they went to bed.

The sky was blue and they all went for a picnic to a little island that was accessible by boat. They had fresh coconuts and shrimp and it seemed like the most perfect day on earth.

When the sun went down they sailed back to her home, they were just disembarking when Tyrese let out a shriek and collapsed. Somporn rushed to his aid, he had suffered a heart attack, it seemed to take forever for the ambulance to arrive and they raced to the hospital along the winding mountain road.

It had been totally unexpected, they had had such a nice lazy day. Marisa travelled in the back of the ambulance with him she held his hand all the way and reminded him that they were the survivors, they were the toughest if anything happened to Tyrese she couldn't handle it. They had been through thick and thin together. Looking at him in the back of the ambulance she realized how he had aged, she had aged too but not much. She had had everything nipped and tucked, on the surface she was well preserved but on the inside she carried all the scars of the past.

They stayed till his condition was stable he had contracted a minor heart attack and was in a stable condition. It was seen it more as a warning than anything. Thank God, Marisa thought that it hadn't occurred on the damn island God knows what would have happened.

Orlando waited till his father fell asleep then caught a taxi back to the house where they ate dinner silently, each one lost in their own thoughts. He had to rest for a month and there was no way he could fly, there was no question about it he would have to stay on the island for as long as took to get better, the rest would do him the world of good Somporn added.

They would hire a nurse just to be sure that he was being properly looked after.

What was intended to be a holiday had turned into a nightmare, Marisa thought that her life seemed plagued with misfortune it was one thing after the other it had been like that for as long as she could remember.

Tyrese had to convalesce in Phuket for two months, they hired two professional nurses to look after him round the clock. Kay, Naret, Orlando and Marisa came to stay alternating their visits so that Tyrese had company, they were all running busy businesses but stayed loyal to their friend, usually they would come for four day periods which meant that Tyrese had company four days a week and stayed with the nurses for three days.

Whilst they commuted by plane from Bangkok, Somporn stayed in Cambodia to sort out the teething problems in their new children's clinic. Marisa missed him, he was the perfect husband and never complained about his long visits to Cambodia he called her almost every second night to catch up with the news of Tyrese.

Meanwhile back at home in Detroit Tyrese's record company was crumbling, bitter boardroom battles prevailed, the four directors were all battling to run the company in the end Tyrese had to hire an interim manager to go in to settle things down. They all knew that he would have to take things a lot easier when he returned and there was no one to fill his shoes, all major decisions were usually made by him and him alone he felt more relaxed when the interim manager had started.

It was strange for Tyrese to spend his days alone lazing around and relaxing, he reflected on his life and both he and Marisa enjoyed going down memory lane. Wasn't it odd how they talked about 'the good old days' the passing of time had softened all the blows that fate had dealt them. They reflected on the good times and the happy times that they had both experienced, Marisa dragged her photo albums and videos to Phuket and they watched them over and over again.

Mostly when Orlando came to visit he would bring Antoine plus all his sketch pads he would sketch from morning till night conjuring up new ideas for his collection.

The last weekend before Tyrese was supposed to return to America Orlando arrived alone, he looked pale and depressed, over dinner he explained to Tyrese that Antoine had returned to France. They had lived together for a year and their relationship was fine, the previous week Antoine's father had called demanding that he return immediately to get married. His family were from an aristocratic background his great grandfather had been a Duke. The family fortune was long gone and as the only child his family had arranged that he marry a rather unattractive heiress the coupling of their family names would secure the future for Antoine's family, his father already bankrupt had lost his family Chateaux, the fact that Antoine was gay was of no importance, his personal happiness was not an issue.

Antoine had not objected, within two days he had packed and left without so much as a second glance, the girl that he was supposed to marry had inherited millions of dollars when her parents were killed in a helicopter accident. The day he married her he would join the league of the super-rich and save his family from great shame. Orlando had taken the split severely he had a heavy heart and felt jilted.

Tyrese was grateful for Kay and Narets' generosity they had been so kind to him and he was sure that they were neglecting their businesses spending so much time with him. As the time drew close for him to return he knew that there would be decisions to make he no longer could forge ahead at full throttle the doctors had warned him to avoid stress and pressure.

Everyone went to the airport to see him off, they sent one of the nurses to accompany him back on the flight, he was reluctant to leave his friends. Over the last two months their relationships had become much closer, how he would miss the azure blue skies, the sound of the sea as it splashed on the hillside, the frothy green palms and the friendly smiles of the Thai people.

He returned to a mountain of paperwork and an even bigger mountain of problems.

He was happy with the work that the interim manager had done, so happy that he offered him a full time position with an irresistible salary.

Somporn's calls became less frequent, Marisa plodded along with her work at the rehabilitation centre and children's hospitals and she had not seen her partner for two and a half months, she missed him he was the sweetest man she had ever known.

One day her lawyer called there was a dreadful mix up and she was being ordered out of her new hospital in Cambodia, she had tried to call Somporn but as usual when he was in the hospital he switched off his mobile, the hospital itself was not answering, the situation seemed strange. The lawyer was insistent the problem was pending and advised her to drive with him to Cambodia.

The journey to Hat Lek was tedious and boring even in the air conditioned Mercedes it seemed uncomfortable, they stopped several times to stretch their legs and drink endless cups of coffee.

To her surprise when they reached the hospital the building was unfinished and unoccupied.

They drove to the condominium block where Somporn lived, Marisa had brought the spare key she was shocked when she entered. The place was dusty and untidy it looked like no one had been there for months. Together they drove to the local bank where most of the funds for their projects were banked, Marisa listened as the bank manager told her that the accounts were empty he gave her a new address where she could find her partner.

As they drove up the tree lined avenue towards the address that the bank manager had given her she was relieved to see Somporn's BMW in the drive.

They knocked on the door for ten minutes, they were almost ready to leave when a sleepy very pregnant woman with a baby in her arms opened the door, she was in her late twenties with long dark shiny hair she obviously didn't speak English and Marisa's Thai was limited. When Marisa asked about Dr Somporn the woman retorted that her husband was busy painting in the Garage, scooping the child up in her arms she walked with them to the garage. When they walked in the door the young woman screamed, Marisa and the lawyer stood frozen in the doorway, Somporn her partner in life, her perfect man, devoted lover. The one she loved so much was dangling from the beams, a noose round his neck, his body lifeless, his eyes popping and staring into space, he had hung himself with a long length of rope.

It took Marisa days to put the pieces of the jigsaw together. Dr Somporn the perfect lover with the bright white smile had not led a double life but a triple life, she discovered he had three kids to a Thai wife whom he kept in Pattaya and a Cambodian wife that was seven months pregnant with her second child. He had embezzled all the money from the trust fund and spent it all in the Casino's on the Cambodian border, it seemed hard to believe that the man who had shared her bed and her heart had so cleverly foxed her. As she stared up at his lifeless body she did not recognize him, perhaps she had been too naive perhaps, she had been blinded by his bright white smile. She never cried a single tear for her loss, she felt more for the poor children that were being evicted from two of her homes. He had also sold the land on which the new one was being built.

The funeral was a quiet one, the suicide story had been splashed all over the front pages of the newspapers, the scandal of the money embezzlement had shocked the trustees of the foundation. Marisa had been devastated by the press, her main concern was not for the loss of her lover but for the welfare of the children that had been dependent on their foundation. After her press release, to her surprise an anonymous sum of five million dollars was deposited in the foundation's bank account, the bank who made the transaction had told her that the depositor had made it quite clear that their name had to remain secret.

The secret donation saved her skin, she had also lost all her personal money. Somporn had cleaned her bank accounts leaving her barely enough to survive.

At the funeral Marisa noticed a woman with three children she was standing at the back of the temple weeping, she presumed the poor looking woman was his first wife, the heavily pregnant woman that had answered the door had not turned up, she had heard that she too had been put out of the home that Somporn had gambled away.

Marisa thanked God, Buddha and every deity known to man for the miracle donation that preserved the three hospitals and children's welfare centres that were still open. Wearing a brave face and dragging her movie star persona out of the attic she campaigned for more money to support her hospitals, the press interviews and television chat shows she used had proved successful and the whole world seemed to pity her and within three months the funds started to roll in.

To her surprise a Hollywood producer offered her a part in a movie, she had promised herself that she had finished with that business and she didn't know if she could pull it off. In her youth she had relied on her beauty and charismatic sex appeal to capture the hearts of the audience, she was old now and although she was in top condition she didn't know if she would attract the kind of audiences that she had thirty years before. The deal was tempting, she had to do four months on location and one month's promotion and for this she would be paid an enormous retainer and a share of the box office profits, it was a compelling role.

An all-star cast would star in the big budget period drama and she would play the leading role.

She had no personal money and her assets were minimal, if she did this movie she could almost finance another hospital single-handedly. Driven by the idea that she could save even more children she eventually agreed to make the movie. She had staff that she could trust to run the clinics, the film would make her financially secure and if it was successful she could use the movie to promote her children's welfare projects. As usual she found that fate had held out its hand to her once more just when everything seemed impossible this opportunity turned up from nowhere.

Simon Draper was the hottest young producer in Hollywood, he had risen to stardom with his first movie stealing glowing accolades. The following three films he had created had been Hollywood Blockbusters, the moment that he had read the book 'Stolen Dreams' he had bought the film rights, page after page as he read the story one face sprang into mind, Marisa Duval. He had watched all of her movies when he was a kid, she had been his fascination and teenage fantasy, she had been in fact the inspiration that had driven him to get into the movie business. As a teenager he lived in a bedsit while he was at college, the walls of his tiny room were covered with posters from Marisa's films, he fell asleep every night staring at her image, the idea of working with the woman who had inspired his dreams was the most exciting thing that he could imagine. When he heard from her agent that she would consider coming out of retirement to star in the movie he was elated.

Thinking perhaps that she might change her mind he cancelled the list of appointments he had and flew to Bangkok to meet her in person.

The morning she had to meet Simon she woke nervous as could be, wanting to look her best she had hired a hairdresser and make-up artist to make her up. She was glad that she had gone to the expense, when they finished with her she stared at her reflection in the antique mirror and thought, 'Not Bad for an old bird,' with her golden honey coloured hair scraped into a neat chignon and make-up made her look glamorous she slipped into the stunning creation that Orlando had made specially for her.

She arrived at the Oriental Hotel to meet Simon for lunch in a bright shiny pink Mercedes.

Mr Draper sat in the reception of the Grande Hotel he too was nervous, it was sometimes disappointing to meet one's fantasy, usually in reality they were disappointing. He wondered if this woman still possessed the magic she had years before, no one had seen her and she had been out of the business for a life time.

The hot Hollywood genius with the unruly hair and dirty jeans sat speechless as the woman entered the hotel, at first he couldn't see her, she was backlit by the strong sunlight outside, she gracefully walked into the foyer and it looked like a scene from a film as she emerged from the doorway. He sat speechless in awe of her grace, she was the only person in the world that could play that character, she was that character, elegance personified a mature woman that possessed something girlish and latently sexual. Accompanied by her agent she walked towards him extending her hand like an Empress.

Feeling confident with the professional make-up and beautiful clothes, Marisa found that she had slipped into the role of playing herself, it was obvious that Simon was captivated by her aura. Over lunch he studied her, the way she moved, the way she ate it looked like a frame from a film.

It was amazing he mused, she still had that ability to light up a room and she was in great condition and would look superb on film he was excited and fascinated by her, she had still this sexuality that was compelling.

Over a light lunch she teased him wickedly when he confessed that as a kid she was inspiration and fantasy. Joking that he was a complete pervert she fed him a spoonful of her crème brûlée, he was captivated.

The agent looked like he was in shock, he hadn't worked for Marisa for twenty years and he was impressed that Simon had offered her a role there would be big bucks in it for him too.

Simon talked excitedly about the book, they would shoot on location in Russia, Tuscany and Croatia. Marisa would carry the whole movie, she had the starring role and would play a Russian aristocrat who had escaped the revolution and who had sacrificed everything for love. It was an old-fashioned Hollywood movie on a scale like *Gone With The Wind*.

Marisa pretended that she was disappointed that she would not have to do any kick-boxing or flying through the sky on a wire, a trend that seemed to be filling the seats at the cinema.

Hollywood actresses would be green with envy she thought, there were a lot of actresses that would die for such a role.

Simon wanted her to fly out to do a screen test, it was he assured her merely a formality.

As far as he was concerned she was the only one that could play this role, this film evidently was the film that was closest to his heart, she was sure he would pull out all the stops and that it would be astounding. She had seen all of his movies and they were spectacular. It was an honor to have this chance she would be mad to have declined the offer.

She had the car take her to Orlando's studio, he was surprised that she had turned up unexpectedly and was impressed that she looked so fabulous when she disclosed that she was going to make a movie he was ecstatic. He couldn't believe it, over coffee she told him all about the role. She was off to Hollywood in a week and needed something absolutely fabulous to wear, her mission was to seduce Orlando into having his staff make three or four outfits in a week. She wanted to dazzle all these young starlets with his unique handwriting.

Orlando's team made her six stunning outfits, four evening dresses and three outfits for day.

His poor staff had worked around the clock and she was more than delighted with the result, she didn't want to hit Hollywood and look like a frump.

A mile long stretch limo was at the airport when she arrived, the studio had tipped off the paparazzi that she was arriving. She had not expected it and was glad that she had made an effort to look fantastic, the press had been tipped off that she had been offered the leading role in Simon's biggest blockbuster yet and they were hungry to see this woman who had vanished from the screen so many years before.

They had arranged a magnificent suite for her at the best hotel in Hollywood. There were roses and champagne in her suite with a note to welcome her and that stated she would be picked up at seven in the morning for her screen test. She ran a bath and switched on the television, it was odd she had just arrived but her face was on television, they had announced on the news that she had arrived, she had been in the country for just an hour and she was on television, 'Not Bad For an

Old Bird.' she mused as she soaked in a fragrant bubble bath with a nice glass of chilled rose champagne.

The driver arrived exactly on time and as she stepped into the vulgar car she remembered how it was thirty years ago when they used to pick her up at five am to take her to the studio.

Simon wanted her in full period dress, the hair and make-up took three hours she had forgotten how boring it was to be in make-up for so long, she was to shoot two scenes, it felt exciting to be in a studio again she could feel the adrenaline kicking in. The feel of being in the spotlight again gave her a thrill. She had butterflies in her stomach as she switched on her movie star persona.

Marisa was nervous as she sat next to Simon in the screening room, she had not seen herself on screen for many years she was nervous that she had lost that magic.

The lights dimmed, the projector rolled and she watched her image on screen, it was weird, the last time she had seen herself on screen she was a young girl, now she studied her image intently. Under Simon's supervision she had sailed through the test, he was in awe of her, she looked good from every angle and she was THE character. With the period hair and make-up and clothing she portrayed the perfect incarnation of his vision. They watched the two scenes twice and Simon took some notes as he watched. Marisa remained silent waiting for Simon to speak when the film stopped.

He had thought that her acting was awesome she had a charisma and on screen magic that only a few actresses possessed, he was delighted with her portrayal of the character, the notes he had made were regarding the lighting, he was not happy with the lighting.

She flew back to Bangkok, and one month later she flew to Moscow to begin filming, then moved on to Croatia. It felt wonderful to be in movies again she had forgotten how she had missed working.

The crew were wonderful and she had the time of her life playing a Russian Aristocrat that defied everything for the love of a poor farm hand.

The months flew by and they completed the location shots in Tuscany, after completing the location shooting she flew to Hollywood to complete the studio sequences.

Simon was delighted that he had chosen Marisa to star in the film, she gave credibility to the role. Playing this movie would be the jewel in the crown of her sparkling career.

The money that they had paid her she used to help finance her children's hospitals.

She had missed all the smiling faces of the children who had become her pride, on the cold winter nights in Croatia she had missed their toothy grins and wide smiles.

There was a lot of hype around the film, everyone was waiting for Simon's new movie to be released, three weeks before the release date Marisa got a call in the middle of the night.

Tyrese had passed away. He had suffered a massive coronary and had died in a deckchair by the poolside of his Detroit home. Marisa was executor of his will, she had to fly immediately with Orlando to America.

The funeral service was attended by three hundred people who had flown in from all over the world, anyone who was anyone in the music industry came from every corner of the planet to show their respect, there were actors, singers, ex footballers and even a man that had been a stripper with Tyrese.

After a sad but wonderful service they buried his body in a marble tomb, Marisa cried as she threw a white rose on the casket, two hundred guests were invited to a lunch in a marquee. Marisa had decked the whole area with hanging baskets of orchids and jasmine, the fragrance filled the tent. How she would miss Tyrese they had been through thick and thin, they had survived everything together his passing away had been a shock to her she felt alone now.

The following day both Marisa and Orlando were invited to a meeting at his record company, they sat at the same table where Tyrese had made all his important decisions and listened as Tyrese's two lawyers read his will.

Marisa was his executor, he had left her the Pippa Curtis Foundation, the schools and institutes that were spread worldwide, the project that helped underprivileged children and encouraged them to study music, he wanted her to amalgamate these schools with her hospitals and projects. The sheer burden of it made Marisa shiver, tears ran down her cheeks as she thought of the responsibility that he had just bequeathed to her.

Orlando his son was to inherit the multi-million dollar recording company, he wished his son to be chairman of the company and run their subsidiaries worldwide. His personal fortune was equally divided with ten million dollars being deposited in The Pippa Curtis Foundation fund and the remaining ten million was being transferred to Orlando's account. He left Kay and Naret a string of properties in London, Detroit and Paris, each of them had a personal letter thanking them individually for their friendship and love.

Orlando wept and Marisa joined him as they walked through the offices that had belonged to Tyrese. Marisa felt that she could almost feel his presence. What a burden she said to Orlando he had just became president of one of the biggest recording companies in the world and she had just become chairwoman of one of the largest charity foundations on the planet. Looks like we won't be getting any holidays for a few years she joked teasing Orlando.

Marisa wore a sparkling gold sheath that Orlando had designed to attend the premiere. As she walked up the red carpet she clung firmly to Orlando's arm for support, the moment they had emerged from the limo the crowds had cheered, she paused at the entrance to the theatre giving the press time to take photos, the flashbulbs were blinding and fans were screaming her name.

"Stolen Dreams" was a Hollywood blockbuster of epic proportions. Simon's best film to date, the movie was nominated for an array of awards. Marisa's compelling performance had made the film a hit, she was regarded as Hollywood royalty, a stream of film offers rolled in, she was flattered but too busy to accept any of the offers. She had thrown herself in at the deep end and had globalised the Pippa Curtis program opening centers for underprivileged children worldwide. The success of the film had given her lots of credibility, she had raised lots of money for her children's hospitals and projects in Thailand, Vietnam and Cambodia.

Simon kept sending her scripts he was desperate that she make a sequel to the film, she declined and worked flat out with the charity foundations.

It was a cold winter's night, Orlando arrived in a smart black dinner suit with tightly cut pants, she was glad to see him she hadn't seen him for almost a year. It had been eight years since Tyrese had died and Orlando had retired from the world of fashion to run Tyrese's Global Empire and as far as she knew he lived alone, sadly it was as she knew extremely lonely at the top.

Marisa looked wonderful in a fifties style vintage couture gown that Audrey Hepburn would have loved, they made a striking couple as they entered the silver Bentley the car sped along Park Lane to the hotel that was hosting the event.

They had a lovely dinner with lashings of champagne, the head speaker made a speech and announced her name, Orlando helped her walk to the stage to receive her award. She was receiving the Linley Blain Foundation Award for outstanding life achievement for helping charity. This was not an award for a film, this was an award for helping thousands of children worldwide. Marisa's eyes misted as she thanked the crowd she clasped the crystal tribute close to her breast and thanked the audience for their kindness.

Orlando escorted her to her Mayfair Hotel suite, she had cried tears of joy as they had presented her with the award. After Orlando kissed her goodnight she lay in the four-poster bed and stared at the crystal statue, it sparkled in the candlelight.

That night she dreamt of many things, of people and places that she had been, she smiled as she remembered all the smiles of the poor children that she had grown to love so much. Their love had been the greatest love she had known. She had in her heyday broken many hearts, Marisa had lived the fairytale life that dreams were made of.

That night as she slept Yoji, Xenon and Tyrese all came to visit her, they were bathed in a liquid golden light and standing at the bottom of the bed their arms outstretched, they beckoned to her, she smiled as she drifted towards the warm golden light glancing only once backwards to say goodbye to the thousands of little children with the big white smiles hat she was leaving behind.

Marisa was not afraid of death, she had been more afraid of life. She saw death not as the end but as a new beginning.

That night Orlando had woken around three am, he had felt a strange presence in his room he had dreamt that Marisa had kissed him on the forehead and whispered good-bye.

At eight am he received a call, Marisa had died peacefully in her sleep about three am, she had been found with a smile on her face clutching the crystal award that she had received earlier.

As Marisa entered the golden light she saw exerts of her life flash past. Her loves were waiting, beckoning her to join them at the end of the tunnel. Just like in the movies she was bathed in light. Her spirit rose higher and higher. She glanced back at the body she was leaving behind and smiled. It had been one hell of a journey she mused as she felt love embrace her.

The light caressed her with a tenderness that was overwhelming, she stole one last look at the lifeless figure on the bed and braced herself, then she was engulfed by the dazzling white light.

'It's Showtime!' she exclaimed as her soul drifted higher and higher beyond the universe.

The End